FEAR
OF INTIMACY

By Dr. Jo Ann Felton Carter

OTHER BOOKS

for you to enjoy by

Dr. Carter:

ABANDONED NO MORE

SHAME IN ME

Secrets & their lies

WHO ME 4GIVE?

VIOLATED

PRAYER 4 THE BELIEVER

Published by Prospering Soul Publishing
5918 Bellevue Road Haughton, LA 71037
www.aprosperingsoul.com

Prospering Soul Publishing is totally committed to publishing works that edify and exhort enabling the reader to prosper in their soul as stated in III John 2.

All scripture is taken from the New King James Version except where otherwise noted.

Published in the United States of America

ISBN: 978-0-9974419-6-3   Book
ISBN: 978-0-9974419-5-6   eBook

Christian Fiction

CONTENTS

Gregory Allen Young

Charolette Ann Thomas

>Gregory
>Charolette

Faith Amber Henderson

>Gregory
>Faith
>Gregory

Janice Catherine Andrews-Woods

>Gregory

Linda Ariana Torres-Ortiz

>Charolette
>Gregory

Divorce Court
Los Angeles, California

His Honorable Judge, Joseph L. Sparks removes his eyeglasses and while holding them, he sternly speaks directly to Gregory Young. "You mean to tell me this is your fourth appearance for Final Decree of Divorce Mr. Young?"

Gregory Young stands staring at Judge Sparks.

Agitated, Judge Sparks yelps; **"Well is it?"** "Yes, your honor." Gregory humbly responds.

Judge Sparks returns his eyeglasses to his nose and glances over the papers in front of him. Again, Judge Sparks removes his eyeglasses and sternly peers at Gregory Young while stating, "Mr. Young, I cannot forbid you to remarry, however I can order you to mandatory Family Counseling. Which is what I am going to do before proclaiming an order of dismissal. Counseling so ordered!" Judge hits his gavel.

Bailiff directs Gregory to the Clerk's Office. Gregory is given a list of offices approved by the court for Family Counseling and is directed to a free phone with instructions to make his appointment.

~~~Gregory Allen Young~~~

BACKGROUND

Gregory was born in the city of Long Beach, California to the short, shapely Phylis Young and the tall, handsome Roland Berry. On the fourth day in the scorching month of August, Phylis Young held her precious baby boy in her arms for the first time and she cried. Why? Because her baby is so beautiful and, for eight months Roland Berry was nowhere to be found.

The day Phylis informed Roland Berry she was pregnant he stared Phylis down for over a good three minutes then says, "I'll figure something out." Roland turned, walked away and there was never a peep from Mister Berry since. After Gregory's first birthday, Phylis received word Roland Berry was in Florida serving in the United States Navy.

Phylis Young was born to Shirley Palmer-Young [Grannie] and Percy Allen Young [Grand Pop]. Phylis was their only child. Percy was raised COGIC [Church of God in Christ]. Percy and Shirley raised Phylis the same; in church with rigid rules. Percy was very disappointed and angry when Phylis became pregnant and having to raise Gregory alone.

Shirley was not always as strict as Percy with Phylis and when Gregory came along, Shirley lovingly spoiled her grandson. Percy spent a lot of time teaching Gregory about God and the Bible. Gregory went to church with Grannie and Grand Pop every day of the week except Mondays when there were no services.

By the age of three Gregory could recite every book in the Old Testament from memory in the order written. Growing up Gregory loved church and the Bible stories he learned. Percy beamed and sometimes called Gregory, "Lil Preacher."

Phylis worked as a shipping clerk for The Port of Long Beach as did Gary Franklin Mays. Mr. Mays worked as a Heavy Equipment Crane Operator and is nine years older than Phylis. Phylis and Gregory lived with her parents and after Gregory's fifth birthday Phylis married Mr. Mays and moved to Seal Beach, California into a two-bedroom apartment.

On Phylis' off days, she cleaned the apartment and did laundry. Gregory was unable to go outside so Phylis bought books for Gregory to read just to keep him occupied while indoors. Gregory began reading books and his love for reading became apparent. At the age of ten Gregory was reading and memorizing scriptures with Grand Pop and thanks to Grand Pop, Gregory had a very good understanding of the scriptures he memorized.

Gregory grew to be six feet one with large hands and feet and has wide squared shoulders. While developing into adulthood, Gregory's long strides convey he is very confident of himself. He observes everything that goes on in a room, he just doesn't say anything unless asked. When he speaks, he is very articulate. A persons first observation of Gregory Young is that he plays basketball. However, Gregory's game of choice is football.

Gregorys' skin tone is the color of a walnut and he has real tight curly hair, so he keeps it cut close. His brown eyes are a perfect oval shape and he has long thick curly eye lashes; protected by eyeglasses he's had to wear since the age of eleven due to his reading constantly.

Gregory has his mother's wide nose and a mile-wide smile he rarely sports revealing those perfect teeth. Being extremely hairy, Gregory started shaving early but his stepfather, Mr. Mays taught him to never use the same razor blade more than twice and take time to clean and dry the blade. Gregory's face is smooth as a baby's behind.

Gregory's sister, Samantha [Sam] Denise Mays was born right after Gregory started first grade. When Sam turned eighteen months old, Jamal Franklin Mays arrived. The three siblings clung close together growing up.

Mr. Mays worked mostly ten-hour days, five days a week and when work picked up to seven days a week, Phylis joined the overtime bandwagon for eight months and saved her overtime paychecks. Grannie and Grand Pop kept their three grandchildren continuously from January until May the year Gregory celebrated his eleventh birthday. That was when Mr. Mays bought Phylis a nice three-bedroom, two bath tract home in Long Beach [LB], California on Stockton Avenue.

Stockton Avenue has a huge backyard, and it was where you would find Gregory with book in one hand and football in the other. One could say Gregory Allen Young grew up on Stockton Avenue experiencing life as your typical Afro-American middle-class family of the seventies and eighties.

WEDNESDAY:
During the drive from the courthouse...

'All I wanted was a divorce. A simple divorce! Lord am I being punished for hooking up with Linda? You would think a forty-one-year-old man could accomplish a simple divorce.   Man!

Last Saturday Mama had all my kids over for ice cream and cake to celebrate their Uncle Jamal's birthday. When everyone left, I felt so lonely. While driving to my place I thought about each one of my kids. I entered my place, sat in the dark and took deliberate consideration of my life…

The summer Mr. Mays moved us on Stockton Avenue I met Ronald Divers. We are the same age. Ronald was born a month before I was, in July. Ronald had a brother six years older than himself and was home alone most of the time, so Ronald started hanging around my house. He lived on Claremont Place, two blocks before you get to Stockton Avenue.

It was Ronald who introduced me to Walter Thomas who was also our age, born in November. Walter lived two blocks behind me, on Willow Avenue. Walter had a sister two years younger than himself and since they only had each other, Walter took his little sister everywhere he went.

Us guys were your typical curious eleven-year old boys and Walter's sister always worked our nerves. Her name is Charlotte Ann [Char] and man was she a pain in the butt. It was like she had a recording inside her that played every single time we all were together, *"Ooh, Walter, I'ma tell!"* It was so bad when Ronald, Walter and I talked about going someplace or doing something Ronald would ask Walter, "Are you bringing Char?"

On the regular Ronald would tell Char to be quiet. Once Ronald told Char, "Shut the hell up!" Walter grabbed Ronald by his shirt collar, almost lifting him off the ground and told Ronald not to ever talk to his sister like that. Walter was protective of his little sister; and that's putting it mild. Walter being taller than both Ronald and I, was the reason we pretty much agreed with whatever Walter told us. Besides when it came to Charlotte, Walter would get up in your face and tell you his sister goes where he goes!

After the shirt grabbing incident Ronald would say things like, "Girl ain't your throat dry from talkin too much?" Or "Do you *ever* shut up?" This would make Char shut up but only for a few minutes. Then she would be spouting off at the mouth about something else. School was the only time the three of us guys had a break from Charlotte.

As soon as we moved to Stockton Avenue Mama befriended the neighbors on both sides of us. The Hamilton's, Roger and Dana lived to our right. They had two sons Bryan, seven, and Sherman, five. Jamal stayed over their house a lot. Sherman and Jamal went all through school together.

Our other neighbors to the left of us, Betty and Calvin Holt had a daughter, Sarah, five years old and spoiled rotten. Growing up, Sam spent a lot of time over there. Miss Betty was a stay home mother and took Sam everywhere with their family however, Sam and Sarah would fall out a lot and Sam would end up in her room with her dolls.

I became the overseer of Sam and Jamal but somehow, don't ask me how, one day and I don't know when, Sam told Jamal and I what and what not to do. I can't figure out how that happened, but it did. Sam would tell us to do something and explain why we should do it. Her explanation would make so much sense, I would scratch my head.

When school started Sam, Jamal and myself were allowed to stay home by ourselves. Mama would lay our clothes out for us every morning, have our lunches made and milk money on the kitchen table. All of us kids in the neighborhood walked to school together up to a certain block where the elementary school kids turned onto the street their school was located while us older kids walked the rest of the way together.

Grannie would pick the three of us up from school and take us to her house. Once there we ate and did our homework before we were dropped off on Stockton Avenue while Grannie and Grand Pop were on their way to church. I wanted to go with them when there was Revival and Mama would let us go so long as our homework was completed. Sometimes I would sit on the last pew and finish my homework during church service.

Every Sunday morning Grand Pop would come take the three of us to their house and Grannie cooked a big breakfast for us before we were off to church. Holy Deliverance Church of God in Christ on Pacific Coast Highway [PCH]. I loved church until I turned twelve, I could not keep my mind focused. It seemed church service was rehearsed, the same thing Sunday after Sunday. *And* it was too long! Gran Pop was an Elder and we had to be early for prayer and stay late for altar call prayer.

I was beginning to drag on Sunday mornings because I no longer wanted to attend Sunday services. One Sunday on our ride home from church I mentioned I wanted to stay home next Sunday. Grand Pop said I was twelve years old and needed to be taught responsibility. Responsible people do a lot of things they don't want too. It is part of life.

The next day, Monday evening Grand Pop and Grannie drove us home and they came into the house. Grand Pop spent over an hour teaching us about the Bible and how it applies to life today. Even though we didn't want to hear it, out of respect we reluctantly listened to what we were being told. Grand Pop was really addressing me because of the comment I made about wanting to stay home from church. That night when I went to bed, I made up my mind to tell Mama I wanted to stay home Sunday.

Up until then it had not dawned on me Mama never went to church. She quoted scriptures to us all the time and the Sundays she didn't work she had us kids ready for our grandparents when they came to pick us up, but Mama would never attend.

The following Sunday morning I asked Mama if I could stay home from church and she didn't have a problem with it. It was Grand Pop who insisted Mama get a handle on me. He said to Mama, "Phylis he is a child and has no business telling you, the parent what he wants and does not want to do!" Mama said, "Daddy I remember giving birth to Gregory, thank you very much!" Man did Grand Pop blow a gasket. That was the day I found out why Mama never attended church.

Grannie and Grand Pop took Sam and Jamal with them to church, but Mama fussed for at least half an hour after Grand Pop pulled off. I sat in the living room on the couch and Mama paced from the kitchen back into the living room telling me in her raised voice, "All that man does is go to church!"

She would pace back into the kitchen talking about Grand Pop and come back into the living room still talking. "He should be perfect by now, all that religion rammed down his throat!" She headed back to the kitchen saying, "I refuse to put my kids through that crap! Those people are a bunch of fakes up at that church. **It don't take all that!**" Mama yelled.

Mama appeared in the doorway and her voice is softened now, "Gregory if you don't want to go to church, you don't have to, you hear me!" Mama was angry and I had never witnessed her standing up to Grand Pop before. I kinda enjoyed it. I liked watching Mama standing up for me because I didn't want to go back to that church.

I loved church now don't get me wrong. I'm not a heathen or anything. It's just as a child I liked the Bible stories and hearing about Jesus' life while He lived on earth. What happened is by the time I was eleven years old; I saw the services being repetitive. I thought there had to be more to church than the same old same old.

After staying home for three Sundays, I missed going to church, so I dressed to be picked up the fourth Sunday. While getting dressed Mama entered our room asking if Grand Pop had coerced me into going to church. I told her "No." After looking my face over, Mama asked, "You sure?" I told her "Yes." Mama turned around and walked out of the room.

When I went to bed that evening Mama came into our room, sat on my bed, and asked, "Gregory do you like going to church?" I told her, "Yes." Mama told me she was forced to attend church and didn't want us being forced. She was just making sure I wanted to attend. Mama said, "Gregory The Lord wants us to love Him, not be forced to be with Him.

Do you like being around someone that doesn't want to be around you?" I nodded my head "No."

"It's the same with The Lord. He wants us to like being around Him, not forced. I want you to love God and not be made a hypocrite. Gregory do you understand what I'm saying?" Once again, I answered with a head nod. Mama kissed me on my forehead and left the room.

Watching Mama leave the room, I recall being nine years old and going up to the alter. I went every Sunday, but this particular trip was different. I fell on my knees as usual however this time when I prayed for The Holy Ghost; I felt a warm sensation fill my stomach. As if I had drank some warm cocoa. A peaceful calm totally apprehended me. Immediately I thought of how sometimes someone in the church would break out singing a song by Hezekiah Walker; *"Won't He make you clean, inside. Won't He make you clean inside!"*

The whole congregation would join in harmonizing the song while faces would be glowing, and smiles would be displayed on every face in the congregation. That Sunday as I stood up to return to my seat I thought, 'this feeling must be what that song means. I feel different inside.' That was my first encounter with Holy Spirit.

Every Sunday service Sam, Jamal and I attended, Grannie made the three of us sit on the pew behind Grand Pop and I would sit and listen to the men pray. Grand Pop being an Elder in the church, was always in prayer. After my experience that Sunday at the altar, I prayed but no longer aloud. I talked to The Lord inside my head all the time. I knew The Lord was with me and I told Him my every thought. That is until I started thinking of the female anatomy. Those thoughts I kept to myself.

From the age of nine until twelve I would spend hours each day after doing homework, studying the Bible. First, I wanted to know about the life of Jesus, then I wanted to understand who Holy Spirit is and exactly what His purpose in my life was. I believe my understanding became enlightened as I encountered one on one conversations with Holy Spirit as I read the Bible. It seemed Holy Spirit would talk to me as I read The Word. He explained the meaning of what I read and gave me references to other scriptures.

During this time while attending church services, I realized a lot of the saints had no idea who Holy Spirit really is. My attitude became judgmental and my idle thoughts began wondering what the difference girls' bodies were from mine.

The summer of my twelfth birthday things changed for me. Walter's family attended a Baptist church and he invited us to his church musical. Sam, Jamal, and I attended that Saturday evening and I really enjoyed their service. The music was great and before each selection, a young man would take the mic and explain to us what the next song was about.

I hummed the songs I heard that evening for the next few days! I would remind Walter to inform me of any and all musicals his church was planning so I could be sure to attend.

Walter would tell Ronald in front of me that I was a "Church Boy" and they would laugh and put their hands together as if praying. I just looked at them. It was obvious neither one of them has had an encounter with The Holy Ghost. I knew they wouldn't understand so I withstood their deriding. After a while they lightened up.

The following summer I started attending church with Walter and his family. Sam and Jamal were still attending church with our Grandparents. By Christmas Grand Pop no longer came to get them, they were going with me every Sunday. I liked the Baptist Church and was amazed they didn't stay all day and they could cuss and drink liquor.

The preacher kept saying, "We thank God for His grace. We are no longer under the law!" I was challenged to read the whole Bible for myself and find out what the preacher meant. Holy Deliverance

Church of God In Christ studied pretty much the same scriptures so attending Morning Star Baptist became my church of preference.

I believe that was the summer I really started praying and asking Holy Spirit to give me understanding of The Word. I began reading the Bible starting with the New Testament, on my own. I attended Sunday School and most Sundays it was the teacher and myself expounding on the lesson. I was almost thirteen years old and had a relationship with The Lord back then. Man…

That year I also figured out Mama did not want to raise us as she was raised with strict rules and that was why she allowed Mr. Mays to be the disciplinarian in our home. If anything went wrong on Stockton Avenue, Mr. Mays handled it as soon as Mama informed him something was out of order.

I wasn't close to Mr. Mays he was and is still very quiet. I would witness Jamal just walking up to Mr. Mays and talk to him about whatever was on his mind. I watched Mr. Mays. I felt he knew everything about life and was the wisest man to ever live. I really looked up to Mr. Mays and always will.

Grand Pop was wise concerning the Bible, but Mr. Mays knew everything else. I respected whatever Mr. Mays said to me and didn't lie to him. Most times he confronted me, he would start with, "Now

Gregory, don't feel you have to lie, tell me the truth son." Now how can you lie to someone after that?

I must say my siblings and I were good kids and hardly did something out of what we were told but sometimes Sam would have Jamal and I do something and after her reason for us doing it sounded so logical, we would do it and end up getting in trouble. I think I was almost fourteen before I figured out Sam was setting us up!

The second year we lived on Stockton Avenue Mr. Mays had a co-worker to retire and was moving to Arizona. He couldn't move his pool table, so Mr. Mays bought it and had an enclosed patio added onto the back of the house. That's when our house became the hangout. There's a park four blocks from us but the pool table kept us home. Ronald, Walter, and I could be found in our spare time, in the back, movin pockets. Oh yeah and Char.

The summer of my last year in junior high school, Miss. Betty went to work so Sarah, Sam's playmate, was being taken to her grandparents through the week to stay because her parents didn't want her home alone. I think that was when Sam and Char became close because when Walter and Char came over to our house, Char always went directly into Sam's room and we hardly saw her. Finally, Char was out of our hair.

The night of my fifteenth birthday Mr. Mays had me follow him to the garage before I went to bed and told me since I was becoming a man, men worked. Mr. Mays said I could cut lawns and wash cars just make sure whatever supplies from the garage I used; I would be sure to put them back. He said, "Gregory you're at the age sex will become important to you. Come to me when you're ready to have sexual relations. Contrary to the word on the street, old people do know a thing or two about sex. Alright?" I nodded "Yes."

A week later I started cutting the neighbors lawns and washing their cars so I would have my own money. Man did I like that. I saved every penny I made and when I needed a new seat for my bike, I bought a real nice one with dark brown stitching, it was really fly.

By then I only attended Holy Deliverance Church of God in Christ when Grand Pop or Grannie spoke on a special occasion. Mother Thomas was very active with the church hospitality committee and Dad Thomas bought her a dark brown Chevy Caprice station wagon. Every Sunday morning Sam, Jamal and I would walk over to the Thomas house and ride with them to church and I precisely remember the Sunday we were all in the living room waiting for Mother Thomas and Char to finish getting ready.

As Mother Thomas walked into the living room she was yelling for Char to hurry. I raised up from the couch as Char appeared in the doorway. She was putting something in her purse. I noticed her white pleated skirt and the wide white belt that really displayed her small waist. I did a double take while thinking, 'Char? Wow!' That was the day Charlotte Ann Thomas took over my every idle thought.

Charlotte was no longer Walter's pain in the butt little sister to me. I have always been what you call "A straight forward guy." I don't volunteer sharing what is on my mind but if asked my opinion, I have no qualms about letting you know my thoughts. It's only when it comes to females, I am hesitant revealing my thoughts. Females tend to get their feelings hurt easily. I kept my eye on Char.

From eighth grade until twelfth, I made a few phone calls to girls and tried asking a few girls at school out, but they were so giggly and offered to give me sex!

As bad as I wanted sex, I want to be the one to control if and when it happens. I was turned off by those girls and thought they were too loose for me. I kept my eyes open for a nice girl and listened to Walter share with Ronald and I about his love making escapades.

Ronald smiled as though his face was permanently etched when he and Pam had sex the first time. Walter asked him several times what happened, but Ronald only said, "Man it was good!" Walter tried to get details, but Ronald would not talk.

Our senior year of high school Charlotte began her first year and after watching her, I knew she was a lady, not rowdy. I decided to let her know I was interested in her. It took a situation to prompt me…

Friday before Thanksgiving all of us; me, Walter, Ronald, Pam, [Ronald's girl] Jamal, Bryan, Sherman, Sam, and Char were all movin pockets and Sam mentioned some guys name and how fine he was. Char giggled and said, "Yeah I remember him. I wonder if he kisses as good as he looks?"

I felt as though a hot flame of fire hit my face. I do not want Char kissing some strange dude. Walter was bent over about to take his shot. With his eyes dead on Char Walter says, "Alright now you keep your mind on this game. Char, you hear me!" I thought to myself, 'that's right set her straight!'

After everyone left the house I went into my room, laid on my bed and mentally went over Char's giggle. I really do not want another guy with Charlotte. I had better make my move on her. Walter said his Dad was taking him to buy some shoes in the morning; alright.

The next morning before cutting my lawns I put on my slacks and plaid shirt, splashed some of Mr. Mays cologne on and walked over to the Thomas house. I am going to ask Char out to the movies.

'Man was that the quickest walk over here. I did not get a chance to go over my speech but one time. Alright.'

I rang the doorbell. Char opens the door. "Hey Greg, what brings you over so early?" "Good morning Charlotte. Just wanted to holler at Walter." "Daddy took him to that outlet for a pair of those new tennis shoes. I'm surprised he didn't tell you, y'all being so tight and all." "Oh yeah, now that you mentioned it. Say, may I come in?" "Sure." As I step inside the house, I watch Char as she steps back to let me in. I feel my heart beating so fast. I think of that boy's name that had her giggling and clear my throat.

Naw dude Charlotte Thomas is mine. "Charlotte, what is your opinion of high school?" "Charlotte!" She exclaims while eyeing me up and down with her forehead wrinkled. She hunches her shoulders while uttering, "Its school, why?" I blurt, "You wanna go to the movies later?" As she jerks her neck back, a question mark appears on her face. She answers, "You asking me out?"

I look her directly in the eyes and purposely answer in my deep voice, "Yes." I heard myself swallow. I think she heard me, but her facial expression changed to serious. 'I can't have her thinking I'm scared.' So, I speak up in a firm tone, "I just thought you might want to see a movie that's all." She tilts her head and asks, "You paying?" "Yes." "I can get popcorn and a drink if I want?" "Sure." She smiles and says, "What time and what are we going to see?" 'Alright! I am in.' Using my manly voice I say, "I'll call you later."

I turn towards the door to leave. Char says, "Okay. But give me plenty time to get ready. You know us girls take more time than you guys." I step down onto the front step and turn to face her just in time to see that beautiful smile. She's holding onto the doorknob. I step down backwards on the porch still gazing upon her and her smile and think, 'Wow, she is so fine!"

While walking home I feel like shouting:

"SHE SAID YES!" To the whole world.

That was the beginning of Charlotte and I.

Walter was cool with me being with his sister, after all I was a church boy. Char and I would sit together, and she would talk about how much she loved art, especially contemporary and black art. She loved talking about art and I loved when she did because her smile seemed to brighten and, I had permission to look at her beautiful face. Char is tall for a female; five feet nine and stacked like a brick house.

Char's smile is so bright and perfect, absolutely no flaws; perfect teeth and lips. She's the color of a hazelnut with almost black oval shaped eyes. She arches her eyebrows and her high cheekbones gives her beautiful face a perfect heart shape. When she dresses for special occasions, she can apply make-up and appear in any room looking like a professional model.

Char is very beautiful and there is an essence of elegance about her as if she is from a long line of royals. She told me she had a boyfriend in the ninth grade for almost a month. His name was Donathan Sanders. They were the same age and had most classes together. They talked on the phone every evening and at school Donathan would carry her books.

When Char asked Dad Thomas if she could go to a dance with Donathan, Walter went to Donathan's house and threatened to break his arm if he didn't leave his sister alone. After word spread around school about Donathan being threatened, no other guy approached Char.

I treated Char like the queen she is, and we were often told we made a great couple.

Mama shopped at the ABC Market over on Cherry Boulevard and I was watching the ad in the window for a box boy. The day after my sixteenth birthday Mr. Mays told me his work schedule and said for me to adjust mine so he could teach me to drive. I jumped on that.

During Christmas break at school I rode my bike to the ABC Market, applied for the job and four days later it was mine.

Mr. Goings, the ABC Markets manager, took a liking to me and worked with my school hours. I would leave school and go straight to the market. After my three hour shift I would head home and get my homework out of the way.

Once I started working Wednesday night church was out of the equation, but I did study a chapter a day of Proverbs after my homework was completed. Grand Pop taught us there are thirty-one Proverbs and usually thirty days in a month, so we are to read a chapter of Proverbs a day and when there were less days than chapters, read the remaining chapters. Grand Pop told us Proverbs is full of life situations and teaches wisdom on how to handle life.

Sundays were my off day at the market. When school was not in session Mr. Goings increased me to six hours a day and I saved my money and was able to pay for my class ring, school pictures and yearbook. Knowing the prom was the next upcoming event, I put money down on a burgundy suit, lavender shirt, a tie, and new dress shoes. Mama told me I had to buy Charlotte a corsage and have money for our meal and pictures.

By then I could not cut lawns or wash cars except Mr. Mays car. I was working at the market so much. I wanted a lot of money saved so Char could have whatever she wanted. I wanted to take Char to the best restaurant and show her off. Since Char and I went to the movies last year in November, we spend all of our Sundays together.

I knew I was in love with Charlotte and there was no other girl for me, and I knew she felt the same about me. I was starting to think of marriage because The Word teaches us not to be fornicators and my body was telling me casual sex every now and then was not going to work with me! After Char and I started kissing it was really hard for me to remember those values. Those were the times marriage would occupy my mind for hours after leaving Char.

Between Walter, Ronald and myself, Walter was the player and he became excited when Cheryl Richbow agreed to be his date for the prom. Of course, Ronald was taking Pam and I was escorting Char. We were all excited about the prom. Walter and Ronald were busy finding a hotel to take the girls after the prom. Walter kept asking me where was I taking Char because I better not even *think* about taking his sister with them. I kept telling Walter I was working on surprising Char and taking her to an art display in Los Angeles.

However, I never verbalized my complete thought to Walter. I was also working on taking Char to a place where we would be alone. Oh yeah, I will end up alone that night with Char, you better believe I will. The fact Walter and Cheryl were well known at school I knew there wasn't a hotel or motel I could take Char without the information getting back to Walter. I had to be creative.

May of my senior year, three days before prom I went to McDonnell Douglas and filled out an employment application for an assembler and used Mr. Mays friend, Harvey Jackson as a referral. I decided to take Charlotte to the recently opened Black Museum of Art, over on East Ocean Boulevard in Long Beach. She loves art and this way while I have Mr. Mays car, after the prom and museum tour, Char and I can go park on Signal Hill. Oh yes, we can kiss and hopefully we won't have to stop with kissing.

At that time Mr. Mays had a 1989 brown Buick Electra Deuce and a Quarter. The six of us are going to The Red Dragon Chinese Restaurant over on East 7th Street, then to the prom. Afterwards it is every couple for himself. Walter kept asking, "You still taking Char to the Museum, right?" I would reassure him that was where his sister and I were going to be.

The day of the Prom I was so excited. Finally, I am going to have my first night alone with Char; I was ready and bought protection. Dinner and the prom went very well and when Char and I left the restaurant as we headed to Mr. Mays car, I grabbed her hand. She is so beautiful in her cranberry carmine taffeta calf length fitted dress. Char had her hair up with small white pearls pinned in it. I wanted to kiss her so bad. I drove Char to the prom and kept my arm around her shoulder during the drive.

Walter drove Cheryl in Dad Thomas 1990 Oldsmobile Royale. Ronald's brother let him use his 1990 Buick Rivera. On the drive to the prom I didn't know what to say to Char I was thinking of us kissing and not having to stop. Man, it was difficult concentrating on my driving.

I parked in the prom parking lot and before I opened my car door, Char reached over and kissed me on my cheek and said, "Thanks Greg I feel like a queen when I am with you." I opened her car door for her and as I watched her get out of the car, I fought really hard not to grab her. I was ready to drive straight to Signal Hill.

Prom was alright, I just felt it was taking too long to be over, I wanted to spend all my time with Char.

On our way to the car after the prom, I told Char I had a surprise for her. Her eyes went really wide and she took on a fearful look. I watched her as I ran to my side of the car, she sat and stared down into her lap. After sliding behind the driver's seat, I glanced over at her. She was sitting so close to her door with her head still faced down.

I knew Char was nervous, so I said, "You are going to really enjoy where we are going. Tonight, will be very memorable for you." I was smiling at her and as she slowly turned to face me, fear engulfed her. I knew the words I had just spoken had a sexual connotation, so I shut up and drove to the Museum in silence.

Man, that seems like eons ago…

~~~Charlotte Ann Thomas~~~

BACKGROUND

Charlotte [Char] Ann Thomas, a tall confident woman. Five feet, nine inches, soft brown skin tone with dark brown, almost black eyes that are shaped like a cats. Charlotte's high cheek bones gives her the appearance of having a lot of American Indian DNA. Born two years after her brother, Walter Junior on May fifth in Los Angeles, California. Miss Charlotte Ann is her father and brother's bonafide princess, and she fills the role to the highest level!

Walter Thomas Senior [Big Walt] and Roslin Harper married after Walter Junior was born. Big Walt had some problems finding a steady job, so the three of them were living in his mother's back house over on Hooper Street in Los Angeles. Big Walt landed a job at a cannery in Terminal Island as a mechanic, saved his money and bought Roslin a house in Long Beach close to his job.

Roslin went to work part-time and when school started for Lil Walt and Charlotte, Roslin quit to stay home.

Both Big Walt and Roslin are from church going families and Roslin found a Baptist church not too far from their home where Pastor Kevin Perryman taught from the Bible. Big Walt liked that, he was not into whoop and holler. Big Walt took his family to church every Sunday morning and on the Wednesday evenings he did not work overtime the Thomas family went to Bible Study. Roslin worked for years on the Hospitality Committee then became active with the Pastors Aide and good friends with Sandra, Pastor Perryman's wife.

Big Walt and Roslin are very affectionate and Lil Walt and Charlotte are also. Lil Walt is always very protective of his little sister being Big Walt taught him to protect Charlotte at all times. Big Walt told Lil Walt and Charlotte when they were very young, "Take care of each other, you are all you have." With Big Walt, Roslin and Lil Walt watching out for Charlotte, she was treated like a princess and most times Charlotte Ann acted like one.

Charlotte's home in Inglewood, California...

"They say hindsight is far better than foresight and whoever *they* are, certainly told the truth!" Charlotte is having a conversation with her youngest daughter, Tammi. "Had I known your father and I would end up hating the sight of each other, I would not have married the man. Tamera Aliyah listen to me now! I am older and wiser than you. When it comes to love, huh, you have no idea what it is.

I know you and Justin think you're in love but what you are feeling is longing for some good sex. This feeling you have will soon pass after a few weeks of rolling around in bed. When he forgets your birthday and anniversary, girl you'll be mad enough to punch his lights out!" Charlotte cups Tammi's chin, softens her tone and adds, "Mark your mama's words."

Tammi looks at her mother in disagreement. "Mom I know what love is, it's what Justin and I have for one another. Just because you and Dad didn't make your marriage work and considering Reece and Charlie not making it; you think my marriage won't work either. I heard your advice and I am going to take what you have said under consideration, but we are getting married in nine weeks. Nothing will stop us. Justin is moving in with me Saturday so we can save money."

Charlotte rolls her eyes up in her head and walks away from Tammi. Tammi adds; "You'll see; our love will last." Tammi walks over and hugs her mother while blinking back tears.

Charece enters in the front door, notices her sister and Mom hugging and as she puts Lexi down on the floor asks, "Hey, what's going on?" Charlotte says, "I am trying to talk some sense into your sisters thick head. Maybe she'll listen to you, I am not getting anywhere." As they all take turns hugging one another Charece says, "I came over to drop the kids off, I'm not in the mood to argue with Tammi. Mom you know she's stubborn like her Dad." Charlotte reacts, "Oh no Reece, I am *not* watching babies tonight. I'm tired, I worked two extra hours today. I am going to bed; no way Jose take them over to their other grandmother."

With face frowned Charece whines, "Mom come on we're already here." Alexis and Tyreke starts running around the living room. Charece says, "Alright Lexi, stop running before you end up falling baby." Charlotte looks at Charece and says, "That's exactly why I can't be bothered."

Charece looks at Alexis and Tyreke and says while rolling her eyes at them, "Mom come on, you need to bond with your grand babies." Whining, Alexis runs to Charece and raises her hands up to be held. As Charece bends down to pick up Alexis, she turns towards Tammi and asks, "Hey Tammi you wanna watch your niece and nephew tonight?"

"Nope! Got a serious date with Justin. He's moving some of his things over. Sorry Sis. Love you." Tammi picks up Ty, kisses him and walks over by Charlotte. As Tammi hands Ty to Charlotte she says, "Bye Mom, I still love you." Tammi kisses her niece and heads for the front door.

Tammi shouts over Alexis whining, "**Okay y'all I'm gone.**" Charece asks, "Mom please just tonight, I…" "No Reece. I am taking a hot shower, pouring myself a full glass of wine and I'm bed bound. You need to call and ask somebody to watch your babies instead of assuming I don't have a life.

The gallery was busy today. We're prepping for Friday and Saturday's viewing and I must get up early tomorrow and do today all over again. Now I love you and my grandkids but you gotta go." Ty starts crying and rubbing his eyes. While staring Charlotte in the eyes Reece says, "Okay Mom. You do me this one favor and I won't ask you to watch them for a month." Charlotte's slowly shaking her head "No."

Charece pulls her cell out of her back pocket and makes a call. "Hey it's me. I can't make it tonight." She turns her back to Charlotte and whispers, "She's tired and refuses to watch them." While listening to the other person on the phone Charece's eyes are moving around the room. She briefly closes her eyes and says, "I know but no one can watch my kids and I can't go. Oh no I can't take them to Charlie's Mom. We are not speaking these days. I'll tell you later. Girl tell me tomorrow play by play exactly how it goes down tonight. Okay, bye."

They all walk towards the front door and Charlotte kisses her grand babies then her daughter Charece, and tells them all she loves them as she closes and locks the door. Charlotte heads for the kitchen and pours herself a glass of Moscato. She takes a sip and sits the glass on the counter and is now headed for the steaming hot shower she has been waiting for since she stepped in the door.

Mentally Charlotte goes over her conversation with Tamera while showering and remembers how deeply in love she was with Gregory. In her kitchen Charlotte drinks almost half the glass of wine, fills the glass to the brim and she's off to her bedroom. Charlotte places her glass on her nightstand, climbs into bed, props her pillows up behind herself, and lies back in total relaxation mode. Her mind effortlessly drifts back to Gregory's senior prom.

Greg was *the* most mindful man I have ever been with and remembering that night makes a smile appear on this face. My heart hurts when that memory clouds my mind. Gregory Allen was a perfect gentleman during our courtship. Anything I thought I might want Greg bought it. Lord help me, I'm getting water in my eyes thinking of that man.

When I see in my mind Greg holding me in his arms and whispering in my ear, "Char I would give you the world with a ribbon around it if I could. I would lasso the moon if it would put a smile on your face." While sipping from her glass Charlotte blinks back tears. As she places her glass down she yells, **"Liars, men are all liars!"** I can't believe I am shouting to an empty room; and I am not drunk! I loved that man and he broke my heart.

Greg loved seeing me smile make-up off or on, the man would beam when I smiled at him. I remember using my smile to get what I wanted him to do for me. He knew I was manipulating him yet he did whatever I asked if I smiled for him. Talk about many moons ago. I'm sitting here smiling thinking about how Gregory Allen could make me smile. All the man had to do was say something stupid and my smile switch would turn on.

The only time Greg said something dumb and I didn't smile was the night of his prom. The two of us were leaving the prom and I thought he was going to take me to a nice hotel. When he said, "You are going to really enjoy where we're going. Tonight will be very memorable for you." I almost burst out crying I was so scared.

Mother told me about sex when my period started, and she said it hurt when you have sex. Her reasoning for telling me that was so I would wait a long time before having that experience. It worked. I was scared to have sex after my talk with her. I thought people hollered when they had sex because it hurt. That's how dumb I was!

Walt and Ronald were talking about going to a hotel after the prom and every time I would enter the room while they were talking, they both became silent. Every night leading up to the prom, Walt would ask me where Gregory was taking me after the prom. I told him the truth, Greg said he was surprising me.

I started listening to Walt and Ronald's conversations a few moments before entering where they were and overheard Walt telling Ronald what I told him about Greg surprising me. Ronald laughed and said, "Yeah, probably taking her to a tent meeting!" Both Ronald and Walt laughed.

I had a feeling Greg was taking me to a hotel because every time we were alone and kissing, he would ask if I were ready to go all the way. I can't lie, I wanted to, but I was so scared it would hurt. I would end up pushing Greg away.

I was half looking forward to having my first time with Greg and half scared. I was saving myself for marriage and the way Greg treated me I knew we were going to get married and live happily ever after. Ha, Ha! It should be taught in school, there is no happily ever after; men are prone to change!

I remember that morning of the prom. When I woke, I was so excited about wearing my dress but when I thought about after the prom and able to go all the way with Greg, I would get so nervous. That evening when Greg came to the house to pick me up, I took one look at him with his burgundy suit and thought, 'Tonight's the night.' He was the finest guy in high school but because Greg was shy, he blended in with the crowd.

I was surprised Greg was interested in me because he was like another brother. Greg and Ronald watched me grow up however Greg never teased me when I wore my first bra or made fun of me while I wobbled my way into the skill of walking in heels.

Ronald on the other hand was always picking on me. Oddly, I had a crush on Ronald, he was always watching my every move. And you best believe Ronald commented on every move I made. Ronald is very outspoken and handsome with his smooth brown completion and seductive smile.

One day we were all over Greg's in the pool room and I had polished my grey flip flops with white shoe polish to match my white blouse. The polish had bled off onto my feet. Sam exclaimed, "Oh my goodness! What's that white stuff on your feet?" When I looked down and saw my feet, Walt and Ronald started laughing at me. Walt says while laughing, "I told you it wouldn't work." Ronald says, "Girl you bout as dumb as they come! Who? Tell me who polishes rubber!"

Everyone in the room was laughing at me. I glanced around the room and when I noticed Greg, he was smiling, looking down at my feet. I shouted at him, **"You gonna take a crack at me too, huh. Go** ahead!" Gregory's smile fell from his face and he looked me in the eyes and said, "Why are you mad at me. I didn't say anything!" That day I realized Greg wasn't as critical as Walt and Ronald and wished Ronald were kind like Greg.

The day Greg asked if I wanted to go to the movies was the day I looked at him differently than a play brother. I agreed to go to the movies with him just for the food and thought we were all going as a group. When Greg picked me up was when I knew it was only the two of us going to the movies.

Greg was so attentive, and quiet. I had no idea Greg was interested in me until we stepped off my front porch, that's when it entered my brain, 'he likes me!' I must admit my first thought was,'why couldn't Ronald see me this way?' After the movie when Greg walked me to the front door of my house, I thought I was dreaming. Kind, sweet, thoughtful Gregory Allen Young was choosing to be with me, Lil Walt's bird legged sister!

I fell in love with Gregory Allen Young. He was so kind and thoughtful. Too bad we married, he worked all of the time instead of spending time with the girls and I. It's strange how Gregory could just put his arms around me and make me feel I was his world.

When we first married, he was so loving and kind and when we made love he was so tender and gentle but before Charece arrived all of Gregory's conversations where about money. We would have made a great life together had he not put making money more important than spending time together... *Men...*

My phones ringing. It's Irene. I answer, "Hey girl what's up?" "Girl, girl. I have us dates tomorrow night. I met this guy, Rance Owens and told him about your Art Gallery Show Saturday. He wants to take me. I asked if he has a friend for you and he said he did. We are to meet them here at my place for drinks at eight-thirty. So, wear something sexy to show that fantastic body of yours and try to be nice Char. Give the man a chance before picking him apart okay?" I roll my eyes up in my head. Irene is always trying to hook me up. I am not looking for heartache, I choose to leave trouble alone.

"Irene, what's the man's name?" "What difference does that make Char; don't be tryin to get out of this date. Besides Rance is fine." I butt in, "Alright, alright, I'll meet this no name guy. But if he's hard on the eyes, it's swallow down my drink and I'm exiting. You hearing me Irene?" "Char do you want to be lonely the rest of your life?" "Irene, let me talk to your man. Come on put him on the phone. Just what I thought. How you look telling me about loneliness? You know you're two months older than I am. Put a sock in it. I'll see you tomorrow evening. Hey! Love you." "I love you to Char. [chuckle] See you tomorrow."

After ending our conversation, I remember the day Irene and I met at high school. It was the first day. I had just finished getting into my gym clothes and secured the lock on my locker when Irene wandered into my cubicle and plopped down on the bench next to me. As I stood up to leave, I said, "All of these lockers are taken." Before I could finish my sentence, Irene snapped, "Oh thank you miss teacher!" "I'm not the teacher." With an attitude and rolling her eyes she blurts, "Oh well excuse me for thinking you were, giving me instructions and all..." I took a step towards her, "Look hefa!"

Irene popped up off the bench so fast. Jackie stepped in between us as she says, "Alright y'all bring it down." Irene quickly spews, "Yeah, tell her something before I give her a trip to the nurse's office!" Monique steps up to Irene and spews, "Oh you're the one goin to the nurse's office Hefa!" I grabbed Mo and Jackie grabbed Irene and pulled her away looking for an empty locker.

When everyone in class was outside lined up for roll call, Irene was late coming outside and Ms. Porter, our Physical Education teacher yelled at her to get in line before she was made to run ten laps. I noticed Irene had tears slowly running down her face.

Mo walked over to me and asked if I saw the waterworks, I told her yeah.

Jackie worked her way over to Irene, said something and Irene broke down. Mo and I walked over to see what was going on. Irene's last teacher embarrassed her in front of everyone just before class was over and Irene had an attitude by the time she finally found the gym building. We took turns hugging Irene and the four of us became, "The Clique."

Irene Dawson, Monique Green, Jacqueline Baker, and I, yes indeed, we hang real tough together all three years of high school. After graduation we all lost touch with each other but when I attended our fifth-year class reunion Irene and I re-united and keep in touch.

After talking to some of the classmates at the reunion we found out Mo became caught up in the drug life and last heard, she was incarcerated. Her mother was raising her three kids. Jackie moved to Arizona for a job as a Social Worker.

Irene married Glen Ferguson, but she said it was a shotgun wedding, they just got caught and her father made them marry. Mr. Dawson told Glen if he wanted to keep his baby maker, he had better show up to the chapel. Irene said her father uttered those words to Glen while twirling his pistol around on their coffee table and staring Glen in the face.

Glen junior arrived nine months after Karol. Irene said the sex was good but the everyday living consisted of yelling and her throwing things at Glen. They were too young.

Irene works for Northrop Grumman El Segundo location. She is very smart and started working there right out of high school. Her being a stickler for detail caused a promotion to the lab department with a big title and raise to match. When Irene's daughter, Karol started middle school, Irene bought a nice three-bedroom two bath stucco home in Fox Hills and does well for herself.

During high school, the four of us started eating together at lunch time and most days our conversations were about the horrible teachers and dumb topics the school board had us learning. Every once in a while, Jackie would share her sex experiences and during the last two months of our sophomore year, Irene started sharing every detail of her first, second- and third-time experiences. Mo and I were still virgins.

Mo was waiting on an older man with money to sweep her off her feet and I was saving myself for Greg. When Greg and I had sex the first time, there was still a month of school to complete of our sophomore year but I never shared our experience with The clique.

What Greg and I shared was so remarkable to me. I felt as though Greg and I became one person. It's difficult to explain the oneness I felt. Besides, it was beautiful and they made sex seem as though it was a typical ride at the Fair. 'Oh yeah we had, we did, and then…' They wouldn't understand what happened between Greg and I.

Talk about a long time ago, Ha!

That Gregory Young was so sweet. Yeah, maybe it was a few weeks after Greg and I attended the movies, we were all over his house playing pool and one by one people disappeared. When Walt left to go over some girl's house, he told Greg to make sure I made it home alright. Greg walked me to the front door and when we stopped to say bye, he reached over and gave me a soft tender kiss on my lips. I was floating the rest of the evening. He smelled so good. We French kissed the first time at school behind the football field.

I never will forget that day…
It was lunch period with the Clique and Mo pointed out the guys on the field, so we all ran over to talk to them. Irene, Mo, and Jackie knew I liked Greg and Irene tried to get me to go all the way with him, but I

was scared and really had no spark for sex, but, we hadn't French kissed yet.

Greg saw us and started slowing his pace as the other guys ran the field. We all talked briefly, said bye and as I walked away from Greg, he grabbed my hand and pulled me close to himself and opened his mouth to kiss me. I opened my mouth and all I thought about the rest of that day and night was our French kiss.

I felt sparks from then on and by the time our homecoming game approached I was having a real difficult time pushing Greg away and telling him that's enough. It's not like Greg and I were ever alone and something could happen, I just wanted our first time to be special.

The Monday before prom while we all walked home from school, Greg told me he was getting Mr. Mays car so the two of us could go someplace special. I became silent after that. I arrived home asking myself, 'Are you ready?' Thursday night before prom when Greg and I were standing on my back-doorstep kissing, I didn't want to stop and felt as though I was ready. The day of the prom, I was back to wondering again. The whole day of the prom I was vacillating whether or not tonight's the night.

Greg came over to the house along with Ronald and Pam and when Walt arrived with Cheryl, we all posed for a whole roll of film. Mother and Mother Mays took pictures until the cameras were out of film. I remember being a little nervous.

I was always the youngest of the group and because Pam was so confident when she spoke and seemed to do everything right, I was a bundle of nerves. We were all dressed up and I felt as though we were on display. Walt and Cheryl left, and we all followed them.

The food was great! My family always order take out at that Chinese Restaurant but by the time Dad gets home with it, it's always cold and after Mother re-heats it, it would be rubbery. That night, the food was absolutely divine!

Greg was so attentive to me during dinner I felt as though he didn't know anyone else was there. He stared at me and passed the Lazy Susan around before I could reach for it. I felt as though I was living a fairy tale. Now we are headed to the prom. After Greg sat in the car I slid over and kissed his cheek. I thanked him for making me feel like a queen. He drove to the prom with his arm around my shoulder and I smiled the whole ride there.

While at the prom Greg was still attentive. He looked at me so tenderly and I found myself blushing. Greg made me feel like I was the only lady at the prom. I love to dance, and hearing music causes me to start moving. Greg's not a dancer and I danced with Walt when my favorite songs played. None of the guys there asked me to dance and after we married, I found out why. Greg gave every guy that came close to me a dirty look as he stepped up to them, making the guys re-think asking me to dance.

I feel so sad now sitting here on our bed alone reminiscing about the time the sun rose and set on me as far as Greg was concerned. Then he changed…

Well as the prom began to wind down Walt and Ronald went missing along with their dates. I asked Greg to tell me where he was taking me, but he just smiled and repeated what he had been telling me for over a week, "It's a surprise but you'll love it!"

We walked to the car and Greg smiled while opening the door for me. After I sat down, I started rubbing my hands together I was so nervous. I was thinking 'You're sixteen Charlotte Ann you are *not* ready for sex yet!' I sat so close to the door; the door handle was poking me in my side.

I glance over at Greg and he is smiling so wide I thought we were headed to the Hotel. I became so scared. Greg said something stupid, but I kept thinking, 'It is gonna hurt! It is gonna hurt!' I grabbed onto the car door handle because it was digging in my side. I had never been that scared ever!

When we pulled up into the parking lot of that small quaint A-framed building, I gasped! I heard myself and covered my mouth that was half a mile wide open. I was so happy I almost cried. And I was a little relieved.

This museum had a write-up in January of this year, announcing its impending grand opening. The newspaper had a picture of the owner and her explaining briefly how her dream became a reality for her. I have loved black art since my seventh-grade class spent a day's field trip at a small Art Gallery in Pasadena.

That trip is etched in my mind. I remember this glimpse of vivid colors out of the corner of my eye. As I turned to see what these beautiful colors were, I left the group and walked totally spellbound over to the painting. I read the title inscribed at the bottom, it was Maxwell Dickson, *"Jazz Musician."*

I stood completely still, studying every inch of the painting. Me being a music lover, I deeply inhaled observing the blue cheeks of Dizzy Gillespie. That was the day my love for the world of Afro-American Art launched.

I smiled so much ambling through the museum with Greg that night, I thought the muscles in my face were permanently etched in the form of a smile. We took our time and walked the whole gallery. I marveled at the art. Some of the paintings revealing our southern plight were very expressive.

While walking to the car leaving the gallery, I asked Greg, "Okay, tell me what captivated you most?" He looked at me and said, "Your smile." When he sat in the car Greg said, "Char, your smile makes my day." He scooted close to me and kissed me so tenderly, I thought I was floating. He slid behind the wheel and started the car. Greg looked over at me, placed his hand around my waist and slid me right up under himself. He drove to Signal Hill and when I read the sign my heart began to race.

Jackie had shared with our clique about Signal Hill. The lovers who frequent the place has nicknamed it, "Motel Hill." When I read the sign I thought, 'Okay Charlotte, you better get ready to go through with this. Greg has done a lot to make you happy so let's make him happy.' Greg turned the ignition off and wrapped his arms around me. Gregory Young kissed me like I have never been kissed by any other man. My heart rate increased and so did my desire. We climbed to the back seat and both of us experienced sex for our first time. Greg held me in his arms and we both cried.

During the drive home, it was so quiet. All that could be heard was the hum of the engine and the flogging of the tires. When Greg pulled in front of my house he says, "Charlotte, I love you and want us to get married. As soon as I get this job at Douglas I am going to save money for us to get a house. You will be eighteen in two years and by then it will happen okay."

I watched his expression as he spoke to me. I saw a different Greg. He was now the man I would spend the rest of my life with. No longer was he Greg, my best friend, he was now my lover and we are connected together forever.

Greg called late the next morning and Walt stood in the doorway of his bedroom with his shirt off asking, "Where did Gregory end up taking you last night?" I covered the receiver and said, "To church, where you think nosey!" I got up and closed the door to my room and laid on my bed while Greg and I talked about getting married for almost an hour. After I took my shower, I entered the kitchen and Greg was talking to Walt about the museum. Walt excused himself and went back to bed.

Three weeks later Greg was called to Douglas and started working. I had two years left to complete high school and half the time I did not want to go to class. Greg and I longed to be together again and when we were alone, he would hold me and tell me it wouldn't take long for him to save up enough money so we can get married. Greg started working ten hours a day including Saturdays and before I knew it he worked Sunday's.

I went into a depression because I missed Greg so much. Every chance I had, I would tell him how much I missed him and could hardly wait for him to have a day off. Greg would always say, "Char I am doing this for us, so we can get married. I miss you too, but this is what I have to do so we can be together." I would always sadly reply, "Greg I know but it's so hard not seeing you. I miss you so much!"

By Labor Day Greg bought himself a truck and on Saturday's he would stop by the house on his way to work. We would sit in the kitchen and talk. Mainly I informed Greg on what was happening since he worked so much and was out of the loop of things. I missed Greg more after I saw him and would go to my room and cry after he left. I think it was Greg's holding me that I missed. That man had a way of making me feel complete when he held me. I felt as though the world stood still while I was in Greg's arms.

Mother volunteered me to participate in various activities at church to keep my mind occupied. She told me to resist depression, it would consume me if I gave it permission.

My senior year's homecoming game I attended with The clique and Mo talked about her boyfriend, Ivan and how he has his own place. She really bragged about all the possessions Ivan had and when Irene asked, "What does he do for a living?" Mo went completely silent. Jackie asked, "Mo, what is it?" Mo slowly answers, "He works from his home."

The way Mo spoke made all of us turn to face her and stare her down. Mo timidly says, "He sells white powder." Suddenly Mo turns defensive. While folding her arms and wobbling her neck she blurts, "What's the big deal, the man in the white house pimps us. We work and he takes taxes from us!" Jackie tells Mo, "That is stupid! Monique Green you know good and damn well you cannot compare drugs to taxes!" We continued staring at Mo waiting for her to reply; she slowly looked away. We eyed one another then watched the rest of the game.

When the game was over, we went to the ladies' room and of course there was a long line. I had to go bad, so I started walking around to keep myself moving and bumped into a guy in my English class, Blake Bell. He apologized so long and held onto my arms thinking he had hurt me because when we bumped, I sailed a few feet away from him. I was too embarrassed to let him know I had to pee really bad and was almost skipping. So, I kept telling him I was alright. Finally, Blake let go of me and went on his way.

When we returned to school after winter break, I ran into Blake again and he asked how was I doing after the accident we had at the game. We laughed and went our separate ways. I didn't realize how we happened to run into each other until we seniors had our "Beach Day."

Blake kept standing around us and when Irene told me our meetings were not accidental; I thought she was being messy. Mo told me she agreed with Irene and Jackie shook her head also in agreement. I told them, "Wait right here."

I walked over to Blake and said, "Hey. My friends seem to think our bumping into each other is not by accident." Blake replies, "Your friends are correct. I hope you didn't put any money on it." I was shocked! I only have eyes for Greg.

I told Blake, "Sorry someone already has my heart." I returned to the clique. When I told them, they were right they all high-fived one another. I turned to look at Blake and he turned from looking at me and walked away. I never gave Blake a second thought. I only had an aching for Gregory Allen Young!

Greg worked so much, and I was lonely most of the time and was preoccupied with prom night memories. Whenever Greg and I were able to be together he always reassured me time would go by fast. He would have money for us to buy our own home soon.

Greg would tell me to concentrate on us having a nice wedding. He reminded me that we would be together soon and for me not to allow depression to take hold of me. Greg would give me scriptures to look up and encourage me. He even went so far as making me visualize some of the items we would have in our place together. Greg always took time to reiterate how this missing one another would be behind us before we know it.

I graduated from high school and yes, Greg missed it. He was sleeping because he had to be at work that night. July fourth Greg phoned me that morning and told me to get dressed, he was taking me to breakfast before he went to sleep. I knew something was up and was hoping it was an engagement ring with a wedding date! Preferably next year, I'll be eighteen in May so a June wedding will be perfect!

I was so excited when Greg pulled up. I was looking out of the window for him. As soon as Greg pulled up I ran to the front door and as my hand touched the doorknob I heard a stern, "Don't you set foot out of that door!" Mother was behind me. I turned to face her as Greg's familiar knock could be heard on the door. He had sprinted to the porch. Mother steps in front of me and opens the door saying, "Well, hello stranger. Come on in."

"Good morning Mrs. Thomas." Greg bends over and kisses Mother on the cheek. She replies, "Gregory you must have a real nice nest egg working so much. How have you been?" Greg looks at me the whole while he talks. "I am working on a goal and a man with a goal is a man determined." "I'm sure," says Mother as she leaves the room. I walk up to Greg and he kisses me so tenderly I feel myself getting goose bumps. He grabs my hand and we're off.

Greg tells me he has an apartment and wants me to go with him to put the money down. "Char my truck is paid for, now I am saving so we can get our own house. I want to get you transportation for your graduation gift. I go Friday to check out a car for you." "Greg you are buying me a car? Really!" I smiled at him and he stares at me with a serious look.

After a few moments Greg says, "You are the most beautiful woman ever created." I drop my smile and stare into his eyes. I'm feeling the effect of our kiss that led us to climb in the back seat on prom night. I feel myself squirming. Greg softly says, "It won't be much longer Char." I feel my smile reappear.

We went to breakfast then Greg took me to Wilmington where our first apartment was located. Our one bedroom furnished, second-floor apartment on Gramercy. After Greg signed the papers, we were told it takes a week to process the paperwork then

Greg would get the key. I was so happy Greg was getting us closer to being together.

Two weeks later Greg pulled up in front of my house in an old dark green two door clunker and blew the horn. Mother and I ran to the window and Greg rolled the window down and waved for us to come outside. After we went through the car, I drove it over to Stockton Avenue allowing Mother Mays to see it. I drove Greg to get his truck and followed him to the apartment. Greg made love to me and I didn't want to go home. I left him asleep, he had to go back to work.

On August twentieth Greg came over to my house on his way to work. He insisted everyone come into the living room before making his announcement. He asked Dad for my hand in marriage. After Dad gave us his blessing everyone cheered and we all hugged. Walt was on the phone and paused just long enough to hug me then disappeared. After Greg left, Dad told Mother and I Greg would make me a good husband; he was not afraid to work and provide for his family. Dad said sarcastically, "Too bad Lil Walt is afraid of work."

Mother told Dad to leave Walt alone he was still young. Dad looked at Mother and said, "If a job was spelled *w.o.m.a.n.* that boy would be a workaholic." Mother stuck her nose up at Dad and walked out the room. I was so happy. I thought, 'I need to get a job and fix up our place. I don't care for the furniture in that apartment.' I spent the next week looking for work.

I became disappointed after my second interview at JCPenney, I did not get the job. Greg and I were on the phone and he asked why I felt I had to work. If I wanted to attend school, it was fine. He would take care of me. That night I thought about going to school, but I didn't know what I wanted to do. I would love to work at an Art Museum.

Pam found out she was pregnant, and Ronald quit college and went to work with Greg. September, I enrolled in art classes. It only took three classes to realize I absolutely do not have an ounce of artistic abilities! I highly appreciate looking at art. I was scared to tell Dad I wanted to drop out of my art class because it cost him money we didn't have to waste.

When I unenthusiastically told Dad I wanted to transfer to another class, he told me one mistake was all I was afforded. After this I would be paying for my own education. I was so nervous because I really didn't know what I wanted to do.

I put in applications to work at Art Galleries. I was hired at what would be my first gallery of four. And, found out quick, cleaning up after artists was all that's available for people like me; not gifted to paint nor draw. Just cleaning up behind those who are.

I started working for a small gallery downtown Los Angeles and I mean they worked me. The good thing about my working was I didn't have time to miss Greg so much.

Thanksgiving Day, Greg presented me with an engagement ring. The day after Thanksgiving I went over to his apartment and we made love three times. I went home and tipped toed into the living room. It was three-thirty in the morning. Mother was laying on the couch waiting for me and I mean she was searing!

Mother leaped up shouting; **"Charlotte Ann, you had better not bring a baby up in here calling me grandmother! I did not raise you to be whoring with Greg. Get a license to go with that ring! You better hear what I'm saying to you Charlotte Ann Thomas!"** Mother's hollering woke Walt and I was so glad Dad was working overtime.

I headed to my bedroom and they both followed me. Mother turned the ceiling light on in my room and Walt stood over me while I laid on top of my bed and he cussed me out good and loud, right in front of Mother.

Walt threatened to kill Greg. He said he was going to beat his ass so bad I wouldn't recognize him! Mother's reply to Walt was, **"Thank you!"** They left my room and after I heard their bedroom doors slam, I got up to turn the ceiling light off in my room.

My mind was made up; 'Six months and I will be eighteen. I am moving in with Greg tomorrow, these people are trippin up in here!

~~~Gregory ~~~

Setting my alarm for nine a.m. so I can get up early and make my first counseling session tomorrow. I am thinking back when Char and I started living together. As I pull cover over myself a flash of her smile crosses my mind. That woman had the most beautiful smile God ever gave a woman.

Out of all my wives Charlotte Thomas is the only woman whose face still flashes across my mind. Sometimes I am not even thinking of her and that smile just appears for no apparent reason. Maybe it's because we were childhood sweethearts…

That woman betrayed me at the highest level and I still see her smiling face, what's the deal with that?

The Saturday after the Thanksgiving Char graduated High School, she appeared at my apartment door with a laundry basket full of her clothes. I was both happy and afraid. Happy Char and I were together and afraid I would have to kick Walter's butt. Char and I started out a good team when we were together and she worked at three different art galleries before being hired permanent.

We lived together saving our money for her dream wedding. The first two weeks she moved in we were getting it on two, three times a day and a few times we had accidents with the protection. Char went to the clinic and started on birth control pills. We had to abstain for a whole week, and it was difficult!

Valentine's Day, Char gave me a "Thinking of you" card. Of course, I was puzzled and when I opened it, I read what she wrote, "*...And how you feel about becoming a father!*" I believe my heart stopped.

My mind immediately went to the balance in my savings. I pictured Char standing in front of a house holding a baby in her arms, but the house behind her was old and shabby. My reason for working was to buy her a new house with warranties on all new appliances. And Char could pick whatever house she wanted.

I realized Char was staring at me waiting for my response. I don't want her to think I do not want the baby, even though I don't want it now. I smiled and reached for her however, before I could say anything she says in a voice just above a whisper, "You don't want a baby now do you?"

She turns around and walks away from me. I jump in front of her, grab both her hands and very softly tell her, "It would be nice if we had the house first."

She started blinking rapidly and I did not want Char crying. I quickly add while smiling, "You know what, babies have no idea where they live. Right?" I start swinging both her hands side to side and she looks away from me and opens her mouth. I blurt, "Char a baby, our baby will be the best thing you can give me."

I grab and hug Char. She cries while saying, "Greg I forgot to take the pills a couple times. I didn't mean to get pregnant. We've worked so diligently to stay with the plans we wrote down." I held her and let her cry. I know we are having this baby. I just have to figure out how to make adjustments financially.

That's when Char became whinny. She complained, this hurt, that's sore. She just whined. I looked forward to having the baby so we could get back to where we were before the pregnancy.

We married May tenth at the courthouse. After the ceremony Mother and Dad Thomas had a small reception for us at the Thomas house. Char was disappointed her grand wedding did not happen, but she never voiced it. The money she saved for the wedding was now being used for crib, stroller and whatever else babies need.

The night Charece Kimberly Young arrived I was elated. The nurses were rolling Char into a room and I walked along side. After they pushed the head of her bed up against the wall and stepped away Char said, "Daddy, come get a good look at your daughter." Char raised Charece up and handed her to me. I was hesitant to hold Charece, but Char adds, "She's yours you won't break her."

I awkwardly held Charece and after drawing her close, her tiny soft body contoured to my arms. That feeling of being one with my daughter evolved that second. Charece was so beautiful to me even though she was wrinkled. I had never held a newborn and holding her confirmed the helplessness of my daughter and her needing me, her father, to take care of her. I thought, 'Look what we did. This beautiful little life. And she is totally depending on me.' I kissed Charece on the forehead and handed her back to Char.

Char laid Charece on the bed and unwrapped her. Her tiny body trembled. I stood over my daughter and felt such a warm feeling cover my heart. I felt water fill up in my eyes. "Isn't she beautiful Greg? She's perfect. All of her fingers and toes. God has blessed us." I blinked back tears, leaned over and kissed Char on her forehead and thanked her for giving me such a beautiful daughter.

I thought God was so awesome to allow us, man, and woman to produce such a magnificent human being. I wondered if I were dreaming. I believe it took me three days to process the gift Charece was to me and my wife, my love.

Man, that was a long time ago.

Char and I had plans to buy her another car then a house but when Charece started walking, Char realizes she is pregnant again. I dreaded going through the pregnancy all over again but so did Char. We discussed at length her getting on birth control again and Char agreed. Breastfeeding Charece threw her body off but after this baby arrives, she will be taking the pill again!

We moved to Lomita into a two-bedroom apartment when Charece was a year old. I wanted my children in a good school district and Char did not like living in that furnished apartment. Everything I read about Lomita was the best choice for us and, it worked.

Char worked for seven months again while pregnant but this time she whined about it. Her paycheck went to layaways for baby necessities and fixing the apartment up with her style furniture. I bought Char a new Sentra sedan, but I had to make payments.

I was saving money to buy her a new house in Carson and was going to surprise her. There was a builder giving first time buyers incentives, paying closing cost. A lot of people were taking advantage of the money being given. So many things occurred, I needed another truck, rent increased, large item furniture had to be purchased. Just life; saving became very minimal.

When Charece started school, Char went back to work, and Mother Thomas watched Tamera. Char was a good wife, she just complained about me not wanting to spend time with her. During the Christmas shutdowns, I asked to be loaned out to other departments for the extra money and my savings was getting up there. My truck was giving me problems and I was contemplating buying myself a new one but that meant car payments.

I had money to pay cash for a used truck, but I needed the money for a down payment on the house. I read not to make any purchases when buying a house. This enabled you to qualify for a larger loan amount. Well I paid cash for another used truck and started saving again for the house. It took me almost two years, but I almost had enough money to put down and extra for Char to buy herself a washer and dryer. I was going to surprise her soon.

I was only eight hundred dollars shy of moving Char into her own house. After Tamera started school, Char started complaining very time we were together about me staying home more. She would tell me to decrease some of the overtime she would cut corners so we could be together. Char would wake me an hour earlier and try getting me to go to the park for half an hour, watch a movie with her. Just crazy stuff. I kept telling her to be patient and we would end up arguing.

Just before Charece had her sixth birthday Char was giving me the silent treatment leaving me notes but to tell the truth, I was glad she was not complaining. Her being vocal always led to an argument. Char had Charece's birthday party at Chucky Cheese in Carson and I left early to go to work. Char was smoking mad!

When Char's twenty-fifth birthday came around, she was still giving me the silent treatment. So, I bought her a large bouquet of flowers and a two-pound box of See's Candies.

Our seventh anniversary was approaching, and Char left me a note; *"If you are interested, our Anniversary is coming up. What do you want to do if anything??"* I ignored her note; of course I am interested. That's what I mean, she is wanting to start an argument.

A few days later she left another note; *"I now accept you being regretful we married. I will no longer bother you!"* I answered back; "I am sorry, I love you, just working and forgot. We can go to dinner Saturday evening; I'll take the midnight shift. Make it happen. Char, I love you, Greg." That night I realized I had worked on our actual anniversary and forgot.

That Saturday evening, we left the house at five p.m. headed to the restaurant to celebrate. Char was silent until we were eating. I held her hand and told her I loved her and how blessed we were to have come a long way from a furnished apartment and two clunkers.

I couldn't say anything right. Man, did she pour the criticism on. Char found a reason my working and paying for what she wanted being what a non-caring husband does. Like I am non-caring!

Almost a month had passed since our anniversary and with Char giving me the silent treatment I thought we were good. I was glad we were not arguing!

Ronald was working at Douglas and I never will forget the night he appeared in my work area. Ten o'clock Ronald came slowly walking up to me acting strange, so I asked what was wrong. He stared me down before saying he had heard a rumor. Of course, I thought he had information regarding a lay-off.

Ronald blurted, "Man Charlotte is cheating on you. I hate to be the one to tell you, but you're my brother. Man, I can't let you go out like that. Pam told me she has seen Charlotte riding around with the dude all over LB. Sorry Gregory, but you need to know. Don't do nothing stupid man. Think before you do anything. We have a lot to lose; you know what I'm sayin?" Ronald stared me down again and left.

I felt as if an eighteen-wheeler was sitting on my chest. I had to prop myself up on a machine. The wind was knocked out of me. Maybe someone doesn't know its Walter Char is with. Maybe…

I don't know. I need to find out what the hell is going on, that I do know!

I tried working until eleven-thirty, but I kept envisioning Char sitting up close to some no faced dude in a convertible and could not keep my mind on what I was doing. So, I told my boss I was not feeling well and clocked out at eleven instead of working until three a.m.

During my drive home, I thought about how Char has been acting lately. For the longest whenever she says anything to me, she has an attitude and rolls her eyes at me constantly. I have gotten to the place I just shake my head at her. I have no idea what she is so irritated about all the time. Char acts as though I want to work.

Here I am thinking her silence is a good thing. When we have sex…Man. She just lies still. Man! I know she is not sleeping with this dude; I know she's not!

I pull up in back of the apartment building and there is a car in my parking space. I don't recognize the car, so I park in front of the building and when I walk to the back elevator, this dude steps out and heads to the back-parking lot. I take inventory of him; I don't think I have ever seen him before. He heads towards where my parking space is so I hold the elevator door open and watch him. Awh naw. Dude is parked in my spot! I let the elevator door go and run to get his license plate, but I didn't make it in time.

I get upstairs and Char is startled as she sharply asks, "What are you doing here?" "I live here! Why are you changing the sheets?" Char gets a scared look on her face. She bends over, picks up the sheets that are on the floor and turns headed to the bathroom. I follow her, grab her elbow, and twirl her around to face me. "Char what the hell is going on?"

My volume is high. She tells me, "Lower your voice Greg, you'll wake the girls!" I pull her close to me and can smell the other man on her. I bet it was that Dude. She yanks herself free from me. I feel my heart beating fast. I am mad as hell! As we stand perfectly still staring into each other's eyes, my face feels like it is on fire. I have never hit a female with the exception of my little sister, when I was a young boy.

As I closely look Char's face over, I am wondering who the hell is this woman and when did she change. Now she has me wanting to change my policy of never hitting a female! I am breathing hard and fast and feel as though I am swelling up. I am going to explode!

I slowly step back telling myself, 'Back off, **back off!'** I want to grab Char and hug her while expressing she has broken my heart and in a split second, I see myself hitting her with my fist and she is falling backwards. I quickly turn around and walk away. **I really want to hit her!**

I left that night and never went back…

The next day Charlotte called Mama and told her I had left her and the girls and she had packed my clothes and would drop them off at Stockton Avenue later today. The next time I saw Charlotte was in court, and she had Dude with her. I never knew she could be so cold blooded.

Man! I can't believe I ever loved her…

~~~ Charlotte ~~~

While lying here in bed I think about how deeply I love Tammi and don't want her heart broken. I see how Justin treats her, just like her father treated me. I knew Greg loved me it's just he changed after we were married.

He never wanted to spend time with me or the girls. It was always work, work, work. I begged Greg to take some time off so we could go to the beach or even a movie. He was either complaining about wasting money to go somewhere or he was throwing up "our budget" in my face.

When we dated, if I asked for chocolate covered ants, Gregory Young would run all over Southern California to find them. I loved that man so. My heart was consumed with love for Greg. I knew the man loved me. He just changed. I guess we all do, that's why I want to protect Tammi.

It's a shame Charece and Charles couldn't make their marriage work. I just don't want Tammi to have to experience the pain of divorce.

As I turn my bedroom lamp light out, I remember the times Greg and I had that were full of laughter and fun. I feel tears slowly drip down my cheek. I think I still love Greg. I really didn't mean to sleep with Blake. I was lonely and, well, greasy hands can't hold things long. I wipe the tears away and remember the day I ran into Blake; January second.

I was at the Carson Mall purchasing a set of flannel sheets that were on sale and just happened to run into Blake. He made me feel so good remembering me. I was comparing the choices JC Penny had for me to choose from so I could get the best deal when I heard, "Charlotte Thomas?"

I looked up and saw this tall fine man smiling at me. I responded, "And, you are?" "Awh that hurts. I have thought of you periodically since we graduated high school. And here you are not even remembering my name."

I search his face trying to place him. It hits me! "Blake? Blake Bell?" "Oh, so you do remember me. I feel better now." He extends his hand out for mine and when I extend my hand to him, he pulls me close and hugs me. I can't lie, it felt so good being hugged. And he smelled so good. I stood back and took in every line and detail of his face. Blake Bell is fine!

Blake asks if I still live in LB and I told him "Yes." He hands me a business card while informing me he works for the I.R.S. up in Tracy California. He was down visiting his Mom for the holidays.

When I took Blake's business card I had no intention of calling him but the next day Greg and I had a huge argument about Tammi receiving her first academic certificate at school and him not attending. I was livid! He can't sacrifice two hours sleep!

I slammed the bedroom door closed and my eyes went straight to my purse. I remembered Blake giving me his card, so I gave him a call. I was angry and felt Greg was taking me for granted and the girls didn't have a Dad.

I agreed to meet Blake for lunch the next day. I have to admit I flirted with the man. I liked having someone demonstrate caring about me. Not one time did Blake mention what the prices were at any of the places when we ate out. Blake went back up to Tracy and put in for a transfer to Los Angeles.

It took eight weeks for Blakes transfer to go through and he flew down every weekend and stayed with his mother in LB. Blake asked about Lomita knowing that's where I lived. Greg moved us there when I became pregnant with Tammi.

I had Blake follow me to our apartment after work to let him get an idea what Lomita entailed. And, yeah, I wanted to have sex with him.

I felt so bad afterwards and broke down crying. Blake held me in his arms never saying a word. When I was able to talk, I told him he had to leave. "Blake, I love my husband, I am so sorry I thought I could do this but now I realize I am angry at Greg, but I still love him, you need to leave."

Blake let go of me and while dressing he tenderly says, "Charlotte I have loved you since eleventh grade. If you need a shoulder to cry on, call me. I'm here for you." Blake kissed me on the cheek and silently left.

After that night I had been with Blake I tried to talk to Greg, but he never made time. Those first three days after Blake and I had been together, I cried like some pregnant woman. I would think about being in Blakes arms and guilt would consume me. Then I would watch how Greg acted like he wanted nothing to do with me and the pain in my heart would cause automatic tears to flow.

That weekend I watched Greg rush to leave for work as if he couldn't wait to get away from me.

That Wednesday I stepped in front of Greg with tears in my eyes and said to him, "Greg we need to spend some time together. I need, I mean we need to get back on track." I reached out to hug him and he grabs both my hands and while pushing me away from him saying, "Char I agree but now is not the time. Why didn't you wake me earlier, now I will have to rush?"

I felt as though Greg could care less about rekindling our love. He was in love with his job and staying on his stupid budget. I know this sounds crazy but, Greg closing the door in my face that afternoon, made me feel as though he had shut the passion we once shared completely out of our marriage. Our marriage has ended. I felt the slam of the door was the bell in a televised boxing match ringing, ding, ding, ding! It's over.

I sat on the couch and cried. If Greg were seeing another woman, I could follow him and fight her, slash her tires, change our phone number. I could do something to fight for my husband's affection. But his job… He runs to it as if she is more important than what he has at home.

I cried so hard I was hyperventilating. When I stood up, I was no longer Charlotte Thomas-Young. I became Charlotte Thomas again, and, single. I had Blake over regularly after that.

At that time, I worked three days a week and the first two weeks I told Mother I was working overtime so I could be with Blake. Mother kept the girls then I gradually let Blake over to have dinner with us. He helped the girls with their homework while I cleaned the kitchen. I would tuck the girls in bed then Blake and I would go to my bedroom and lock the door. Eleven p.m. Blake would get up shower and head home. I would change the sheets, take my shower and crawl in bed.

...I think I wanted to get caught so Greg could see where his shutting me out had driven me... into the arms of another man.

~~~ **Faith Amber Henderson**~~~

BACKGROUND

Faith's birth to Fannie Mae [Mae] Henderson and Shelton Ingalls was kept secret for months, being Shelton was married to a close friend of the family. Mae had Faith's sister, Shelia three years earlier by a long-haul truck driver, Terrence Warren. Mae and Terrence lived together until Terrence realized Mae was not pregnant the second time by him.

Born January first, two minutes after the stroke of midnight. Faith was the first baby born that day and she has no problem whatsoever being the first at anything.

After Terrence left Mae, she worked as a waitress and did Day Work for a few families in Bixby Hills Estates. After Faith celebrated her fifth birthday, Mae took a live-in position that paid better. Mae's younger sister, Essie took the girls to stay with her. A short time later Terrence died in a work-related auto accident.

Faith's Aunt Essie was married to Alonso Stover. At the time Shelia and Faith moved in, their four children, Jasmine, was nine; Zachary, eight; Dylan, six and Lauren was five. Alonso became Youth Pastor at The Rock Baptist Church located in

Seal Beach and the family was always going on trips to the beach and historical field trips with a lot of young teens.

Hanging around older boys Faith learned at an early age she could get things from boys because of her looks and Faith worked her looks to her advantage. Shelia on the other hand wanted nothing to do with boys and buried herself in books, mainly Romance Novels.

When Faith and Lauren were thirteen, Jasmine and Shelia dared their younger sisters to shave their eyebrows off. All four girls took a razor to their brows at the same time. However, Faith's eyebrows never grew back. Faith draws her exotic shaped eyebrows on every day. She has a small flat nose like her fathers and it truly enhances the presentation of her full, lively smile.

Faith is short like Mae, five feet five with beautiful smooth mahogany brown skin just like Ingalls. Faith is built with hips and thighs that made Gregory's eyes enlarge with interest when he first glanced her way.

When Gregory made his entrance into Faiths' life, she had two sons and lived on Housing Assistance.

Faith's two-bedroom Section Eight apartment located in LB...

I'm standing at the door shouting at Harold's back, **"Yeah, and don't bother to come back!"** Harold slams the door. I open it so _I_ can be the one to slam it! There, that'll show him who's boss. I go into the boy's room and quiet them down.

When Harold and I argue my boys, Jaheim and Dameon start screaming and crying. Harold makes them go into their room. I get them calmed down and let them sleep with me tonight. After I get the lights out, I slide in bed thinking, 'I'm getting me a job and leaving Harold. He thinks having his boys I can't go anywhere; I'll show you Mr. Paulson!'

I wake up the next morning and again Harold did not come home. Probably over there with that north side hefa Monica.

After I get us ready, I walk the boys to school. On my way home I start thinking. Olivia phoned yesterday and told me she was going to fill out an application at McDonnell Douglas Aircraft, they are hiring women for assemblers. I think I'll go too. I have had enough of Harold and his cheating on me. Seven years is enough of his lies, he will never change.

I stopped to pick up a pack of cigarettes and came home, made a cup of instant coffee, and did some serious thinking.

I called Olivia to see if she had left to fill out an application yet. She was just getting ready to walk out the door headed to Douglas, so I had her swing by to pick me up. On the way to Douglas Olivia asked if I want to work. I have known her five years, Harold introduced us.

Olivia Murphy is a professional Booster. She met Harold when he sold her, her car. After Olivia and I had been friends for awhile she told me Harold was like her, they want to live life to its fullest and not settle down. Olivia knows since I have been with Harold I have never worked.

I said to her, "Girl, I have had enough of Harold's cheating." She sarcastically stated, "Yeah like you haven't said that a thousand times before." I couldn't reply, Olivia is right. I thought I could tame the man. I knew he was a cheater when we met because he was cheating on Gloria every time we were together. To Olivia's comment, I thought to myself, 'Okay. I can show you better than I can tell you!'

Olivia and I filled out the applications and the lady asked if the phone numbers on our applications were good, we told her "Yes." Olivia dropped me off at home. I looked around my apartment and realized how I could use extra money to get things like pictures on the walls and chairs to match the couch I already have. A fancy set of end tables and a cocktail table would be nice.

I can't believe it has taken me this long to realize Harold will never settle down. I met Harold when I was living with my sister Shelia over on Atlantic Avenue. I was twenty-one and going to California State Dominguez Hills College for my Associates Degree in Business Management. I was having a ball partying and loved the college life.

After I graduated high school I worked at various cafes because Shelia told me how good the tips were. I overheard a family talking about grants for college and checked into it. I was thinking of applying for a grant and when my co-worker Huey, one of the cooks, kept sexually harassing me, I quit and started school.

Denice Webb was in my English class and I met Harold at Denice's twenty-first birthday party. I fell hard and fast for the man. Harold is five feet nine inches tall, the color of midnight, fine, sexy and, he knows it. I don't know if Harold being a salesman and telling people what they want to hear helps when he meets women or him telling women what they want to hear makes him a great salesman.

Anyway, Harold knows what, when and how to smooth talk a woman and make her fall like lightning for him. After I introduced Shelia to Harold she started fussing at me about how he wasn't any good and I could do way better. Shelia really got on my nerve, but I didn't have to pay her rent or anything, so I had to put up with her fussing.

Shelia's father was a truck driver and died when she was ten. The owners of the trucking company whose truck he was driving was found negligent. They had insurance and paid quite a bit of money. When she turned eighteen, Shelia was given some of the settlement. My mother, Mae wasn't married to her father, so his parents received a check and set aside some money for Sheila.

Shelia's grandparents had the insurance monies paid out in increments. So, when Shelia reaches eighteen, twenty-five and thirty years old she gets a certain amount of the money. Her first check was forty thousand dollars and Shelia moved into her own place a few months after the first check. Shelia told me Mae was on her every day for some of that money.

Shelia was working odd waitress jobs and after buying herself clothes and a year-old Honda, her first check was almost gone. Having to work for another restaurant she decided she wants to be a Registered Nurse so when her second check arrived Shelia leased her a place, enrolled in Nursing School, and started living on a budget.

I moved in her first apartment with her because she lived so close to Dominguez College that I walked. Harold would spend the night with me and if Shelia were up when he left, she would snap at him about paying rent in his own name somewhere.

Harold and I broke up when I told him we had been dating for a year and it was me or Gloria. Two months later he reappeared on my doorstep saying how I was his one and only. I had stopped taking my birth control pills when he left and a month after we were back together, I was pregnant. When I told Harold about being pregnant he told me to get rid of it. His job was looking shaky and he would not be able to take care of it.

Harold took me to the clinic and paid for it. The man took me home and left me. When I told him, he needed to stay and take care of me, he said for me to get my mother or sister to do it, sick people made him nervous. I cried when he walked out while I was yelling at his back that my mother and sister were at work and he was the father!

Harold Paulson opened the front door, turned around looked me dead in the eyes and sarcastically asks, "Father of what!" I was so mad at him I wouldn't take any of his phone calls and when he came over I refused to let him in; I listened to him apologize through the door.

After a month of his apologizing I caved in and why did I get pregnant again! I told him I was not going to any clinic; he was going to be a daddy again. He told me the child support he was already paying made it impossible to pay for my kid, so I had to tell the County I didn't know where he was. I did and at first Harold gave me diapers and cases of formula but by the time Jaheim was six months old, the diapers and formula stopped coming and so did Harold for two weeks. That's when I knew he had a new chick.

Well we broke up and again I stopped taking the birth control. Jaheim was nine months old when I took Harold back and, once again I was pregnant. Nothing we used to prevent pregnancy worked. I thought this time Harold would marry me, but he told me not to count on him for any support instead of proposing.

Harold works as a salesman for Dodge Moss Motors on PCH [Pacific Coast Highway]. He started that job right out of high school. He is twenty-nine and one smooth talker. My two boys makes four sons Harold has fathered and I don't need to tell you, he **does not** pay child support for any of his sons. After Dameon arrived one night in bed Harold slipped and told me his checks were not steady, so he never pays child support.

When Harold meets a new chick, he stays away from me for a week or two. When he gets serious with whomever he is with, then he is gone every other night. During the seven years we have been together Harold has been serious three times. Gloria, Rosalind and now Monica.

I know this because I always get a phone call from Harold's new chick. They call to say how they are now with Harold and have no intentions of trying to keep him from seeing his sons, you know, wanting to be up front. I just listen to them to figure out what it is they have Harold is after.

Gloria, her family has money and she keeps Harold dressed so when they go places, he is not dressed like a pimp. Rosalind manages property and keeps him in his own place. Me, I give him love and Harold confides in me. I knew he was no good when we met. Gloria was right there when he took my phone number but what can I say, the man is some fine package of dark chocolate!

Patricia Bennet has Harold's oldest son, Harold Junior. They were high school sweethearts and when Patricia became pregnant her parents had a phone conversation with Harold's mother and planned to meet so they could discuss planning a wedding.

Crystal, Harold's mother is first runner-up for Ms. Ghetto! The day they all met was the day Patricia found out Harold had no intentions of getting married. Both her parents forbade Patricia to have anything else to do with Harold. They informed him if their grandchild didn't have a father in the home, the father was not going to be in the child's life period! Now you know that was just what Harold wanted to hear.

Sonja James has Harold's second oldest, Tyrell. Sonja works for the DMV and hooks Harold up with difficult sales due to driver's license glitches. He uses all of us baby mamas to his advantage. The two best qualities Harold has is talking and making love.

Harold and I have been on and off again since we have been together. I have had enough of him and this life. Our relationship nor this County Assistance living is taking me where I want to go!

I think I'll put Harold's work information on my County papers this month. Yeah, Ms. Monica can go without something and Harold can pay for my boys. I am finally done with his two-three-timing behind!

Yesterday I received a phone call from Douglas, I have an interview tomorrow morning. I called Olivia to see if she received a call. I don't have a car so if she doesn't have an interview I will catch the bus. She is not answering her phone.

I go get the boys from school, come home, and fix us some mac and cheese and hot dogs for dinner. I'm ready to get off the County. The Fourth of July is in two weeks and I'm tired of having hot dogs because money is tight. I want to have ribs like most people do on the Fourth of July.

~~~~Gregory~~~~

I am sitting in this counselor's office and don't know why I am so nervous. Alright my name is being called, let me get this over with.

Mrs. Judson, my counselor introduces herself and reads the court order aloud as if I were not there when the judge issued it to me. She looks me directly in the eyes and says very sternly, "You can make this difficult or easy. The truth is what will turn the light on the root of your behavior. Mr. Young I am trained and qualified to help guide you to the truth. It is up to you to embrace it."

I thought to myself, 'She must be a Christian quoting The Word like that.' I nodded my head. She says, "Alright. Let's begin with how you met your first wife and remember what is said in this room is kept in confidence." Mrs. Judson pushes play on her remote control causing the video camera sitting on its tripod to start. She looks at me like, ready, get set, go!

I told Mrs. Judson about Charlotte and I. On my way to work I stopped at a red light and realized a tear was on my cheek. I cannot believe I still hurt when I think about Char. She broke my heart in half but for some strange reason, when her smile flashes across my mind, for that split second she never hurt me.

The night I almost caught Char with Dude; I went straight to Mama's. I rang the doorbell and thought Mama was sleep. Mr. Mays answered the door. I was surprised they were both still up. Mr. Mays asks, "What brings you here this time of night? Something wrong?" He headed to the back room and hollered to Mama, **"Phylis, Greg's here."** They were up watching a movie together. Mama met me in the hallway and asked, "What's wrong? You okay?" Mama put her arms around me, and I broke down. I felt Mr. Mays hand on my shoulder.

I stood straight up and said, "Char and I are through. She is seeing another man." Mr. Mays says, "Come with me." I wiped my face with my arm as I followed him to the kitchen. I observed Mr. Mays reach up in the cabinet over the refrigerator and pull out a bottle of Wild Turkey Bourbon. He looked into my eyes as he sat the bottle on the table then took two small jelly glasses from the cabinet and handed me one.

Mr. Mays poured his drink and handed the bottle to me. He sat down and I followed his lead. I took a swallow and shivered; it was so strong. I looked up at Mr. Mays, his eyes locked on mine. "I need to stay here for a bit until I find a place." He nodded his head. I downed the rest of my drink and went to my old room which was now Jamal's. As soon as I opened the door I could hear Jamal snoring.

As I closed the door, Mama appeared in the hall next to me.

"Take Sam's room." As I step into the room Mama hands me some sheets and adds, "Sleep tight." I look at the sheets and have a flashback of Char holding those crumbled-up sheets in her arms. I threw the sheets on top of the bare bed and felt myself feeling relaxed, so I laid on top of Sam's bed. While mentally rehashing what had just happened with Char, I drifted off to sleep.

Sam lives in San Diego with her husband Rick, Richard Larkins and their three kids. Leslie, Lauryn and her infant, Lil Ricky. Rick is an Officer in the Navy and Sam teaches elementary school. My little sister has her bossy ways and when she told us she wanted to become a teacher, I thought, 'If that don't fit her. She will have a room full to boss.'

Sam turned out to be a great mother and Rick must love her bossy ways. She and Rick married five years ago, and she became pregnant soon after they married. They all come up for the holidays and Sam and the kids stay a week with Mama during Christmas.

When I woke the next day, Mama told me Char had called to say my clothes will be dropped off here later. I went to JC Penny and bought myself a shirt, underwear, and a pair of jeans. I showered, ate the feast Mama cooked for me and went to work.

For three weeks after Char and I split, I worked until I was made to go home. Every Friday I dropped off a seventy-five-dollar money order at the Thomas house for the girls and only thought of Char when I climbed into an empty bed and when I woke in the afternoons. I kept myself busy with work.

Mama would sit in the kitchen across from me while I ate, and we would talk. That first morning she told me I need to start back attending church and inquire of The Lord what I need to do. Mama wanted me to get back with Char, get some counseling and allow both of us to forgive one another. I just listened.

It hurt too much to think about how I could have busted Char with another man. I would have killed whoever he was with my bare hands. I do know The Lord kept me away until eleven-thirty which kept me from serving prison time. I am grateful for that. However, what Mama said made me think about once I slow down with the overtime I will start attending church.

Two months after I left Char I moved into my own studio apartment in Bellflower. Char served me with divorce papers in the parking lot at work two days after my twenty-ninth birthday. Holding those papers in my hand, I briefly thought 'maybe we could work it out.' Then a mental picture of Char holding those sheets flashed in my head.

The thought of Char in bed with another man, no way can I have her comparing me to him. Especially a man who knew she was married. I became so angry I told myself Char and I would never get back together and she could slowly roast on a rotisserie in hell!

When I went to court for the finalization of the divorce, that was the day I realized "Parking lot Dude" was Char's man. She had him by her side and holding her hand in court. I looked him over and wondered, 'what kind of man must he be sleeping in *my bed*. You know what, they deserve each other!'

The day after court I went to work and noticed a pretty brown skinned short brick house. She was stacked and attractive, so I watched her. After observing her and her friend Murphy, I found out her name is Henderson. I watched her every time she entered the break room and took notice of how she shook off the guys that would approach her. She pretty much stayed to herself and worked, I liked that about her.

One day during lunch break I strolled over to her and Murphy and introduced myself. I sat and we all introduced ourselves and talked about how fortunate we were to have a job. When we stood to go back to work, I asked Henderson for her phone number. She told me she would think about it and let me know at the end of the shift. I informed her I worked twelve-hour shifts. She said she would find me.

The next day after an hour into my shift Faith appeared in my work area. After saying, "Hey." She handed me a piece of paper, turned, and left. I liked that, not too mouthy. Of course the paper had her phone number written on it. Olivia, Faith, and myself spent our break and lunch together after that. I called her the next day from Mama's since I did not have a phone in my apartment, I was hardly there.

Faith and I hit it off. She is almost three years younger than I am and wants to have a house and understands you must work to get it. The only problem I had regards to Faith was she had two sons. Dameon five and Jaheim six and they were out of control by my standards.

The fact Faith was so fine made it very difficult to dismiss thinking of her. When I passed up Saturday overtime, I knew then I had moved on from Char.

Our first date, I took Faith to a supper club on the Redondo Beach Pier and she loves to dance. I am not much of a dancer. I believe my upbringing in the Holiness-Pentecostal denomination makes it difficult for me to party which includes drinking, smoking, cussing, and dancing. I am not experienced in any of those arenas. Faith does them all and she attends church on Easter, Mother's Day, and Christmas. Faith explained to me her philosophy of religion.

Faith believes each person is put on this earth to be tested as to whether we deserve to spend eternity in heaven or in hell. Faith says, "God looks at our heart as we live the life we are given to see if we are sincere when we do things for others." She also believes living our lives is a test as to how we accept what we are given in life. Faith thinks God judges us highly on how we can better ourselves without hurting others.

Faith strongly believes God knows her heart so there's no need to attend church all the time. She wants her boys to understand there is a God and wants them to learn about who He is. She sends them to church so God will be part of their life foundation. Her mothers sister takes her sons to church most Sundays. I realized after living with Faith that she has no clue about Holy Spirit; she was totally carnal minded.

The Saturday night we went to Redondo Beach Pier, Faith said her boys were spending the night with her aunt and going to church. The way she said it I knew it was an invitation to spend the night. We left the supper club and went to her place.

Faith kept offering me a drink. She certainly is no Char by any means personality wise. When Faith drinks, she gets loud and flirty. With or without alcohol Faith is wild in bed. The next day, after church her aunt dropped off Faiths sons. Faith fixed them boxed mac and cheese. I left headed home and stopped at a nearby burger stand and ate. I went home and slept; I did not get much sleep at Faith's.

I spent less time at my place and more at Faiths, so I picked up a cell phone.

Oh, did I meet Harold Paulson! After Faith and I were together a month we were all awakened seven-thirty in the morning by forcefully loud pounding on the door. I jumped up and followed Faith.

Harold was upset his key didn't work. He saw my shirt was off and pushed Faith aside. When I stepped up to him saying, "Hey! Don't handle her like that." Harold froze in his tracks and while eying me up and down sarcastically says: "I am the father of her sons. Don't put your hands on them or it's you and me!" The boys came into the living room crying and ran straight to their mother. Harold turned to leave and said to Faith, "I'm watching you."

Faith slammed the door and calmed the boys down. I put my clothes on getting ready to leave. Faith came into her bedroom and asked me to please don't leave. She told me how her relationship was with Harold and promised she was through with him. I didn't think he would return knowing I was here. The way he coward down when I stepped to him I knew he was a chump. Harold left Faith alone after that incident.

I wanted to see how my daughters and Faith's sons would get along. I told Faith I wanted us all to go to the Pike Saturday to give our blended family a trial run. Faith was all for it.

Saturday I took my truck to Mama and picked up her car. Char told Mother Thomas I could blow twice for the girls at her driveway so after I went to pickup Faith and the boys, we headed to Chars. I am praying she stays inside and there will be no hollering and cussing in front of the kids. Char only rolled her eyes after hugging the girls bye.

Faith had no breakfast foods at home so now we all head for Denny's. The girls have already eaten so only the non-breakfast food household eats and I am thinking, 'This is going to cost me a pretty penny!'

Maybe an hour into the rides the girls are hungry. I grab their hands and ask what sounds good when Faith interrupts me.'Uh they should have eaten when we did." I interrupt Faith. "No way am I going to have them tell their mother I refused to feed them; No way!' I turn to the girls and smile asking them what sounds good? I glance at Faith and she is pissed!

While waiting for the girls food order Damien sees cotton candy and starts jumping up and down for some, so I treated both him and Jaheim to cotton candy and all of the kids are happy. Faith even hugged me and I knew she was no longer peeved.

When we dropped the girls off that evening, I vowed to never cause an expense like that ever again, and believe me, I did not bring up another blended family outing ever again.

When the first of the month rolled around Faith and I had agreed on my moving in with her so we could save our money and get married. I gave her money for rent so she could pay the sitter and save. By then I had over five thousand dollars saved but for some reason, I did not let Faith know. I told her I had a few hundred saved. Our plan was to save enough money to get married and buy a house to put apartment living behind us.

By me giving Char money every pay day and putting money away I had stayed true to my budget. After a month living with Faith I realized I was broke the day before payday because she only cooked box mac and cheese like it was a vitamin the body required.

Four months living with Faith I noticed a lot of additions. There were now pictures hanging on the walls, nice tables in the living room, a twenty-inch color television, coffee maker and a countertop microwave oven. Faith also has expensive taste. Plush rugs in the bathroom and the bath towels were thick and heavy.

One November afternoon while Faith and I were getting ready for work I asked, "Do you have any money saved?" Faith snapped! "Why you asking? You not asking me for some money are you?" My response was, "Just wondering. Maybe it's time to take this relationship to the next level."

She smiled and teasingly asked, "Why Mr. Young. You asking me to get hitched?" I shook my head "No" as I told her, "We need to plan for a wedding. When I ask you to marry me, you will know you have been asked." Her smile dropped... UH OH!

Faith was silent the rest of the time we were getting dressed. We each drive our cars to Douglas because I work overtime and Faith goes home to *her boys*, as she calls them when her shift ends. On my way to work I stopped at a liquor store and bought a box of chocolate candy to take to Faith. I knew she was mad and thought the candy would soften her up.

Faith was a little frosty during break and lunch and Murphy was not surprised so I knew Faith had told Murphy what had transpired with us earlier.

When I left work my plan was to leave the candy on her nightstand but when I walked in the door there Faith was sitting at the kitchen table. She was playing solitaire and I noticed her drink and cigarettes on the table.

I nervously smiled as I handed her the candy. She did not move. I laid the box slowly down on the table. "Pack your things and get out. You think because you can have the milk anytime you want the cow is free. Get the hell out!"

I headed to the bedroom and saw my clothes stacked up on the bed. Faith came into the bedroom and threw several paper grocery bags at me. I gathered my things up into the bags. As I reached the door leaving, I heard, "Key! Put it on the table." I did as instructed and left without uttering a word. As I unlocked my car door I thought, 'I just wasted six dollars on some candy.'

Being at work with Faith was difficult. I sat several feet away from her and she avoided eye contact with me. When Olivia sat with her, Olivia would turn and watch my every move and it seemed she was telling Faith what I was doing. This went on for almost a month. Then one night I heard the buzzer for second shift to end and a few minutes later Faith appeared by my side.

"Gregory." I removed my safety glasses and responded, "Hey, how are you?" Faith replied, "Pregnant." Totally shocked I responded, "Really!" "Really, and it's yours." I had a mental picture of my son sitting at her kitchen table eating box mac and cheese. "Come by the house when you get off so we can talk." She reached over and kissed me on the cheek. 'Maybe this will work.' Is what I told myself.

When I arrived at Faith's place I only knocked once, and she opened the door. She was waiting for me in her sexy lingerie. As she locked the door she grabbed my hand and led me to the bedroom. The next afternoon I rushed to LB to get ready for work. I waited for Faith in the parking lot. We walked to the building together and she told me we will talk tonight.

Lunch time she invited me to sit with her. Faith told me she was keeping the baby and wanted to know my thoughts about becoming a father again. I just looked at her and kept my mouth shut. She says, "I'm ready to go on that budget you want to put me on." I replied, "Is that right?" She shook her head "Yes."

I tried to keep my mind on my job, but I could not stop this short video playing in my head. My kid sitting at the table with Dameon and Jaheim shoving box mac and cheese down. By the end of my shift I decided to marry Faith and be there for my kid. I left work, went to LB, and packed up most of my clothes.

This time Faith opened the door wearing an apron, nothing but the apron. It took us until Sunday to finally, "talk." When I woke up, Faith was sitting in bed smoking. I told her we need to talk over breakfast. We got up and I asked if she was cooking. She says, "Please, this room is where my talent lies." We went to a cafe and ate. She told me to write down a budget and promised this time to keep to it.

We went back to her place and was in bed until the boys were dropped off by her aunt. I took them all to eat out. Dameon is spoiled and Jaheim, he is just bad. Faith tells me they are just being boys.

It took Faith and I a week to decide December shutdown, we were driving to Vegas. Olivia and the man she was dating at the time, Curtis Monroe rode with us to Vegas. I rented a Ford Escape and they had an open container in the back seat.

When I got a whiff of the liquor I told them to put it away I was not getting a ticket. Faith told me to calm down it was okay for them to drink they weren't the ones driving. They all thought what Faith said was funny. I looked at her and up into my rear-view mirror and told them: "If you don't put a cap on it I will pull over and pour every drop out! I mean it, right now." They handed Faith the bottle and she placed it in the glove compartment. They were all silent for at least half an hour.

After our honeymoon Faith and I had a rocky start in our marriage. By the time she was seven months pregnant I knew I had made a mistake. When Faith started to show I begged her to stop smoking until the baby was born but she insisted she had cut down. She told me she smoked while pregnant with the boys and it didn't bother either one of them.

Faith went on maternity leave and every day I came home from work there sat a new box containing something she had bought for the baby. Knowing Faith was home everyday spending money, I was about to explode. The word "budget" no longer existed to Faith.

During Faith's last month of pregnancy, she developed Braxton Hicks and was bed ridden the last week. I asked Mama to come over and cook for us and she did, willingly. Mama was always commenting on my weight loss and figured it was due to Faith not being a cook.

I would give Faith money for groceries and she still bought boxed mac and cheese. She just stepped it up with hot links or hamburgers, so I made a grocery list. That was a waste. She purchased the foods on the list and let it spoil in the refrigerator. When I mentioned the spoiled foods she snapped, "I bought them thinking you were gonna cook!"

While Faith was healing from giving birth to Kozet, Mama came over daily for two weeks and cooked for her house and ours. Faith raved about how good the food was. I thought she would get incentive to cook, but that was asking too much.

It was less stressful for me to take us all out so that's what I did, I just grunted the whole while we ate. Faith and I would argue in restaurants. I would tell her to order one meal for the boys to share, they wasted more than they ate. She would tell me they each wanted something different.

I could not win with Faith. When we walked away from the restaurant tables, I would look at the foods left and felt like cussing.

Kozet Rena Young was born July eighth and she was a beautiful sight just as Charece and Tamera were. Before Kozet was a month-old Faith started drinking again. She returned to work in September and I was working all the overtime I could get my hands on, even working in other departments. The DC 9's were keeping us busy. The plant was preparing the line for tooling the MD 80, it was scheduled to start running in October.

Faith could mentally turn off kids noises. The boys would holler and scream at each other and she would act as if they were on another planet. Sometimes I would hear Kozet cry and not hear Faith say anything, so I would get up to see what was going on. Every single time Faith would be sitting right in the room with Kozet like she was deaf. I would pick Kozet up and ask Faith why was the baby crying.

Faith would piss me off saying, "She's probably teething. Put her down you have her spoiled." I felt Faith would allow Kozet to cry for long periods of time so I would get Kozet often and each time that happened, Faith would roll her eyes at me.

Our first wedding anniversary we were not speaking. Faith was mad at me about something she wanted to buy, and I told her it was too extravagant.

It was real bad with our relationship. Faith and I hardly spoke unless it was important. By then Dameon or Jaheim were our interpreters; "Ask Uncle G this. Tell your Mother that." Our second anniversary we were not speaking, you know why; she wanted to spend a lot of money!

I stayed at work as much as I could during the shutdown. When I was home, there was so much tension. Right after New Year's Faith told me she was checking out three-bedroom apartments on the north side so Kozet could have her own room.

We moved the first of February and I saw stacks of boxes still in their delivery containers. When I asked Faith what were they, with an attitude she tells me, "Things I bought for the new place!"

By Valentine's Day Faith had our new apartment looking like a model home. My savings was down to three thousand dollars and some change. I was going broke and when the end of the month came, Faith asked me for three hundred dollars, the rent was increased. I almost cussed her out!

Memorial Day we were all going to Mamas for barbecue later. In fact, we had all celebrations there because Faith could not cook. I had just stepped out of the shower and heard Kozet crying. By the time I was completely dressed, Kozet was still crying. I went into the kitchen to see Faith on the phone.

Kozet was in the living room sitting on the couch and the boys were sitting on the floor in front of the television. I sat next to Kozet and asked what was wrong. She pointed at Jaheim and was trying to tell me something and I became so pissed. I jumped up, turned towards Faith, and yelled, "**You need to be tending to our daughter not gossiping on the phone!**"

Faith ended her conversation saying, "Girl I gotta go this crazy ass fool has lost his mind! Bye."

Faith walked over to the back of the couch and yelled, **"You have her a spoiled brat. I watched the whole thing. He was just playing with her. What's really your problem Gregory you have been distant since we moved here. What's your problem?"**

I was at my limit!

As I stood I hollered back, **"You really want to know? You. It's you and your no cooking, no cleaning, always drinking, smoking and on the phone self!"** She came back at me with, **"I don't have a noose around your neck Mr. cheap ass!"**

A light bulb came on in my head. I thought, 'she's absolutely right!'

I rushed to the bathroom and took my toothbrush and shaving supplies and shoved them in my travel bag. I hurried to the closet and grabbed a handful of my clothes and walked out. As I closed the door behind myself I heard Jaheim ask, "Where Uncle G go'n?" I drove straight to Mamas, right back to Samantha's room which was now mine!

Faith and I avoided one another at work. Every Friday I would go to the Credit Union to cash my check before clocking in. I had money orders made out to Char and Faith. Saturdays on my way to work I would stop by the Thomas house and drop off the money for Charece and Tamera.

Every payday I slipped Faith an envelope at lunch time with a fifty-dollar money order in it. Considering I paid Faith's car note I figured two hundred dollars a month was enough for Faith to feed my daughter.

After a month passed when I handed Faith the envelope she said, "Hi." I responded with a "Hi." That was the sum of our communication. Every other week I would ask how Kozet was, Faith always responded with the same, "Oh she's good. Growing." I thought Faith might try and get me to come back home but saying "Hi" was all we ever said to each other.

Just before Labor Day I was called to the office, there was an emergency phone call for me. It was Faith.

She was at Long Beach Memorial Medical Center with Kozet in emergency. Faith was crying and I became nervous as she said Kozet was being transferred to the hospital. I clocked out and drove like a maniac to emergency. When I arrived, I was led to the back where Faith and the doctors were.

The doctor explained to me Kozet has asthma and had suffered a severe attack. One of the doctors specialized in Juvenile Asthma and explained in detail the severity and risks. I became so angry. Kozet must suffer with asthma because her mother smoked during her pregnancy. I was heated!

Gradually I became somewhat relieved since asthma can be dealt with. Seeing Kozet lying still in that oxygen tent in such a defenseless condition. I thought of her being very active and now she's sedated. My anger worked itself up again and I became angry enough to slap Faith; her and her cigarettes!

The Nurse allowed me to stay with Kozet for a while. I went home and told Mama about Kozet having asthma. I asked if anyone else in our family has it. Mama told me "No." We had an aunt who dipped snuff, but no one has ever had asthma. That really pissed me off.

I decided since I was off for the rest of the day I would go around to the Thomas house and see Charece and Tamera. No one answered the door, so I went back to my truck and just as I was driving off, Mother Thomas pulls up in the driveway with Charece and Tamera. They have grown and man are they pretty. Charece has Char's smile. I stared at them both but Charece had my attention most of the time. She reminds me of Char at that age with the exception of Charece having my skin tone.

The girls are very articulate. Char had them in preschool and it is definitely paying off. After seeing

Kozet then Charece and Tamera, I felt so lonely. I love my daughters, but their mothers makes it difficult for me to deal with spending time with them. That causes me to miss out on hugging them and watching them grow up. I was really down after seeing my two older daughters.

I spent the rest of the day watching television; however the truth is television was watching me. My mind was so deep in thought. I assessed what I wanted; to be able to provide for my family. I had no idea I would not *be* with my family, just a provider for them. I asked The Lord where did I go wrong?

Jamal came by to drop off some ribs for Monday, Labor Day. He challenged me to a game of basketball and whupped my butt. Working all the time has me rusty. Jamal told me on the walk back from the park how I need to get a balanced life. All work and no play makes a lonely man.

Jamal met and moved in with Tina Moore while they were attending Claremont McKenna College. They were both taking classes in engineering. As soon as Jamal went to work for Raytheon in El Segundo, they had a small wedding at a Chapel in Los Angeles.

Tina went to work for Hughes Aircraft in Culver City so she and Jamal ended up moving closer to her job in Ladera Heights. Tina is from San

Bernardino California and is number six of eight children, so she does not want a family. They give my girls very expensive gifts and they both drive BMW's.

One afternoon right after Labor Day, I woke up crying. I dreamed Char and I were in our first apartment together and we were getting ready to make love. When I reached for her, she disappeared. I sat on the edge of my bed and let the tears fall and I mean they came spurting out. I kept telling myself it was over with Char. I need to move on. I can't figure out why she runs across my mind!

Then I thought about what Mama said to me about going to church and find out what The Lord has for me to do. By the time I walked into my building at work, my mind was made up; I am going to start going to church on Sundays. No more Sunday overtime for me.

~~~~Faith~~~~

Oh, my goodness! That's Douglas Aircraft. I happened to glance up at the news being broadcasted and there's a story on with Building 1-A in the background. Wow, seeing that building brings back memories.

I remember it as if it were yesterday…

My first day at Douglas went by so fast. That place is huge I didn't think I would ever remember my way around. Olivia and I were in the same group being trained but I'll need to get my own transportation.Olivia is working to draw unemployment later, me, I'm working to get ahead, change my life's course.

Olivia is a good friend, but I don't want to rely on her to drop the boys off every day and pick them up during our training. I'll get Harold to find me a good running car. I am so excited! I can finally buy what we need around here. Now it is time for me to do better.

"In my Bible learning days I remember Luke 14:26. *"For which of you, intending to build a tower, does not sit down first and count the cost, whether he has enough to finish it—"* My Sunday school teacher, Sister Simmons told our class, "The Lord has a purpose for each of our lives and no matter where we are in life, we must believe we are being led to do better. We must prepare ourselves, before stepping into our purpose." I am ready to do better. My mind is made up.

I am ready to improve my surroundings. Yes, it's time for a positive change!

The first night after training I laid in bed and thought about how Harold staying with Monica has opened my eyes. I realize every moment I have spent with Harold has been borrowed. I cried last week when I woke up alone. I've been doing some soul searching and realize I hang onto Harold to keep from feeling like a failure.

A woman must have it going on if she has a man, right? This realization came to me when I faced the truth about why I keep holding onto this so-called relationship.

Having Harold's two sons I thought he would want to raise them with me. Since I am his only baby's mama to have two of his sons. It might have been three sons had I not taken that trip to the clinic.

Anyways, when I looked in the mirror at Faith Amber with raw truth glasses, I saw how Harold is only a sperm donor. He will never marry me. I wept when I faced that fact. I was holding on to him to keep from accepting the truth; I am another one of

Harold's silly women. Harold Paulson married? Ha! He couldn't be faithful if his life depended on it.

A week had passed when Harold came over. After we had sex I told him this so called relationship was getting old and he went right into his "con-man act." As I looked at Harold uttering his rehearsed presentation, and realized I'm with him to save my own face. I told myself I am not wasting anymore time loving him.

Truth is I am almost thirty years old and it's time to face the facts so I can move on. I want out of this impoverished living. I want to have something of substance, a house, and car. When Harold was done with his rehearsed speech, I told him he needs to grow up. He jumped out of bed and asked, "Who have you been talking too?"

OOO that pissed me off! I jumped out of bed and told him I have a brain! Harold put his clothes on so fast and headed for the door telling me he didn't have time for foolishness. I let him have it!

I told him he was selfish and only wanted to do what was good for Harold and could care less about his sons, nor their mothers. The look on his face told me I had gotten to him. He strolled out of my apartment cussing. I cried after closing the door. I felt so disconnected from Harold; I really felt lonely…

The rest of the day I took inventory of why I hold onto Harold. I concluded my reason is; so I won't look like a fool. I also realized I have wasted seven years of my life. Later that night while lying in bed, I accepted my being prideful and caring too much about what people thought of me. I prayed and asked The Lord to forgive me and told Him that I am ready to move on. In my heart I am ready. I'm scared of what's ahead of me but I'm ready to see what it is.

Three days later Harold shows up at my apartment before I went to bed. I told him we were through. He was like, "Awh Fay, I gave you some time to cool off. Come on baby you know you missed Big H!" He was half right. I miss him but I'm also tired of his two-timing behind. I want a committed relationship and a house. Staring my thirtieth birthday in the face, my mind is made up. I'm getting out of low-income housing for good.

Harold stayed the night, but I made him leave as soon as daylight hit the room. I don't want the boys to see him. He knows now I'm serious about being through with him. I tried my best to make him give me my key back. Okay, I'll tell the manager I lost my keys and have the locks changed.

I'll show Harold Paulson. Yes indeed, he will get my message. While Harold dressed to leave, I told him to find me a used car because I'm looking for a job. He rolled his eyes at me while leaving.

I am so happy to be working again. These two weeks of assembly training are during the day so I'm going to have to find a sitter that will keep my boys late. All of us in training will be on second shift. I can drop the boys off at school, but someone will have to pick them up and keep them until almost midnight.

After I put the boys to bed I stayed up and made myself some instant coffee. I looked through the sales papers that came in the mail. I saw a coffeemaker I'm going to get me one with my first paycheck.

Olivia is yapping about the men here at Douglas. She looks at all their left hands to see who's available and who isn't. All I see is how everyone acts on Friday's; payday. I started a list of things I want to buy, and the list changes everyday. I work my butt off so I won't get laid off. To Olivia, this is just another means for her to draw unemployment but to me, it's a ladder climbing up to a better life. Maybe if she had kids she would feel the same way.

At the end of my two-week training the boys and I came home to find Harold in my apartment and on my phone. I thought he had a car for me to go see but turns out he remembered me telling him I got paid. He left after our heated shouting match ended. I worked and he thinks he's my pimp! Here I am trying to make ends meet taking care of his two kids and the man is seriously looking for me to give him money, ain't that a blip!

Harold told me I need to stay home and take care of his sons. I didn't need a car. Oh, okay, now I know I have to find a car on my own. Harold wants to keep me here so when he gets an itching I'll be here to scratch it!

The next day I picked up one of those Car Mart free papers and found a used Ford Focus. Most of my check went to purchase the car. Nothing on my many wish lists was purchased but I need transportation. I had to let my jalopy warm up every morning and pump the brakes every time I wanted to stop. And I had to run the heater to keep it from running hot, but I didn't have to catch the bus.

Olivia started seeing this guy Paul Clayton, who worked in the spray area and she was late a lot coming to work. She was spending her breaks and lunch with him when one day she runs over to my work area and tells me to talk her out of using her drill motor on Paul.

"Faith he's married! He just told me his wife has been in Texas with her sick father all this time. She's coming home today; he's picking her up at LAX!" My supervisor eyed us, so I told her to get back to her area. Olivia and I started riding together again the next day and we were taking our breaks and lunch together.

The lady I had watching the boys told me she couldn't watch them anymore. It took me a week to find a good sitter, my sister Shelia. I was able to work overtime going in early and getting off at the shift end. Shelia agreed to get the boys out of school and keep them at my place making sure homework was completed and the boys were in bed by nine p.m.

Shelia didn't mind keeping the boys because she was able to do her homework when the boys did theirs. Her only complaint was having to leave her car parked that long outside my building. She would park her car where she could look out of the window every so often. She had to move her car a few times to make that possible.

My block and building is Tiny and Blues' turf so, that Sunday I had them come up to my apartment. I introduced them to Shelia and after we explained our sitting arrangements they offered to put the word out about her car. Shelia relaxed and our sitting arrangement worked great. I didn't have to pay her she enjoyed being with her nephews.

One day during first break Olivia noticed this tall guy in our break area. He was handsome, around six feet tall and some change, and he was always reading. He kept to himself and didn't wear a wedding ring on his left hand, so Olivia watched him. She allowed him to see her watching him so he would approach her.

Well it didn't take but a few days before he began noticing us and after a week of watching, he approached us but to both our surprise the man spoke to me! I thought he was a gentleman and after my drama with Myles and Harold, gentleman looked real good on Gregory Young to me.

I gave Gregory my phone number and after talking to him on the phone for over a week, I thought he was worth my dating, at least until he took off his "Nice Mask." My problem was, I was looking so hard for a mean, harsh, selfish Gregory but by the time I realized Gregory was not wearing a mask and he really was caring and thoughtful; I was in love with him.

Gregory is what you call a man's-man. He can make you feel like a queen. Gregory makes a woman feel as though he can take on the world on her behalf and win; You just feel protected. His quiet mellow disposition makes you feel safe. You know he's got you!

The morning Harold introduced himself to Gregory I felt as though Gregory was all dressed up in shining armor. Gregory stepped up to Harold and I saw Harold back down for the first time and knew at that moment I was rid of Harold for good. Harold didn't see anything wrong with him fooling around with other women, but if I looked at another man or another man looked too long at me, Harold would want to take me home.

I knew Gregory and I had a solid relationship; it took almost five months before I found out our relationship was not as rock solid as I thought. We were doing great together looking forward to buying a house together in the future.

One Sunday afternoon while we were getting ready for work, Gregory told me he wanted to spend some time with his daughters. He wanted to take all our kids to The Pike Amusement Park next Saturday; he would take the day off. This way we get to see how our kids get along. I didn't have a problem with it. I thought he was serious about getting married and I will have to meet the girls eventually. So, I agreed to us going on a family outing.

Gregory was so excited Charlotte told her mother he could pick the girls up in front of her apartment Saturday morning at eleven a.m. That morning we get up and Gregory asked if I was making breakfast for us, so we all didn't have to eat three meals out. I told him I didn't keep breakfast foods except cereal, and we could all eat some before leaving.

Well when I went to the kitchen, there was only enough milk for one or two small bowls of cereal. Gregory grunted and said, "This is going to cost a pretty penny." Then he grabbed his shoes and stormed out of the bedroom. Now I'm agitated. I'm thinking, 'Man you the one wanted this to happen. You thought it was going to be free!' I thought it I didn't dare say that to him.

Gregory took his truck over to his mother's and brought back her Oldsmobile. We went and picked up the girls. Miss Eye Roll'n Charlotte looked at my boys like they were dirty or something. When she stood on the sidewalk watching her girls climb inside the car, Charlotte's eyes were all over my boys. When she glanced my way, I let her see she wasn't the only eye roller, I rolled my eyes right back at her.

Just because she lives in a nice neighborhood, she call herself looking down on me and my boys. Huh, she don't know, I'll jump her over my boys!

Four kids in the back seat and three seat belts. The little girl, Tamera, was whining, "Daddy, he won't let me have the seat belt. Daddy, he won't move over..." Finally, after telling her to try and sit back and share Charece's seat belt, Gregory was on the freeway. After adjusting his rear-view mirror to look at her, he gently says, "Make room baby it's crowed for everyone, okay baby."

For at least twenty minutes it was baby this and baby that. I turned around, looked the little brat square in the eyes and asked, "How old are you? Don't you think an eight-year-old should act better?" The older girl pulled her sister close and rolled her eyes at me. Oh, so eye rolling runs in the family I see!

We all went to Denny's and the girls weren't hungry, so Gregory, the boys and I ate and after an hour into the rides at the Pike, these hefa's are hungry! I looked over at Gregory and he was so nice as he says, "Okay baby let's get you two something to eat." I stepped up to him and said, "Uh, they should have eaten when we were at Denny's."

He says to me, "Faith what do you want me to do, let them go hungry so they can tell their mother I didn't feed them. Awh naw." Gregory began shaking his head "No" and grabbed both his girls' hands and told them, "Come on baby what do you want Daddy to get you to eat." I felt my mouth fall open. And I'm talkin a jaw dropping experience!

This penny pincher wants my boys to share their food. These little princesses whimper and all rides stop! I'm pissed now and want to see if they have to share a plate!

Of course, the girls get whatever they want. When Damien saw the cotton candy he started jumping up and down screaming, "I want some, I want some!" Gregory bought him and Jaheim cotton candy. I wrapped my arm around Gregory's arm and gently laid my head on his upper arm. Gregory really is a good-hearted man.

I know Gregory spent almost a hundred dollars that day when it was over. We ate at a small family restaurant after we left the Pike and he never spoke of picking his girls up again.

Gregory would go over his ex-mother-in laws and spend time with his girls or his mother would call and say the girls were at her house for a while. The girls were always at his mother's on holidays when we went there but Charlotte never came inside the house. In fact, Gregory would be so angry when he had to talk to her. He would shout at her over the phone and a few times I heard him swear. Other than Charlotte angering him, Gregory never cussed. You know, Gregory was a good man, he was just so CHEAP!

One morning after the first Labor Day Gregory and I spent together, Mr. Young made it known to me marriage was just a bone he was dangling in my face. He brought up his, "Rigid Budget Plan" and me not keeping it so marriage was not going to happen. He really pissed me off. It's bad enough the man is cheap, now he's threatening me with money!

On the drive to work I realized I don't need Mr. Young anymore financially. I'm on my feet now. He gave me four hundred dollars a month for my rent that was only a hundred seventy-five. Now I can move into a better neighborhood. So, his tight behind can go fly a giant kite!

During lunch at work I looked at Gregory as if he were a stranger and not as a man I was interested in having a relationship with. It's amazing how that day I saw him for the workaholic he truly is. When my shift was over I stopped to get cigarettes and headed home to pack his things.

Shelia knew I was mad about something and followed me into my bedroom. She watched me throw Gregory's things on the bed, she asked, "So, is it over?" "Yep!" "Faith you want to talk about it?" "Look, I have tried to be patient and understanding with Gregory, but he is all about money. The budget is all the man cares about, and I can't have no cheap man.

I like nice things and can't have a man turning over every price tag on what I bring in my own house. Besides I'm the one paying for it. It's not like I ask him for money. I don't interrogate him about what he buys. I'm done!" Shelia looks at me and takes a seat on the bed and starts folding the clothes and stacking them in piles.

After Shelia left I checked on Jaheim and Dameon then poured myself a drink. I sat at the kitchen table, played some solitaire, and gave deep thought as to where I want to move. This housing living has played all the way out for me. In four months I will be thirty years old and for the first time in my life, I'm making good money. I need to get up out of this ghetto.

After I put Gregory out I really started missing him. Having to take out the trash and sleeping in a cold bed. I had to remind myself to put gas in my car because Gregory always did that for me. Every morning while getting the boys ready for school they would ask where was Uncle G. Gregory really is a kindhearted man and very thoughtful. I began wondering why does Gregory have to be so doggone cheap!

Even though I was on birth control pills when October rolled around I realized I was pregnant. For two days I wondered if I wanted to keep it or not. I'm just getting on my feet and Jaheim is six. The thought of changing diapers and being up in the middle of the night rocking a baby didn't seem appealing at all. I went to work and saw Gregory briefly in the lunchroom and thought how sweet he is and knew he would make a good supporting father.

Gregory gives money every week to his ex-wife for his two daughters which is more than Harold does. I won't have to take care of this baby by myself that's for sure. The more I thought of how responsible Gregory is, the more I knew I was keeping this baby. The next day at work, I told Gregory I was pregnant, and we needed to talk; we were back together.

Everything was going great and December twentieth we made a run to Vegas with Olivia and her man at the time. Gregory spent money on me like he wasn't on a budget and we had a great time. I thought we were doing good and in January the man had the nerve to ask me to stop smoking until after I had the baby. I almost cussed him out!

I noticed whenever Gregory was alone with the boys he would ride them for every little thing they did. My eighth month of pregnancy while on maternity leave I went off on Gregory. I told him they were babies not men for god's sake, let them be boys! He never said anything else to them.

A few days before Kozet was born I was in bed taking a nap. I heard the boys making a lot of noise and wondered where Gregory was. I went to see what the noise was about. Jaheim and Dameon had toilet paper all over the room. I hollered at them to pick it all up and put it in the trash. Gregory was sitting at the kitchen table reading. When I asked why didn't he stop them? He sarcastically said, "They're just boys remember."

After Kozet arrived, the first two weeks Mother Mays came over to our place Monday through Friday and cooked for us. One day she made a banana pudding that took over an hour to cook on top of the stove and Gregory ate a small bowl before leaving for work. When I tasted that banana pudding, I couldn't speak for two whole minutes! My eyes were rolling around in my head.

I told Olivia about it and she dropped by and between her, the boys and I, well, Gregory didn't get any more banana pudding. I put a portion in the refrigerator for him but before I went to bed I finished it off. Gregory was so mad, but I told him Olivia ate it with her greedy butt.

One day Mother Mays baked a pan of oxtails and I kid you not, I ate what was left after Gregory ate and took his lunch. She had dirty rice, fried cabbage, and a long pan of sweet cornbread. I ate so much I thought my stomach was going to pop!

Mother Mays made grocery lists for Gregory and she used turkey ham for greens, beans, cabbage, peas, and green beans. I didn't even know there was such food as turkey ham! I grew up on cereal, mac and cheese, hot dogs and can soups.

That little, short woman could fry corn that made you want to stand up and sing the pledge of allegiance a' cappella! The last day she cooked for us

I hugged her before she left and almost cried. I was missing her cooking and she hadn't even left yet!

That's when Gregory started tripping about me cooking. I couldn't believe he wanted *me* in the kitchen, me! I think Gregory had in his mind that a wife was supposed to be a cook. We always went to Long Beach for holidays and special occasions and it was apparent all the women were good cooks. I even heard Charlotte was a great cook.

When our family ate at the cafes or restaurants and the bill would come, Gregory would make this grunting sound. He would complain about how money was being wasted and would insist the next meal eaten by the boys would be one plate; split. "They waste more than they eat!" That was Gregory's recording that clicked on when we went to eat. The man was used to staying home eating greens, yams, cornbread and chicken or beef roast.

My mother, Fanny Mae Henderson, had Shelia and three years later I arrived on the scene. Mae was a waitress and day worker until she moved up in Bixby Hills as a live-in. What I remember about those times is Shelia and I were home alone most of the time and we stayed in the house and was not allowed to open the door or answer the phone.

Shelia and I were pretty much on our own all the time. We ate cereal, boxed Mac and cheese, hot dogs and can soups. Cooking five course meals in our house was a foreign language.

When Shelia and I moved in with Aunt Essie, she had a house full and did all the cooking. Aunt Essie did not cook like Mother Mays. We ate a lot of spaghetti and beans and rice and fried chicken. Jasmine my cousin and Shelia did the cleaning and that left Lauren and I with nothing to do but stay cute. I am not much of a housekeeper or cook but there is more to life than cooking and cleaning, right?

After Kozet was born Gregory became distant towards me. We used to talk about our plans, what our next phase we would save for but after the wedding Gregory never brought up our buying a house or savings again. I sure wasn't bringing up anything about money to Gregory. I was not going to set him off intentionally on one of his budget tangents.

I knew in my heart Gregory and I were drifting apart and I also knew my not being a good cook like his mother and Charlotte had a lot to do with the distance between us. By then, I knew I was not Gregory's definition of a wife.

Hey, I am who I am and love, loves the person for who they are. I felt if Gregory couldn't love me the way I am, then I'm sorry.

Gregory made good money and eating out and hiring a housekeeper was affordable for him. The man was just stingy. The point of having money is to live the life you want, right? I decided I was never going to be who Gregory wanted in a wife and just did my thing. My money was mine to spend and I spent my money on what I wanted.

Gregory and I were together for just over two years and when he was home and awake, it was always tension between us. He complained constantly about the boys wasting and needing more discipline. Or he would complain about me leaving lights on and how high the bill was. Kozet was the only person Gregory found no fault with. He had her rotten. If she whimpered, he would pick her up.

At first I would explain to Gregory Kozet was smart and was whining so he would pick her up. He always told me, "Faith, she is a baby anything could be hurting her." Then I thought he was finding fault in my parenting Kozet, just as he does with my parenting the boys! I was the one with Kozet most of the time and having to hold her all day was not possible. Gregory would enter the room as if he were Superman coming to rescue Kozet from her non-caring parent! I would evil eye him every time he came running to rescue her.

Our first wedding anniversary I asked Gregory for a new wedding ring set. Our rings were bands and I saw a set in the paper that had three pieces, totaling three carats and his ring was a thick band made of white gold. They were almost four thousand dollars, but Gregory could make payments. He put his foot down, "Absolutely NO and you better not apply for credit. If four thousand dollars is going to be spent, it will be for a house, not some ring!"

Gregory's voice was raised when he said it and that pissed me off. We weren't even speaking when our anniversary came around and I didn't want to go anywhere with him. He gave me a card and some flowers. I bought him a "Thank You" card the next day but I didn't get him anything, not even an anniversary card. Gregory was cheap and I was hoping he would ask where his anniversary card was so I could tell him, "It cost money!" But he never asked.

Now that I'm thinking about this, we weren't speaking on our second wedding anniversary either. My Ford died right after I had Kozet and Gregory bought me a new Honda Accord and he had it financed. He said I needed a dependable car to get where I needed to go with the kids. He did not want to worry about me being stranded. Then that Thanksgiving, his transmission went out in his truck and he bought a used Toyota Tacoma.

I felt we should go to Vegas and spend the weekend celebrating our second-year anniversary but he said having bought two automobiles, we couldn't afford the trip. Gregory had money saved but he was too tight to spend it on us. I was so mad at him because I felt our wedding anniversary comes once a year, come on, we can't splurge once a year!

I was really tired of hearing the same old recording: "We can't afford that." I had an attitude from our anniversary in December until July; oh yes I did!

I did get Gregory to move into a nice area. All I had to say was Kozet needed a room and he gave me the green light.

The Fourth of July I was waiting for Gregory to wake up so we could head over to his family's for barbecue. I was in the kitchen on the phone with Olivia; she was telling me about her new man, and I could see the kids while they were watching television.

Kozet was on her blanket on the floor playing with her doll. A commercial came on and Dameon turned around and snatched Kozet's doll from her. She started whining and Dameon threw the doll back at Kozet. She cried louder and looked towards me.

Jaheim lifted her up onto the couch and gave her doll to her. Gregory came into the room, sat down, and asked Kozet what was wrong. Kozet pointed at the boys and Gregory went off! He doesn't want Kozet to cry at all.

I watched the whole thing and Gregory acts as though I'm not a good parent. I told him how he had Kozet rotten. One thing led to another and he stormed out. To be honest, I was glad to see him go, things were so tense when he was home. Gregory had changed so much from the sweet thoughtful guy I had fallen in love with into a quarter inspecting, penny auditing warden!

Being at work and seeing Gregory was very awkward so we avoided each other. Olivia had gotten laid off, her attendance was raggedy, so she won't be back. Gregory and I used to spend our lunch together so now we're not together, I ate alone. He stopped coming in the break room but on Fridays when I headed back to my work area, he would hand me an envelope.

After a month or so I spoke to Gregory and he replied, but by then it didn't bother me to see him. I was back bar hopping with Olivia and had met Oliver. Gregory would ask how Kozet was doing as he handed me my envelope and I would tell him she was good. It bothered me Gregory never asked about the boys. Jaheim asked about Gregory every morning while I was getting them ready for school, even after Oliver started staying over.

Shelia started working as a nurse at Long Beach Veteran's Hospital and I found an older woman a co-worker referred to me, a Ms. Dawson to watch the kids. One day in November, Kozet had a hard time breathing and Ms. Dawson called 911. I left work and after the doctor told me her diagnosis was asthma I called Gregory.

When the doctors told him Kozet had asthma Gregory responded very loud, "Asthma! Asthma?" He looked over at me and rolled his eyes. I could tell he blamed me for smoking while I was pregnant. I watched Gregory as he almost cried while looking at Kozet. She looked so helpless with that tube down her throat and the oxygen tent over her little face. Gregory held her tiny fingers and rubbed them as he blinked back tears. All I could do was cry. I hated seeing my baby like that.

Kozet was sedated and good thing, she would have had a fit for Gregory to hold her had she been awake. Kozet was walking around the apartment calling out, "Daddy?" I leaned on Gregory, but he didn't respond so I stepped away and wrapped my arms around myself.

Watching Gregory with Kozet; I realized I was witnessing firsthand the love a father has for his little girl. I became quiet and noticed the other babies in ICU and their visitors. The parents were obvious to spot giving their babies gentle touches and soft, "I love you's."

Later that night I laid in bed thinking how much Gregory loves Kozet and how he expresses his love to his daughter. I thought about how Shelton Ingalls never called me baby. Ingalls never hugged me, and I don't remember my father ever asking me how I was.

Nope! The first time I recall seeing Ingalls, Mae came in the room and told me my father was at the door and wanted to see me. I remember the door being wide open and as I approached it this tall dark man saw me and smiled. I can still see him bending down while saying, "Hi Faith!" As he stood up Mae says, "You can pick her up." I noticed his smile dropped and as his eyes left mine, he looked to his left and right then behind himself and shook his head 'No'. He says, "Eyes are everywhere Mae. I better go."

After Shelia and I moved in with Aunt Essie, Ingalls would drop by on my birthday, waving a twenty-dollar bill in his hand. Then we would see him the day before Christmas with another twenty in hand. After my fifteenth birthday we never saw my father again.

Ingalls would always knock on the front door; he never rang the doorbell. He would wait for me to appear and as soon as I came into his view, he would smile and wave the twenty-dollar bill in his hand. All I remember about my father is his smile and the twenty-dollar bill for me. Hum…

Maybe if Ingalls hadn't been married to Mae's close family friend, he may have had a chance to hold and coddle me and be a part of my life.

Mae would come stay at Aunt Essie's every six months for a weekend and I would wake to the sisters sitting in the dining room sipping on their coffees. Before going downstairs, I would sit on the top step and listen to their conversations. Aunt Essie would catch Mae up on the happenings.

One morning I overheard Aunt Essie tell Mae that Shelton was seen with some woman again. Mae said, "Shelton will always be a dog. Dorothy's nose is open so wide she's blind. Girl no other woman is gonna put up with his running around. If Faith didn't look like him, Dorothy and I would still be close. Just think, three minutes of pleasure cost me a good friend." Aunt Essie came back with, "Dorothy probably knows Faith is Sheltons. I have noticed how she looks long at Faith. She doesn't say much to me either."

Remembering that conversation made me weep. My baby is in the hospital and I wish her father were here to comfort me. I wept because I realized I have no firsthand knowledge of what a father's love is for his daughter. I wondered if my life would have turned out differently had I been loved by Ingalls.

My first love was Myles Washington. Myles was the weed man at my high school. He drove around while we all walked home and when he stopped at a traffic light someone would run up to his window and make an exchange. Lauren and I admired his car and Myles always smiled at me when he drove by.

One day Myles pulled up alongside Lauren and I and asked if we wanted a ride home. We both told Myles "No" and he said, "I won't do any business with you ladies in the car, promise." His smile was more convincing than his words. I looked at Lauren and we hopped in the car; me in the front seat, Lauren in the back.

Myles dropped us off in front of the house and put the car in park. He reached into his cars center console, pulled out a twenty dollar bill and handed it to me. As I took it I asked, "What is this for?" He smiles while saying, "I like you. Think about me when you spend it." He took off burning rubber.

I thought about Myles all the time. He was five feet seven, wore a long Jerry Curl and was brown skinned. His eyes were dark brown but the white of Myles' eyes were yellowish, not white. He had a thin mustache and a short-pointed beard. Myles was not fine but when he smiled his intoxicating smile, you gave Myles Washington every bit of your attention. He was street and the bona-fide definition of "Bad Boy."

Lauren told Jasmine about our ride home and Aunt Essie got wind and told Uncle Alonso. Myles was picking me and Lauren up in the mornings and taking us home after school. Every Tuesday Myles handed me a twenty-dollar bill before I left his car and he always told me to think of him when spending it. And I did.

Maybe after a month of Myles giving us rides, one Sunday evening Aunt Essie and Uncle Alonso told everyone to go upstairs to their rooms they were going to talk to me. I knew it was about Myles.

I was told by my uncle that Myles was bad news and I could get caught up in some dangerous stuff. Uncle Alonso told me to have Myles come talk to him man to man then the three of us will have another conversation about me and Myles. And I was not to see Myles until after he talked to Uncle Alonso.

I was okay with it. I thought they would talk, and everything would be cool. But, when Myles came to pick us up for school the next day, I told him what Uncle Alonso said and he went off. "Who the hell is this man thinking he's my daddy? I am a grown man and will see who I want!"

As we left his car Lauren says to Myles, "He is my father and he is a real man!" Lauren purposely slammed the car door and told me, "Come on Faith!" I looked at Myles, he was looking at Lauren and was not smiling.

That day at school while I was at lunch Myles parked close to the fence and was walking around to get my attention, then waved me over. I went over to him. He told me that he really liked me a lot and wanted to spend time with me without Lauren around, just the two of us.

Myles told me to just leave the campus and he would bring me back and no one would know I had left, we need to talk about us.

I was so scared as I walked pass the office leaving campus. Myles was parked at the curb and opened the car door for me. When Myles sat behind the wheel he told me he loved me and pulled me close. We went to his house. His mother was at work and Myles took me to his bedroom but before we entered the door I pulled back.

Myles Washington hugged me and assured me oh so sweetly that nothing would happen that I didn't want to happen. I gave in to Myles entering his bedroom and to his tender kisses. We had sex and Myles said we were one now and no-one could ever separate us. If Myles Washington had told me the sky was orange I would have believed him. I was so in love. Myles and I made a weekly routine of that day's events and, the Tuesday twenty-dollar bills stopped.

After a few weeks Aunt Essie was informed of my ditching school. Lauren and I walked in the house from school and Aunt Essie hugged me then Lauren and told her to head upstairs for a few minutes. She started our conversation with, "Have a seat Faith something has come up and we need to talk." I'm thinking this is about girl stuff because Uncle Alonzo is not involved. She continued, "The attendance office called to inform me you are ditching fourth, fifth and sixth period. I'm thinking you must be seeing Myles. Are you?"

I told her the truth and she said for me to stop seeing Myles then she asked if we were sexually active. I lied and told her not yet. She told me she was taking me to the family clinic to get birth control pills then she got up and left the room. I knew she was mad, and I also knew she knew, I lied. If she caught me in another lie it's going to be my behind!

Essie Leigh Henderson-Stover is the personality type who will ask you direct questions and if the truth is told she is good. But if she thought you lied to her, she would give you a look and for a couple days she would watch you like a hawk. When you would do or say something to make her mad; Aunt Essie would jump you like white on rice and only Uncle Alonzo could get her off you! I'm talkin fist fight'n windmill you; pulling your hair kind of jump on you! I was so scared.

Myles and I never talked on the phone; we always saw each other through the week on school days. Lauren and I would walk to school and I would meet Myles in front of the school after my lunch period.

The day after my conversation with Aunt Essie as soon as I sat in his car I told Myles that today was my last day being with him. He says, "Well all good things must come to an end!" I was mad because the words he spoke were cruel, cold, and distant. I knew that I meant nothing to him. I was in love with Myles and he lied when he told me he loved me.

I opened the car door and jumped out. He says sarcastically, "Bye, nice knowing you!" I stood holding onto the car door and yelled, **"Go to hell!"** I slammed the door as hard as I could and kicked it. Myles yelled, **"Bitch!"** And got rubber leaving me standing at the curb calling him every name but a child of god!

I cried. I went to my class thinking how I really loved him, but Myles only used me! As I sat in class I thought about how Myles stopped the spending money after I gave him what he wanted. The crying stopped and the real pissed off took over!

Several months later Myles was busted for drug trafficking. We all followed his trial in the paper but I don't think anyone but Aunt Essie knew about Myles and me.

...I think I have never had a man to love me like Gregory. Maybe if Ingalls had held me and told me he loved me or called me, 'baby,' I might be able to hold onto a good man like Gregory. Gregory was a loving father and in fact; he was even loving to me. I just couldn't take his being so cheap.

I thought I had met Gregory's twin in Carl Johnson. Carl was so kind, thoughtful and fine! He spent money on me like no one else I have ever dated. After Carl moved in with me I figured it out. Carl was into moving large quantities of cocaine and needed a place to stay; I just so happened to be his bee hive.

Unlike Gregory, Carl never said anything to the boys about their behavior. In fact Carl was always asking me if I had someone who could watch the kids so we could be alone. When I told Carl I was pregnant he asked if I intended to keep it. That was a giant red flag for me. He was Harold Paulson when it came to kids.

The money Carl had was good and I was intending to move to Inglewood into a house after the baby arrived. I found out I was carrying twins, a boy and girl. I was happy but Carl never got excited about any baby arrival talk. He was all for the move as long as everything was in my name. I knew it was a matter of time before he was caught but I decided to enjoy it while it lasted. Besides enjoying my life, I was putting cash away.

Carl was picked up and his two friends, Abdul and Vince rushed into my apartment throwing things around looking for Carl's stash. It was three-thirty in the morning and they scared me and the kids so bad, I started having cramps and lost the babies.

The money I had saved to move was in my closet and Abdul and Vince took it. Not only was I grieving the loss of my babies, I was depressed my way out of the ghetto was taken from me also.

…I think I have never had a man to love me like Gregory. Maybe I should find another man like him; a responsible, caring man…

I prayed for my baby everyday while she was in the hospital and I also prayed that I would someday be loved like I am the apple of a mans eye.

That was the night my mind was made up' I am going to find a love that is like no other and he is going to put me and my kids in a nice house.

Wow! Here I am eight years later and still looking for Mister Right! Let me go call Gregory and see how Kozet is doing.

~~~~Gregory~~~~

Why is it after I leave Mrs. Judson and her so called counseling session, I rewind the session, as if it were not painful enough the *first time* I sat through it! Man…

After Faith and I broke up, I worked and went home but I had no feelings at all. I forced myself to engage in conversations and pushed myself to go through the motions of everyday life. I would read but could not concentrate on what I was reading.

My mind kept sweeping up the same script. I could not rid my thoughts of me being thirty years old, living with my mother. Here I am with two ex-wives and three daughters. Daughters I cannot hug, bounce on my knee, or talk too. I kept thinking, 'there has to be more to life than this.'

I thought Faith was different, not like Char. I really thought she wanted to work towards having a house for the family. I thought Faith wanted what I wanted. Faith worked and never complained about me not spending time with her. How did we become strangers?

I wanted to talk to Mama about marriage number two going down the drain but I realized Faith's body is what attracted me to her and, well

Mama would tell me to get myself back in church and allow The Lord to guide me.

Mama has always been a woman of few words but she gets her points of view across. My Mother is ninety-nine percent right when it comes to people and had I shared my questions with her as to why my marriage failed, she would have told me I never should have hooked up with Faith. I did not want to hear that.

Grand Pop had a severe stroke right after Faith had Kozet and Mama started attending church mainly to help Grannie with Gran Pop. He was left unable to speak and the right side of his body was weakened but he would stomp that cane of his to get his point across.

Mama told me the church was having its annual cookout next Saturday and I should come before going to work. It starts at eleven a.m. and there would be good foods. I had no intentions of going but the day before the cookout she told me if I wanted to eat tomorrow, she would be at the park at nine a.m. so, I had to attend the cookout.

Jamal woke me and I followed him and Tina to the park. There was a lot of people and food. I sat by Mama's blanket and saw some people I knew as a child and was I surprised to see Janice Andrews. Man was she looking good. She still wore glasses but had filled out in all the right places. Janice had a body on her.

Mama was right, the food was good. I kissed her bye and went to work thinking about attending church tomorrow. There was overtime in my department but I declined it and went home at my shift's end and set the clock for church. The next morning, I found myself energetic again about going to church.

It is a shame I have not attended church in years but I am ready now to start including The Lord in my plans. It pains me to admit it, but it is obvious my way of doing things does not work too well. The rest of the time getting dressed, my mind was on Janice Andrews and her shapely body.

Holy Temple Church of God in Christ off PCH and E. 7th street in LB is my grandparent's church of choice since they married. It is an old church building and very large. I have a lot of childhood memories there. I used to do homework on the left back pew growing up and was always sleep when it was time to go home. I loved the music but felt church was too long.

Morning Star Baptist church would have been my choice of church to attend however, due to Char and I not on good terms, I do not want to take the risk of seeing her there. I believe that is the reason I avoided going to church altogether.

When I saw Pastor Lawson the day before at the cookout, I mentioned to him he might see me today. When I arrived I recognized an usher and three deacons. It seemed nothing had changed since I was a young man except now there was grey hair on the familiar faces. Pastor Lawson taught us from Luke 15: 11-24 and it reads,

"Then He said: "A certain man had two sons. [12] And the younger of them said to his father, 'Father, give me the portion of goods that falls to me.' So he divided to them his livelihood. [13] And not many days after, the younger son gathered all together, journeyed to a far country, and there wasted his possessions with prodigal living. [14] But when he had spent all, there arose a severe famine in that land, and he began to be in want.

[15] Then he went and joined himself to a citizen of that country, and he sent him into his fields to feed swine. [16] And he would gladly have filled his stomach with the pods that the swine ate, and no one gave him anything. [17] But when he came to himself, he said, 'How many of my father's hired servants have bread enough and to spare, and I perish with hunger!

[18] I will arise and go to my father, and will say to him, 'Father, I have sinned against heaven and before you, [19] and I am no longer worthy to be called your son. Make me like one of your hired

servants.'   [20] And he arose and came to his father. But when he was still a great way off, his father saw him and had compassion, and ran and fell on his neck and kissed him.

[21] And the son said to him, 'Father, I have sinned against heaven and in your sight, and am no longer worthy to be called your son.' [22] But the father said to his servants, 'Bring out the best robe and put it on him, and put a ring on his hand and sandals on his feet. [23] And bring the fatted calf here and kill it, and let us eat and be merry; [24] for this my son was dead and is alive again; he was lost and is found.' And they began to be merry."

Pastor Lawson explained: "The whole fifteenth chapter of Luke is about loss. Lost sheep, lost coin, and lost son. Today we are focusing on the lost son. This young man desired what was not familiar. Similar to the sinner who desires a lifestyle out of the plan God has predestined.

This son craved the experience of life outside of the life he was destined to have. Like us, especially when we are young and long for the things and lifestyle contrary to what is profitable for us. So, today we can relate to this son's longing.

The father being wise, allows the son to have his inheritance; knowing his son has to gain his own testimony. Work out his own salvation! The wise father knows what his young son does not. The father also knows this longing his son has for the lifestyle outside of his reach must be dealt with by his son.

The son must experience what is detrimental to him so he will know, the lifestyle his father has provided is the best lifestyle for him. However like us, the son must find out for himself. The hard way.

You know our heavenly Father is wise just as the father in this example written for our learning. Our Heavenly Father knows this flesh longs for what is not good for us and, He is wise enough to know we cannot be told **'No, no, that's not what's best for you.'** Our heavenly Father knows like the father in our example today, we must find out for ourselves. That longing inside us must be reckoned with.

Saints, most of us in here today are parents and just as a toddler must find out exactly what, *"hot,"* means by getting their little hand burned; so it is with the younger generations. They, like the son in today's scripture must find out for themselves, the lifestyle God has designed with His wisdom, is what's best for us.

Today's society has our young folk and even some of us grey heads, enticed by what's so readily available now days. This flesh yearns to try what the eye sees. I stopped by to tell you this morning, don't squander your youth on enticement. Hunger and thirst after righteousness and you will be filled.

Parents pray for your sons and daughters. Saints pray for our youth today. Plead the Blood of Jesus over them and decree they will live and not die. Pray their soul will be satisfied with the lifestyle of holiness and producing the fruit of the spirit. Let us come together in prayer and bind this strongman that is out to destroy our youth because they are the next generation to carry the church forward with the gospel of Jesus Christ."

Pastor Lawson opened the doors of the church and invited all who want to walk in the spirit and not fulfill the lust of the flesh to come to the altar and get it right. Pastor Lawson prayed for all of us including himself to repent of our past deeds and request a clean heart so we may be able to serve The Lord with gladness and delight ourselves in Him and His way. Pastor Lawson prayed we would be witnesses to the good lifestyle God has ordained for us and others will see The Lord through us and want to walk as we do.

Yep, Pastor preached today!

I thought about how I had stopped going to church and no longer read my Bible daily as I did when I lived at home. I sat on the pew and repented of wanting what was different for me than God's plan. God knows my heart and how I want to provide for my family. I did not go to the altar but I did pray for a clean heart and gave an offering.

When we were dismissed I looked to see where Janice was so I could say "Hi." I also wanted to see if there was a man hanging around her. I spotted her and was working my way over to her but people kept talking to me asking how have I been. Good seeing me, hope to see me Wednesday night and make sure I come back. By the time I was done talking to everyone Janice could not be found.

Mama had cooked one of Mr. Mays favorite meals; smothered chicken, collard greens, rice, cornbread, and she bakes a pound cake or a cobbler for Sunday dinners. Today it was blackberry cobbler. While we ate Mr. Mays tells me he was glad I came to church today. Mr. Mays has never been much of a talker but today he was talking and we all listened.

Mr. Mays looked me in the eyes and said, "When you children were young I worked a lot of hours to make sure you had what you needed. I didn't want you to go without and be teased like I was as a child. After you left the house Gregory, I realized I missed spending time with you so I slowed down with work and spent more time with Jamal and Samantha. Son don't make my mistake. Give The Lord His time and He will bless you with your children. You might keep your wife happy too." Mr. Mays looks over at Mama and continues eating.

While eating I asked Mama about Janice and she informed me, "Janice is a Woods now. She came into a service over three years ago and said she wanted to re-dedicate her life to The Lord. I believe her husband, Melvin has been missing for a couple years now and if you ask me, him not coming around is a blessing.

That young man would beat her bad but it made Janice more sincere about her rededication. She asks for prayer all the time. She's believing The Lord to send her husband back to her and that her marriage will flourish. Gregory, you'd best to look somewhere else son, there's no sap in that tree for you."

I must admit Janice had me feeling alive again and looking back I should have listened to Mama. I was lonely…Genesis 2:18 tells us; ***And The Lord God said, "It is not good that man should be alone; I will make him a helper comparable to him."***

I attended church faithfully every Sunday but it was not for the sermons, it was to see Janice. She was working with the children during the services. When we talked, she told me her daughter Sybil, wouldn't go to anyone when it comes to church.

Janice began to sit with her baby in the children's class and ended up being the Teacher. Janice loves teaching the babies and always talked about them. I could tell she loved what she did.

I noticed how Janice always talked about Melvin and spoke life to her marriage and I really admired her faith. I kept thinking about the incident in the Bible of the valley of dry bones when Ezekiel spoke life to them and they came back to life. Janice felt that way concerning her marriage.

Ezekiel 37: 1-14 states:

The hand of The Lord came upon me and brought me out in the Spirit of The Lord, and set me down in the midst of the valley; and it was full of bones. [2] Then He caused me to pass by them all around, and behold, there were very many in the open valley; and indeed they were very dry. [3] And He said to me, "Son of man, can these bones live?" So I answered, "O Lord God, You know." [4] Again He said to me, "Prophesy to these bones, and say to them, 'O dry bones, hear The Word of The Lord!

[5] Thus says The Lord God to these bones: "Surely I will cause breath to enter into you, and you shall live. [6] I will put sinews on you and bring flesh upon you, cover you with skin and put breath in you; and you shall live. Then you shall know that I am The Lord."' "[7] So I prophesied as I was commanded; and as I prophesied, there was a noise, and suddenly a rattling; and the bones came together, bone to bone. [8] Indeed, as I looked, the sinews and the flesh came upon them, and the skin covered them over; but there was no breath in them.

[9] Also He said to me, "Prophesy to the breath, prophesy, son of man, and say to the breath, 'Thus says The Lord God: "Come from the four winds, O breath, and breathe on these slain, that they may live."' "[10] So I prophesied as He commanded me, and breath came into them, and they lived, and stood upon their feet, an exceedingly great army.

[11] Then He said to me, "Son of man, these bones are the whole house of Israel. They indeed say, 'Our bones are dry, our hope is lost, and we ourselves are cut off!' [12] Therefore prophesy and say to them, 'Thus says The Lord God: "Behold, O My people, I will open your graves and cause you to come up from your graves, and bring you into the land of Israel.

[13] Then you shall know that I am The Lord, when I have opened your graves, O My people, and brought you up from your graves. [14] I will put My Spirit in you, and you shall live, and I will place you in your own land. Then you shall know that I, The Lord, have spoken it and performed it," says The Lord."

I admired Janice and recalling this now, I realize her faith was also what kept me pursuing her. I needed hope and encouragement about what The Lord would do for me to make my future better than my past. It also helped Janice was good looking, shapely and had a sweet disposition.

I was still working twelve-hour days but I did not work on Sundays. Faith was laid off so I did not see or hear from her unless Kozet needed something. I started mailing my money orders to her until the divorce finalized then the payments were taken out of my check.

Faith called every time she moved and the places she lived made me feel sorry for Kozet. So, a few months after she moved into another housing development, I started mailing Faith fifty dollars twice a month. I cannot have my daughter going without. I am a man who takes care of his responsibilities and my daughter will not go hungry!

Charece was skipped to the sixth grade and Tamera was in the fourth. I was so proud my daughters are not only pretty; they are also smart. Mother Thomas would sometime stop by Stockton Avenue Sunday evenings with the girls on her way taking them home from church so I could see them.

I had mixed feelings. I was so happy to hug them and listen to what they were into. It was when they left I would feel inadequate as a father and immediately look forward to the next time I would be able to see my daughters.

Faith started dating some guy by the name of Tyrone and she called me one night at work asking me to come by when I left Douglas. She was afraid

Tyrone would come back to her apartment. He had jumped on her and left mad.

I left work at the end of my overtime shift and drove over to Faith's place. I saw how he had blackened the side of her face and her eye was red and swollen. When she hugged me I could smell liquor on her and the more she spoke, slurring became noticeable; Faith was drunk.

I offered to take her to the hospital but she refused. I asked if Kozet was alright and told her I would in no way accept Tyrone upsetting Kozet. Faith said that was why she called me. She knew I would stand up to Tyrone.

Kozet was sleep when the fighting started. Faith had Kozet in bed with her and allowed me to see my daughter. I was shocked to see how much Kozet had grown and how healthy she looked. It is very obvious Kozet will be tall.

Kozet is so pretty and has big fat rosy cheeks and there are dimples in her tiny hands. I leaned over and kissed her. The last time I saw her, was in the emergency room. I looked at Faith and told her I would pray she does the right thing in regards to this Tyrone guy because my concern was for my daughter. Faith asked me to stay with her until she took the boys to school in the morning. I slept on her living room couch. Tyrone did not show up.

Faith getting the kids ready for school woke me. Kozet hardly knew me. My feelings were hurt she was hesitant coming to me. Dameon is slightly taller than Jaheim and as he walks closer to me he asks, "You back?" I shook my head "No." Jaheim stood in the doorway staring at me.

Dameon spoke in a raised voice, while hitting his right fist into his left hand. "Don't worry, I got Tyrone's ass!" Faith tells him to stop cussing. Dameon keeps talking, "Mama stopped me from jack'n him." Faith says, "Dameon! Stay out of grown folks' business!"

Faith directs her eyes to me and says, "Dameon woke up and jumped on Tyrone's back. Tyrone shoved him off and Dameon went into the kitchen, got the butchers knife, and cut Tyrone's hand. Tyrone left swearing to come back and deal with all of us. Thanks for being here Gregory. I need to drop them off. I have an interview this afternoon and must fix my face."

I left Faith wishing Tyrone had come back. I need to punch him out for jacking Faith's face up and he better be glad he did not hit her in front of Kozet. As bad as I wanted to slap Faith when we were together, I kept my cool. No man should *ever* hit a female. A man has way more physical strength than a woman and can do serious damage to her.

I did some thinking as I drove home.

I have always been tall, in fact, I was teased as a child. People thought I was older than I was because of my height. Being skinny, Mr. Mays signed me up for Pop Warner Football so I could learn to defend myself. I did not much care for fighting but by the time I turned nine, I had to fight.

Mr. Mays told me the boys would choose me to pick on until I proved to them I would fight back. He told me it didn't matter if I won, it mattered that I defended myself. I found out he was right. After my talk with Mr. Mays the next kid to bully me was a classmate Michael Pierson. After he shoved me I balled my fist and punched him in the stomach. When I saw the look of shock on his face, I hauled off and punched him in the jaw. I hurt my hand, his face swelled and we both went to the nurse's office.

Principal Harper came into the room and told us to find other ways to settle our differences. He looked at me and said my Dad should invest in boxing gloves for me and he walked out of the room. His words were a confidence booster for me. I had a confident walk and reputation after that.

Junior high I had to fight again twice but I was not afraid and felt I could outlast any contender. I never started the fights but like Mr. Mays said, I had to defend myself.

My high school football coach told me my height was intimidating and I need to learn how to use my height and upper body strength to my advantage; people are automatically afraid of me.

I try to avoid violence, it makes me angry I am put in a position being made to fight. However, if I have too, I will defend myself and my family. My concern is that Kozet will not be living in a violent environment. I will start a fight with Tyrone for sure when it comes to my daughter!

On Sundays Sister Butler would give Janice and Sybil a ride to and from church. Sister Butler did not attend church one Sunday and had sister Payton to pick Janice up in her stead. I was talking to Janice after church and she told me to excuse her, she needed to remind Sister Payton to take her home. I told her I would drop her off and she agreed.

I asked if she wanted to stop at IHOP with me for lunch. Janice told me her budget did not allow eating out. I told her I was paying for her and Sybil. She agreed to go. While we ate I asked how she met her husband and she told me. The way Janice eyes enlarged as she told me about their coming together, I believe it became apparent to her that Melvin had issues with women even before they met.

Janice began sharing how Melvin's mother and younger sister were always gone together and Melvin was left alone at home quite a bit. I said, "Maybe you two are unequally yoked." She became silent and watery eyed so I changed our attention to her baby, Sybil.

When I dropped Janice off I told her to call me if she wanted to talk and started reciting my cell phone number to her. She stopped me and said, "Let me put it in my phone, hold on." After she finished with my number, she smiled such a sweet soft smile as she waved me off. I thought of her the rest of the day.

The following Saturday I told Mama I was inviting Janice over tomorrow after church for dinner and for her to cook extra foods. The next day I went into the Children's Church and invited Janice to the house for lunch after church, and she accepted the invitation. On the way to the house I was thinking of how to let Janice know I liked her. She was quiet so I kept my mouth shut and decided spending time with her would be all I needed to do.

I watched Janice as she went straight to the kitchen with Mama. Apparently the two of them pray together they were like mother and daughter; like watching Sam and Mama together. Janice even helped Mama warm up the food. I decided to just observe her and figure out the best time to let her know I am interested in dating her.

Mr. Mays was so engrossed with Sybil. Just so happen Mother Thomas brought the girls over and Mr. Mays hugged them and asked about school. Mama told Mother Thomas she would take the girls home and Charece and Tamera went to the kitchen with Sybil. As the girls left for the kitchen Mr. Mays says, "Gregory, be prayerful as to your next move. Let The Lord guide you."

I looked at him and replied, "Yes sir." However I wondered what he meant by that. Jamal and Tina arrived and we all had dinner.

Us men went to the back room and watched the game. The pool table is on the grass in the back yard and Mr. Mays' thirty-two-inch color television and a small sectional is now in its place. Half time I went into the kitchen. The girls were talking about school just starting and what their favorite subjects were. Janice is a natural with them and I am glad.

During the ride taking Janice home, I asked if Saturday after she gets off work, would she like to see the movie everyone was talking about; "Collateral," and reluctantly she said, "Hm, okay."

I had enough money saved to buy a house in Carson but the divorce was not final and I did not want Faith to know about the money because she was entitled to half. It was almost six months since I filed and the divorce was about to be finalized. I told my attorney I had a thousand dollars saved and would gladly give Faith five hundred dollars. It's not that I did not want to give Faith anything, she was so extravagant I knew she would run through my hard-earned money in a heartbeat.

By then I was mailing Faith a hundred dollars a month while sixty dollars a week was being taken out of my paycheck for Kozet. Considering I was still paying Faith's car note I had to budget my money. My taking Saturday and Sundays off prevented me from saving. Janice and I dated four months when my divorce from Faith became final.

It was right after New Years and I was to the point of frenzy wanting to kiss Janice. She was very easy to be with and the more time we spent together the more I was convinced we made a great couple. Janice and I talked about the Bible a lot and she instigated prayer before we left each other because my mind was always on what she looked like without clothes. She never touched me but her tone and soft smiles let me know she liked her some Gregory.

I asked Janice one Sunday night while driving her home, "Have you filed for divorce?" She turned her head away and after hesitating a soft, "No I haven't," was spoken by her. I wanted to ask why not, we had been dating for almost five months but I was a little perturbed and did not want to come off angry so I kept my mouth shut.

February third Sybil was turning three years old and Janice was giving her a birthday party at Fashion Island, Farrell's Ice Cream Parlor the Saturday after Sybil's birthday. I asked Janice what I should buy Sybil for her birthday. She said some money would help her pay for the ice cream. So I gave her thirty dollars.

I only see my two older daughters briefly on Sunday afternoons. Mother Thomas brings them by on her way taking them home after church and dinner. I was looking forward to spending time with Charece and Tamera that Saturday at Farrell's. After picking up my daughters the three of us went to get Janice and Sybil.

We were at Farrell's having a good time. There were some church members and the babies from Janice class in attendance. We heard commotion at the entrance of the parlor and when I looked where the noise was coming from I saw a man leaving, he seemed upset. I noticed Janice had a look of horror. I asked, "You alright?" She nodded "Yes," and returned her attention to the children.

After we dropped the girls off at the Thomas house Janice told me the man that caused the disturbance at Farrell's had a resemblance to her husband Melvin. I asked if she had invited him. She assured me she hadn't she had no idea where he was.

Now I am wondering how then did he know we were there! Huh.

I carried a "totally knocked-out" Sybil upstairs into Janice apartment and this being my first time inside, I followed Janice as she led me to Sybil's baby bed. We went into the living room and Janice talked about Melvin being abusive with her. She explained he would sometimes show up at her apartment when she wasn't there demanding the manager give him the key to her apartment.

The neighbors would tell Janice that Melvin reeked of alcohol when he came around and reassured her they had her back. Melvin would slap Janice around and show up banging on her door refusing to leave until she let him in so she moved to where she lives now. When I asked if she were afraid he would find her, she shook her head "Yes" and began to cry.

When she started crying I moved over to her and held her close to console her. Realizing this was my chance to kiss her, I made my move to her lips. We both became pretty worked up and that was the first time Janice and I had sex.

Janice told me what had just happened could never happen again. We had just committed adultery and we both know better. I did not say anything but I was thinking, *'that's what you think!'* After that day, I never looked at Janice the same. Lust was on me like white on rice, man I tell you!

From that day on I never worked Saturdays or Sundays. I made sure Janice and I spent every weekend together and Sybil and I began to bond. I would look at Sybil and think, 'At least I get a chance to enjoy her.' Sybil was asking a lot of "why's" and I found myself enjoying sitting with her answering her questions. She was so captivated by what she was learning and sometimes I would initiate some of her interest.

While spending time with Sybil I would reminisce of my times with Charece and Tamera when they were that age. Sunday mornings while Char dressed them for church was my time with them. They would come jump in bed with me after they had breakfast and Char would bathe them in our bathtub and dress them and comb their hair in our bedroom while they each informed me of their past weeks events.

Watching Sybil, listening to her expressions made me feel like a father. Even though I felt like a father to some other man's daughter, still I was being afforded that luxury.

Valentines fell on a Saturday so I made reservations and Mama kept Sybil while Janice and I went to dinner and I devised a way of spending the night with Janice. My plan worked. When I took her home I locked my car door with my overnight bag in the trunk. Janice had a bottle of sparkling apple juice in the freezer. While we toasted to better days ahead, I put my glass down and kissed her. That night we made love three times and each time she would say, "Gregory, we mustn't …" I tenderly placed my finger over her lips and held her in my arms and caressed her.

I wanted to spend every eye opened moment with Janice. She was on my mind all the time. I started bringing clothes to her place a little at a time, and Janice never said anything. We gradually began semi-living together. Saturday afternoons I went over Janice's and took my suits and the three of us attended church as a family on Sundays.

Mama cooked for all of us on Sundays and after Janice helped with cleaning the kitchen and the game was over, we would leave for her place. During the drive to her place I always asked if she were working on her divorce and she gave me the same hesitated answer, "working on it." I wanted to tell her so bad to put a rush on it but I did not want to spoil the love making mood.

Janice was working for a boutique within walking distance to her place and Sybil's sitter. Mondays while she would get herself and Sybil ready for work and daycare, I would get ready heading to

LB. Just before we all walked out of the door I would ask Janice, "Gonna work on that divorce?" She always hesitated before answering me and her usual responses were the same; "I'm working on it; Trying;" or, "It's not easy." Janice would kiss me on the cheek and tell me to have a blessed day.

The last Sunday in March was Easter and the church has an annual shut-in on Good Friday until Sunday. I stayed in LB and missed Janice so much I decided to tell her on Sunday how much I loved her. Sunday right after church Janice avoided me. I spoke to a few folks and found out Janice caught a ride home so I went to LB and decided to let her call me and tell me what was going on.

I am thinking the shut-in made her feel guilty about us sleeping together. I decided to let her handle her guilt. I want her to divorce Melvin and marry me, so there was no guilt in my head. However I had questions about why she was dragging her feet divorcing her husband.

Tuesday I stopped by the boutique on my way to work. Waiting for her to make a move and call me *was not working!* As I entered the room Janice caught glimpse of me and became very fidgety and avoided eye contact. I held her hand and asked what was wrong. She pulled her hand away and said, "Gregory please leave. I'll call you later and explain everything." I asked, "Is it Melvin? Has he come back?" She rapidly blinked back tears. She bit her bottom lip while shaking her head "No" and walked to the back of the store.

I followed her. When Janice turned to face me she had tears streaming down her face while saying, "Gregory you must leave now, I will call you later this afternoon and tell you what's going on. Leave please before I lose my job." She wiped her face and I resisted the urge to hold her in my arms and reassure her everything was going to be alright. Janice turned her back to me while pleading, *"please leave!"*

I was racking my brain trying to figure out what happened to make Janice change so abruptly towards me. She is so soft spoken and I did not want to be harsh with her but I was tired of sneaking around as though we were teens. I felt as though we needed to make our relationship legal. I thought maybe I was pressuring Janice but I want to get married. We love each other. We get along so well.

I decided to put my foot down and demand Janice get her divorce. I will even pay for it. Maybe she is worried about the cost. Man, I wish she would call and tell me what's wrong!

Wednesday while I ate, Mama asked what was going on with me and Janice, did we fall out? I told her my plans about getting married but Janice was avoiding me. She never called yesterday like she said and I was thinking all sorts of things were wrong. Still married to Melvin maybe he found her and is making her stay with him. Mama told me to call Janice since I was a nervous wreck. I jumped up from the kitchen table and made the call.

Janice did not answer her phone so I dialed the boutique and she answered. I started in on her, "Janice do not hang up. I will come straight over there if you do. Is Melvin harassing you?" "No." She promptly replied. "Gregory meet me around the corner at the donut shop in fifteen minutes and we will talk okay?" I did not reply, just hung up and left headed to the Boutique. I am thinking, 'this will be resolved today!' I had to calm down. I kept thinking this has to do with Melvin and if he is harassing Janice, his butt is mine!

I get to the donut shop before Janice does and stand near the counter in the rear facing the door. Janice walks in and sees me. Man does she look good. She has on her red long sleeve dress with the satin lapel. She is five feet six, smooth pretty brown skin and the softest round brown eyes. She has a small waist so this red dress is showing off her shape.

I reach out to hug her, she ignores my extended arms and sits down. I get seated and Janice leans in and says, "Gregory this is difficult for me so please let me finish before saying anything. I need to get this out." I took her by the hand and looked into her beautiful eyes. My heart was beating so fast. "Sure." I replied. She opens her mouth but nothings coming out.

I lean into her and say, "Janice, I love you and want to spend the rest of my life with you." She took on a frightened look. I asked if she were alright. She placed her free hand up to her mouth and shook her head up and down as her eyes became so large. We look at each other. In a shaky voice Janice says, "I don't know how to tell you…" My heart stopped. I squirmed and swallowed so hard. For some strange reason I was so afraid she was going to tell me some bad news and I was trying to prepare myself. "Gregory, I'm pregnant."

I felt myself breathing again.

No Melvin? No being harassed. I sighed aloud. I look in her eyes and envision her lovingly holding a baby in her arms, my baby. Now gazing into her eyes, I ask, "How far along are you?" She still has that look in her eyes while, "I'm keeping it!" Bluntly flew out of her mouth. I felt myself jerk back a little and I guess a question mark appeared on my face because she crossed her arms and looked at me with squinted eyes.

I leaned forward and asked, "Janice, will you marry me?" She broke out with a soft smile while saying, "Of course I will!" We reached for one another as I say, "Of course you will have to divorce Melvin." She pulled away from me, looks into my eyes and softly says, "Of course." We were both smiling. She told me she had to get back to work.

As we stood, I grabbed her and kissed her on the cheek. She looked embarrassed as she walked away from me. I watched her leave the donut shop, man she is fine! I headed to work thinking. I need to buy us a house, I am going to be a father again! I was so happy Janice is my match. Finally a woman who does not think saving is ridiculous! Thank You Lord. And she loves The Lord.

I signed up for Saturday overtime, I need to save and buy Janice a house! We talked on the phone every day during her lunch and I decided to get her rings and present them to her Saturday. I picked the rings up Friday and Saturday after I ate, Mama wished me the best as I left LB headed to the boutique on my way to work.

Janice was elated when I revealed the rings. She hugged me and thanked me so many times. I made her so happy. I left for work riding high, man was I happy. Sunday I noticed Janice had her old wedding ring on her finger but I kept my mouth shut, I do not want her upset over a ring.

The next two months were a little tense because I asked Janice every other day if she had found an attorney yet to file for her divorce. Her answer was always, always a hesitated, "Not yet; or I'm working on it."

Fathers' Day Janice was looking pregnant and just before church dismissed Deacon Mecum came to me and said Pastor Lawson wants to see me in his office right after service today. I found Janice and told her to wait for me Pastor Larson wanted to see me. She said, "Me too." I knew then what this meeting was about. I waited for her and we went into pastor's office together. I grabbed her hand before opening the door.

Pastor was removing his robe as he spoke. "It's time for the three of us to talk. There is a lot of whispering going on and I need to shut it down but I have to know what your intentions are." As he stood waiting for a response, he pointed for us to be seated. I was half glad he wanted to know what our intentions are because I wanted to know where Janice was with her divorce. But I felt the church had no business in ours.

I spoke up; "Pastor, Janice and I are planning to marry." He asks, "Gregory you divorced?" "Yes sir I am." As he sits he directs his eyes to Janice, "Janice?" She squirmed as a soft, "I'm working on it." Was spoken.

Pastor takes turns looking in our eyes while saying, "Well you both know you are committing adultery and we are Bible believers here and do not take adultery lightly. I can't defend you two and you are not living according to The Word. I'm going to ask you Janice to step down from the Children's Ministry. After you divorce and marry Gregory, we will have another meeting and discuss reinstatement. Are we all in agreement?" Both Janice and I answer, "Yes Sir."

We left pastors office and I noticed Janice was blinking back tears so I grabbed her and hugged her. She only let me hold her a few seconds then forced herself from me while saying, "Let's not give them more to talk about." Janice would not look me in the face. I went to my truck and waited for her and Sybil. The ride to LB was tense but Sybil told us about her class, that's our routine. Janice had tears flowing down her face until we reached Mama's.

We all sat in the back room until Mama and Janice called for us to come eat. Jamal and Tina were waiting along with Mr. Mays, myself, Charece, Tamera, and Sybil. While walking to the kitchen to eat, Jamal pulled my arm and asked, "Hey, you alright?" I told him "Yes," and kept walking. After Mr. Mays blessed the foods he says, "Gregory, is there something you'd like to share?" To tell the truth; I was pissed. During the whole time the game was on I kept thinking of how Janice was treated by the church. It angered me to see her cry on the way here. I am just angry.

I clear my throat and answer a short, *"Nope-ah!"* Janice comes right behind me and says, "I'm pregnant." Mama, Jamal, and Tina all say at the same time, "We know!" Mama says, "We're not blind. Your belly been talking way before your mouth." Jamal and Tina laughed. Mama continues, "Y'all a little late today did pastor say something to you?" I looked at Janice and she moved her eyes to mine. I told them what was told to us. Mr. Mays asked, "So what you two plan on doing?"

I said, "We plan on marrying as soon as Janice gets her divorce." I followed Janice with my eyes as she stood up and left the table. I thought she was embarrassed so I stood up to follow her. She returned to the room with her ring I had given her on her finger and her hand was extended. "See, see the beautiful ring Gregory bought me?" I stood looking at her, she is glowing. Tina walked over to Janice and the "oohing and awh-ing" began. The both of them slowly walked over to Mama and the women became excited.

Charece and Tamera looked at the ring and I had a brief image of what their mother's reaction might be. I am sure they will inform her. I watched Janice as she smiled and modeled her hand, she was so happy. I felt so good that ring had turned Janice's day around.

I noticed Mama and Janice were in the kitchen for a long time washing dishes and on the ride to Janice's I asked if Mama had given her some advice on marriage. She says, "Gregory I have been married before. Mother Mays told me to have my lawyer file for desertion. And she also gave me some advice on how to hold my head up high when I go to church. I am not the first woman this has happened to and I won't be the last."

I replied, "Good. So you have found an attorney?" "No, not yet." I felt myself getting upset. I am thinking, 'why the hell not!' However I kept composed and asked, "You need some help? Because I will pay for everything…" She cut me off and placed her hand on my shoulder while saying, "Gregory I have been trying to find Melvin. I felt so embarrassed being with you and married, then being pregnant by a man that's not my husband and I'm *supposed to be a Christian.*"

I pulled into the parking space at her apartment complex, turned the ignition off, pulled her into my arms and quickly replied, "Felt?" "Yes, but not after your family embraced me today."

Janice wore the rings I bought her from that day on.

~~~~Janice Catherine Andrews-Woods~~~~

BACKGROUND

Janice was born to Margret [Margie] Ruth Palmer and Albert Ulysses Andrews while living in Beechwood, Mississippi. Albert worked on fixing cars in his neighborhood and enlisted into the Navy working on vehicles and learning the craft of a Diesel Mechanic. He was always referred to as, *'the best, as good as they come!'*

September twenty-sixth Janice Catherine entered the world. Six minutes later her twin brother, Jamison Carlton followed. Jamison arrived with his cord wrapped around his neck and did not survive. Janice was loved and considered a miracle by her mother and father who vowed to always appreciate God's blessing to them and they spoiled Janice.

After serving Uncle Sam three years, Albert could not find a job in Mississippi so he applied for the Coast Guards and was hired as a Machinery Technician and moved his wife and daughter to Long Beach, California.

Moving to California with her nine-year-old, Margie stayed home with Janice and they were inseparable.

Janice noticed her mother would pray all the time. She would hear Margie praying aloud binding the Jezebel Spirit and praying in her heavenly language. Margie even taught Janice to pray aloud. When Janice entered the ninth grade she became concerned her mother was talking to herself and not praying. One day Janice asked her mother who was she talking to. Margie went into a rage and told Janice to stop asking foolish questions. The woman over there, the hussy trying to take her husband was who she was talking to!

After Janice mentioned to her father about Margie's behavior she noticed a sitter would be at the house when she arrived home from school. Monday through Friday her father would bring her mother home after four p.m. Margie would go straight to bed and stayed there. Janice noticed Margie took a lot of medications that made her sleep.

When Janice started eleventh grade her father sat her down at the kitchen table and told her, her mother was ill and had to stay in a hospital close by. Janice realized Margie had a nervous breakdown. Janice would catch the bus and visit Margie weekly. Margie never acknowledged Janice; however, Janice would sit for an hour emptying her feelings out while Margie laid in bed staring at the ceiling.

That was the year Albert sent Janice to church and no longer attended. The few times Janice did not attend church her father would leave the house. After Thanksgiving of that year, Albert brought home Patricia Hayes and introduced her to Janice as his friend.

Janice knew they were lovers the way her father would hold Patricia. She didn't care too much for Miss Patricia Hayes. Oh, so Miss Hayes was the Jezebel my mother was "telling off" all the time before she was sent away!

Miss Hayes never reached out to Janice until the day her father announced Miss Patricia Hayes was soon to be her stepmother. A week later Albert and Patricia were married at the Courthouse while Janice was in school. It was the last week of high school and Janice was rehearsing for her commencement. The day after graduation Albert sat Janice down and told her she was going to have a sibling.

That was the day Janice decided to get a job and move out of Miss Patricia's house. Her father acted as though Janice was invisible. Patricia Hayes-Andrews was now running things.

A week after graduation Janice landed a Clerk Typist job at a large insurance company downtown Los Angeles. Melvin Woods worked in the mail room. A month after Janice began working she found a small studio apartment close to her job. Three months after Janice started her job, Margie died in her sleep.

Albert had a quiet service two days after Margie transitioned and none of the family in Mississippi were invited. Janice knew then, just as her mother no longer existed in her father's life; neither did she. Albert clearly dismissed Mississippi being a part of his life.

Melvin would stop by Janice desk and make her laugh. He said she seemed so sad. Janice thought Melvin was sincere when he told her he really liked her and they began dating. Janice realized she lived a sheltered life being a church girl because Melvin would say, "Jan you are country as all get out!" And Melvin told her that every time she didn't understand what he had to explain to her.

Janice thought everyone attended church because that's what she was brought up to do, give God praise and thanks for all He had provided. Melvin attended church with his mother only on holidays, Easter, Mother's Day, and Christmas.

Melvin had a car and took Janice to church once while they dated. They went to the church her mother would take her to while growing up, Holy Temple Church of God in Christ off PCH and E. 7th street in Long Beach.

After two months dating Melvin Janice had sex with him and four months later, she was pregnant. When she told Melvin she was pregnant he told her to get rid of it, they couldn't afford a baby. Melvin had moved in with Janice after they started having sex, his reason was, "Jan, we can save money and get married."

While Janice was on maternity leave she started attending church and drove Melvin's car. Janice began praying for her future because she had the feeling Melvin was dragging his feet about getting married. Melvin said he was laid off and his car was repossessed. Because Janice lived in Los Angeles city limits and the only church she was affiliated with was in Long Beach and busses did not run on Sunday, Janice no longer attended church.

Evangelist Ester Walker was running a two-week revival. Mother Harris gave Janice a ride every night and the last night of revival Janice went up for prayer. Janice asked for the prayer of agreement that Melvin would marry her before the baby was born. Evangelist Walker told Janice to leave him and when Janice informed Evangelist Walker the apartment was in her name; Evangelist told Janice to kick him out and stop living in sin.

Janice broke down crying and a few of the Mothers of the church took her in the back room. They anointed her head with oil and prayed for her strength to give Melvin an ultimatum; "Get married or get out!" Janice left that church with her courage built up and ready to kick Melvin out.

Janice arrived home from the Revival to find Melvin in bed asleep. She woke Melvin by pulling the covers off him. He thought the house was on fire and jumped up running. When she told him he had to get out, he had no intentions of getting married! He told her to calm down. Janice sat down and very calmly repeated herself. Melvin asked who had she been talking too. When she answered, "The Holy Ghost!" He went silent for a few seconds. Melvin told Janice she was being brainwashed by those church people.

Janice interrupted Melvin saying if he didn't get out she was calling the police to throw him out. Her name was on the rental agreement and being pregnant… He interrupted her and agreed to get "Hitched," as he called it. They were married two weeks later. Sybil was born a month later and has her father's last name.

Melvin was distant towards Janice after the marriage ceremony and the day Sybil was born Janice had no idea where Melvin was. Miss Butler who lived in unit one-twelve gave Janice a ride to the hospital. Janice came home from the hospital to find Melvin in bed and asleep. Mother Mays and Mr. Mays were who picked up Janice and her newborn from the hospital.

By then Janice had told Mother Mays all about her relationship with Melvin and Mother Mays would go over scripture and pray with Janice. Janice was determined to make her marriage work. Mother Mays would sometime ask Janice if she were sure she wanted to stay in the relationship, did she think perhaps The Lord wanted to give her a husband that treated her better. Janice was determined to stay with Sybil's father.

After Janice unemployment ended she went on County Assistance. When Sybil was beginning to walk, Melvin seldom came home and when he did he would be sloppy drunk or high. Melvin would demand Janice give him money and when she didn't he would slap her around, sometimes real bad. Sybil's first birthday Janice realized everything of value in their apartment was missing. It was then she faced the realization her husband had a problem.

Janice moved to another low income apartment in Long Beach to be close to the church. Melvin began going to the church looking for Janice. She stopped attending church for a few months and everyone there told Melvin Janice no longer attended, which was not a lie. Melvin's harassment became very unpleasant.

Melvin was going to the church every day and would get hostile when there were no men around. He was looking and smelling as though he was homeless. Eventually Melvin stopped going around the church and Janice had different people come give her a ride to and from church. She prayed constantly for her husband to be delivered and made Sybil and the church her life.

Janice reminiscing at her desk while at work...

I remember the day Gregory Young came to our church cookout. That night after I took Sybil to her bed, I found myself thinking how well Gregory looked. It had been ten or fifteen years since we saw one another and I believe it took Gregory a minute to realize who I was.

He was married but Mother Mays told me he was back home waiting for his divorce to finalize. Mother Mays was cooking good home cooked meals for Gregory, he had lost weight being with his last wife that couldn't cook.

The day after the cookout Gregory came to church and I noticed him looking for me. Gregory has always been quiet but because he is so tall, he stands out in any crowd. He has always been good looking and when we were young, I had a crush on him. His sister Samantha and I had the same Sunday School class for years growing up but Samantha was popular and very outgoing and those kinds of people never notice me.

I am what Mama called, "Ash brown" skinned, five feet six and there's nothing noticeably flattering about me. My having worn glasses since third grade and braces from seventh to twelfth grade has taught me to blend into a crowd.

Not being outgoing and more of a follower instead of a leader, most people don't notice I am in the room. I figured that out in first grade. I was quiet, I guess I still am. Mama used to tell me to speak up for myself or else people will run me like faucet water when they get the notion. I'm just not combative and will always side with the path of least resistance.

The summer my body began filling out, Mama taught me to cover up and be chaste [morally pure]. Mama said men were easily aroused and showing off my curves and large breast would cause men to lust after me. That's when I started wearing baggy clothing and not wearing make-up. I pretty much went unnoticed. Mama taught me a woman was to be sexy and provocative only behind closed doors with her husband.

Mama explained God designed Eve just for Adam and we women are designed just for our husbands. A wife should sexually satisfy her husband only and no other man. I was to keep myself pure until I married. I followed Mama's instructions.

When I asked Mama what was sex about she sat me down and explained the act to me and told me men want sex with women who arouse them but never want to marry women who gave them sex before marriage. A man wants a wife who is respectable and makes a good wife and mother to their children.

When I became fourteen Mama made me memorize Titus 2: 1-5; *"But as for you, speak the things which are proper for sound doctrine: [2] that the older men be sober, reverent, temperate, sound in faith, in love, in patience; [3] the older women likewise, that they be reverent in behavior, not slanderers, not given to much wine, teachers of good things— [4] that they admonish the young women to love their husbands, to love their children, [5] to be discreet, chaste, homemakers, good, obedient to their own husbands, that the Word of God may not be blasphemed."*

For several weeks Mama and I went line by line dissecting this scriptures meaning. Mama taught me Christians; people who want to be Christ-like, are to learn The Word *and* live by The Word. Paul wrote this letter to Titus because the church Titus was leading had religious trends and Titus encouraged the people to walk as being led by the spirit and not by old traditions.

At the time of the scripture writings the new believers were so accustomed to doing whatever they felt made them feel better. Now Titus comes and teaches them sound doctrine. The people were emotionally tied to one another and a lot of gossip and adultery was rampant among them. Holy Spirit sends Titus with guidelines for a godly life.

Titus 2:1 Paul is instructing Titus to teach the older men and women to be examples of what they were teaching. Women were to love their husbands and children with an unconditional love; a love that covers faults and not slander and tear one another down. The wife was to *be* discreet [wise and careful] in her home. Demonstrating how to balance love and restraint.

Mama told me this scripture means a chase wife only has sex with her husband and no other man. The wife keeps her house clean, cooks and takes good care of her husband and children. Mama said a wife does not compare her husband to other men nor does she tear him down. A wife builds her husband up and encourages him to be skillful in whatever area he is the strongest.

I believed everything Mama told me and lived by her words. That is until Melvin Sullivan Woods came into my life.

Before Mama became ill, she would say how California women were not chaste! She had a tone when she said it. I didn't understand then, but I sure do now…

Yes, I remember that particular summer very well. My bra size increased and so did the Bible memory verses. I tell you; Margie Ruth Palmer Andrews taught her daughter well!

I noticed Gregory watching me and was flattered the day he offered us a ride home after church. I think it took me a few months spending time with Gregory before my prayers changed from, "Father I speak life to my marriage," Too, "Father I pray your will regarding my marriage to Melvin." I remember thinking…

Gregory treats me so kind. I feel appreciated when I'm with him. He asks my opinion and I don't feel as though I'm dumb for not knowing what he knows. Gregory reads a lot and knows so much. I liked being around him.

Gregory is good with Sybil and she likes him. He asked me to go to the movies and I almost said "Yes" so fast I had make myself hesitate answering him. I can't have him thinking I am an easy woman. However, Gregory makes me feel safe when I'm with him and the way he treats me, I know he likes me. We are a good fit together.

We like to do the same things and he never hollers at me, belittles, or treats me harshly. Gregory is always a gentleman. He's never tried to kiss me or has said anything inappropriately to me and I can relax and be myself with him. I was a virgin when Melvin and I had sex and thought that was how sex was supposed to be. When I had sex with Gregory, I experienced love making. The man is so patient and tender. That's when I began to understand why women get jealous of their husbands.

Gregory is also a hard worker and puts family first. After Gregory gradually moved in with me, he started asking every Sunday evening like clockwork if I had thought about divorce. I didn't know how to tell him I did not know where Melvin was and when Gregory would bring the subject up, well it made me feel guilty about us committing adultery.

When I was with Gregory, I felt as though we were married, joined together. I felt we were two of the same person and we had so much in common. However he made it clear every Sunday evening we were not married and I needed to get a divorce.

Our first Easter together I realized I was pregnant. Oh my goodness did I have some emotional issues going on with me! At first I was scared God was punishing me and I would have a baby born with some defect. Then I thought Melvin would kill me and Gregory if he found out I was pregnant by another man. Then fear took a really strong hold when I thought the church was going to kick me and Sybil out.

I thought of getting rid of the baby so no one would know about me being adulterous. My mind was wondering how Gregory was going to react to my being pregnant knowing how he hounds me about getting a divorce and me not knowing where Melvin was. I thought Gregory might make me get rid of the baby. My mind was constantly going over all of these scenarios and being pregnant again was all I thought about.

During the church's annual shut-in I decided to keep the baby. Holy Spirit spoke to me that I was loved even when I make mistakes. Almighty God choses who will live and the baby I was carrying has a purpose. I was to forgive myself and get divorced.

I felt a weight had been lifted from my heart. I repented and told myself over and over, 'God has forgiven you, now forgive yourself.' When Elder Richmond prayed the closing prayer for our shut-in, I heard his words loud and clear; "Jesus as you rose from death to life, so shall we!" I praised and thanked The Lord so much I got happy! I danced and thanked The Lord so much I became hoarse. I am so thankful redemption is available because of the Blood of The Lamb, Hallelujah!

Easter morning when Gregory walked into the sanctuary looking for me I became so scared I almost threw-up. He waved at me and I ignored him. Honestly, when I saw him, I wanted to tell him about being pregnant. I didn't want to wait I was so nervous! I knew I wouldn't hold what I had to tell him until tomorrow and surely didn't want to tell him in church. Our adulterous affair has me pregnant and church is *the last place* Gregory needs to find out about it.

I had Sister Joseph drop Sybil and myself off at home. Gregory didn't bother to call or come by and I was glad because me keeping my baby and allowing Gregory to be part of its life was going to take some figuring out. Gregory misses his daughters so much and sometimes beats himself up not being able to spend time with them. Gregory is a good father. Also I avoided him because my plans on how to handle this wasn't fully figured out.

Gregory ended up coming to my job and before I finally told him I was pregnant, he asked me to marry him. I was elated and afraid if I couldn't find Melvin how was our lives going to be affected. We love each other but knowing we're committing adultery keeps a feeling of temporariness hovering over our relationship.

I had no idea how to get a divorce if Melvin could not be found. I had been praying for Melvin to show up but I didn't want him to find me. I wanted someone to tell me they had seen Melvin. The day Gregory found out I was pregnant, he offered to pay for my divorce so we could marry right away.

I found a lawyer in the phone book after I prayed just before opening the yellow pages. His practice was in the Wilshire district. Melvin had to be found and Attorney Aaron Mordecai had skip trace capabilities. I knew The Lord led me to the right attorney. Gregory took me to the attorney's office and after I filled out the paperwork, he paid every red cent of my attorney's fees.

The Wednesday before Labor Day we received the phone call. Melvin Woods was found and was willing to sign the papers if I paid five hundred dollars. Attorney Mordecai told us Melvin tried to extort us but my attorney threatened to file charges against him along with the divorce. Melvin signed the papers with no more threats. It cost almost seven hundred dollars but Gregory worked all the overtime he could so we could get married.

We were hoping to be married before the baby arrived but it didn't turn out that way. December twelfth David Allen Young was born. Gregory gave my social worker a legal affidavit stating he was the father of my baby and Young is on David's birth certificate. Gregory was so happy he had a son.

April nineteenth Gregory and I were married in Las Vegas, Nevada and July first the Young family moved into our very own brand new three-bedroom; two-bath tract home located on Cloverleaf Court in Carson California.

Gregory had saved money for the down payment and two thousand dollars for our own washer, dryer, refrigerator, and a new couch for the living room. Except for automobiles Gregory paid cash for everything. He told me and the kids, "Remember, always pay cash for what you want and never live above what you bring home. When you use credit cards, you are paying more money for what you are purchasing."

I saved my money earned at the boutique and bought the baby furniture. Gregory told me to stay home with David until he was two years old then I could go back to work. That was the plan but I was pregnant again three months after we moved into the house. David was almost ten months old and trying to walk.

Sybil was enrolled in a Christian Day Care close to our home three days a week when James Ivan Young came into our lives, May twenty-sixth. David was potty trained and James was crawling when I found out I was pregnant again. This time we wanted to know the sex of the unborn so we would know which room to add a bed too, Sybil's or the boys.

We found out we were having another boy and four months later Jonathan Guy Young was added to our tribe. Gregory started telling me to take birth control but I loved having his babies. The man is a great lover and I love babies. Gregory is a great provider and I save as much as I can to help his money stretch. I had no idea he was feeling pressured about me getting pregnant again until the miscarriage.

After we moved into our house Gregory talked to Mother Thomas about picking the girls up on Saturdays and them spending the day with us. I would pick them up from Charlotte's apartment at nine o'clock in the morning, take them to our house, then wake Gregory for a big country breakfast I had prepared. Gregory would spend time with the kids before leaving for work then at five p.m. I took the girls home.

After a few months of this routine, Gregory had me pick the girls up on Friday evenings and he would take them to Mother Thomas Sundays after church and our family dinner together. I absolutely loved having the girls over. Sybil enjoyed them because they spent time having tea parties, dressing up, polishing nails, and combing each other's hair.

Just before James turned a year-old Gregory told me he wanted to include Kozet in our family weekends. Gregory was concerned I would not be able to handle another three year old; being I was pregnant again. I had no problem with Kozet coming over. Because Kozet did not remember Gregory, Faith suggested Gregory spend half an hour with Kozet on Saturdays on his way to work in Kozet's environment and when he and Faith felt Kozet was comfortable with Gregory, he would bring her to our house for a few hours.

I did have a moment when the thought of Gregory being with Faith might ignite some flame between them. But Gregory was so happy about having his children together I couldn't see him jeopardizing breaking us up as a family. The one picture Gregory carries in his wallet of Kozet is with Faith and Kozet cheek to cheek and Faith is a very pretty woman. I had gained so much weight and the picture of Faith revealed an air of sexiness about her but like I said, Gregory wouldn't break up his family.

My gaining weight made me wonder if Faith was fat or not but I didn't let thoughts of Gregory being around Faith get out of control. It helped that Gregory reiterated how he wanted all of his children to know and love one another.

Every time Gregory left to spend time with Kozet he made sure to hug me and tell me he appreciated me being a loving, caring wife, and stepmother. The first time he spent time with Kozet, Gregory called and told me what took place during the visit right after he left Faith's apartment. The next day during his breakfast he told me how Faith left him alone with Kozet. I knew he was reassuring me he had no feelings for Faith and I was comfortable with him going over there.

After a month spending time with Kozet at Faith's place Kozet warmed up to Gregory. Kozet was almost four years old when Gregory would get up on Saturdays, eat breakfast, and go pick up Kozet.

By this time I had the house furnished so no more lay-a-ways meant Gregory could take off on the weekends. He started spending time with us as a family. Gregory is a great Dad. He listens to our daughters and lets them know he will always protect them. Our sons, Gregory teaches them about The Lord and how to behave. We were a picture-perfect family back then.

The first day Kozet came to our house she stayed in Gregory's lap. I talked to her and Sybil gravitated to Kozet right away. However Kozet stared at us and watched Sybil's every move. Gregory had Kozet on his lap and picked Sybil up and placed her opposite Kozet. Kozet buried her face in Gregory's chest. Sybil tried giving Kozet a small stuffed bear but Kozet shied away. Reece and Tammi stood in front of Gregory and stared at Kozet. David kept asking why was Kozet crying.

We sat all of the kids down in the family room and Gregory explained they were all brothers and sisters and he was their father. I think Charlotte had already explained the situation to her girls because they both accepted Kozet with no questions.

The next Saturday Gregory brought Kozet home Reece and Tammi tried to include Kozet in their doll playing, Kozet wasn't having it. I told them all to give her time to know we were not strangers and she would warm up. The third Saturday Kozet came over she warmed up to me. Then as Sybil shared some of her toys Kozet warmed up to her. When Gregory took Kozet home that day she was not ready to leave.

A month later Kozet began spending weekends with us but she ran with Sybil most times and having two older brothers at her house, she allowed David to give her instructions, unlike Sybil. When Jon was born Kozet stayed with me the whole time he was in my arms watching me breastfeed and care for him.

Saying it was rough having seven kids in a three bedroom, two-bath home every weekend is definitely putting it lightly, but we managed. Gregory is a great father and having all of his children together had him feeling as though he were ten feet tall. What we don't want to talk about is traveling in an automobile!

Gregory had to buy me a Chrysler Aspen eight passenger SUV after Jon was born and even still Sybil and Kozet had to share a seatbelt when Gregory drove us to church. I am not complaining, truthfully, I loved every moment of it. I would have given Gregory seven babies or more. He loves his children and I love him and his children. Gregory is the kindest, thoughtful, most gentle man and all of his loving attributes radiates when he is with his kids. I really loved my Gregory!

Gregory and I talked constantly and kept our focus and goals written down on target. After Kozet entered third grade Faith started calling me at home some Friday mornings asking if I would pick Kozet up after she came home from school. Faith's speech was always slurred and I felt sorry for Kozet. She was a sweet little girl and Sybil looked forward to her coming so I added picking Kozet up to my taxi driving on Fridays.

Three-thirty p.m. every Friday I took the babies to get Sybil from school then picked up Kozet. We would come home and I would fix them a snack, fix dinner and six-thirty we were all off to Long Beach to get Reece and Tammi.

One Friday I was ten minutes late picking Kozet up and Faith had left her alone and I was pissed! What mother in her right mind would leave an eight-year-old alone in an apartment. Especially in that neighborhood! I woke up when Gregory came home and told him we need to file for custody, Faith didn't want Kozet, just the money he gave her. Gregory had to calm me down I was so angry with Faith.

The second time I went to get Kozet and no one was at the house with her, I took her to our house and made them all a snack. Let me mention I was mad enough to spit hot coals! While cooking dinner I made my mind up to get Kozet's clothes and we were keeping her. This was the last time Faith was leaving Kozet alone!

The apartments Faith lived in were questionable. Some homeless looking people would sometimes be standing in front of the building. I believe this was the second time in less than a month Faith had left Kozet alone. No way is this going to happen again!

After picking up Reece and Tammi I headed back to Faith's. I had Reece watch the kids in the van while I took Kozet inside Faiths apartment and we put most of Kozet's clothes in grocery bags. I was flaming mad when I walked out of that apartment! Kozet stayed with us all the time from that day on.

I must say, Faith has very expensive taste, her apartment was decorated like a model home.

Kozet has not had an asthma attack since she moved in with us nor has she had a breathing treatment since none of us smoke. Also, I admire the relationship Kozet and Sybil have as if they are blood sisters. There was that one time they had a falling out. Well that was the day Kozet told Sybil, "Gregory is **MY FATHER, NOT YOURS!**" It was just before a Father's Day; I think they were around ten years old.

Sybil came running into the kitchen ordering me to tell Kozet Gregory was her father too. I stopped cooking and sat Sybil down. Kozet stood in the doorway listening so I told her she could come sit and listen. I explained to Sybil, Kozet was right, her father and I divorced. Sybil asked who her father was and where was he. I told her Melvin Woods was her father and he loves her very much. We didn't know where he was. Melvin and I didn't get along too well. When Gregory and I married he already had Reece, Tammi and Kozet; they have different mothers.

Sybil is nine months older than Kozet even though Kozet is larger than Sybil and I think Sybil was embarrassed Kozet knew something she didn't and for a few days Sybil walked around the house with an attitude. Kozet looks up to Sybil as the older sister. Because they have so much in common, they get along very well. However they have different personalities.

Sybil does dolls, paper dolls, tea parties and spends time dressing up and playing house. Kozet plays most of the time with Sybil however, Kozet prefers reading a book and listening to music. When Reece and Tammi are at the house Tammi and Kozet will be found in the back-yard reading with the radio on. Reece would be in the bedroom with Sybil painting their nails or playing dress-up in my high heels and make-up.

The boys would be found outside throwing balls, tackling, leap frogging or practicing swinging a bat. Gregory had me put them in football, baseball, and soccer as soon as they were large enough to play. He said it would keep them active in boy games and not painting their nails and applying make-up on their sisters. Gregory told me sports would teach them how to get along and grasp "team" skills. Boys think differently and having four sisters, they had to be involved in male activities.

Gregory voiced he was not raising a fainthearted man. He talked to the boys about how to treat girls and explained in detail how girls think differently than boys and it was okay. Me not growing up with other siblings, I learned a lot from Gregory about males and how to raise them differently. I tell you this blended family is a lot of work and there is definitely *"an art"* to managing the different personalities!

Reece turned twelve and I guess that's the age girls begin fighting for independence. She started throwing her, *"I'm the oldest!"* weight around the house and I had to let her know, **"I"** was the oldest. For a few months I had been complaining to Gregory how Reece had been spouting off at the mouth when she came over, "My mother lets me do this at her house!" I would tell her that was there and the rules here on Cloverleaf Court will be carried out here!

Reece would get in a huff and march straight to Gregory and tell him I was mean. He would sit her down and ask the same questions, "What makes you say that? Why do you feel that way?" The fact Reece had Gregory wrapped around her finger didn't take Tammi long to use the same tactics on her father also.

I stood my ground with Reece and would tell Gregory every Sunday while getting ready for church, he was allowing the girls to cause friction between him and I. He refused to see it. I prayed constantly not to have an attitude with Gregory. The girls I could handle, I just had to make sure they didn't cause friction between the other kids and that kept me constantly watching Reece and Tammi when they were with us and listening to their every conversation.

It was so stressful when Reece and Tammi were around on the weekends and to tell the truth, by then I was enjoying Monday through Thursday, when they weren't around. School breaks, Reece and Tammi were with us, there were arguments every day!

Between David, James and Jon playing tricks on one another, scaring the girls, and bringing cap guns and spiders from the garage into the house, I was refereeing most times. The boys were doing Kung Fu wrestling in the house and, they were breaking every wooden obstacle that happened in their way.

Reece was wanting to talk on the phone the whole while she and Tammi were at our house and had an attitude when I limited her time on the phone. I finally broke down and added "call waiting" to our service so Reece could switch over when a call came in for Gregory or myself.

I found out at church Reece was telling the people who called for Gregory or myself while she was on the phone, that I was busy and couldn't come to the phone or, Gregory was sleep and for them to call back later. I understood her behavior was her age but I stayed on her letting her know she had rules to follow and other people had the same rights as she did. Her attitude was terrible! To top it off, Reece and Tammi would go home Sunday evenings and tell Charlotte I was a mean stepmother and let them tell it, I treated them like they were Cinderella.

Charlotte started phoning me Sunday nights after nine p.m. and would cuss me out. Charlotte never said "Hello," she would light into you after she heard *you* say "hello." I would answer the phone and she would start with; "You had better not be mistreating my daughters. They told me how you had them washing all the dishes. Hire a damn maid for your litter or wash the dishes your damn self!" Or

"Reece told me how harsh you speak to her. If you make her cry one more time, I will drive over to your house and let you see how it feels to be made to cry!"

Once after Tammi and I had an argument, I told Tammi, "This is *my house* and you young lady are not grown. Tell you what, when you buy a home, that would be the time for you to call the shots. *All children in my house will do as I instruct!* No teenager is going to call shots in *my home* and you had better learn how that's done!"

Tammi smiled as she rolled her eyes at me. Later that night Charlotte phoned and told me if I made Tammi cry one more time; I would find sugar in my gas tank! And she slammed the phone in my ear. I was so mad. Gregory took all Sunday night phone calls after that one.

The following Sunday night when the phone rang, Gregory answered it. He listened for a few minutes, cussed at Charlotte, and hung up on her. She called back. He simply lifted the receiver and slammed it back down. She called again; he repeated the slamming in her ear. And Charlotte called again. Gregory slammed the phone in her ear, reached down and unplugged it. We were too mad to go to sleep that night. All of Gregory's conversations with Charlotte ended with him cussing and hanging up on her.

Reece had her sixteenth birthday party at Charlotte's house and I was very uncomfortable going on Charlotte's turf. Reece had been causing a lot of dissension in our home since her twelfth birthday. I would tell her to "calm down, it is not that dramatic."

By Reece having Gregory wrapped around her finger, I was stressed. Gregory took everything said by Reece as if she were quoting the Bible. When I tried explaining what or how the matter actually happened, Reece would interrupt saying I didn't like her and Tammi and mistreated them. Or; I was treating her and Tammi like Cinderella's stepchildren.

Gregory heard of a possible lay-off and became stressed. My being stressed about Reece and Tammi being around made it extremely tense at our house. To make matters worse, Reese and Tammi would go home then Gregory and I waited on needles and pins for Charlotte's phone calls. So, the thought of being in Charlotte's home for Reece's birthday party had me in a nervous knot.

Reece was the Belle of her ball and when someone asked what she had wished for; Reece announced in front of everyone attending her party that she no longer wanted to spend weekends at her fathers house. She was old enough to make her own choices!

Gregory was so hurt. I believe the combination of Gregory seeing Reece in the light I had to deal with combined with her telling him in front of everyone attending her party was what hurt him. We left the party not long after that announcement, not making it obvious Gregory's feelings were bruised.

Charlotte was cordial to me but I held onto Gregory the whole time we were in her house. Mother Mays walked us all out to the van and as she hugged Gregory goodbye she told him Reece was at the age of trying to find who she is and not to take what she said personal. Gregory listened but he was quiet the rest of the evening.

Gregory and I both were so busy, him with working overtime Monday through Friday and me busy taking care of the kids and the house, there wasn't time for any extras. I was making sure there was nutritious breakfast, lunch and dinner for my family *and* clean clothes *and* a clean house. My mind was always on what was next to get done. In between those duties I made sure the mortgage, utilities and car notes were paid on time. It wasn't until Jonathan started kindergarten I had a chance to slow down.

Jon was on the morning class schedule and after driving back home from dropping the kids off for school, I was able to sit still for an hour and drink a cup of coffee. That's when I realized Gregory and I hardly spent time together.

In August, Gregory started working three to three, Sunday through Friday and left the house for work at two-fifteen every afternoon. He was saving so we would have a cushion to tie us over financially and my spending was very minimal. There was a rumor of a big lay-off. When I asked Gregory what was so special about this lay-off rumor; he told me management was preparing for a giant lay-off this time. Gregory was stressed.

You have to know Gregory, he's low key; not quick to speak and very laid back. When he went around the house turning out lights, saving his plastic lunch bags for me too wash and reuse, I knew he was troubled. He made a big deal over junk foods being around the house but what he referred to as junk was small, packaged chips, cookies and small boxed raisins the kids took for their lunches.

I had never seen this side of Gregory. In fact Gregory never stressed over anything and now our communication consisted of, "Good night, good afternoon." And "Bye, be careful." He left me notes, "Pay the phone today, mortgage due, need razors." Stuff like that. He would slip in bed, put his arms around me if there wasn't one of the babies in it, we had sex otherwise he would start snoring before I could say anything to him.

Saturday nights were Gregory and my nights of romance. After the kids were in their beds was when

Gregory and I had "Our Time." Gregory was a reader. He had books in his truck, the bathroom, on his nightstand and in the garage. He took books to work. They were used books but he loved to read. I started noticing when we were in our room on Saturday nights, I would talk and Gregory would have his nose in a book or his mind would be somewhere else.

Gregory would only comment on what I said when I asked him too. Even then he would say something like, "What do you think? Or "What, I don't care what you do, I trust your judgment." Or "What do you want me to say?" I even noticed how Gregory would sit with the kids but his mind was far off somewhere else.

At first I thought he was acting distant because Reece and Tammi were no longer with us on weekends but as I watched him I realized this was now Gregory's behavior. Now I have mixed emotions because I was relieved he wasn't just distant with me yet; I was bothered he was being so distant.

I was beginning to miss the Gregory I fell in love with. Now the only conversation we had with more than five words was about the budget. I thought about going back to work, the boys were now five, six and almost eight. Sybil was eleven and Kozet was soon to be eleven. The boys would never do as Sybil told them; they were resentful all of their sisters were older than themselves.

I was going to have to get a sitter. My not having a college degree and the only work I knew outside of teaching children was typing so school was a must for me. I had not touched a typewriter in so long the corporate world was now using computers.

I knew I would have to make more money than what I would have to pay a sitter for five kids. I gave it serious thought and wanted to go back to school. Jon was going to first grade and would be in school all day. I could go to school while the kids were in school, yeah, that should work. Now let me see what courses I want to take…

I decided to take the introduction to computers course, hone my typing skills and give the City of Los Angeles a try, they were hiring Clerk Typist's at the time. When I mentioned the idea to Gregory he agreed because the union was scheduling a meeting in two months to go over the new contract. I took an eight-week course at night and it was hard and that's putting it lightly!

The problem was not the class, the problem was the kids. Mother Mays came over every evening at five-thirty Monday through Friday and I went to Cerritos College. Mother Mays had to grab up David. He was trying to pull the wool over her in regards to his homework. David was telling his grandmother he had none. She told him to read a book and David thinking his grandmother was old, tried to outsmart her. When I received a phone message from David's teacher his homework was not turned in, I let him have it.

Mother Mays is not the type to be made a fool of. She let David know he may be taller than her, but she is his grandmother. James and Sybil told me Mother Mays jumped up and grabbed David by his shirt collar and pulled his face down and became nose to nose with him and told David she would set his butt on fire the next time he lied to her! David never lied to his grandmother again.

Mother Mays washed all the dishes and Sybil never attempted to pick up a dish. Mother Mays saved all of the pots and pans and told Kozet to leave the kitchen while Sybil finished up. By the time my class was completed, the kids all saw their grandmother in a different light.

Gregory smiled when he found out Mother Mays had the children walking a straight line. He told the kids his mother was a strong little woman and they had experienced a sample of how he had been raised.

During class our instructor told us we were on the brink of digital phones and cell phones being used for everything in the future, landlines were soon to be extinct. I finished my course and received my certificate just in time to get an application in for the

County of Los Angeles Assessors Office. I took the test, passed the interviews, and landed the job.

The pay was okay. Mother Mays would arrive at our house every morning at six forty-five and send the kids off to school. I paid her fifty dollars a week but I had to beg her to take it. She loved being with her grandkids. This worked out for me and she cooked for all of us and left Gregory a plate in the microwave for his lunch. I passed my six months probation on the job and absolutely loved it.

Gregory was laid off, OH BOY! He went into a frenzy looking for a job.

Most mornings Gregory would get up with me and the kids and gripe about us wasting. "Look at the milk left in this bowl, who left… Turn out the light when you leave a room, I'm not Warren Buffett!" It was so bad we all tip toed around Gregory so he wouldn't look us over and find a reason to complain.

The days Gregory went job hunting Mother Mays would come over and be home when the kids arrived from school. Those were the days Mother Mays would call me later and ask if Gregory was in a better mood when I came home. She would talk to Gregory but he thought I was complaining to his mother and would give me the silent treatment or would snap, "Just had to tell my mother on me!

Every time Mother Mays would try and make him open up, Gregory and I would go at it! The nights before Gregory had to walk the picket line, he wouldn't be able to sleep. Then I couldn't sleep. It was really bad in our home because the kids would hear us arguing and they would start arguing. Talk about a dirty snowball effect.

Our happy, loving home had turned into a verbal war zone. I prayed for us to be loving and considerate of one another again. Believe me I was walking by faith because the arguing became worse.

I wanted Gregory to talk about "US" and how we needed to communicate better instead of being defensive but he was always in a bad mood. I would cry some mornings on my way to work because I felt like Gregory was slipping away from me and I loved him so. I began praying for my marriage and the fire we once had be restored. During my prayer time Holy Spirit revealed to me my weight was a major turn-off to Gregory.

I know my gaining weight after the boys were born had a lot to do with Gregory not wanting to have sex but he never said anything. I think if I had been motivated to lose weight earlier on having my babies, my weight may not have gotten out of hand.

The few times I asked Gregory if I were too fat or did he think I was too big to be attractive to him, he would say, "You need to be happy with yourself in order to be happy." Or "You look fine. If you're not happy, do something about it."

When Gregory and I started dating I wore a size twelve and still had my shape. After I gave birth to David I wore a size fourteen. I was breast feeding and lost the weight but became pregnant as soon as I stopped breast feeding and gained the weight back. After being pregnant with James I needed size sixteens.

I watched everything I put into my mouth as to not gain any more weight. But here comes Jonathan. Size sixteens became tight on me and I had gained weight everywhere not just my stomach and hips, but face, arms, thighs, and my feet grew half a size.

When I had my physical for the job at the Assessor's Office, I was wearing a size eighteen. I had gradually gained the weight and really didn't notice how big I had gotten. It wasn't until I realized Gregory no longer approached me for sex that I took a long look at myself.

After I started working, I would cook the next day's meal in the evenings after we finished dinner. I started eating various kinds of salads for my dinner meals. The weight didn't seem to be coming off so, I began eating half sandwiches for lunch and some of the boxed raisins. But I couldn't see any weight being lost. Then I started drinking lemon and water to keep myself full at all times. That only kept my kidneys flushed. I begin to feel defeated all the time. No weight loss and no passion in our romance.

While Gregory was still laid off my boss called me into his office and I was informed there was an opening in the department for the collections and the supervisor over there was interested in me working with them. My boss at the time, Mr. Yeager told me Mrs. Henry had her eye on my work and thought I would be a perfect fit personality wise. I applied for the position and after two interviews, was hired with a nice hefty raise.

Now you know it's bad at home when you are scared to tell your husband you were promoted. Knowing Gregory wasn't working and his unemployment barely kept our utilities on let alone paying Charlotte and Faith money. Yes I said Faith! It was lean in our house.

The night I eased in the conversation I had been promoted and will start my new position in two weeks was the night I found out Gregory was paying Faith a hundred dollars over and above his court ordered child support. Kozet had been living with us for years. The man had been mailing a money order to her!

When I asked, "Are you still in love with her?" He stood still as his eyes looked me up and down before a, "No I am not." Slowly slid from his mouth. I felt as though small bombs were exploding in me. One in my stomach and one in my head!

All this time I trusted him with Faith. I felt like a total fool. Here I am scraping nickels and dimes and he's paying Faith behind my back! That's what bothered me. Why would he keep that from me?

We became extremely loud and I believe I blacked out I was so angry. I don't remember walking from our bedroom into the closet I was so mad! I was stunned when I realized we were standing in the closet arguing. I couldn't remember walking into the closet or what I had said if anything.

As I stood astonished wondering how I ended up in the closet, Gregory took that opportunity to grab his pillow and slam our bedroom door, he slept on the couch. Frightened I had blacked out, I didn't care Gregory left our bed. I climbed in the bed wondering if this is what happened to my mother!

I wondered if I was losing my mind just as she had… After contemplating how my father drove my mother crazy concerning another woman, I decided *I was not going to let no man, even Gregory put me in an insane asylum.* Okay, I'm leaving Gregory alone. I'm going to keep my sanity. I prayed for peace for a long time before dozing off.

The next morning Gregory and I passed each other. I was headed to the kitchen; he was headed to the bedroom. Neither of us spoke a word.

I arrived home from work and Gregory had cut a few flowers out of our yard and had them on the kitchen counter, placed in a coffee cup with a note in front of the cup. He had written, "I am sorry , please forgive me. Love, Greg." I smiled as I bent over to take a whiff of the fragrance from the flowers. I had my Gregory back.

My husband entered the kitchen all cleaned up and hugged me. I cried. I was thanking The Lord for answering my prayer, my husband was back and I am not crazy. He held me tighter as I cried. The kids were standing in the kitchen doorway watching us when I opened my eyes. Sybil came into the kitchen and pretended to get a glass of water because after pouring water in her glass she stood and looked me in the eyes. Gregory says, "Okay you all come in here."

They all entered the kitchen quiet and scared. Gregory continued, "I know I haven't been the person you want around these last few months but I want you all to know I am sorry for how I have behaved. I have been under some stress from being laid off and I should not have taken it out on you all.

Please forgive me." He looks into my eyes and with tears in his he asks, "Forgive me?" I smile as tears stream down my face. I hug him and answer, "Yes." Each one of the kids hugs Gregory all at once. We looked like a football team in a huddle.

During dinner the kids are all talking about their day. David and James start throwing food at each other until Gregory tells them to cool it. The girls are telling Gregory about a Sadie Hawkins dance coming up soon at school and I felt a very sharp cramping in my stomach.

I get the dishes started for the girls and Gregory pulls me into our bedroom. He closes the door and tells me he is proud of me but the way he's talking, I feel as though he's holding back, like he wants to totally open up but he has rehearsed his words and can only say what he has rehearsed.

We sit on the bed and when he's done talking I tell him I love him and understand. He is the head of our home and wants to provide for us. I told him I thank The Lord constantly for him because he is the best provider any woman could ever ask for.

For the first time I have ever known Gregory, he opens up and becomes vulnerable in front of me. He told me he was embarrassed, my getting a raise and he is the man and his responsibility is to be the bread winner, not me. He felt less than a man living on unemployment.

Gregory said this morning he realized he was angry because he is not working and knew he owed me an apology. He also knows not attending church nor studying The Word has contributed to his bad attitude. My Gregory promised we were all going to church this Sunday as a family. After getting the kids to bed we talked until after eleven. He went to take a shower and I fell asleep.

The next few days I was awakened with sharp cramps and when I checked my calendar it was a week before my cycle so I planned to make a doctor's appointment. We were at our old happy family status again minus Charece and Tamera. Gregory and I still didn't have sex but at least he wasn't angry all of the time anymore.

The third night we were getting along I brought up the subject of him not paying Faith any more money and we need to file for legal custody of Kozet. Gregory went silent on me again. I was so mad. Instead of going to sleep all I could think about was Gregory still having feelings for Faith. Kozet has been living with us for years and he wants to keep giving Faith money!

The next morning, I just left for work without saying anything to him.

I get to work and a few ladies in the collections department came over to introduce themselves to me. I thought they made a nice gesture and was happy the rest of the day. After their welcome, I looked forward to going to work because my love life was miserable. I started praying for my marriage to be healed and Gregory and I become one again.

Friday morning I rushed to the bathroom from the sharp pains and started hemorrhaging. Gregory called Mother Mays and had her come get the kids off to school while he rushed me to the hospital. I was given an ultrasound that revealed I had fibroid tumors and a Tubal or Ectopic Pregnancy. The baby burst my fallopian tube.

I was losing my baby and a fallopian tube. I was shocked I was pregnant. The doctor explained to Gregory the baby was growing in my fallopian tube and he responded, "Baby!" After displaying a disgusted expression, of course he then went silent. I was so hurt.

I had surgery to remove the fallopian tube and the fibroids and was hospitalized for three days. The mess started when I went home.

Sunday morning Gregory took me home from the hospital and made sure I was comfortable. He left our room saying, "I'll be back. I'm going to pick up Charece and Tamera so they can help around here while you're down." But Gregory made them come and they brought a big harsh attitude with them. I kept my bedroom door open at all times to hear the conversations.

Our bedroom is a little ways down the hall from the family room. I heard Reece tell Jon she was going to whip him if he didn't move from in front of the television and the way she said it sounded like she was getting ready to do it. I hollered, **"Put one hand on him and I'll be the one doing the whipping on you!"**

I inched myself out of bed and stood in the family room doorway. Jon was sticking his tongue out at her. Reece looked up at me and that made Jon turn around and when he saw me, he was startled. I stepped to the couch and picked up the small pillow and threw it at him. Gregory stepped inside the kitchen door just as Jon ducked. Gregory hollered, **"I *will not* have you all fighting one another. You are siblings and had better learn to get along!"**

Reece stuck her tongue out at me and I headed for her. Tammi jumped in between us and Gregory asks, "What the hell is going on?" Sybil shouts, **"Reece threatened Jon and stuck her tongue out at**

Mom." Tammi starts walking towards Sybil telling her to shut up, it's none of her business. Kozet jumped in front of Tammi and told her to shut up! I turned around and went back into my room. My stomach was starting to hurt.

Reece told Gregory what happened and Jon denied what he had done. Tammi took up for Reece, and Sybil and Kozet told Tammi to shut up it wasn't her business. They were all yelling at one another and when Gregory yelled for them to "**SHUT UP! ALL OF YOU!**" They all went silent. I didn't hear another word out of any of them but boy could I feel the tension between them, all the way in my room.

Gregory came in the bedroom and asked if I were alright. I told him to take Charece and Tamera to their mothers, they don't want to be here and cause too much friction amongst the other kids when he brings them here. He insisted they should be here to help me. I let it alone. Gregory took his two oldest daughter's home that evening and Friday evening he brought them back to Cloverleaf Court.

All weekend it was two against two and Gregory had to break up Charece and Kozet, they were physically fighting. When I saw Kozet's face I cried. She is such a pretty girl and for her to have a face full of scratches, my heart ached from seeing the anger inflicted on her and, from her own sister.

It took all the Holy Spirit I could muster up to hug Charece and Tamera goodbye. I told them I loved them as they walked out of my room. I was so glad to see their backs as they were leaving! I cried and prayed Gregory would never pick them up ever again. He didn't.

The next four weeks Mother Mays and Mr. Mays came to our house and she fixed dinner for all of us every evening. The kids did their homework in the bedroom with me because when I came home from the hospital I stayed in bed. The few times I did get up my stomach hurt so bad I couldn't stand long.

The third week of my recuperating I went into the family room for an hour and sat with Gregory when the kids were in school. I talked to him about painting the house and fixing up the back yard. He was supportive but didn't have any suggestions. I was just happy there was no more friction to deal with.

Gregory took me to my doctor's appointment for my month check-up and during the drive home he told me the strike might be over soon. I had mixed emotions. I liked having my sweet thoughtful husband back. He was very caring and kept the kids quiet for me to rest.

When Gregory and I came home from the doctor's office, he brought in the mail and there was a letter stating he was to report back to work on the coming Monday. Gregory was a different man that evening. Instead of complaining about the lights and running water too long, he just turned the lights off and walked to the kitchen sink and turned the water off. I was so happy to see him not worried about money.

I was able to have sex and realized I had lost weight; my clothes were real baggy on me. I took a shower and put on a sexy gown and let Gregory smell my perfume. He came into the bedroom, commented on what was that perfume that smelled so good and took his shower. When he slid into bed I slid over to him but while turning his back to me he said, "Tired, gotta get some rest. Goodnight."

I felt deeply rejected and undesired. I have never felt such profound penetrating hurt in my life.

Even when Melvin slapped me and pushed me I never felt this extreme harshness before. I felt as though my heart had been stabbed by cruelty. I actually gasped from the pain. While focused on Gregory's back, I slid all the way to the end of my side of the bed, turned over and balled myself up in the fetal position. I allowed my salty tears to slowly travel down my face.

Here I am a woman and my husband does not want me anymore. Being an unwanted wife is being spurned at its most excessive level. The disdain conveyed to you creates a deep continuous agony in your heart…

I sniffled a few times and Gregory threw the covers off himself, grunted, took his pillow, and left our bedroom. I talked to The Lord silently. I sang Donnie Mc Clurkin's song; "Stand" over and over in my head. I began whimpering as I told The Lord I was tired of Gregory vacillating back and forth with me. Gregory doesn't want me anymore and it is now so very obvious so I asked The Lord to take my desire for Gregory away from me. I need to be free from wanting someone who has made it clear he no longer wants me.

I cried myself to sleep.

For the next two weeks Gregory was very distant towards me. I kept thinking about how a woman is made for her husband and how my husband didn't want me and I felt less than a woman. These thoughts only entered my head when I had some quiet time and before bedtime. I felt bad not being wanted by my husband who I loved so much. I never approached Gregory again and slept on the edge of my side of the bed after that.

Gregory started back to work with the overtime but he did take Sundays off and attended church with us. He would interact with the kids. It was just me he slighted.

I went back to work and my department has balloons and cake for me, it is my last day with them. I had forgotten about my promotion with all that's going on at home. An hour before time to sign out Mr. Yeager handed me the sign-in/out sheet and told me to sign out and I could pack up and take my things to my new department.

I put my things in a plastic grocery bag and walked to my new department. After Mrs. Henry revealed my desk, my co-worker who sits next to me enters the room to sit down, his name is Jerome Mixson. I sat my bag on my desk and he introduced himself and told me to ask him anything I wanted to know. He was my trainer and only the two of us will be handling Second Phase Collections.

Jerome was very patient with me. Every day we ate lunch together while he told me the ropes and pitfalls of our job and after a week working with him I found myself looking forward to going to work and made extra effort with my hair and clothes in the mornings.

Mr. Jerome Mixson is very handsome. He is six feet tall, the color of pale brown with light brown eyes. Jerome is very hairy with thick eyebrows and long thick curly eyelashes. He has curly hair that he keeps activator in at all times and he dresses neatly. Always slacks, no jeans and a shirt and tie every day.

Jerome wears glasses when he uses the computer. One could say Jerome Mixson is in the "fine family."

After my six weeks of training I bought new clothes that fit, size sixteens and moved to the desk across from Jerome. Every morning Jerome entered our department, he would stop by my desk and check to see how it was going with me being on my own. There are five of us in this department and our supervisor sits in her office behind us.

One of my co-workers, Velma Franklin, gave me the cold shoulder when all of us females had break together. I couldn't figure out what problem Velma had with me and after a month Diane Walls, another co-worker stopped at my desk and turned her back towards Velma and whispers, "Miss V has a crush on Jerome and he has a crush on you. That's why she hates you. Meet me in the bathroom in ten minutes I'll fill you in." I was shocked and speechless!

I met Diane in the ladies room and she ran it down: "Jerome divorced last year and as soon as it was finalized Velma gave him her phone number. They dated a few times but he stopped asking her out. She told us everything the two of them did while they went out but when he dropped her, she told us he wasn't her type.

We can all tell that's a lie. She looks at him like she would throw rose petals down on the ground for him to walk on. We all listen to her chatter on and on about his shoes not matching what he has on, or he's in need of a haircut. No one confronts her.

We all notice how Jerome's eyes follow you when you leave the room and it's so obvious he likes you the way he talks to you every morning as if you make his day. Watch your back because Velma will nitpick your work just to frustrate you and make you transfer."

I was so flattered Jerome had an interest in me. Gregory only touched me twice since my surgery just to satisfy himself.

I knew I was wrong to start a relationship with Jerome but, I felt as if my marriage was over. Gregory no longer desired me and Jerome did. Gregory no longer had dialogue with me and when I spoke to him he would look at me until I finished my sentence then walk out of the room. I started to say something to Gregory but we were not arguing so I left conversations alone. This only fortified my theory of Gregory not wanting me so…

The Monday before Thanksgiving Jerome told me there are certain procedures we had to do for year end and he wanted us to go over the different forms before December first, this way I would be able to catch on and not slow him down. We started meeting in the cafeteria for lunch. Jerome would bring a folder with him and go over the forms we had to fill out for the December thirty-first mailing.

Thursday, a week after Thanksgiving, we were in the cafeteria and Jerome started going over forms and when I told him we had already gone over that particular form, he pulled out another. I asked why was he going over what I already knew. Jerome says, "Janice, I'm sorry but I have a grown man's crush on you." He looks me in the eyes and waits for my response. I realize while looking into his eyes how fine he is.

I feel embarrassed as I tell him, "I am married and don't appreciate you talking to me like this!" I stand up, grab my purse and storm out of the cafeteria. I go straight to my car and sit until lunch is over. I'm seriously blinking back tears and thinking to myself, 'Girl you are married and lusting after another man!' Then I hear, 'Yeah because your husband doesn't want you, you'd better take Jerome's affection. Huh, some affection is better than none.'

I prayed out loud as I yield to the tears. I felt myself desiring Jerome's touch and played a recording in my mind of Gregory turning his back to me when he slid into our bed. I told The Lord, "My husband doesn't desire me anymore. He can't hide it. I want to be loved and made love too."

I enter the office after lunch and avoid Jerome's eye contact. I look at Diane and she's looking at me with an inquisitive look. I look away from her and get into my work. Break time, Diane walks up to my desk and tells me to come go for a walk with her. I did, she is not going to leave me alone. We get off the elevator and instead of going to the cafeteria she pulls me over by the pay phone and asks, "What happened today between you and Jerome, he entered the office red faced after lunch and you came in later?"

I told Diane what happened but left out my thoughts. Diane turned serious as she says to me, "Janice you have almost what, eight years of marriage? Make sure you can handle losing that before you leap into another mans bed. You just might be experiencing the seven-year itch and end up regretting scratching yourself! I know some Bible, not a lot. But I know somewhere it says a man and a woman become one soul when they lay with one another. Girl be sure you're willing to let what you have go. Be very sure okay."

She hugged me as "Okay" glides out of my mouth. I'm thinking, 'What do I have to lose? Gregory has made it quite clear he does not want me anymore.'

I fought back tears and went to the rest room before entering the office. Jerome's eyes met mine and

I felt myself get flushed. On my drive home I thought, 'I will give Gregory one more try!'

I cooked Gregory cabbage, yams and baked chicken with fried hot water cornbread and made his lunch for tomorrow before I went to bed. I left him a note taped to the garage door as he entered it, **"Left you some food for your lunch in the fridge and, dessert is in our bed. Wake me. XOXO "**

I had my sexy teddy on however Gregory didn't wake me and when my alarm clock went off he pretended to be asleep.

I was so hurt. No, wait, I was past hurt. I was numb. I felt a severing. While getting ready for work I felt Gregory and I had just separated ourselves; the oneness we shared had just been severed. On the drive to work my mind was taking pictures of times Gregory slipped into bed and deliberately turned his back to me.

I remembered when we first began sleeping together. Gregory has a very high sex drive and after experiencing being made love to a few times by Gregory I enjoyed love making and hoped every time we were together he would make love to me. After a few months with Gregory I realized I was initiating making love and felt so guilty. Still being married to Melvin and desiring Gregory day and night.

After years of marriage and becoming busy with life, when I sat down long enough to think about our passion, I could see very clearly Gregory seldom reached for me. In fact driving to work I see Gregory's back replaying as he lay next to me, uninterested.

I sat at a red light and heard myself; "Holy Spirit show me a sign. I want Jerome because Jerome wants me. I'm married and in need of love and want to be made love too. Lord, I have a husband that doesn't want me but another man does… You better stop me from being with Jerome because if Jerome still wants some of this, it's his for the asking!"

I realize tears are trickling down my face. Here I am working every day with a man who wants me and sleeping in the same bed with a man who doesn't. I say aloud, "Work this out Lord, I don't know how much longer I can endure this. Work this out!"

I walk into the office thinking, 'Gregory has made it very clear I am no longer desirable.' I sit at my desk preparing for work, struggling with these tears trying to erupt from me. Jerome said good morning to me as he walked pass my desk. I turn towards him saying, "Good morning Jerome. We still need to go over those forms today at lunch?" He turned and looked me in my eyes, and replied, "Sure, you ready for the next step?" "I'm as ready as I'm gonna be." He shook his head "Yes" and said, "Okay," as he sat down.

I looked down in my drawer and slightly over at Diane. Her mouth was open but she was looking at Jerome then she looked at me, closed her mouth and looked away. I glanced over at Mrs. Henry's office then slowly at Vera. Vera was mad, squinting her eyes at me. I rolled mine at her and started working.

I'm thinking, 'No man can judge me. My husband has made it perfectly clear he is through with me. That's why the Bible says God will judge the adulterer. No one knows I'm being neglected, no-one!' [Hebrews 13:4] " *Marriage is honorable among all, and the bed undefiled; but fornicators and adulterers God will judge."*

Lunch time Jerome and I ate in the cafeteria then he drove us two blocks away and parked on the street. We sat in his car for the rest of our lunch. He asked about my marriage and told me about his and what led to their divorce. Jerome said, "Janice make sure this is what you want to do. I really like you and I am not talking about a one time situation. I am looking for a relationship with you. Alright?" My reply was, "Alright."

He reached for me as he asks once more, "You sure?" As I reach for him, I answer, "Yes I am." We kissed and I was so aroused. Jerome says, "Man!

We've got to put this fire out! Tomorrow, okay?" I quickly replied, "Tomorrow it is!" We went back to work but I had a difficult time concentrating the rest of the day. That kiss definitely ignited sparks!

The next day Jerome and I ate in the cafeteria and left together headed to his place over in Pico Gardens. If I were to grade the three lovers I have had, Gregory would get an "A plus" Jerome would get a "B" and Melvin would get a "C minus." I told myself what we had just done may not be right but Jerome wants him some Janice and Janice needs to be wanted!

Two weeks before Christmas Mrs. Henry told Jerome and I we had to work overtime to get the forms prepared for the last Friday of the years mail. She asked Jerome if two hours overtime Monday through Friday for the next two weeks be enough time to get the forms completed, he told her it would.

The first week we worked from eight a.m. until seven p.m. and Jerome said we were almost done. The following Wednesday we worked from eight a.m. to six-thirty and Jerome took me by my hand and led me into Mrs. Henry's office we kissed and fondled and he begged. The next day, six-thirty Jerome asked if I could follow him to his place for half an hour. I agreed so fast.

During the two-week shutdown Gregory was only home three days. Then he went to work for another department. He let us have a good Christmas, he didn't complain one time about the money being spent. Gregory and I didn't argue any more but by then I was thinking of Jerome every idle moment I had.

Jerome was very patient and would listen to me try and analyze where I failed twice as a wife. I had no intentions of marrying Jerome. He talked about us marrying but I just wanted to be held, heard and made love too. I wanted to feel like a wife and a woman, not someone my husband *once loved*.

I didn't notice Gregory and I weren't sexually active anymore since my surgery until our eighth wedding anniversary came around. Gregory forgot about it and to be truthful, so did I. The Saturday before our anniversary the kids and I were off to the grocery store when Sybil and Kozet asked what their dad and I were doing for our anniversary this year. I didn't even feel guilty for forgetting. Gregory and I are through.

The day after our anniversary Gregory walked into the bathroom while I was getting ready for work and said, "Yesterday was our anniversary. You never said anything. I think we need to talk about what we're doing. We don't have a marriage in fact I don't know what this is. I am tired of going through the motions. Let me know what you want to do." He used the bathroom and crawled back into bed. I stood in front of the mirror and watched him.

On my way to work I was thinking about Kozet. She's going to stay with me. I'm not letting her leave with Gregory. I may not have given birth to her, but having Kozet in my heart since she was three years old, makes her my daughter.

I know Gregory will pay the mortgage so that his children will have a home to grow up in. I can handle the rest. My van is paid for and I paid cash for everything I did in the house. By lunch time I was already divorced in my head from Gregory.

Jerome and I went straight to his apartment that day for lunch.

~~~~Gregory ~~~~

Mrs. Judson and these counseling sessions are taking me back in time. Man!

Okay, so Janice finally found a lawyer that handled skip traces so Melvin could be served and we were able to get married. Janice later told me she felt guilty whenever I brought up divorce or Melvin. We were committing adultery and she was ashamed.

David Allen was born before we were married but he is not a Woods, he has the Young signature! Man I have never been that happy in my life, a son, an heir. Long after I am gone from this earth, there will be a David Allen Young. The Young name will be around when I am not. I was so happy, a son!

I thanked God so much he gave me a healthy son and turned out looking just like me but with a slightly better grade of hair.

Janice and I had agreed to budget and she stuck to it. I was able to buy her a car and a brand new three-bedroom house for my family. Janice cooked every day, made me lunches, cut out coupons and bought items we needed when they were on sale. We worked together really well.

Her car was going to be paid off in two years instead of three because I had her add an extra fifty dollars to the payment so it would be paid off sooner. We moved into our home and wanted to get the back yard landscaped with a patio cover and outdoors patio furniture and a custom made built-in barbecue grill. But...

Right after we moved into the house Janice tells me she's pregnant again. I am thinking, 'Five kids, six with Sybil. I may as well forget saving for college tuitions. With child support, the mortgage, car payment and utilities taking most of the money I brought home. Groceries were like a magic trick; however Janice cooked delicious balanced meals for all of us.

James Ivan arrived so now there is no way Janice could go to work. The cost of infant care was exorbitant. Our plans were shot clean out of the water.

Often I would thank The Lord for the way Janice loved my kids. She was so tender with them in fact Janice was a very sweet tender hearted woman.

When Janice told me she was pregnant for the third time, I told her we need to use birth control. I don't like using protection so her taking a pill made better sense. She frowned and told me she wants to let The Lord bless us with as many babies He has planned for us. Besides taking the pill causes a lot of health issues, pills have side effects. I became hesitant making love to her for fear of another mouth to feed occurring.

Every time I would bring the subject of birth control up, Janice would shy away from the subject, but her being so fertile made me afraid to touch her. With the arrival of Jonathan Guy overtime was now mandatory for me and my boss knew it. He would loan me out to other departments because everyone knew I needed the money and I did not mind working.

The guys at work would tease me and say they lied on their tax exemptions and I was probably the only employee in the plant that really had nine dependents.

I believe Janice gaining so much weight was a deterrent also with me not wanting to make love to her. Her waist was completely gone and her face had gotten so big, she didn't even look like herself. Her personality was the same she never complained but when she asked about her weight I would skirt around it. Now, how you gonna tell your wife, the woman you made pregnant, she needs to stop having babies and lose a lot of weight? Yeah well, I was not going to be the one to tell her.

I just didn't want her pregnant again and when I looked at her size, well, it was easy for me to look away. Her being busy all of the time and having a baby in our bed when I came home made us not have much sexual contact.

One night I came home to just her in the bed. No babies or toys and when I began to love on her, she was on her monthly. Talk about pissed. I decided then to just leave her alone. That was the night I realized Janice was no longer coming to me four times a week.

…Now that I am thinking about this, I might have been angry most of the time because Janice and my relationship was fading. I loved Janice there just wasn't any fire in my pants for her anymore. The woman I married was lost inside this increasingly huge body. When I looked at Janice I saw this unrecognizable woman with "Pregnant Magnet!" stamped on her thighs!

Early on in our marriage I wanted my kids to know each other and had Janice pick up Charece and Tamera on Friday nights so they could spend weekends with us and get to bond with Sybil and their brothers. They loved each other when they were young. I cannot figure out what caused the change.

I had to trade Janice car in for a van so the Young tribe could ride together. When I told Janice I needed to pick up Kozet on Saturdays so the kids will know her, Janice was all for it. I was concerned because Janice was pregnant with Jon and I didn't want to overwhelm her. I have to give it to Janice; she is a natural with kids. Having Kozet was never a problem for Janice. I am thankful for that.

Faith wanted me to spend time with Kozet alone because Kozet didn't remember me. Faith was living in Lakewood with some dude named Carl Sanders and he made real good money. I wondered what Carl was into because every time I spoke with Faith, Carl was always there.

The first time I visited Kozet at Faith's apartment, when Faith opened the door I noticed she was pregnant, real pregnant. I congratulated her and she thanked me. Faith had me wait as she went to get Kozet. When Faith told Kozet I was her Daddy and wanted to spend time with her, Kozet shied away from me. Faith directed us into the living room and Kozet and I had our visit, Faith left the room.

The second time I visited Kozet I noticed how alert Kozet was for her age. She has always been very pretty. I was surprised how healthy Kozet looked with dimples in her hands, she looked well-cared for.

When I hollered at Faith I was leaving, she walked me to my truck and told me Carl was into some pretty heavy stuff and asked if Janice would mind keeping Kozet for a month after she delivered.

Faith asked about Janice and when I inquired what Carl was into, Carl yelled out of the window for her to come upstairs. Faith quickly left.

The following Friday I did not hear from Faith but Saturday I went over to see Kozet. When Faith opened the door she had her face turned away from me and I had a feeling something was wrong. I looked around for Kozet and when Faith closed the door and locked it, I turned to her asking where Kozet was and noticed Faith's long robe and, her big stomach was gone. I commented, "Had the baby I see." She broke down crying. I stood watching her. She told me while trying to control her tears, "I lost the babies. I was expecting twins but they didn't make it.

Carl was picked up making a delivery. Gregory I don't know what I'm going to do. I can't seem to find a man with money that has a legitimate job. Let me get Kozet for you, wait here." She left and came back with Kozet. I held my daughter and sat in the living room and made conversation with her.

Faith didn't return to the room until I yelled to her I was leaving. I visited Kozet for two more weeks and Faith moved. She moved into a lot of different apartments and ended up back on County Aide, living in Housing. By then I had Kozet living with us. Even though child support was being deducted from my check, I still paid Faith extra. I felt sorry for Faith.

When Kozet had her first Christmas with us, she was always hugged up with Sybil. By the time Kozet started school she and Sybil were inseparable and she calls Janice Mom. By then, Charece was giving Janice problems not wanting to come to the house anymore. Tamera started smart mouthing Janice and Janice told me to leave them with Charlotte on weekends.

At Charece's sweet sixteenth birthday party she told everyone there, she was old enough to decide if she wanted to come to my house and she made it known she elected *not* to be with us any longer. She broke my heart.

I felt like a failure as a father…

I wanted my children to know and love one another. I tried to understand Charece by listening to her but Janice told me Charece was spoiled and I needed to put my foot down with her. I wanted my oldest daughter to know she could talk to me about anything and we could have a close relationship. I felt if Tamera saw my relationship with Charece, then she would understand she could also come to me.

Janice felt as though Charece and Tamera were disrupting our home as they became older and I was allowing it. After Charece's birthday party Janice no longer went to get Charece and Tamera for the weekends. The upside of not having Charece and Tamera at the house was there was no more drama.

That is until Janice and I started arguing. Yeah, it was peaceful for the first five years of our marriage.

I remember Janice being excited about getting a job. She told me she wanted to paint inside the house, get new drapery in the living room, new carpet and put floor tile down on the floors where the carpet was worn in heavy traffic areas. I really did not see what she saw. Janice was a clean woman and the house was never nasty. Sometimes the house would get cluttered from the kids having school projects but never for too long.

Janice insisted on showing me why we needed things around the house. She would get so mad when I didn't want to get up and see what she wanted to show me every time she found another reason she should go to work. I didn't have the heart to just come out and say to her I really did not care. I would reluctantly get up and follow her as she went on and on about whatever her point was.

To tell the truth; all I knew was if there was going to be any new whatever, I was not going to be the one to purchase it. My check was already stretched to the limit and saving was down to only twenty-five dollars a week.

Janice went to work. Now I was able to save a hundred dollars a week. The Lord was with us because when I was laid off there was enough in my savings to pay the mortgage for seven months!

Janice and I were not communicating at all. We were only shouting at each other. The straw to break the camel's back for me with Janice was when she found out I was paying Faith extra. Two hundred-fifty dollars a month child support was taken out of my check for Kozet. Plus the hundred dollars I mailed Faith.

Well the night I told Janice I was paying Faith extra money, she accused me of sleeping with Faith and insisted I was still in love with her. I tried telling Janice about Faith's living conditions but Janice started hollering over me and I realized her mind was made up so, to keep from slapping her, I went to sleep in the family room on the couch.

I was so upset I tossed and turned for a long-time telling Janice off in my head and shaking her until she shut up! As I calmed down I realized we have had Kozet and Faith has never said she wanted Kozet to move back with her. Maybe Janice has a point. If I file for custody that two hundred-fifty dollars will help around here. Huh, Janice thinks I am sleeping with Faith and that's why I am giving her money. Okay, I see her point.

The next morning I realized Janice needs my reassurance that Faith no longer means anything to me. I cleaned up myself and cut her some flowers from our yard and apologized to Janice and the kids. We were once again happy. It was when Janice wanted to get romantic I recoiled. Janice is a baby magnet and refuses to use birth control. I have to leave her alone. There are enough mouths to feed around here already.

The following Friday I went to the credit union as usual to cash my check and get my money orders. Char kept our child support payments as it was. She declined automatic payments from my check when we divorced so I mailed the money order to Char for Charece and Tamera every Saturday. That was the day I noticed a new teller, Linda Torres. Wooh, man is she fine!

It was stressful at the house so I worked as much as I could. Janice and I stopped communicating altogether and I only touched her when I absolutely needed too and, I made sure she wouldn't get pregnant. Both of us were just going through the motions in the marriage. Our living conditions resembled roommates instead of husband and wife; non-speaking roommates.

One morning Janice jumped up out of bed running. I was startled until I heard Janice scream. I ran to her and when I saw the blood I became scared! I rushed her to the hospital and when the doctor told me Janice had a miscarriage; What! I hardly touch her! My god, this woman is super fertile.

While at home with the kids for the three days Janice was hospitalized I realized our marriage had decayed. Marriage number three is no longer working!

Janice arrived home from the hospital on a Sunday and I picked up Charece and Tamera that afternoon. Man was that a mistake! They helped with cleaning the kitchen and gathered the laundry up for me to do Monday but man did they have attitudes! Eye rolling and short snappy "Yes!" Or "No!" answers were given to whomever asked them a question.

Later on the drive to their house Charece asked if they had to help me again. When I answered, "Maybe, why are you asking?" Charece sarcastically replies, "We do have lives you know!"

The following Saturday when I picked up Charece and Tamera, it was attitude all over again. That afternoon I heard rumbling sounds coming from down the hall. I could see the boys in the back yard. I followed the sound and stood in the girls' bedroom doorway. I couldn't believe my eyes. Charece and Kozet elbows hitting up against the dresser. They are bent over, each with their hands pulling the others hair. They were huffing and puffing, panting like animals! I yelled, **"What the hell!"** I stormed into the room and tore them apart.

Both of their faces were covered with bloody scratches and there were large chunks of hair on the bed. Kozet had pulled chunks of Charece's hair out and scratched her face up some. Charece had scratched Kozet's face up really bad. As I took inventory of my daughters, I almost cried. My daughters: sisters, fighting like they hate each other.

I looked each one in the eyes while blinking back tears. I calmly said, "I will never pull you two apart ever again. Understand!" They both uttered, "Yes," in unison as I almost ran out of their room. I went to the garage and paced while rubbing my hands together.

I glanced down at my hands and the first time these hands held Charece flashed in my head. Then holding Kozet in these same hands for the first time flashed across my mind. Now, here they are fighting each other! Man was I hurt!

I dropped my two oldest daughters off that Sunday evening and fought back tears on my way home. I never called to pick them up ever again. I felt as though I had lost my daughter's relationship and like a father… I hurt.

Janice and I were avoiding each other. I let her know I was not interested in having sex with her. I didn't even feel bad letting her know. My spare thoughts were about where I was going to live. I will leave Janice the house for our children to be in a stable environment. I was only home physically my mind was always on my next move.

The weekend I moved back home with Mama and Mr. Mays was the end of April. I talked to Mr. Mays about having to pay child support for seven kids and explained to him I did not have money left over to pay for an apartment but I would give Mama some money at the end of every month for my room and board. He simply responded, "Oh you bet you will. Can't live anywhere for free. Gregory, seek the will of The Lord for yourself. Find out what plans The Lord has for you." He patted me on my back and left the kitchen.

This time when I moved back home, Mama insisted I go to somebody's church. She told me I needed direction from The Lord because it was obvious I did not know what I was doing! I never uttered a word but the way Mama became ignited over my marriage ending, I think Janice had been in her ear.

I agreed with Janice to pay the mortgage. My kids need a home and the schools there are rated in the top percentile. The kids have enough to adjust too with my leaving why move them. What I would have to pay Janice in child support for four kids was just a little less than the mortgage anyway and I can write the payments off my taxes. I filed for custody of Kozet so that money will no longer be taken out of my check.

I thought about Faith living like she was and decided I can no longer give her money. I have six kids to pay for and Faith is a grown woman. Here I am thirty-nine years old and living with my parents. That's shameful for me, not that anyone but me is concerned.

Sam was coming home every weekend with her kids and the noise was making it difficult for me to sleep until eleven a.m. on Saturday and Sundays. Every Sunday morning seven-thirty Lauryn and Lil Ricky were making so much noise arguing, every week like clockwork!

I would go back to sleep and was so tired when my alarm went off I was barely getting to work on time. I like to be early; rushing is not my way of starting anything. When I rush to get to work, I feel rushed for hours. Every time I felt rushed I would tell Sam off in my head. I was ready to move from LB, so saving my money was an absolute necessity.

David, James, and Jon were fighting one another and I figured it was because I was absent. This was their way of getting me to come to the house and break up their tiffs. David called me to say James was fighting him and Jon. I stopped by Cloverleaf that afternoon on my way to work. It was a holiday and there was no school so the kids were all home.

I pulled up in the driveway and saw David in the window. He let me in the house and I stepped into the living room to see Janice sitting on the couch next to some dude. The man stood straight up and walked toward me with his hand extended. "Hello, I'm Jerome." I didn't shake his hand. I thought about how I was paying the mortgage and this dude was playing house with my wife!

I asked David where was James and Jon. Both boys slowly appeared into the room. I looked at my sons and realized it was not about me coming over here to see them, they were fighting to get me over here to stop Jerome from coming to see their mother.

I became furious! Janice has Jerome in *my* house. I took it out on the boys. I told them very sternly, "If I have to come to this house one more time to break up brothers fighting each other; I will return with my belt in hand and will beat every ass in this room!" I turned around avoiding having to face Janice and Jerome and left Cloverleaf fighting mad!

Janice has lost weight in her face and looks good. I kept asking myself on the drive to work, "What the hell have I done!"

The middle of June Sam and her kids came to spend the summer and Sam and I were at it constantly. I told her to teach her children to respect my privacy and she told me to move to the back room. That was the enclosed patio where the pool table used to be. I had a fit. There is no insulation at all back there and besides that's where the television is.

When I told her to put her kids back there, I thought Sam was going to hit me. The way she popped up in my face like Mama, her fist were balled up. Man, I don't need this!

Charece and Charles Kennedy were planning their wedding the first Saturday in July. Janice phoned me because the invitation was addressed to Mr. and Mrs. Young and Family. She was concerned I hadn't receive an invitation. After hesitating a few seconds, Janice asked if I had a date to accompany me to the wedding. I told her "No." She asked if I would mind sitting with her and the kids. She was still fearful of Charlotte.

I agreed to spend the afternoon with her and the kids for Charece's wedding and reception. I must admit, I enjoyed being with my family for that day.

During the year-end shut down I worked on loan for the Spray & Bake Department and Sam and her kids spent the duration with us in LB. Mama told me Sam and Rick were having marital problems and she was thinking things over. Sam and I were constantly going at it.

I was adding my money daily so I could move as soon as possible. When we were paid that first Friday in January I went to the credit union but my mind was on how much money I was away from making my move and how much I could put into savings.

When I stepped up to the teller's window, I looked up and realized it was Linda Torres' window. I heard myself think, 'Man! She is fine!' While Linda spoke to me I took a good look at her. She is light skinned with the darkest perfectly rounded brown eyes I have ever seen on anyone that fair and her eyebrows and hair are black as coal. She has long eyelashes and layered color make-up on her eyes. When she walked away to go type my money orders I looked at her shape. She was a brick house for sure!

I'm thinking, 'Ump, ump, ump!'

She returned and counted out my money and as she handed me my money orders I looked at her name tag, "Linda Torres." I found myself rewinding Linda Torres walking away to the typewriter every idle moment I had after that day. She did not look Latin with all of the padding she carried on those rounded hips nor did I detect an accent when she talked but her last name is Torres.

All that work week Linda was on my mind. Next payday I happily went to the credit union looking for Linda. The third payday I let people go in front of me just so I could be waited on by Linda. I walked up to her and she says, "Hello." I replied, "Hello." She says while smiling, "You do know all of the tellers here are capable of handling your banking needs, right?" I shook my head up and down. I am trying to think of a line to give her.

I conclude my transaction and she says, "Thank you for banking with us. By the way I look forward to you getting in my line." She smiles a flirty smile and looks away from me to the next person in line. I exit the credit union smiling.

I thought of Linda all the time. Wednesday I started getting my mack together for Linda. Thinking of her made me feel as if I were brand new. I was so energetic and everyday seemed less and less dreary. Man I was becoming vibrant and alive again. I decided to introduce myself and ask if she were in a relationship and if not, I was going to ask her out to dinner.

That Friday I walked up to her window and my heart was racing so fast I inhaled deeply and heard myself swallow trying to calm myself. 'Come on Gregory, you're thirty-nine years old. Get it together man.'

Linda smiled and asked how was I today? All I could do was shake my head up and down. When she went to type out my money orders I caught my breath. She counted out my money and thanked me for my business while giving me her flirty smile. I opened my mouth to ask her out but she looked away towards the line. I walked away.

I was so mad at myself and decided I do not need another female in my life now anyway. But I couldn't keep the image of Linda's walk with her curvy body out of my head.

The following week I did the same thing when I stepped up to Linda's window but I did manage to ask how she was doing. That time I walked away I thought, 'Okay Greg, take it slow with her.'

Payday all employees received notification in our check that payroll was changing to bi-monthly. The first thing I thought of was I could only see Linda twice a month. I had to ask her out there is no way of getting around it. I went to another teller that day; I must approach her correct. As fine as she is, I am sure she can smell a one-night stand real quick.

All that week I talked myself up daily going over different possible scenarios of when I asked Linda out. I decided I had no choice but to ask her Friday.

On my way to the credit union I psyched myself up. 'Today is it. It will be two weeks before you get to see her again.' I stepped up to her line, looked into her eyes and did not give her a chance to talk. I placed my check on the counter and dove right in, "Hello Linda, how are you today?" She smiled as she slightly jerked her head back and says, "My, my Mister Young you're out of character today. What's going on with you?"

"Well Linda I heard about this great blockbuster movie and I really want to see it but, I don't have anyone to see it with. How is your weekend looking?" She is looking me in my eyes. I am thinking, 'Man are you fine!' She softly says, "Well Mr. Young I am a sensitive woman and like good movies that don't make me feel sad."

I jumped right in, "Oh no worries, you can choose the movie." I am thinking, 'Okay Greg pump your brakes, let's not sound hard up.' She's looking my face over. She taps her finger on her lips and says, "Hum… are you a gentleman Mr. Young?" I look deep into her eyes, "Always." She takes my check and completes my transaction.

When Linda reappears at her window, she slides my money orders to me, counts out my cash and instead of allowing me to pick it up, she lays her hand over the pile and says, "Wait, you'll need my number."

She grabs a piece of paper and pen and as she writes her phone number down I'm thinking, 'YES!' She looks up at me and smiles while thanking me for banking with them. I grab everything on the counter and leave feeling like I am ten feet tall.

By the time Linda and I went out for the first time, it was the first Saturday in February. Linda and I talked every day that week and I took the weekend off work. She gave me her address and directions to her house; she lives in Torrance, CA. I must say I was impressed with where she lived, clean and well kept up houses and her apartment building was nicely kept. She must make good money working at the credit union.

Linda came to the door dressed in a short tight skirt that displayed all of her curves and her blouse was nice and low. She invited me in and as I stepped inside her apartment a young girl slowly appeared into the living room. "Mr. Young this is my daughter Izabella. Izabella say hello to Mr. Young." I hear a soft, "Hello Mr. Young."

Linda says, "Very good Mija." Izabella sits on the couch while looking me over. The door opens and this lanky young man skids inside and slams the door. Linda and I are standing at the door and the young man looks at Linda and shouts something in Spanish with his hands raised. Linda yells back in Spanish to him. She faces me and says, "And this Mr. Young is my son Pedro. And believe me he's stubborn as a rock! Pedro say hello to Mr. Young."

Pedro turns my way, looks me up and down, looks back at Linda and says, "I told you we have rehearsal today get someone else to watch her!" Linda grabs her purse and looks at me while softly saying, "Come on Mr. Young I'm ready." Pedro yells in Spanish and Linda rolls her eyes at him as we walk out of the door. I am thinking, 'Rude *and* he talks to his mother that way; it is a miracle he has all his teeth! Definitely not raised by Phylis Young.'

12 Years A Slave was the movie we watched and having read the book; I thought the movie was pretty good. Linda laid her head on my arm when she was moved by some of the scenes. I had to hand a few napkins to her, she is sensitive. We went to dinner and she explained she was Black and Puerto Rican. Her mother was black however she knows very little of her Mothers history, she was raised Puerto Rican.

Linda commented on how she thought the movie was exaggerated for effect. I told her the movie exposed truth of what a lot of slaves endured. I was surprised she was not knowledgeable of her African American heritage. I asked if she were ever married. Linda told me about her ex-husband, Omar.

Omar is from Puerto Rico, Dorado Barrio. He worked in his family's business. They have a very well-known Architectural and Construction Company. Omar worked as an electrician there and here in Culver City until four years ago. Her daughter had her third birthday party and that was the day Linda found out Omar was mixed up in drug trafficking. He was picked up that night.

They lived in Culver City and was living very large. Omar built their four thousand square foot home on their two acres and had garages built on their property for his trucks and equipment. Turns out his drugs were also being stored there.

Linda took care of her family while their maid kept the house up. Linda could cook but her specialty was native Puerto Rican foods. Could she cook black-bean soup! Man oh man.

Linda's mother, Ernestine Bailey has family roots in Kentucky. Ernestine married Louis Gian Ramon Torres and had Linda. When Linda became two years old her mother died giving birth to her baby brother, who was stillborn.

Because Linda was so young Ramon sent for his mother in Puerto Rico to take care of Linda here in the United States, and he buried himself in work. Linda was raised influenced by her Puerto Rican culture and speaks both English and Spanish fluently. Her mother's family mails her birthday cards, other than that she knows nothing about them.

When Linda was about to have her eighteenth birthday her grandmother told her the family had a friend in Puerto Rico whose son would make a great husband for her and Linda protested until Omar came to America and she saw how fine he was. He was twenty-three and just graduated with an architectural degree and spoke very good English.

Nine months later Linda and Omar were married. Omar is now serving his ten year sentence up in Vacaville Federal Prison in California. He was to get out last year on probation but stabbed an inmate and now has to serve his full term. She divorced Omar a year after he left in order to get a new start.

I really liked being with Linda. Her sense of humor was entertaining and we had a lot of fun. She has this saying, "Exactly!" However she can say the word four different ways. Exactly, Egg-zactly, Zactly, and E-zactly. And Linda is sexy with that coke bottle body. She likes to flirt. I dropped her off at home after our first date and thought of her the rest of the night.

The next day after church I phoned her and we talked for over two hours. She had to ask me to hold on a few times as she shouted at her son but she apologized each time she returned to our conversation. I asked if her son was always difficult. She told me he was just a very passionate boy.

Puerto Rican culture allow males to be expressive because at age twelve boys are considered men. Pedro was just being the man of the house that's all. After our conversation ended I thought, 'any other culture, Pedro would get his butt whupped! Puerto Ricans are definitely different people!'

By Memorial Day Linda and I decided since I was looking for my own place, I would move in with her and stay in her guest room for three months and buy myself a condo. We were not sexually active and she said I could not sleep in her room because she did not want to live wrong in front of her kids. I was just a friend she was helping for ninety days, that was all.

I agreed thinking I would ease into her bedroom after I moved in. Pedro was the problem. When we told both him and Izabella I was moving in, Pedro went ballistic. He stood up over Linda yelling at her in Spanish. I jumped up between him and her because I thought he was going to hit Linda. She never flinched which should have given me indication this was a constant in their house, but oh-no, I did not see it! I was too busy gawking at Linda's low-cut blouses and slits up her thighs.

When they finished shouting Pedro left the house and Izzy went into her room and shut the door. I asked Linda if she was okay and she said, "Yeah." With an attitude, like, why would I not be okay. I told her I was going to check on Izzy. I knocked on her door and she said for me to come in. I left the door open and asked if she were alright. She asked, "With you moving in or with them fighting?" I was shocked she knew the difference. Izzy is so quiet. I just thought she had no clue what was going on around her but that day I found out Izzy was a very intelligent seven-year-old.

My answer was, "Both. Tell me what you think about me moving in here and about your Mom and Pedro fighting." Izzy speaks very slowly as though she is giving thought to what she is saying to me. "I think you should move into Pedro's room. Aunt Maria stays in the guest room when she comes to California. Pedro is the man and has a right to his opinion. That's what I think." I told her I agreed with her but Pedro should not talk to his mother that way. Izzy told me Pedro was acting like the man of the house, and that was okay. I left Izzy's room scratching my head.

I moved in with Linda and took thirty-minute cold showers every day Linda was around. She wore low cut everything and splits on her robe up to her thighs. I was having a hard time sleeping at night knowing she was in her bed right next to me sexy as hell.

I took on more overtime. Janice was having trouble with the van and was paying a lot on repairs. She needed an extra hundred to keep the cell phone on. I gave her the money; she has to transport my kids and I do not want them stranded. Janice is a great mother and I knew she was not wasting money.

Three weeks after I moved in with Linda she started knocking on my door looking for something in my room after she took Izzy to school. Pedro hardly ever stayed at the house. He was in a band and stayed with the lead singer most nights. He would come home in the evenings, get clothes, and stay gone until he was in need of more clothes.

After I would come home at three-thirty in the mornings and take my shower, Linda would come into my room asking if I had seen something she was looking for. Dressed in teddies and matching see-thru robes. I knew exactly what *she* was looking for so I grabbed her and man oh man what great sex. After our first time Linda started crawling into my bed when she heard me come home at three-thirty in the morning.

Izzy had to wake her mother in bed with me a few times and Linda would be in a bad mood on those days. She cared a lot about her daughter seeing her living with a man she was not married too. I did not understand what the big deal was. I thought Linda was worried about her reputation. But I found out it was way more to the equation when Maria came into the picture.

During our love making we had several mishaps when we used protection and three weeks before my fortieth birthday Linda told me she was pregnant. I was not surprised. I told her we were adults and could raise the kid together. She laughed at me. "You are at work all the time. How can I depend on you for two o'clock feeding when you are at work?"

I looked at her wide eyed and she sounded out, "Egg-zactly! Now if you don't want to marry me it's okay. I will take a trip to the clinic and take care of this, 'situation.' But Mr. Young, you had better be gone from here when I return from the clinic. I will be angry enough to help Pedro cut you into little pieces!" She got up and left my room.

Man did she jack my head up! Linda was something else. I had never seen this side of her. I was too scared to go back to sleep. I got up, showered, and left for LB. I need to talk to Mama.

During my drive to LB I kept thinking about Linda getting rid of my kid. I have seven kids; six I have fathered. My two oldest daughters no longer receive my support. If Linda has this baby child support will increase again. Wait! I have not received my final decree of divorce from Janice. Man, what have I gotten myself into?

I told Mama about Linda being pregnant and she went totally somewhere else with the conversation.

First she said I had no business messing with a Latino girl. They have a different culture and some of their brothers, father and uncles threaten men who knock up their daughters, sisters, and nieces. Then she went Bible on me. "Gregory Allen, I raised you better than to be jumping in every perfumed woman's bed. Get into The Word of God and find out what His plans are for you. Paying child support and making more babies is not what God has in store for you Gregory Allen!

Now I love every grandchild you have given me but you listen to me good. You need to get back in church on your knees praying more and humping less!" Mama stood up from the kitchen table and went to her room and I heard her slam the door. I sat at the table thinking, 'What the hell got into her?'

I went to work that day and thought about Linda being pregnant. I cannot be made to marry Linda like I am some eighteen-year-old boy. I am a man and will take care of my kid. No one is making me, Gregory Allen Young, almost forty years old having a shotgun wedding. Nawh man, that is not happening!

From that night on Linda poured the sex on and I knew what she was doing and thought, 'This is great and with no protection! All the sex I want, yeah this might could work!' I was telling myself that every time we finished making love.

Well my divorce was final with Janice in October and Linda was four months pregnant. One early November Saturday morning we were all awakened by the ceiling light being flicked off and on and Maria yelling, **"I heard a rumor. Linda is pregnant. I have come to see for myself!"**

Izzy ran into our room, "Aunt Maria!" Izzy hugged Maria and Maria reached down and kissed her on the forehead and said, "My princess, my Mija! How have you been without me?" Linda jumps from the bed and hugs this crazy woman who almost got jumped. She scared the mess out of me. It was five-thirty in the morning.

Linda went into the kitchen and all I heard was laughter coming from the both of them. Maria stayed in the guest room and Izzy slept with her. Some nights Maria did not come home. Maria is Omar's cousin from Puerto Rico. She helped Linda with our wedding at City Hall on November twentieth. After we were married all of the good loving was rationed out. Linda got me!

I was so mad at myself for falling into her trap. She worked her body like magic on me. I was walking around in shock from being played. By Christmas I was thinking about how comfortable the couch in LB would sleep for me.

Christmas Day Linda, Izzy, and I went to LB and Mama had an attitude with Linda. She embraced Izzy but not Linda. She called her a man trapper when Linda left the kitchen and I know Linda heard her. Tamera and a friend, Alisha drove over to drop off our Christmas gifts and when Mama told her to have a seat for a few moments she copped a very visible attitude.

Mama brought Tamera a plate and introduced her and Alisha to Izzy. Tamera took one look at Linda and stared at her with arms folded. Linda noticed the staring and told me she was ready to leave. Janice came by with the kids and gifts. She was with some dude named Willie. He looked old enough to be her father.

I sat on the couch and watched my kids, my ex-wife and her man and my new pregnant wife. Janice looked so good her face was back to normal and all she had was a stomach. Janice was nice, she even asked Linda if she knew what we were having. Linda had an attitude that matched Tamera's.

Kozet and Sybil were the only ones not mad in the room. I looked at both of them. They are very pretty girls. Kozet is a little thick. I remember Charece and Tamera being like that and they outgrew it. I took inventory of my family and decided I need to consider The Lord on what I need to do next. I have totally made a mess of my life and the lives of my children.

Well, the last six weeks of Linda's pregnancy we had to abstain from sex. Maria comes back in town February first to help Linda with the baby. Anna Marie Young was due March twentieth but she decided to make her appearance on March fifteenth instead. She weighed eight pounds, three ounces so she was good to come home with Linda. Anna is the most beautiful baby I have fathered; she looks like a doll. I held and kissed her. She smelled so sweet and I could not take my eyes off her.

I messed up really bad. I mean real bad…

When Maria returned in February whenever the three of us were home she would leave the bathroom and bedroom doors open when she changed her clothes. She would tease Linda when I was around about how we could not have sex. Maria would get so graphic Linda would tell her something in Spanish real harsh and Maria would shut up.

Maria started making long glances at my body and allowed me to see her looking. Maria dressed like Linda before she was pregnant and the day Linda gave birth, I left the hospital, went home, showered, and crawled in bed. Later that afternoon Maria slid into bed with me. There was absolutely no resistance from me at all.

Maria told me Linda shared with her how great a lover I was and she just had to see for herself. I should have felt guilty afterwards but some kind of way I felt Linda was getting back what she deserved. She tricked me and now she has gotten tricked. Maria and I had sex twice.

The only problem is a week later I started having burning and pain when I urinated. I had to see a doctor and was told I had a sexually transmitted disease and had to be celibate for at least six weeks. If I were exceptionally active it would be best to go eight weeks.

I am thinking, 'I do not want anything to do with Linda nor Maria. I am checking out of here. I am going back to LB and get on my knees. As I waited at the pharmacy I made my mind up. I need to ask The Lord what my next move should be. It is apparent I cannot make good decisions on my own.

I prayed during the drive to work and during my shift. Three-thirty in the morning I entered the house and there Maria was wearing a red see-thru Teddy with her finger over her lips for me to be quiet. She grabbed my hand and I jerked it away from her. She whispered, "Linda will not hear us in my room and the baby just had her feeding half hour ago, come on Poppy. We need to get our tensions handled now before you go into your room."

I reached into my pant pocket and shoved the prescription in her face. I whispered, "I would not touch you with a ten-foot pole!" Her eyes became so large. She snatched the bottle from me and walked over by the night light that was visible over the stove and read it. I snatched the bottle from Maria and went into our bedroom, took my shower, and slid into bed with Linda; man was I mad. Mostly at myself.

I kept my head on work and it was what I needed to keep my mind off sex with Linda. I would be so tired when I went to bed I fell asleep as soon as my head hit the pillow. Anna was a good baby, she hardly ever cried. Maria was rolling her eyes at me and kept saying some word at me in Spanish [*cobarde*]. I made sure Maria and I were never alone.

After Linda had been home for three weeks she started wanting to fool around when I slid in bed. I was trying to avoid her and Maria. One night I left our bedroom and went to Pedro's room but he was home of all nights! I laid on the couch and Maria woke me just before the sun came up. I pushed her onto the floor and went back to bed with Linda. I almost cried, what have I done!

Linda started letting me feed Anna before I left for work and when I held my daughter I fought back the urge to cry. I knew holding Anna were moments I had to treasure, I was not going to be in her life. I did not love Linda I was in lust for Linda...and Maria. It was only a matter of time before Linda would find out I had an STD and the fan would be plugged in and particles would soon head straight towards it.

Every night I slipped in bed Linda started with the fooling around. I had to think of some way not to go home. I started lying to Linda to keep from having sex with her.

The fourth week after Linda had Anna while at work I texted her a lie. I told her Mr. Mays had taken a fall and Mama needed me to help her lift him. I figured I would leave work and go to LB for the next three weeks so I could remain celibate. Mr. Mays fall was good for two of those weeks. I had to do what was necessary to keep Linda from finding out about Maria.

I started praying for Maria to go back to Puerto Rico so I would be able to stay in the guest room. But that did not happen. One good thing with me staying in LB, I had time to think without seeing half naked bodies I craved for. Linda only had a stomach from being pregnant but she was firm everywhere else. I texted Linda every day and added happy faces.

Two weeks later Linda texted me at work she had her six weeks check-up today and the doctor gave her the green light for sex. She texted: "I will have candles lit and my body ready for you. Come straight home." I couldn't touch Linda; she would get what Maria gave me for sure but what excuse could I use… I did not reply, I was contemplating.

Seven more days, all I need is seven days! So, at ten-thirty I texted Linda, "So sorry, Jamal has had an automobile accident. Nothing too serious, a fender bender. I am going to Ladera Heights to be with him at his house. I will call you tomorrow and update you, Greg."

I knew Linda would not talk to Mama; she knows Mama does not like her so I thought I was good. Linda texted me back, "OMG is he okay? Was Tina hurt too?" I knew then I had made up the wrong story. I texted; "Do not worry, I just want to be there for him. Tina can go to work tomorrow, Jamal cannot he is sore that is all. See you tomorrow before work, Greg."

I was so nervous. I need one week before I can touch Linda, she knows how I am, she will suspect something if I make it obvious I cannot touch her. Man, what have I done!

I left work headed straight to LB and went to the cabinet over the refrigerator. I poured myself a drink and took it with me to the back room. My mind was moving so fast however when the liquor kicked in I felt myself relax and fell off to sleep.

The next morning Mama asked what was going on with Linda and me. I told her the baby keeps me up and asked about Charece and Charlie's splitting up.

Charece is a Computer Programmer and she is extremely good at what she does. She was always good in math and figuring things out so she went into programing. She loves her job. She says she became pregnant after she and Charlie married but, Alexis was born eight months after the wedding. Alexis was eleven months old when Tyreke appeared on the scene. I remember thinking the day Anna was born, 'Here I am a father again with two grandchildren!

Mama told me Charlie had a roving eye. Charece gained a lot of weight getting pregnant with Ty after Lexie became two months old. Now that her and Charlie has split, Charece has lost weight. I do not get into my daughter's business. I just make it clear to them I am here if they need me. However, when I stayed in LB after Anna was born I talked to Mama, or should I say listened to Mama talk about Charece and Charlie being so nasty during their split.

Listening to the shenanigans Charece and Charlie were up too, I realized I do not want to be nasty with Linda. It is bad enough Char and I are nasty. After Mama left the kitchen my mind regressed to what a mess Charece and Charlie's wedding rehearsal and wedding day was for Char and myself.

At the time of Charece's wedding Janice and I were recently separated and because Janice was afraid of Char, I went to the rehearsal alone. Char was sitting on the front row in the sanctuary when I entered so I sat behind her, a few rows back. Char and I only shout at one another, we never talk civil. She starts the hollering and I finish it. Afterwards I feel so bad allowing Char to take me there but I get so angry at her for having Dude *in my bed!*

Anyway, at the rehearsal Char stood up to leave the room and rehearse being escorted in and noticed me. She rolled her eyes. After rehearsed being escorted inside, seated on the first row, Char asked, "The father doesn't have to sit near me, does he?" I loudly said, "Oh please do not worry. The father does not want to sit anywhere near the mother!" She turns towards me and says, "Oh that's right, you probably won't make it being at work and all!" Charece says, "Alright you two! I need both of you to act like adults. If you can't, just don't come to my wedding!"

Charece started crying. Tamera and Charlie stood next to Charece and tried to console her but Charece looked at me, then her mother and said, "I mean it! Do not come to my wedding and jack-up my happy day memories. Both of you can stay home and grow up!"

Char stood up and reached out to Charece but Charece broke down crying and Charlie hugged her.

Char turned completely around facing me, put her hands on her hips and yells, "**YOU CAN STAY AT WORK, I WILL PERSONALLY MAIL YOU PICTURES. NOW YOU'VE MANAGED TO UPSET CHARECE!**"

I yelled back, **"ME! YOU STARTED IT..."**

Tamera yells, **"BOTH OF YOU SHUT UP!"** She lowers her voice and says, "Look, I mean no disrespect, but both of you need to grow up. This family is shot to hell because neither of you wants to be the adult!" I felt like Tamera had just given me a whupping. She was right! But Char did start it. I shut my mouth after that. Tamera started crying and Char consoled her.

Every time Char and I locked eyes, she rolled hers at me. Char was shooting shots at me the rest of the evening but I bit my lip. I think my not saying anything pissed Char off. When I left the church and thought of how my silence made Char mad, I smiled. I got her butt!

The next day was the wedding. Janice sat so close to me she almost shared my chair. Char was with some dude she kept rubbing on and laughing all loud while throwing her head back. I could tell Char was performing as though she and dude were a happy couple. I also noticed Dude kept looking my way. He knew her performance was just for me.

When I announced I was leaving I overheard Char say something about me having to take my litter home. That comment pissed me off.

Now, Mama comes back into the kitchen and hands me her cell phone. It is revealing a picture of Tamera and some handsome young man cheek to cheek smiling at the camera. Mama says, "His name is Justin Moreland. They just got engaged. They're planning a wedding next year." Once again I am dreading having to tolerate being around Char. I remember being delighted for Tamera and hoped her marriage would work. But my life was in such shambles then. I was ardently trying to stay one step ahead of Linda so she would not suspect anything.

Today the lie I made up for Linda is my truck had to go to the shop for a few days. Now my stomach is upset I have told so many lies. While I get ready for work I realize it is Wednesday, only four days left before I can go home.

Well, that night when I walked in the house after my shift, I was surprised to see Mama up sitting at the kitchen table with her Bible. I know something is wrong, Mama is up at three-fifty a.m.! I thought it was Grand Pop.

Mama said very sternly, "Gregory Allen *SIT* down…" She watches me sit and as I stare in her face, I feel like I am ten years old again. She is mad at me!

Mama continues in a heated tone, "I got a phone call today from your Latino wife." I hear a loud, 'UH OH!' In my head.

Mama continues, "She asked if Mays was better. I hesitated to answer, but I managed to say, "Yes he is." I figured you had lied to her but to say Mays fell and hurt himself. You didn't have enough brains in that big head of yours to tell me so I could back you up!"

I opened my mouth and Mama pursed her lips and lifted her fist up in the air. I shut my mouth. I thought she was going to punch me in my face. She continued, "AND, you put Jamal in a car accident! I had no idea you were such a great liar. Let me tell you something!" Mama stood up with both hands on the table and she shouted, **"DON'T YOU EVER LIE ABOUT MY HUSBAND AND BABY AGAIN. IF YOU GONNA MAKE UP LIES, LIE ABOUT YOURSELF!"**

Mama slapped the napkin holder on the table over. She was hot with me! She walked away and stopped in the doorway, turned to me, and said, "Gregory Allen, take your ass to church and get on the altar! Lord this boy got me cussin!"

Mama disappeared and I was scared. Linda knows I lied; she is very intelligent. I did not sleep that night at all. I thought of more lies to tell Linda.

Finally I came up with; I was experiencing erectile disfunction and was ashamed to tell her.

The sun was coming up and I was too tired to think of any more scenarios of Linda asking me questions. By then my erectile dysfunction lie sounded real good.

I decided not to contact Linda, I will let her call me. The next day I texted her "Missing U" and smiley faces everyday but no voice contact. Linda never responded to my text and I copied and pasted the same text to her daily. I buried myself in work to not think about my home life.

Monday, I woke thinking, 'I get to go home tonight and I have mixed emotions now not having heard from Linda.' Four p.m. that afternoon, I get a text from Maria: "Emergency, come home!" I thought something was wrong with Anna and I flew home I was so scared. I get to the apartment elevator and another text comes through from Maria: "We are at the hospital, Lomita Avenue. Hurry!"

I hurried to get there. Linda, Maria, Pedro and two tattooed, bandana wearing, Latino goons were in the back-waiting area. I had no idea what I was walking into.

Maria was sitting on the bed with Linda and Linda was holding Anna. Before I could ask what was wrong, Pedro started yelling at me as he walked up in my face. He threatened to let one of the guys standing there have a piece of me. I took off my jacket and started cussing like a sailor. I have had it with him! *Come On! Bring it on!* I yelled. Nurses ran over and told us guys we all had to leave; security was on the way.

Pedro started yelling stating I had better get the hell out of the hospital before he made sure I needed a bed in ICU. 'This piss-ant!' I punched Pedro in the nose. The two goons grabbed me and punched on me good. I fought them off until security came and took all us guys to a private room. I went to jail because Pedro said he was a minor and I had hit him. My hand was swollen and red and Pedro's nose and clothes were bloody, so off to jail I go.

Mr. Mays came to bail me out. It was after midnight when we arrived home. Mama said Linda phoned her earlier, around eight p.m. and ran everything down. Maria told Linda I had come on to her and gave her some disease. Linda called Pedro. Omar has two brothers and they make sure Pedro is protected so I am to stay away from the house for a few days so they won't follow me and put me in the hospital.

Mama said Linda apologized and was crying over the phone but Mama thought Linda was crying because she messed up her chances with a good man.

Mama never has anything good to say about Linda, ever. Mama said looking at me, "Now I know why she was sorry. That man beat you real good!" Mama made me sit at the kitchen table while she cleaned my face. She left to get rubbing alcohol, cotton balls and Neosporin. While dabbing at my wounds I told her "I gave those two guys a run for their money!" Mama stopped wiping my face and said, "Two guys did this to you?" I nodded. Mama grabbed me tight and said, "Lord thank You. They could have killed my baby! Thank Ya!"

When Mama finished cleaning my face I went into the back room. I sat on the couch hoping Mr. Mays would come into the room, I need a Dad right about now. How could I have made such a mess of my life. Mr. Mays appeared behind the couch. "Gregory, you are not thinking of doing something stupid are you?" "No sir. What *I am* thinking of is dropping to my knees and crying out to God." My voice is trembling.

Mr. Mays adds, "Son, I am here if you need me." I slid all the way down on the couch lying flat on my back and did not fight the tears falling from my eyes. I placed my forearm over my forehead and whimpered. I couldn't fight it anymore. I rolled onto my side and cried like a baby.

I know this is crazy but I felt as though the tears were a river. My tears felt like they had been dammed up inside me for years and now all the debris that held them back has finally been removed.

Visions began flashing in my head. I saw Char's face as she held those crumbled sheets in her hands. Faith as she sat at her kitchen table cigarette in one hand, drink in the other. Janice, as her face inflated into this unrecognizable person. I saw Linda behind the tellers' window at the credit union as she walked away. Then Maria laying on the guest bed with a sheet partially across her naked body.

I heard myself cry out, "Oh God, what have I done!" I heard myself sob. I could not stop the tears. They kept pouring and pouring from me. The more remorseful I became, the louder I cried.

Finally, I am able to stop crying. I pulled the throw pillow up under my head and prayed. I talked to The Lord like I used to when I was young. I told The Lord everything I had kept inside me for years. I heard myself sounding so selfish and childish. I realized; this is all my fault. I need to get a grip on my lust.

I promised The Lord I will start going back to church Sunday's and I am getting back in fellowship with Him. I fell off to sleep and slept good.

I woke to the smell of coffee. When I stepped into the kitchen there were grits, bacon, scrambled eggs, and toast. Mama spoils me. Mr. Mays was at work and I asked Mama if her and Mr. Mays were tired of me coming back home. She told me "No, but Sam and Rick decided to divorce and she's looking for her own place around here.

San Diego is not too far for Rick to come see his kids. I sarcastically said, "At least his kids want to see their father." Mama interrupts, "Now Gregory stop feeling sorry for yourself. You can't help it if these women nowadays don't know what a good man is.

Reece was smelling herself pay no mind to her talk. You need to ask The Lord to give you a wife." Mama sat down, watched me eat and told me all about Tamera searching for a place to have their wedding reception. On my way to work I realized; I do not know what I want. I do know I am getting divorced and leaving women alone!

Wednesday before getting out of bed for work I get a phone call from Linda. She apologized and told me she was remorseful of all that has come between us. All I could say was, "Me too." Linda told me Maria lied and said I approached her and gave her an STD. Linda asked if I were alright and told me to take care and she ended our conversation. I kept hearing her soft voice as she apologized and it messed me up. I felt I owed Linda an apology as well. But I never called her back.

Friday after eating breakfast I went to the credit union and made a money order for Linda and decided to take it to her. I may be a jerk, but I am a man. I will own up to everything I have done. Saturday on the drive to Torrance I thought about filing for divorce but this time I am using a Paralegal.

Pedro opened the door with tape on his nose and I could see purple around his eyes. I said, "Hey Pedro." He says, "Hey yourself!" I stood at the door and as he walks away from me, I add, "Pedro, I am sorry." He was standing almost by the door to his room, turns around to face me and says, "You put one hand on my mother and your mother will bury you." Linda yells from the bedroom, "Pedro!" He points at me and adds, "You heard what I said!" He enters his room and slams the door.

Linda appears in the doorway. She has on some long sleeveless dress with slits up both sides. "Did you come to get your things?" We make eye contact. "May I see Anna?" "Sure, come on." After I entered the bedroom Linda closed the door and I thought she was going to let me have it. I walked over to Anna. She was lying on my side of our bed. I stood over my daughter watching her sleep. Linda sits on the bed and tells me I can pick her up.

I lifted Anna in my arms and slowly gazed over every inch of her. My beautiful daughter. She is beginning to look like Linda. She smells so sweet. I kiss her forehead and cannot stop. Anna squirms and opens her little eyes. For a second she looks directly at me. My heart felt as though a fraction of it melted.

Anna opens her eyes again and looks into mine. The feelings going on in me. I automatically smile. "Hi there angel." I say as she smiles at me. I thought I was going to burst! I was elated. Linda says, "She likes to be talked to." I start talking to my daughter and decide to take advantage of the moment.

"Anna, your father has made some stupid choices lately and your beautiful mother needs to know I did not solicit Maria. She was the instigator and *she* infected *me*." I was looking Linda in her eyes. "Linda, I am so sorry. I never want to hurt you but Maria is bad news." Linda interrupts me. "I know. She's gone and for good this time. Izzy is taking it very hard.

Maria has always been in Izzy's life all of her life and the two of them have been close. I did not handle putting her out too well. I jumped her. Gregory, we both made mistakes. Do you wanna start over?" I say, "Yes, that sounds good." Linda walks over to me and I lay Anna on the bed and hug my wife. Linda cries in my arms.

I returned to Linda's but it was strained living there with Pedro's sarcasm. He made sure to stay home every day and night now. He would talk to Linda in Spanish while she cooked me breakfast and her facial expressions led me to believe he was talking about me. A lot of times I would stand up in his face and ask, "Why aren't you working, huh, big man Pedro can't do any work beside running your mouth, huh." Linda would always step in between us.

Pedro always departed from our brief talks headed for his room while spitting out something in Spanish. That was the norm for Pedro and me, sarcasm. I stayed in the guest room for another week to make sure I was clean. Linda and I had sex but it was different, not passionate. We were just overdue. After a week of me being back in our bed, she cried after we had sex. I knew something was going on with her so I asked, "What is it Linda."

"Gregory, Maria kept filling my head with lies about you must have another woman because you were avoiding having sex with me. The day I called your mother and asked how her husband was doing I could tell she had no idea what I was referring to. I put your mother on speaker and went to Maria and let her hear the rest of our conversation.

I asked if Jamal was better after the auto accident and your mother hesitated before saying, 'I'm sure Gregory told you everything. I have to go now but I'll tell him you called. Bye.' Maria agreed with me, your mother was covering for you. She had no idea what to say to me. Maria said you were probably somewhere with another woman all this time.

Gregory I am so sorry. I thought you were cheating on me and I had Pedro stay with Anna and Izzy that Friday and Saturday night before you hit Pedro. Maria and I went to the club. I slept with some guys. I am so sorry. I was so angry with you Gregory, I am sorry." Linda began sobbing.

My heart stopped…

Linda was in my arms. I abruptly removed my arms from around her and moved to the edge of the bed. After I was able to catch my breath I started interrogating her. Who are they, what nationality, where did you go, how many times, have you seen them since? I was mad.

I showered and headed straight to the guest room. I felt like I did after Char and I broke up. This time I felt as though I deserved being cheated on but I still hurt. Linda was the second wife to cheat on me. My mind went all the way back to when I was fourteen.

I read up on the female anatomy and discovered the female body has many trigger points of arousal. I studied the female body for months before Char and I had sex, I wanted to give her pleasure. I pride myself in being a good lover but having two wives prefer another man...No other pain impairs like betrayal.

Linda and I were trying our best to make this marriage work however it was getting more and more difficult to keep us together.

We started talking and she wanted us to go out like we were dating to build the passion and trust back in our marriage. Okay, I was like, 'Gregory this is your fourth wife so let's do this. Take it one day at a time.' So I am trying to be the good guy and since we discussed Linda staying home for a year with Anna, I went to the apartment manager.

I told the young man Linda and I were married and asked for the necessary paperwork to add my name on the lease so I could pay the rent. The guy tells me Linda knows the owner and I need to talk to her about that. I thought I was going to surprise Linda but turns out I was the one surprised.

I asked Linda did she know the owner of the building and she looked as though I had just drained all of her blood from her veins. I knew she was lying as she told me the owner was close to her father. She asked why I asked. I told her the truth; I want to pay the rent since she was not working. Linda went silent on me.

I asked what was wrong. She said she thought Anna was crying and left the kitchen. When we were getting ready for bed I asked again about the owner of the building. She blurted, "There is no owner. Don't worry about the rent, it's taken care of." She gave me a lap dance and I forgot about the rent.

The next day I thought about how evasive Linda was about the rent and after our conversation I noticed she had the same look on her face when I asked her other questions about money. I suspected Linda was lying to me. Now I want to know why. How does she pay for everything around here.

Linda is my only wife to never complain about wanting to purchase things. I started watching more and asking less questions. When the end of the month came around I asked her before turning out the light to write the apartment owners name and phone number down for me in the morning, it was time to pay the rent.

Linda never mentioned the rent again. My forty-first birthday Linda gave me a watch while we were all over Mama's. Jamal and Tina both said, "Whoah" at the same time when I pulled the watch out of the box. I knew it was expensive by their reaction so I looked it up on the internet, it was a *Seiko Prospex LX*. And yes, it was expensive. And no Linda was not working.

September, I started with the seven-day overtime again but noticed in the mornings my right shoulder would hurt and thought I was sleeping wrong on it.

Linda and I hardly interacted and when we did spend time together, she had an attitude because I did not spend enough time with her. She would say, "Oh I get my turn!" Or "Wow, Linda's turn. Yay!" I grew tired of her nagging.

Our first wedding anniversary I took Linda to brunch the Sunday after our anniversary and she tripped because I stopped to buy her card *before* we went to eat. I went silent. All I wanted to do was get through the brunch and go to work. We ate in silence while she rolled her eyes the whole time.

As soon as we get home I walked into the bedroom to change into my work clothes. Linda follows me and stands in the doorway. She asks, "I just wanna know why do you work so much overtime." I responded, "Linda, Anna makes five children I have to support." Linda folds her arms and says, "I've seen your checks remember, I used to cash them for you. Where does the rest of your money go. You don't buy things."

My reply was, "I have a savings." Linda quickly shoots to me, "How much do you have saved?" My eyebrows go up as I say, "Tell you what." I turned around to face her. "I will tell you how much I have in savings when you tell me how much rent is here. Yeah, how does that sound too you. Fair Linda?"

She turns to leave talking to herself in Spanish. I yell, **"Yeah, just what I thought!"** She came back into the bedroom and closed the door. Linda walks up to me and says, "Who owns this building is none of your business. You live here for free so what's the real reason you want to know who the owner is."

I stood right in front of her and asked sarcastically, "Is he your man? Is that why you do not want me to know who he is. Are *we* living here free because you give the landlord a little once a month." She hauled off and slapped my face!

I grabbed her hand at the wrist and stared at her. For a split second I envisioned shaking her until all of her hair was standing straight up. I wanted to shake some sense into her but I thought, 'Gregory! She is a female, don't dare hurt her!' I pushed her hand away and grabbed my wallet, cell and left for work; mad enough to put my fist through a wall.

The following day Linda came into the bedroom while I dried off from taking my shower. Linda quietly sat on the bed and told me her father was the owner of the apartment building. She collected the money from Donte' and mailed it to her father. I knew she was lying and called her on it. She was shocked I called her a liar. She stood up and said, "Gregory I own this building. Why are you making this rent paying such a big deal?"

I told her, "I am a man. I do not mooch off anyone, especially a female. I work so I can pay for whatever my family needs. That answer your question?" "Yeah. Gregory why are you so angry?" "Because it has taken you this long to tell me the truth. How are we supposed to make this work if every time I ask you a question, you lie to me?" She started shouting, **"Lie, me? You're the one who lies. You slept with Maria right under my nose, In my bed! Me, the liar!"** I went silent.

I dressed and left the house. She threw Maria up in my face after having one-night stands. After that day, every time we argued, I ended up in the guest room. Linda and I were off again, on again until after our second anniversary. I slept in the guest room so much it became my room; most of my clothes were in that closet.

After Anna had her first birthday Linda went back to work but at a credit union close to the house. June first, I had to go to the doctor for my shoulder. It was hurting all of the time and I had to rub ointment on myself to get relief. The pain increased and I was not able to sleep. After several tests the doctor told me my Rotator Cuff was torn and I needed surgery. I optioned for shots and therapy instead.

October rolled around and I could barely move my arm and my neck was increasingly sore. The Thursday before Thanksgiving I went to the surgeon and December seventh, I had the surgery. Linda took off two weeks from work. I came home from the hospital and went to our bedroom and Linda made me very comfortable and I slept until the meds wore off.

The next morning I heard Linda's phone moving on her nightstand, she was in the bathroom. She came into the room and went straight to her phone. She did not know I was awake. I closed my eyes and pretended to be sleep but I peeped at her. She read her phone message and smiled as she returned her phone to the nightstand and left the room. I went to use the bathroom and headed straight to her side of the bed to read the text. Her phone was locked. I watched Linda because I suspected she was cheating on me.

I remembered when I started working week-end overtime Linda complained all the time about us not spending time together. By the time I went to have surgery Linda was no longer complaining. I was relieved. Now I remember Char acting the same way. I began watching Linda's moves. If that surgery were not necessary I never would have had my suspicions. Suspecting your wife is cheating on you and knowing your wife is; is a whole new circumstance.

When what you suspect becomes truth, that is indescribable pain. Man…

After the morning Linda had her phone on lock, I watched her every move. I took mental notes of when she would leave the house and how long she would be gone. She had a routine. Monday, Wednesdays, and Saturdays, she left the house and was only gone for over an hour. Tuesday and Thursdays she would be gone for almost three hours and she always smelled of soap and looked as though she had just taken a shower unlike the other days.

Animosity was mounting fiercely in me towards Linda. If she wants to be with him, just let me know and I will leave! I did not believe anything she said to me and she knew it. The tension was so thick it was visible! We were not speaking *to* one another just *at* one another through Izzy or Anna.

Pedro was staying in his room all of the time with some girl he brought home that could only speak Spanish. Valentines was on a Thursday but when I phoned the local nice restaurants they were booked. So I made reservations for Linda and I on Saturday. We were getting dressed for dinner to celebrate Valentine's. I asked Linda why were we getting dressed so early.

She informed me Pedro was not watching the girls. When I asked why not, she had an attitude and said, "That airhead he bought home wouldn't know what to do if the house caught on fire. I'm not leaving my baby with her." The sitter Linda had taking care of Anna through the week was going to watch Izzy also tonight.

Miss Valorie stays ten minutes away by the four-o-five freeway so I was driving us to Miss Valorie's to drop off the girls. I stopped at the CVS to pick up some mints and parked right next to the handicapped. When I backed out Izzy says, "Oh look Mom, there's Mr. Hall." I noticed Linda had turned to face Izzy in the back seat but she was shaking her head, "NO" at Izzy. When I commented, "Oh yeah. Izzy, who is Mr. Hall." Linda says, "Just a guy who takes his kids to Miss Valorie." Izzy asks, "Who?" Linda turns around and says, "Izzy don't get your dress dirty and watch Anna. Mija ....."

Linda went into speaking Spanish. I looked at Izzy in the rear view mirror and when Linda stops speaking, Izzy says, "Oh, okay." Izzy darts her eyes my way. She sees me looking at her and looks away from me. I was mad enough to cuss Linda out. Having Izzy and Anna in the car made me go silent. But internally what was happening was, I was back hoeing my frustration up onto a volcano.

We dropped off the girls and headed for the restaurant and it was a quiet ride. I am wondering why are we going through the motions? Once we are parked, I open my car door and say, "Linda, hold up." I shut my door; she shuts hers. "Why are we pretending there is a marriage here?" As Linda looks me in the eyes I realize she is a totally different person than who I married.

Linda looks different. She softly says, "I need a father for Izzy and Anna. Gregory you are a good man. You just bury yourself in work as if work is your life." I abruptly say, "I bury myself in work to provide for my family. I want you, Izzy, and Anna to have whatever you need. I want my sons and daughters Janice is raising to go without nothing. I take my responsibilities seriously."

"But Gregory why do you work so much. You have a savings with plenty money." "Linda I hoped to buy a house for us, have a back yard for Izzy and Anna. I would love for them to go outside and be able to play and leave their toys outside. I want all of our children to know each other and be a family. But you lie so much I cannot trust you."

"Gregory all I want is for you to stay home and hold me, us. Anna and Izzy, but saving is more important than being with me. Gregory do you hate me that much?" Linda starts crying. I wait until she stops. "Gregory I am married to you and I am lonely. When I was single I wasn't this lonely. You act as though you're tired of me. Are you tired of me?" "Linda, I do not trust you. Who the hell is Mr. Hall?"

At first I thought she was not going to respond; it took her a minute. She leans towards me and slowly says, "My lover." She sits back and says, "You are my husband and he's my lover. You work and he loves on me, makes me feel like a woman." I raise my hand up. "Alright now! That's enough Linda! Your point is made."

I put on my seat belt and start the car. While backing up I'm thinking, 'Marriage number four is over!' We get to the apartment and I go into the guest room and Linda goes into the bedroom and I hear her talking to Mr. Hall, she is not hiding either. I close the guest room door and wonder where am I going to go. Sam and her three kids are still with Mama and Mr. Mays.

Linda left and I heard her and the girls return, it was eight-thirty.

The next morning I woke up with attending church on my mind. Linda cooked breakfast, I ate and dressed. I kissed Izzy and Anna bye and Izzy asked where was I going. I looked up into Linda's eyes and said, "To church. It has been a while since I have attended." Izzy says, "Poppy, pray for Mom okay. She cry's when you're not home." Izzy hugged me and I dashed out of the house before Linda saw me blinking back tears. Man.

That was February of last year, it is now mid-May. I ended up renting a room at an extended stay hotel. The rates were reasonable enough for me to rent until I found an affordable studio apartment. I filed for divorce a month after I left Linda and we have been civil.

I realize there is not going to be a condo or house for me to purchase, so I bought myself a new burgundy Silverado truck, loaded. I am spending my savings and calling my apartment, "My Place."

Last year in March first, I returned to work however I have been on light duty. My incision developed lesions and treating them took almost nine months before they healed. Light duty affords me quite a bit of time to do some serious thinking about my life and the mistakes I have made.

Having to attend counseling has me thinking about my actions, mainly my motive for why I do what I do. I have also made the conscious decision to leave women alone for now. I *see* women but I don't *look* at them. Know what I mean!

My relationship with The Lord has strengthened. I spend time in The Word, prayer and worship. I have been praying and asking The Lord to show me what I am to do helping build the kingdom of God, but so far I have not heard anything from Him so I am keeping still and obedient to His Word until I do.

~~~~Linda Ariana Torres-Ortiz~~~~

BACKGROUND

Linda stands five feet six inches and has a small waist even after giving birth twice. Her hips are full and her legs are large like her breast. Linda is very comfortable in her female skin and she walks and dresses confirming this.

Being bi-lingual, speaking English and Spanish fluently Linda is mixed with African American and Puerto Rican. She is one lovely lady! What makes Linda stand out is she knows she is beautiful and smart. She likes to flirt, dance, and have fun.

Linda's mother died during childbirth with her brother, he was stillborn. At that time Linda was two years old. Her father sent for his mother from Puerto Rico to come to America and help raise his daughter while he buried himself in work. Having her grandmother rear her, Linda's Puerto Rican roots are very dominate. However Linda has not one clue of the plight of African Americans at all.

On the phone in her Torrance apartment...

"Okay, so this real tall handsome light skinned black guy comes into my credit union and watches me the whole time while he's in line. I don't know anything about black men but this guy is so good looking. I wouldn't mind connecting with him and learning some black history!" Maria replies, "Oh yeah black men are great." There's a beep. "Oh Mija, gotta go, that's my ride. Vaya con Dios."

As I end my call with Maria I'm thinking, 'I really don't know about black people and need to find out about my black heritage. I mean firsthand not just something written in a book.'

I know everything about my father, Louis Gian Ramon Torres coming to America when he was seventeen and only for the sake of working to help his family extend their construction business to America. He met my mother, Ernestine Bailey in Kentucky. She worked the fields and Papi built a smokehouse on the same property she worked. Papi said Mami was very pretty and sweet. She was shy and smart and also taught him English.

They caught the bus to California when they found out she was pregnant with me. They went to Tijuana, Mexico and married. Papi wrote to Puerto Rico about his marriage and me on the way and my grandfather made some connections with other Puerto Ricans he knew in the same area where Papi and Mami lived.

Those connections my grandfather knew made sure Papi worked. I appeared on the scene December third, and because Papi was not a lazy man he moved up in his company. He told me Mami was very content with whatever he bought her and he wanted to give her whatever made her heart skip a beat.

Mami became pregnant again with my brother Axel after I turned two and she died during childbirth. My brother did not make it. Abuela [Grandmother] came to America from Puerto Rico to take care of me. Papi wanted me to grow up in America. He thought Puerto Rico life was too limited for his little girl.

Abuela's name is Gabriela and she writes me once a month still. Mainly to keep me fluent with reading and writing Spanish because we talk on the phone often.

Abuela and I had wonderful times together and growing up I thought everyone had a live-in grandmother. Abuela is very direct and I have never known her to be shy about any subject. Life to her is to be lived and we are to take life as it comes. What else can you do? Abuela would tell me whenever we saw someone sad, "See, can't take life as it comes!" In Spanish to me: "Mira, no puedo tomar la vida como viene!"

After Omar and I married Abuela stayed with Papi until Omar and I shared our sixth month anniversary then she said to me, "His sperm is weak, you should be pregnant. I'm going home and come back if he is able to give you a baby." The eighth month we were married, I became pregnant with Pedro. By then Abuela was too sick to come, she had fallen and fractured her hip. It took her almost a year to recover and by then I knew what to do as a new mother. Abuela phoned me every Sunday morning to give me advice.

Omar and Papi were very close when Omar first arrived to America. After Pedro had his first birthday, Papi became distant with Omar and when I asked Omar what was going on with him and Papi, Omar said Papi was old fashioned when it came to work methods. At that time I had no idea Omar was trying to persuade Papi to smuggle drugs to make lots of money. I found out the hard way after Izabela was born.

I knew we were having a lot of money to spend and when we had our home custom built in Culver City, Omar told me it was cheaper to build from the ground up and besides he was in the contracting business and knew where the discounts were.

Just before Pedro started fourth grade Papi informed me he was moving back to Puerto Rico and asked if I wanted to move with him. I was so upset Papi was leaving us and tried to get me to leave my husband. Little did I know Papi was trying to protect me. After Papi arrived in Puerto Rico he wrote me a letter and enclosed a name and address of a family I was to contact if I needed anything. I thought it strange at the time and figured he and Omar had a falling out. But I did save the letter as instructed.

I had to call the Ochoa family Papi wrote to me about after Omar was arrested. I had no idea Omar was that underhanded until I found out all of the things he was into, including a Karina Gonzales and her sons, Jorge, twelve and Miguel, ten who both look like Omar and Pedro!

I felt as though my whole life with Omar was a lie. I swore to kill him and piss on his bones! My kids and I stayed with the Ochoa family for almost a year. They told me they had to wait for Omar to be sentenced before giving me the money they had for me, nine hundred sixty-thousand dollars. I phoned Papi and he told me to buy myself an apartment building, live in it and get a landlord to collect the rents so no one would know I owned it.

I had half of the top floor in the building converted into my apartment. I have a large master bedroom with its own walk-in closet and bath. Also three large bedrooms and two and a half baths with a laundry room and a large kitchen for me and my kids to live in. No one knew I had the largest apartment in the building because no one in the building visits.

Donte' lives on the first floor and pays half of the price for rent because he has the title of Property

Manager. If there are any problems, Donte' takes care of it and puts all bills in my mail slot. I told Donte' my father owns the building and I keep my father informed of what's going on.

Omar has three brothers and two female cousins he was sending money to in Puerto Rico when he smuggled drugs and they are loyal to Omar and vowed to watch over Pedro during Omar's absence.

When Pedro became a man at twelve years old, Fabian, Ricardo, Angel, and Maria; Omar's cousins, paid us a visit. The guys kept Pedro in his bedroom and spoke Spanish to him for a week straight and when Omar came home at night, he would join them. Pedro was acting like he was the boss of everyone from then on. I had trouble with him cussing out teachers and refusing to do what he was told.

When I went to slap the back of Pedro's head like I always did, he stopped my hand and coldly said to me, "I am a man now Linda Ariana and you will treat me as one from now on!" His eyes were fiery and he scared the crap out of me. He was almost my height but what scared me was the strength he had when he stopped my hand!

Omar and I had long conversations about Pedro. Well not exactly. I did all the fussing about how Pedro needed to respect me. Omar said I had to cut my apron strings. I phoned Papi and told him what happened and insisted Pedro go live with him. Papi told me I had to respect Pedro coming into manhood, but teach him to respect others. Later that evening Papi talked to Pedro for over an hour on the phone and Pedro was scared to resist me after that but he is part Omar and gets very passionate when he has an opinion.

After Omar went to prison, Pedro was acting like my husband instead of my son. He would cuss at me and order me what and what not to do. I bought a baseball bat and told Pedro I would hit his head off and put his body in just poured cement if he disrespected me one more time!

Pedro ran to phone Angel and I guess Angel told him to do as I say, so Pedro called Papi. Pedro has never used foul language around me after that day but Papi and Pedro had private phone conversations weekly until two years ago, Pedro's seventeenth birthday.

I remembered Omar getting fiery on the phone with his business associates but he seldom raised his voice to me. But Omar cussed all the time, I did all of the yelling. I allowed Pedro to be Pedro while raising him, it was him becoming a man I had issues with. Papi was right, I taught Pedro to be respectful of others feelings. Should he go off on someone as passionate as himself, a situation could get turbulent.

Pedro graduated from West Torrance High and wanted to continue the band he and a few friends started in tenth grade. Pedro is very intelligent and I wanted him to attend college and become an architect but he took music in high school and learned to read music. My son is a great guitar player and was set on performing and becoming famous. He never had a grade lower than "B" on his report cards and was qualified to go to a university.

I really thought Pedro was into music for the girls. He and his friends talked about the girls they met all of the time they were at my place. Pedro would close the door when they went into details and I was glad he respected me and Izzy enough to do that.

...I think Mr. Young is trying to approach me and ask me out but is having difficulty finding his words when he steps up to my line at the credit union. I must admit I unbutton my blouse a button lower when I know it's time for his arrival. He is very good looking, walks slow and sexy. Hmm… I would love to sample what he's packing.

Finally we have a movie date. Gregory is even more fine when he cleans himself up. He is about six feet tall, the color of a walnut, thick eyebrows, short haircut with a thin mustache and wears wire rimmed glasses. Gregory has a warm smile; however his personality is one of being serious and he very seldom exposes that beautiful wide smile of his but when he does, it makes you feel like you are his world! He walks real slow and sexy and his long strides when he walks makes him seem very confident about himself.

Gregory not being a smiler but he softens his demeanor when I say something makes me feel important to him. Mr. Gregory Young is a gentleman and makes me feel he can handle the world if it ever came against me. I like being with Gregory.

The movie was sad in a lot of scenes but I used it as an excuse to lay my head on his shoulder. I want him to miss me when we're not together. I like me some Gregory Young.

We went to dinner and I found out Gregory has too many kids for me! All those money orders he makes are child support payments, the man is a baby making machine! I think I'll drop him. He has too much baggage. Three ex-wives, *no para mi!* [not for me!] I made the mistake of giving him my cell number and he calls sounding so sexy its real hard for me to turn him down.

I love the way Gregory holds me when helping me step down off the curb. I find myself thinking of him when we're apart. Oh please let me just spend one night with him and he be on his way, *no para mi!* That's what I kept telling myself when I thought of those money orders.

Gregory took me out to eat, for walks in the park and we sat at my place and listened to music and talked. Every weekend for almost two months we were together and I was loving me some Gregory Young. The end of our first week together I asked where he stayed and he told me about his living arrangements.

He lives with his mother and stepdad in Long Beach. Gregory shared with me about the tension at his mother's because his sister had moved in with her three kids and the kids kept a lot of noise up making it difficult for him to sleep until eleven in the mornings.

The second month we were dating Gregory and I were talking on the phone and he received a call and asked me to hold. I did and hung up because he took so long getting back with me. I'm thinking "ex" right? One of his ex-wives was having it out with him but no, it was his sister. Gregory called me back and he was mad.

You have to understand, Gregory is so low keyed and this was the first time I experienced him being angry. He told me earlier that morning his nephew and niece were going at it and woke him. He was upset because this is a daily occurrence he has told his sister about.

He got out of bed and told the kids to be more respectful of him and his sister, Samantha told him not to yell at her kids. Gregory told her to teach them how to behave and Samantha told him not to tell her how to raise her kids. Their conversation turned into a shouting match between them and his mother had to make Samantha shut up.

Gregory was so upset he couldn't get back to sleep until after ten a.m. and when his clock went off he overslept. He left Samantha a nasty note in her room and she called him when she read it. That was her on the phone he had to set straight.

The next three days Gregory looked for a place to move and that Saturday he wanted me to look with him. When he came to pick me up I took him into my guest room and told him it was available for him. He hesitated responding. Gregory looked me up and down then said, "I don't think that's a good idea. We might get in trouble." I smiled my sexy smile and told him, "Trouble is not always bad you know. Sometimes trouble can be fun, exciting, maybe even memorable. Who knows!"

His response was, "Let me think on it." I said, "Besides, how much trouble can come about in ninety days?" The next week he and Samantha were at it again about her kids and when he shared it with me I told him to just move in and look for a place while staying here. By Friday Gregory told me he would pay me rent while staying here. It would only be for three months. I wanted to have sex with Gregory. I love being with him he's so attentive and the man is sexy!

While dating I flirted with him every chance I had but Gregory was still a gentleman. We were staring at each other for longer lengths of time before he left my place but he remained a gentleman. I was fantasizing about us being together every night and going crazy when Gregory put his long strong arms around me. So yeah, I wanted him to move in with me for my own reason.

Gregory finally agreed to move in for only ninety days and the next morning he moved his clothes into the guest room. Until Gregory moved in we had only pecked each other on the cheek, like I said he's a genuine gentleman. Gregory moved into the guest room where Maria stays. I figured when she comes to California she can bunk with me. Besides once we share our love I'll kick him to the curb. That many ex-wives has to come with drama.

Why does Gregory act so serious as though his move-in is strictly business. I'm going to show him!

Now that Gregory's moved in we hardly see one another until Sundays. He works a lot of hours and only took off weekends to take me out. The third week he moved in, I set my alarm on my phone to be awakened when he arrives at four a.m.

After Gregory showers I go into his room telling him that I'm looking for something. This happened three nights in a row and Gregory finally caught on and told me he had just what I was looking for.

Ay Dios Mio!! [Oh My God!] Do I understand why the man has so many babies! I thought throwing Gregory Young to the curb would be most appropriate but now after sharing our love, I never want him to leave. I have a dilemma now.

I don't want Pedro or Izzy to see me living with a man. All of my men in my past have had their own places and none of them had six kids. Pedro will tell his uncle Angel and Omar will find out and there's no telling what he will have done to Gregory. Omar can have two children outside our marriage but me sleeping with another man living with me, Omar will not swallow that pill without choking.

Also, I don't want Izzy to think it's not wrong to live with men you're not married to. My head was in a spin with my dilemma every day and every night I couldn't wait for Gregory to come home.

Even though Gregory and I used protection, we had a few accidents with it and I ended up pregnant. I told him we needed to get married but he was still working on his divorce. It took nine months for his divorce to finalize. When Gregory's divorce was final, I was four months pregnant and we went to City Hall.

I just wanted my baby to be legitimate and not some bastardo. I knew Gregory and I were from two different sides of the track but I am half black and thought we could have fun and I would learn a little more about my roots on my mother's side. Gregory was very helpful filling me in on black culture and we didn't argue a lot but, he was hardly home.

Whenever Pedro came into the house, Gregory's veins would get very large in his neck and he would look at me and shake his head while leaving the room and slamming the door to our bedroom. Gregory thought Pedro was too disrespectful and he wanted to make Pedro respect me. Gregory would yell at Pedro and tell him, **"She is *my* wife and you *will not* speak to my wife that way!"** Pedro would reply, **"She's my mother and if you don't like it, leave!"**

Pedro would walk up to me sometimes when we disagreed and Gregory would step in front of Pedro and when Pedro backed down, Gregory would look at me in disgust. When Gregory and I would go to our bedroom, he would tell me I was allowing Pedro to be disrespectful. Then Gregory and I would go at it. However Gregory and Izzy bonded, but Gregory has that way with females. The man is so gentle and thoughtful; when he's home that is!

Maria busted in on us early one morning in November, she has always had a key to my place. Gregory didn't like the fact she could show up anytime and disrupt our lives like she did. I assured him I would have a talk with Maria about being considerate now that I have a husband living here.

Maria agreed to respect Gregory but wondered why he didn't tell her to her face. She called him, "Cobarde!" [Coward] every time Gregory would leave the room where Maria and I talked. I really thought she didn't like him because he was a stranger, you know, not Puerto Rican.

It was after Anna was born I found out the truth. I still get a little feelings of hurt when I think of how close Maria and I were. I have never had a sister and Maria was the closest I had to one. I loved our time together and treasured every moment. Gregory was distant with me the last two months of my pregnancy.

He has a high sex drive and I thought his being distant was his way of handling having to abstain so I allowed the distance between us. When I came home from having Anna he was so attentive but he didn't try to sneak and fool around when he slid into bed with me. He never held me or even held conversation.

After almost three weeks of him slipping into bed I approached him. He pushed my hands away and acted like his mind was somewhere besides where he was; lying beside me. I thought he might be scared I would get pregnant again so I mentioned we could use protection. He pretended he was tired but he was aroused and kept tossing and turning until he got out of the bed and I heard him snoring on the couch.

The following week he texted me, not phoned me, texted! Mr. Mays had taken a bad fall and his mother couldn't lift him so he was staying in Long Beach for a week to help her. Mr. Mays is tall and big like Gregory and Mrs. Mays is shorter than I am. So I thought he was being sweet helping his mother.

Just before Gregory was due back home he texted me again. Jamal and Tina were in a fender bender and he was staying with Jamal and Tina to help Jamal because Tina was returning to work. I thought, 'Okay, maybe a few more days and Gregory will be home and ready for us to fool around.'

Gregory didn't come home and the next morning he texted his truck was acting up and he took it to the shop, he would see me in a few days. Gregory had been texting me every day asking if we were all doing alright and signed off with smiley faces. But when the text about his truck came, my eyebrow lifted. Hmm, this is one too many excuses.

I thought Gregory was tired of me sexually. I thought about him not responding at all to my teasing and flirting. I thought maybe he was having an affair with someone at his job because he worked so much.

My mind went back to when I texted him the doctor gave me a clean bill of health after my six-week check-up. Gregory didn't respond like he should have after us not making love for two months. Yep! I know it's another woman. I was so wounded. Now I know Gregory has a mistress. I cried as I imagined Gregory satisfying another woman in bed!

While tears were drizzling down my face, I went into our closet and rambled through Gregory's things. Then I went through every drawer of his. Nothing. So, I went into the guest room and started going through the drawers looking for a phone number, address, or some clue as to who this woman was that had my husband not wanting me anymore. I came across a prescription for Maria. I thought it strange she never mentioned she had an infection.

Maria is three years older than I am and has taught me how to meet guys and size them up. I looked up to her and she's very experienced sexually. She lives in Florida and travels back and forth to

Puerto Rico. Maria taught me the ropes of dating and having one-night stands.

I know Maria keeps protection on her at all times so her having an STD never entered my mind, I'm thinking kidney infection. I kept the prescription bottle in my hand so when she returned from the grocery store I was going to ask her what was going on with her.

When Maria walked in the door I was standing in the doorway to the kitchen, she looked down at my hand and when she saw the prescription bottle she walked towards me and asked who had I talked too. I asked what did that have to do with her taking this medication. She put the grocery bag on the counter and told me some guy gave her something and snatched the bottle from my hand. I asked what was it and could anyone else get it, I have a newborn and want to protect her.

Maria told me to calm down and what it was she had and started preparing dinner. I went to look up what Maria had and when I saw it could only be transferred sexually I felt better. I still had this question in the back of my mind, 'Why didn't Maria tell me? We share everything…'

I ate and Maria asked what was wrong with me. I told her Gregory texted me with a lie about his truck. I had been keeping Maria abreast of Gregory's texts so she understood I was now suspicious he had a mistress. I had to find out who she was. Maria suggested I call Gregory. I decided to call his mother instead and find out if he were in fact even in Long Beach.

Why did Mrs. Mays hesitate answering me when I asked if Mr. Mays was better? I had the feeling Gregory wasn't over his mother's at all, he was with some woman. I pushed the speaker on my cell and walked into the kitchen and let Maria hear Gregory's mother. When I inquired about Jamal being better after his accident, Mrs. Mays stuttered and hurried off the phone. Maria and I looked at one another. I knew then it wasn't my imagination.

I ended my conversation with Mrs. Mays and told Maria, "He's laid up with some desvergonzada [hussy]. I just gave birth to his daughter and he's moved on with someone else." I broke down crying I was so angry and hurt. Maria has never taken up for Gregory and when she consoled me by saying the both of us should go out like we used too. I thought, I need to move on, since Gregory already has. I agreed with Maria to going out Friday night.

I left Gregory alone. I didn't text or call him. I figured if he didn't love me anymore I was not going to force myself on him. Secretly I was hoping Gregory would call or text me. I wanted him to care about me.

The next day was Thursday, I wrapped Anna up and Maria and I took Izzy to school then went shopping for me an outfit for tomorrow. I felt like a woman again. Shopping was just what the doctor ordered for me. Friday night we went to a new club in Redondo Beach and met two guys.

We went to the hotel close to the club and half hour later Maria texted she was waiting in the lobby. When I arrived in the lobby I asked if he was a three-minute man but she didn't think what I said was funny. Maria was in a mood so I left her alone.

Saturday I told Maria I was ready to hit another club and she gave me a strange look. When I asked if she were ready to talk about last night, she snapped at me, "None of your business! In Spanish. We went to one of our old hangouts and Maria was distant and snappy with me. After she had a lot to drink she became quiet.

Maria has always been animated. I didn't know what was going on with her. Two guys came and sat with us and I was flirting with the guy sitting next to me and Maria cut her eyes at me. I decided I was going to have me some fun. It felt good being wanted even if my husband didn't want me. Jose' was ready to leave and Maria and Enrique' followed us.

We went to a nice hotel and again Maria texts forty-five minutes later she was waiting for me. This time during the cab ride to my car, I asked what was going on with her. She scolded me in Spanish telling me I had a husband and was acting like there was no infant at home needing me!

I thought this had something to do with her being on medication and drinking alcohol. Why is she upset with me? Is it because she was limited being on medication and I wasn't. I left her alone until Monday afternoon.

I asked if she wanted to go eat after we get Izzy from school and she snapped at me again. I stood over her as she sat on the couch and told her to tell me what was going on in her head! Maria jumped up and turned to me and yelled, **"Your husband forced himself on me and he's the one that gave this disease to me! Linda you need to be checked to make sure he hasn't given it to you and god forbid something is wrong with Anna Marie!"**

I freaked out! My beautiful baby girl might be sick because of her un-faithful baby making father! I ran to my room and undressed Anna. I went over every inch of my baby, then, I phoned Pedro.

Making this phone call, I knew I was giving my son permission to do to Gregory what he's wanted to do the day Gregory entered my life. I told Pedro Gregory forced himself on Maria and now she has some disease and Gregory may have given it to me and Anna. Pedro was so glad now he had permission to jump Gregory. I told him Gregory would kill him, he had better get some help. While I'm talking to Pedro Maria tells me I need to go to the hospital and take Anna! I became enraged! If my baby is sick; I will kill Gregory Young myself!

I told Pedro to meet us at the hospital over on Lomita. I cursed Gregory all the way to the hospital, I was fuming. When we were called to the back, Maria said she would phone Angel so he could have his guys find Gregory and take good care of him, she went outside to get a connection.

Pedro arrived at the hospital with two of Ricardo's boys. Maria came back into the room and a nurse took blood from me. I was beyond shocked when Gregory entered the room where we were waiting for the doctors to examine me. The scene that took place, watching Gregory lose it and him get beat down. All I could do was cry. I was half glad he was getting hit but at the same time, I didn't want him hurt. After the police took him away I asked myself, 'how did Gregory know where we were?'

I asked Maria what did Angel say when she phoned him and she lied. I have been around Maria too many times when she has lied; I know that look. I thought about her prescription bottle having a Florida label and Maria calling Gregory a coward. She came here taking that medicine. Now her calling my husband a coward has a different spin on it. She was trying to get to him, not him trying to get to her.

With an attitude I ask, "Maria how did Gregory know we were here?" She could tell by my tone I had her number. She stared at me then said, "You kept telling me how great he was in bed. Anyways he was wrong for you. You see he couldn't be faithful." I raised up and told her to get out! I swear I could have killed Maria with my eyes. She went to the front waiting area. After the doctor examined me I sat in the front and we waited for Pedro to get stitches.

Pedro had Maria drop him off at a friends and she took us home. As soon as we walked in the door I told her to get out of my house and to never come back. I told her to forget I existed and to leave all keys she had of mine on the kitchen table.

After I put Anna in her bed, I went into the guest room and jumped up in Maria's face and grabbed her hair and pushed her down on the bed. We wrestled until we ended up on the floor fighting. I scratched her face up and kicked her while she used her fist hitting me in my face and pushing me off her.

I felt energy inside me giving me strength I never knew I had. Maria wiggled herself away from me as I caught my breath. She slid away from me and stood up. As I stood up plunging myself into her, she stepped aside and spit on the floor and told me good riddance! I was so startled. Spitting is indication of death to the person.

As I looked at Maria I saw a different person, not my sister. She walked over to the closet while keeping her eyes on me and threw her suitcase on the bed. I realized she was packing so I left the room and stood in the kitchen. I began pacing the floor thinking about Gregory and how Maria was constantly in my ear about him being a coward and realized Maria wanted Gregory from day one.

I heard her leave the guest room and turned to watch her pull out her phone and call Angel. She raised her voice for me to hear her tell him make sure Gregory was dead when they find him.

I was mad enough to murder Maria. I thought of spending the rest of my life in prison. And Izzy and Anna not having a mother to be here, just as I had no mother to be here for me. I turned to get a knife out of the drawer. Maria heard the drawer open and told me she was leaving.

As she hurried to the front door, Maria says; "You always thought you were better than Omar and his family. Hell you're not even full-blooded Puerto Rican. You have never known what a hard time is!" As I plunged towards her, I jabbed the knife at her. She slipped out of the door before I could cut her. I was out of my mind with anger and heard myself cussing in Spanish, loud enough for her to hear me. Then I broke down and cried. I was so mad!

I leaned against the door and slowly slid down to the floor, I began to tremble.

The only sister I have ever had never liked me and I didn't see it. I remembered how Gregory never cared for Maria. Gregory! I got up and called Mrs. Mays and told her what happened and for her to keep Gregory away from the apartment for a week. I know she was glad to hear that, she never liked me.

I heard a text come to my phone and when I read it, it was from Maria; **"Your keys are at your front door. I did you a favor. He's not one of us. Take care half breed. Ha, ha!"**

So, she thinks I wasn't one of them because of my mother. I cried so hard. My heart was torn I hurt so bad. Today I lost my sister and my husband.

I couldn't sleep that night thinking about Gregory and him sleeping with Maria. Those thoughts made me remember Omar being unfaithful and fathering two sons with the same woman. I laid in bed thinking how much I trusted Gregory thinking he was a gentleman, not capable of what Omar was. I realized Maria had instigated their sex but had Gregory loved me and held our marriage sacred, he would not have given in to Maria's advances.

The theory of a man cheats when a wife doesn't do what she's supposed to in the bedroom is not always true. Then I remembered my motive getting with Gregory was to have a one-night stand. I had to admit our marriage should have never happened and I only married because I wanted Anna to be legitimate.

I cried so much as I accepted my responsibility for marrying Gregory with the wrong motive. Maybe I was getting what I deserved.

I spent the next few days inside the house. My face was badly bruised and swollen from Maria hitting me. I did a lot of thinking about our marriage and called Gregory, apologized, and told him very sincerely, how sorry I was. All he said was, "Me too." A week later Gregory came to give me money for Anna and to see her. We ended up getting back together and decided to start all over.

I was truthful with Gregory about my one-night stands but I never should have told him. He couldn't handle it. He could have sex with Maria and I handled that without making a trust issue out of it.

I think because I had sex with another man, Gregory never forgave me. Our relationship wasn't stable. He would ask me questions as if he were interrogating me. We would argue and he would sleep in the guest room more than he slept in our bed. Can you believe he had the nerve to tell me I was a liar and he couldn't trust me, me, the faithful wife!

Gregory worked all of the time and said he was saving his money so he could buy us a house but I felt he was saving to build his savings. Gregory liked nice things, he just believed in paying cash for purchases. If any one of his kids needed anything, Gregory came up with it right away and he paid cash.

He never made time anymore to talk about our future. I complained to him constantly how we never spent any quality time together. We didn't go out just the two of us. I began to feel lonely as though Gregory wasn't missing being with me. Abuela told me I was bored and should take up sewing or quilting.

I decided to return to work. So after Anna became a year old I started working close to the house. When I first went back to work I thought I had made a mistake and was going to quit when Izzy started back to school. I thought about working on her school campus to keep from being bored. That was my plan, however Anna was enjoying being at the little school I had her in and Izzy attended after school.

I was referred to this lady, Miss Valorie who lived just on the other side of the four-o-five freeway from where we lived. Miss Valorie has a small daycare in her single-story home. She also taught the children and I really was sold on that. Izzy did her homework there and actually tutored two of the younger children to memorize their alphabet.

Anna was the only toddler there and Miss Valorie promised me she wouldn't take another toddler while Anna was there. Anna was talking more after she went to Miss Valorie. Miss Valorie had a fourteen-year-old daughter and a son, eleven. Both of them loved Anna and never allowed her feet to touch the floor when they were home. Anna was loved and she was learning there.

When August came around I thought twice about quitting my job so I told myself, 'I'll work until Christmas. Maybe I'll save my money and surprise Gregory with a trip to Cancun while he's off during the shutdown, then I'll quit.' But…

Being the last hired I was elected to early lunch, eleven to twelve was my lunch time. I would go across the street every day to the local cafe and sit at the counter and have my lunch while reading a book. August was a scorcher and I was wearing a lot of sleeveless dresses and no nylons.

One day I ordered a vanilla shake with my order and was engrossed in my book. When I picked up my shake without paying attention to the container being full and without a top, I spilled milk shake on my chest.

I jumped up off my seat and at the same time Lyle Hall who was sitting next to me, jumped up and grabbed a handful of napkins and handed them to me. As I laid the book down on the counter I quickly glanced up at him and thanked him while taking the napkins from his hand.

After I cleaned myself, I looked at Mr. Hall and said, "Well, I've had my bath!" He looked me up and down and said, "So delighted I was able to watch." We both laughed and he extended his hand out while saying, Lyle." Our eyes locked as I replied, "Linda." Lyle has a deep voice, a sexy deep voice. We shook hands and I felt myself blush. I have always been a flirt but Lyle; Lyle was my match. The way he slowly took in my body made me feel like a woman, a wanted woman.

Abuela raised me to be feminine. She taught me a female was made for a male and women are to be honored and proud we are a man's gift. I like being a woman. Dressing in sexy clothes and being pretty and feminine.

I was missing Gregory. He was working so much. I was starting to feel more like a means of relief for him sex wise and not loved and appreciated. Add lonely on top of the list and now you have set the alarm on the clock labeled,"Affair." It's just a matter of time before it goes off!

Realizing I like the way Lyle looked at me, I immediately felt embarrassed. Feeling like a woman appreciated by a man that is not my husband. I sat down and picked my book up but I was peeking a look at Lyle. When I stood up to leave, he said bye. I didn't answer nor did I look back at him. Lyle was sitting to my left so I knew he noticed my wedding ring.

After that day I went out of my way to spend every moment I could with Gregory. I would get him worked up every night after he climbed into bed but after the fourth night, he said he was tired. His words were cold enough, but it was even worse when he turned his back to me…

I fought off thoughts of Gregory not loving me. I pulled myself close behind Gregory and he said, "I'm tired." I said, "Gregory do you still want me?" He sighed and said, "I'm tired Linda. Let's not start the drama." As I scooted over to my side of our bed I thought I am missing love in our marriage. Why am I doing all the work to keep this marriage together?

I was getting up an hour earlier cooking Gregory pancakes, hash browns with biscuits. Foods he liked. I would make meals at night for him and leave notes on his pillow. He would leave responses; "That was good, I liked the extra sour cream." Or "Thanks for the superb breakfast." I was going online and learning to cook greens and macaroni and cheese for him on Sundays.

All I wanted was for Gregory to want to be with me and for him to hold me, wrap his arms around me. I felt so complete in his arms. All I received were notes. It takes two to make a marriage and all I want is for him to want to spend time with me. He thinks its drama, drama! I'm done!

I noticed Lyle every day after my spill and after a few weeks of saying "Hello," to one another, Ella placed my check in front of me and Lyle reached for it at the same time I did. Lyle held his hand over mine while saying, "I have this. You have a good day." His voice mesmerized me. His hand was so warm and his touch was gentle. I kept my hand under his for almost a minute.

It was obvious Lyle was holding my hand and we were staring at one another so I slowly moved my hand away. Very softly I told him "Thank you." I went into my wallet and left three dollars on the counter for Ella while glancing quickly at Lyle, I left. While opening the door to leave, I glanced at Lyle. He was eyeing my body. I had to fan myself before crossing the street.

Lyle is the color of milk chocolate, maybe five feet-nine and has light brown eyes, curly hair and is clean shaven. His deep dimples in his cheeks are revealed when he speaks and smiles. Lyle has an oval face and the body of a football player and he's always on his cell phone reading. We carried on conversations about the weather, what we each did for a living, general topics. After Lyle paid my bill I never paid for another meal, even the tip.

Lyle told me he was separated from his wife of seven years and common law for almost seven which makes their relationship almost fourteen years. Eboni was his second and last wife. They have a son together, Kyle, twelve years old and Lyle knows his son needs his father so he spends Monday and Wednesday's with his son and they spend weekends together.

Kyle was playing football with a local league. When Lyle found out Gregory worked second shift, he invited me out to observe his son's practices. I told him I was a married woman and he asked if I were happy. His question caught me off guard. I felt myself blinking back tears. I grabbed my wallet and almost ran across the street to my office. I still had twenty minutes before my lunch was over so I went into the break room and thought about being happy.

Gregory is a good responsible man and a caring father but he can be so distant. Omar had his mistress on the side but he still was loving to me. I was so confused after Lyle asked me that question. Am I happy?…

When Gregory came home that night I waited until he showered and turned the light on. I told him we need to talk. Of course he wanted to talk in the morning when I got up. But I knew we wouldn't talk so I told him we were going to talk now; our marriage was in trouble. He grunted as he slid up against the headboard.

Gregory stared straight ahead and I asked if he was listening. He said with an attitude, "I am up, aren't I. Linda what is it now with you." "Now! You act as though this is a regular thing with me. Gregory we need to spend time together…" He cut me off. "This again!" He threw back his covers and I knew he was off to the guest room. As I fought back tears I thought, 'Okay, he could care less.' As he shut the door, I turned off the light and made my mind up; Izzy, Anna and I are going to a football practice and I am going to find out how good a kisser Lyle Hall is!'

The next morning Gregory was complaining about his shoulder and asked if there was any pain ointment around the house. I didn't want to care, but he is Anna's father. I was so angry at him yet I longed to be in his arms. When I said, "Gregory." To him, he sighed. That was it. He doesn't want to hear anything

I have to say. I could have wanted to talk about the weather for all he knew.

That day I came to the realization that Gregory Young cares nothing about my feelings whatsoever. "What is it Linda." "Nothing. Are you working overtime tonight?" "No, my shoulder is hurting. I will come home after my shift is over." He asked about Izzy and Anna. I finished getting ready for work and he went back to bed. I never bothered Gregory after that, Lyle consumed my idle thoughts from that day on.

I found out when and where the football practices were being held and took Izzy and Anna with me to the park. Izzy is very observant and I had to keep my conversations with Lyle very cordial which was beginning to get more difficult as the time we spent with each other increased. We were both wanting to spend private time together.

I was to the place of fantasizing about being with Lyle in my spare time, which I had a lot of at night. We began talking on our cells for hours at a time. Gregory was having pain in his shoulder and the overtime stopped. He worked from three to eleven-thirty and would come straight home. Most nights I would be in bed but on the phone with Lyle so Gregory coming home early gave Lyle and I less time to talk.

A week before Thanksgiving, Lyle and I agreed we would spend the day together at his house. I took Izzy and Anna to Miss Valorie then went to the nearby park, called in sick and waited until Gregory went to work then went home. I took a bubble bath and fixed myself up. I put my black Teddy on under my dress and off I went to Lyle's place. We spent our first time together at his small Condo in Redondo Beach.

Lyle is a Mortgage Loan Officer and has a sharp eye for details. He was very attentive but Lyle is not your quiet gentle type. He's vocal, outspoken, and flirty. I only became close to him out of loneliness and he knew it from the start. I wasn't in the dark either, I knew he was not looking for a wife so our relationship worked.

The only problem I had with Lyle was, he would flirt with other women in my face and I felt disrespected and, I told him so. We would argue and he would remind me I was flirty also and our relationship wasn't going to end in matrimony so what was the big deal? It was those times when Lyle would say things like that to me that I felt criticism consume me. I would think, 'I'm a married woman who has a lover. Even my lover wants other women. What's wrong with me?'

I would take long looks at myself in the mirror to see what men saw, what Omar, Gregory and Lyle didn't desire exclusively. At night I would lay in bed and evaluate my relationship with Gregory. My conclusion was my husband would rather be at work than home with me, his wife. So, for me to feel like a woman loved and wanted, Gregory was forcing me to take a lover. I had to tell myself this regularly to keep myself together.

I would be cordial to Gregory, cook and do laundry for him and when I went to be with Lyle I had not one ounce of guilt because I was keeping my end of the marriage up. It was Gregory who wasn't keeping up his. I am not going to beg a man to want to be with me. When Gregory and I were together he was distant, always in a book or staring into space.

I would have divorced Gregory but he was good with Izzy and Anna. I felt a sense of security when Izzy would say, "Poppy Young" or when Anna would say, "Daddy." I felt as if we were a family. My daughters need that.

Gregory had to have surgery it could no longer be put off so I took two weeks off to care for him. I thought he would be full of pain killers and Lyle and I would still be able to keep our times together because Lyle only lived fifteen minutes away.

Gregory was alert three days after his surgery and was reading everything he could get his hands on. Lyle and I still kept our lunch times at his place and because I was on vacation at work, the extra time we had was great.

Gregory being home made it tense around the house and that tenseness intensified when Pedro came home. Pedro was bringing his girls to the house and with his music being loud and the sounds of the girls giggling coming out of Pedro's room I knew Gregory would blow like a volcano; so I would watch Gregory.

Gregory would grunt, throw his book down or tell Izzy and Anna to go to their room for a while then Gregory would go bang on Pedro's door and yell for him to turn the music down. Most times Pedro would turn the volume up or, open his door and he and Gregory would verbally go at it. I didn't want Gregory to hit Pedro so I ended up standing in the middle of them.

After Gregory began therapy for his shoulder at the clinic, it was less tension at the house but I would talk to Pedro. I told him Gregory has a point in telling him to be considerate of the rest of us living in the house. Pedro would always say, "Then *he* can move out!"

When I spoke to Gregory about not being so defensive towards Pedro, he would tell me I was protecting Pedro and Pedro was a man and should be living in his own place. The first few times we had this conversation, I added, "Like you." That led to him wanting to pay the rent and how big of a liar I am. So I started rolling my eyes at him and walking away.

Pedro started drinking more and I tried to get him to talk to me but he would always look at me and walk away or leave the house. One night while Gregory was at Cloverleaf, Pedro's lady friend came running out of his room screaming. She was in her underwear, standing in my bedroom doorway. She had her dress in one hand and shoes and cell in her other hand. Izzy and Anna were on my bed. Izzy was reading to Anna and I was folding laundry.

The girl was screaming, **"He's not breathing! He's not breathing!"** I ran to Pedro's room and he was stretched out on his back on his bed. I thought he wasn't breathing and jumped on top of him and pushed down on his stomach. I was going to give him mouth to mouth when he came too, waving his arms around. I realized he has passed out from being drunk and I jumped on the floor and slapped his face!

Pedro sat up in the bed and with slurred speech says to me, "Oh, so you *can* fight!" I stood looking at him, he was not my son, he was not Pedro Venturo Torres Ortiz. I was looking at a total stranger!

Standing in Pedro's doorway was his lady friend. I watched as she pulls her dress down and steps into her shoes saying, "I'm outta here. I don't need this!" She grabbed her purse and cell phone and left with her indignant attitude. She yanks her dress down over her butt. Izzy and Anna were standing in Pedro's room and I didn't want them to see him like he was. So I took them to their room and helped them get ready for bed.

Izzy asked what was wrong with Pedro, he was acting strange lately. I asked what did she mean? She said Pedro was drinking a lot and when she asked him any questions, he was mean to her. Oh yeah! Now I'm going to let Pedro have it, upsetting Izzy! Before covering my little angels, I heard the door shut. Thinking it was Gregory returning home, I kissed them and turned out the light.

I finished my laundry alone. Pedro had left the house. Now I'm worried about Pedro driving under the influence. Gregory came in after nine p.m. and he was silent. He went to the guest room and I stood in the doorway and asked how the kids were. Without looking at me he says, "Fine."

I watched as Gregory grabbed his book and pounced on the bed never looking my way. As I walked away from him I thought this is no marriage, I am a statistic now. I'm one of those women who stays with her husband for the sake of the kids. As I looked for my phone to call Lyle I was wondering how long Lyle would be in my life.

I talked to Lyle about how I was feeling regards to my so-called marriage. I heard myself say, "Gregory and I have been together almost two years and we don't talk to one another. He and Pedro are always at each other. Gregory doesn't trust me and says that's why we don't talk, I'm the world's biggest liar.

We don't even share a bank account. He sleeps in the guest room all the time now and we haven't had relations since last year in October." Lyle listened and when I finished talking he asked why don't I leave Gregory.

I told Lyle the truth about me having family money and owning this apartment building. I told him after Anna was born Gregory wanted to pay the rent and after several months I told him I own the building. Since then Gregory refers to me as a liar.

Lyle paused before saying, "Linda I am not criticizing you, but, I have known you for only four months and you have told me everything about yourself. Have you told Gregory everything you have told me?" I answered yes, but I realized at that moment I hadn't told Gregory everything about myself. I changed the subject. I told Lyle about how Pedro was giving me a hard time. After Lyle and I talked, I asked myself why have I kept things from Gregory?

After hours of analyzing, I realized I never planned on marrying Gregory from the start of our relationship. I have always felt we were never going to be until death do us part. I want a marriage but after Omar deceiving me, I really don't trust men. My relationship with Lyle works because we both know we will never have a future together.

I wept while facing that.

Well, Valentine's Day was coming and I didn't expect anything from Gregory. Lyle and I celebrated it during our lunch. The next morning Gregory mentioned Valentine was yesterday and if I wanted he would make a reservation for us Saturday before he goes to work, I agreed. Saturday I woke feeling as though we were going through the motions and it was getting pretty pitiful. I felt as though we were an acting cast and it was time to perform. Little did I know it would be Gregory and my last performance.

Gregory stopped for something at the CVS Lyle frequents and when Izzy saw Lyle getting out of his car to go into the store, she remembered his name and pointed him out to me. Gregory asked who was he and I said he was one of the fathers who sends his kid to Miss Valorie. Izzy promptly asked "who?" I had to tell her in Spanish Gregory doesn't know any of the kids at Miss Valorie's so don't mention it to him, he wouldn't understand who we were talking about.

But Gregory was suspicious and before getting out of the car at the restaurant he asked who Lyle was… and I told him. I told Gregory that Lyle was my lover. He sat there as if he didn't care one bit. We never made it inside the restaurant for dinner. Our so-called marriage was done. No more scripts to go over.

Gregory left the next morning headed for church and came home later that evening and moved most of his clothes out. The next day he came over after I came home from work and took the rest of his things and asked if he could come pick up Izzy and Anna on Sundays after church and take them to Long Beach to have dinner with him and his family. I agreed.

As Gregory turned to leave, he stopped when he put his hand on the doorknob he asked with his back to me, "Linda was I such a horrible lover?" I uttered a soft, "No." As I walked over and stood next to him. I added, "You are a great lover. Maybe that's why I wanted to spend so much time with you. I love being in your arms. Gregory, you have a mistress and her name is McDonnell Douglas. She gives you money and that's more important to you than holding your wife."

He looked at me and said, "Thanks. You were a good wife and mother. Maybe too good to Pedro. You do know grown men work!" He lifts his hand up and says, "Okay. I'll leave that alone." He left.

Gregory texted me every Saturday evening informing me he would be by to get the girls tomorrow. They love being with him and his family. The first Sunday Izzy came home talking for over a half hour about the fun she had playing outside in the back yard with Anna and how everyone tells her how pretty she and Anna are. That night I went to bed and after talking to Lyle I cried and didn't know why.

It took me talking to Abuela a few times for me to figure out… I miss family. I began spending time soul searching and concluded after two marriages and three kids, I need a mother.

I began asking Abuela more questions about my mother and after a few months of questioning her, she told me before hanging up, "It's time to talk to your father. You need to know who your mother was. She's a part of you and you need to be completed now." I started crying as I shook my head "Yes" over the phone. Abuela knows exactly what I need. I wanted to go through the phone to hug and kiss her.

I thought deeply of the words Abuela had spoken to me and realized she was right. After a few weeks of tossing around in my head how I was going to confront Papi about my mother, I phoned him. I told him I had two failed marriages and need to know about my mother. He said he understood and he needed a few days to compile all the information I would need. April first Papi phoned me with a phone number and told me it was a good number, he had spoken to my mother's sister, Bertha Lee.

I called my Aunt Bertha. She was so happy to hear from me. She became really serious and asked if I were alright. As tears streamed down my face I told her in a trembling voice; I need to know my roots and was thinking of making a trip to Kentucky. She didn't hesitate to tell me, "Come home chile. You have a place to stay. We take care of family down here. Just let me know when you are coming and how you are coming so I can pick you up. Suga we can't wait to get our arms around you and your babies." I broke down. It felt so good to hear those words. This half breed was on her way to Kentucky.

I told Pedro he could stay here in California if he wanted I was going to get some history about his grandmother and didn't know how long I would be gone. He told me he would stay here and take care of the house. I put in my two weeks notice and told Lyle my plans. He wished me the best and told me my grandmother was right, I need to know who I am so I can be the best of who I am.

After Pedro knew Gregory was gone for good he stayed away from home like before Gregory moved in. We hardly saw him but I would hear when he came home to get more clothes and when he left the house.

Two days after the school year ended Izzy, Anna and I left for Kentucky. Pedro came home early that morning with his clothes in a bag and said he was leaving with us. He was mad so I left him alone. I decided to take the train to Kentucky. That way Izzy could see some of the states and it would give me time to get my speech ready for my family I didn't know.

We had a beautiful trip seeing the country. The first day on the train Pedro slept most of the time and the next day he sat next to me and put Anna in his lap. After an hour riding he leaned into me and asked, "Linda, did you know who my father really was when you were married to him?"

"Yes Pedro, we had an arranged marriage, but we dated for almost a year before we married." Almost whispering Pedro says, "Well hold onto your hat. Omar had a wife and family in Hermosa Beach and I have two brothers!" He looks my face over. I'm thinking he has found out about his father and thinks I don't know.

I tell him the whole story of Omar and his dealings. Pedro was shocked I knew. "Why didn't you tell me I had brothers?" "Pedro she was a mistress not a wife, I was Omar's only wife, me, your mother. Your two brothers are bastards. Besides Omar cheated on me, not you. He loves you and always will. You are his first-born son, you Pedro Venturo Torres Ortiz."

With raised voice, Pedro says to me, "Linda, I have a right as a man to know my family history just as you do. From now on you will not keep any secrets from me. You understand?" With an attitude I come back with, "Pedro what I understand is, you are the son, I am the mother and, I don't care if you become a grandfather, I am your mother. Do *you* understand!" My voice was getting high pitched.

"You still don't accept my manhood." I sigh and turn to him saying, "Pedro, you must realize a man respects his mother. In fact it takes a real man to do that." I grabbed his neck and pulled him down towards me and kissed his cheek. When I let go of him I said, "Mijo!" After a few minutes I asked, "Pedro when did you find out?"

"Aunt Maria was texting me after she left California and told me you were a half breed and my brothers are whole Puerto Rican because my father and their mother are whole Puerto Rican, you aren't. Why would she say that about you, you were like sisters." "Pedro, I found out Maria called Gregory "coward" because he fought off her advances."

Pedro's eyes became so big while he says, "But she said he forced himself on her." I instantly replied, "Mentiras! [Lies!] And, you still have some growing-up to do my son." The look on his face let me know he was in shock. I added, "Pedro, I will love you always. Even while you yet grow into the man I know your father and I will be very proud of."

His smile he gave me, made my heart leap inside me. I noticed he wasn't as angry after our conversation, but I was boiling over inside and told Maria off in Spanish *and* English in my head.

Kentucky is so breathtakingly green! Aunt Bertha Caldwell has a nice four-bedroom single story home. They say, "Ranch Style" down here in Kentucky. Her children are all grown and away in different states so Pedro had his own room and the girls had theirs and I had a room.

The next morning the rest of the family came over for breakfast. Fried potatoes from the garden, Canadian bacon, cheese grits, scrambled eggs, and homemade biscuits. Pedro was upset I woke him for breakfast and was smarting off at me for being made to sit in on meeting people he didn't know…

While he was in the middle of his sarcastic speech to me, my aunt Natalie walked over to Pedro and hauled off and slapped the side of his face. She put her hands on her hip while saying, "Young man, if you want to live to be an old man shut up talking to your mother like that!" Pedro was rubbing the side of his face she had just slapped and the look of shock was so deep on him, I started laughing. My family all looked at me with total confusion.

I explained to them Puerto Rican custom allows a son over twelve to speak their minds. My Uncle Ralph spoke right up while directing his attention to me. With his heavy Kentuckian accent, "Well baby, we don't take to back talk down in these parts. Save the boy's life and slap some respect in him."

Uncle Ralph looks directly at Pedro and continues, "Son we want you to have an opinion, just learn how to keep your opinion to yourself until someone asks you for it. Then watch your words. We don't ever disrespect one another around here. Welcome to the Bailey side of your family."

All of my family started laughing and each one took turns hugging Pedro, then Izzy and myself. Anna was already being handled like a newborn from one set of arms to another.

We ate and they took turns telling me about my mother and who she was growing up. We sat looking at pictures of my mother, aunts, and uncle until after six p.m. Aunt Dorothy helped Aunt Bertha fix us supper. Collard greens, corn bread, yams, macaroni and cheese and ham that melted in my mouth. I remembered how Gregory would tell me about this kind of foods and realized why his mouth would water when he spoke of it.

Uncle Ralph drove me over to the old tobacco farm house and I saw the actual smokehouse my father built when he met my mother. On the ride back to Aunt Bertha's, Uncle Ralph told me, "That smokehouse was the beginning of Ernestines life. She wrote Bertha letters of her adventures with your father and we listened to Bertha read them after our Sunday suppers. Had Ernestine stayed around here, there wasn't much for her to experience. My sister lived a relatively short life, but a full life none the less. She was happy."

That was almost a year ago. Uncle Ralph took too Pedro. He let Pedro spend days with him and taught Pedro to work. My son was slowly changing into a respectable young man, and we became closer. Pedro had his twenty-first birthday and decided to join the Air Force and is now stationed in Germany.

Pedro has a wife; Vinita and they just found out she's pregnant! I can't believe I'm going to become a grandmother with a three-year-old, but maybe by the time the baby arrives I'll be ready.

Izzy loves it down here in Kentucky. I am beginning to see she is very smart for her age. Aunt Dorothy shared with me Izzy has to be smart to be able to speak two languages. Aunt Dorothy is a retired schoolteacher.

Anna is so beautiful and I see she's going to be tall like her father. Anna has very thick and curly hair like Gregory's. And she loves books. She is learning phonics and counts up to twenty. Aunt Dorothy tells me Anna gets her smarts from the Bailey's, her grandmother was smart enough to experience life outside of Louisville.

Gregory phones us on special occasions to check on us and I take pictures of Anna and Izzy and send him copies from my cell phone.

About nine months after we arrived here during our phone conversation, Gregory asked me to forgive him. He was doing a lot of soul searching and realized he was lonely when he approached me. He also said when he went to get our divorce finalized the judge ordered him to family counseling and he thanks The Lord for it.

Counseling has helped Gregory understand I was a rebound relationship. I told him I forgave him but Anna is such a blessing to me so our relationship wasn't a total waste. I asked for his forgiveness also. I had no intentions of getting into a lasting relationship when we met. We were both silent before he told me he had to get some sleep before his next shift.

After our conversation that evening, I mentally reviewed my relationship with Gregory and since I attend church here in Louisville, I am starting to understand God has purpose for each and every life.

When I envision Anna being a successful grown woman, I have no regrets having her father in my life. I wouldn't be here in Kentucky if Gregory and I hadn't met.

I am very happy now and have The Lord and Gregory Young to thank for that.

~~~~Charlotte~~~~

Why did I tell Irene I would stop by for drinks tonight? I have a thousand and one things to do before Saturday. Sometimes I think I need my head examined! Let me jump into the shower real quick.

Who's calling me now? "Hello. Hey Irene, what's up, did they cancel?" "No Charlotte, I'm making sure you don't back out. You coming? Girl don't have this man come and be a third leg." "I'm gonna jump in the shower and get dressed Irene, I keep my word. I hope mister no named does also." "Okay you sound like you'll show up. See you in an hour, bye." An hour! Yeah, I can make that happen.

I changed dresses three times. I have been blessed with a nice body and I have never had to exercise but these skinny calf legs! My thighs are beautiful it's just my calves, they're like stilts. Gregory told me everyone on the block called our house the crane house. We all have skinny legs except for Mother. All the Thomas' have long skinny bird crane legs, it's a Thomas trait.

I want to show off my shape but that means I have to show off my legs. I tried on a pant outfit but only my sleeveless blouse shows my full breasts. I ended up putting on the first dress I tried on and left the house with my phone ringing. I know its Irene and don't bother answering it.

As I enter Irene's living room two men stand and turn to greet me. Irene is saying, "Gentlemen our late guest has arrived. Charlotte Young; meet my date, Rance. Rance meet my best friend since high school. Charlotte this is Nathan Howard." Nathan extends his hand to me as he utters, "Nate is good. Nice to meet you Charlotte."

Well, well. I will not be rushing home tonight. Nate is fine. He's slightly taller than myself, dark brown skin with touches of grey hair on his face and head. He's a little heavy in the middle but he's well groomed and his slight smile tells me he's wise. Doesn't trust until he see's some evidence you can be trusted. He asks if I would like a drink, if so, could he get it for me. "Sure, I'll have a glass of Moscato please. Thanks" I notice he is headed to the bar.

As I sit I check Nate out. He's dressed in a Stacy Adams two-piece polo knit light and dark green casual suit. The suit has slight black in between the strips and Nate has chosen black shoes. Very nice! He hands me my drink and is careful not to touch my hand. He has good moves. Not treating me like I'm a one-night stand.

As Nate sits I think, 'Charlotte you have been on way too many dates. You know all the moves and signals. Somewhere, that's considered a shame.' Nate starts, "So Charlotte you've been friends with Irene since high school. What school and what year did you meet?" Smart move, women love talking about themselves. We all ended up talking about our high school days.

Turns out Rance and Nate have also known one another since tenth grade. They are the same age also, just two years older than us, forty. They both grew up in Pomona, California, and attended Garey High. They ended up going in different directions being married and all. While attending their five-year class reunion they re-connected just as Irene and I and have kept in touch.

The four us ended up doing some dance steps we remembered while growing up and I had a great time. I wanted Nate to ask for my number. He smelled so good. He was a perfect gentleman. Nate reminded me of Gregory. Might have been Nate's height and eyeglasses.

As I walked to the door leaving, Nate walked with me and asked if I mind giving him my number. I smiled and told him I wouldn't mind at all. As I stood directly in front of Nate reciting my number, I looked into his light brown eyes and realize Nate has bedroom eyes. You know, low, sexy, and inviting.

Irene walked up to me grinning as she hugged me goodbye. I left leaving Nate at the door watching me. Before I could get in bed Irene texted, "Jackpot! He likes you. Charlotte: don't mess this up, love you."

I woke up running. Today is my gallery's pre-showing. We have our private guest list attendees tonight for their own special preview. This list consist of big money and I have a list of five things to get accomplished which means five different places must be visited by me. Ugh, someone please remind me why I love this line of work!

After my driving marathon I went home and ate, showered then went back to the museum with half hour to spare. I made sure everything was in place and had time to calm down. I don't drink at these functions, some of our clients are non-drinkers and I want them to know we don't all drink. However after these previews and shows, I take my whole bottle of Moscato into my bathroom and soak in the tub while sipping to the movie I allow to play in my mind of that nights events.

My boss, Pamela Hastings, loves the way I set everything up. After breaking up with Blake I was a total wreck and that was the only time Pam was worried I wouldn't be able to pull off my job.

I remember the gallery had a showing in a week and Pam pulled me into the ladies' room and told me this coming show was more important than any of the other shows and if I couldn't do it, let her know now. This was not the time for her to be let down by me. I promised her I could do it. I spent fifty dollars more than usual that night, it was perfect.

Pam had me keep the guest occupied in the north section while she took a client on private tour of the south section. I found out later her client was some billionaire and keeps himself anonymous. He made a purchase that night and she was given a very substantial commission from that transaction. Pam gave me two thousand dollars extra just for doing what I love to do.

Pam does that every once in a while. She'll add a few thousand dollars in my pay envelope, cash so I don't have to include it on my taxes. Pam was who encouraged me to buy my own home to raise the girls in.

I was shocked to find out two years ago Pam was never married to Marvin. They were living common-law but she had him pay her palimony when he dumped her. His picture was in every local newspaper with a younger woman hanging on his arm. Pam is very wise and I've learned a lot from her and she has never made our different race an issue.

I noticed Nate when he walked into the gallery. He is so handsome and walks with distinction. Nate is very confident like Greg. My goodness I have to stop comparing every man I meet to that man. I worked my way over to Nate and we acknowledged one another and I kept moving.

Every time I noticed Nate he was looking at me. I felt myself blushing. He never turned from me, he let me know he was watching. I felt good knowing a man wants to look at me. I was dressed for him too. I spend money on my clothes and write it off because it's work related. You don't want to know what I spend on my shoes. I stand for very long periods and cannot afford hurting feet.

Before the closing Nate disappeared and I found myself disappointed. I wanted to talk to him and maybe go for a drink before heading home. I thought about him all the way home. While in bed drinking my second glass of wine Nate was on my mind. His text woke me at seven a.m.

Nate asked me out for a nightcap tonight after the show. He apologized for texting me so early but he was headed to work. I replied to his text agreeing to a nightcap. Later Irene texted informing me her and Rance were planning on joining Nate at the viewing and she reminded me to be nice!

I think I smiled all morning. I finally meet a nice man; it's about time. I'll get the low down of Nathan Howard tonight. Nate is sexy. I think I want to sleep with him. I'll see.

I noticed Irene when she walked in with Rance but there's no Nate. I felt disappointed. As I worked my way over to Irene we speak and she says, "Nate informed Rance he will arrive later. Charlotte you do amazing work. Girl this place looks fabulous!" I respond with a, "Thanks" and kept it moving.

An hour before closing Nate enters with the largest bouquet of assorted flowers I have ever seen not delivered. He works his way towards me and as he hands the flowers to me he says, "Hi Charlotte, these are for you. I hope you have a place for them." He smiles a full smile and the man has me smiling now. I thanked him and took the flowers to the kitchen.

As I return to the exhibit Nate is standing in the doorway. He turns towards me and says, "You look beautiful. I hope you won't be too tired for a drink later." I could smell his cologne. Hmm, this man looks as good as he smells. I'm wondering, where has he been all my life. I want to get to know him. "I won't be too tired." And I glided away from him. I could feel Nate's eyes on me as I mingled.

Nate and I agreed I would take my car and flowers home then ride with him. He took me to a nice supper club and ordered buffalo wings while we drank. He drinks Hennessy on the rocks and says he's not much of a drinker. Two drinks and he was done.

Playing basketball in high school deterred his attraction to drinking and smoking.

He started telling me how he met his first wife and how badly messed up he was when she left him and their three kids. His ex, Jasmine worked at Hughes Aircraft as he does and they had a whirlwind romance that caused Brandon to arrive.

They married when Brandon was five months old and before he became a year old Jasmine was pregnant with Charles and a year later came Amber. Nate told me Jasmine was a great wife and mother but when Amber celebrated her fifth birthday, Jasmine became overprotective. That was the beginning of the descent of their marriage.

Jasmine resented him suggesting anything to her about "Her babies." They had agreed Jasmine would return to work but by the time Brandon started school Jasmine wanted to stay home because she didn't want anyone taking him to school. She was paranoid of Brandon being kidnapped.

Nate didn't find out until after the children arrived, Jasmine had been abused as a child and her so called mother was her aunt. Jasmine kept a lot of what happened in her childhood to herself and when her "babies" started growing up she was afraid what happened to her would happen to them. It became so severe Jasmine would keep the kids home all day and would not let them go to school nor outside to play.

Back in those days there were Truant Officers who would come to your house and investigate why children were not attending school. Well it was a phone call that made Nate aware of the problems going on with Jasmine.

Nate shared with me how hard he worked and the long hours he invested into being the provider for his family. He really went into detail about the struggles he experienced being brought up by a single mother. His uncle took him under his wing and taught him to do honest work so Nate could live without having to look over his shoulder for the law. Nate shared while proudly smiling, about being a provider was what an honest, caring husband and father does; take good care of his family.

He explained the pride he experienced making sure his wife and children lived in a safe environment. And how making sure his wife and children never having to go without what they needed is really what a responsible man makes sure to do. Nate bragged about being honored even blessed having The Lord enable him to make sure his family was very well taken care of.

Nate turned sad when he explained how his working so much kept him unaware of the change in Jasmine. First she accused him of informing the authorities she kept her babies home, then she accused their neighbors. Jasmine thought everyone who did not agree with her was in conspiracy to take her babies from her.

Finally Jasmine's aunt called a family meeting and made the decision to have Jasmine tested for mental illness. Jasmine was institutionalized for two years and when she was released Nate was dating someone and her babies who were now eleven, nine and eight, were afraid of her.

Jasmine was staying with her aunt and called Nate one day out of the blue, told him to file for divorce and she would sign it. After the divorce was final Jasmine told her sister she was going for a walk and never came back. Four years passed and Arizona PD called to notify the family Jasmine's body had been found. No one knows how or when Jasmine went to Arizona and it is apparent no one will ever know.

Brandon will be eighteen and plan to attend UCLA. Charles is almost seventeen and graduating next June. He plans to also attend UCLA. Amber is almost sixteen. Jasmine's aunt raised them because of Nate's work hours. I listened to Nate and felt sorry for him. He seems to be a good man.

After explaining his second wife's death caused by an automobile accident two years ago, these days Nate has been burying himself in work and church.

Nate said he just happened to say "Yes" to Rance about Thursday and he is very glad he did. The look Nate gave was saying he likes me. But my mood changed.

I kept looking at Nate and became silent. After a few minutes Nate asked if I were tired and ready to go home. I answered softly, "Yes." I felt so sad.

Nate dropped me off and while undressing I began to cry. I had no clue as to why; but I wept.

I wasn't myself for the next few days. I didn't feel like talking to anyone. I stayed in my robe all day Sunday and thought I was sinking back into depression but I had no clue what pushed me here. I started going over everything I had done to figure out what it was I had lost that made me feel this way. I concluded I was feeling sorry for Nate.

Sunday afternoon Nate called and texted but I didn't answer nor respond. I like Nate but it may be because he is so much like Gregory Allen. All day I kept going over what Nate said about him working to be a good provider. The picture he painted of a loving, caring responsible husband kept being rewound. One o'clock Monday morning a light bulb came on in my head. I sat straight up in bed.

Greg worked a lot of hours to provide for us. That's it! Nate painted a picture for me of Greg…

I cried myself back to sleep.

I awoke up at five-thirty a.m. and remembered crying like this when I broke it off with Blake. But why am I crying now, I haven't ended a relationship?

OH NO! I realize Nate reminds me of Greg. Nate gave me insight into Greg's mindset of taking care of the girls and I. Unbelievable! I laid back and allowed the video that had already began to occupy my mind to play…

I would follow Greg from room to room, begging him to spend time, make time to be with us.

I didn't understand it when Greg and I were married because I was too busy accusing Greg of not wanting to spend time with me and the girls. I made our marriage not working all Greg's fault.

But today…   today I understand…

I destroyed my marriage; totally misunderstanding Greg was being responsible. All I saw was my side, Greg not wanting to be with me and the girls. I felt Greg didn't love me anymore and was taking me for granted leaving me alone all the time. The way Nate broke it down about a responsible man takes good care of his family…

Now I feel guilt totally consuming me for breaking up my marriage. All because of me wanting Greg to prefer being with me instead of being at work. Greg, like Nate, was being responsible and making sure we had what we needed. I was too young and blind to see Greg's side.

Wow, this realizing *I* was the one to break up our marriage is causing my heart to hurt…

No wonder Greg is so angry with me. I have been blaming him and he has never confronted me about it. I have accused him of changing on me but, Greg has always been a provider, even before we married.

…Lord, what have I done! Why didn't I see then what I see now? Why didn't I listen to Mother when she told me not to ride Greg about working?

I cried until I drifted off to sleep.

Monday's after a showing is my off day. I needed it today. I slept until ten-thirty and that's only because Nate called. I didn't take the call. What can I say to him. "Your losing your first wife made me realize I broke up my marriage." Yeah, and he'll think I'm Jasmine all over again; crazy.

My past can destroy any chances of Nate and I having a future. What really hurts is… is… I hurt Greg.

I committed adultery to make him give me some attention!

Facing the truth is making me cry even harder. I'm crying so hard I'm whimpering and I am talking snot flowing with these tears!

Mother used to tell me, "Gregory isn't out with other women or gambling grocery money, he's making a good life for you and the girls."

Oh my god! I feel so bad. I hear in my head Mother reciting Proverbs 14:1; **"The wise woman builds her house, But the foolish pulls it down with her hands."**

Oh god help me! Lord I repent for breaking up my marriage and I am so sorry for using Blake. I have ruined my life and blamed Greg. Oh Lord help me! I have caused death to my own marriage! Greg is a good man and… I hurt him… I purposefully hurt him.

Now memories of Greg and I being happy together are flooding my mind.

I have cried for hours. I am exhausted from shedding tears! I swear I have no more water left in my body.

Okay now my phone is ringing. It's Tammi let me take this.

"Hi baby how are you today?" "Wow Mom, are you coming down with a head cold?" "No baby just a little stopped up. The question is how are you today?" "I'm doing very well Mom. Ask me why." "Okay, why?" "I saw my father yesterday and he agreed to give me away. Yay!"

I feel as though my heart has stop beating. "That's great Tammi. You know I need to apologize to you. Tamera if you and Justin love each other, baby go for all the gusto you can. I want you happy and loved." "Mom are you okay, have you been drinking all day?" "No. Baby I mean it. I've been thinking and, love is truly a beautiful thing.

Most people never get to experience true unconditional love. I'm sorry I gave you a hard time. I don't want you hurt Tammi. I love you." Both Tammi and I are sniffling over the phone. "I know you do Mom and I love you for loving me so much." Sniffles.

"Tammi where did you see your father?" "He was at church yesterday. He met Justin. Oh and he tried to say he didn't get an invite. But he has agreed to give me away. I am so happy. We may not have a huge wedding, but we will have a royal one. We will never forget it and will make memories we can tell our grandkids."

"I'm happy for you Tammi. Justin seems to love you and that's the main ingredient to a marriage. It covers faults." "Okay Mom, I gotta go, love you." "Back at you!" Dial tone. Hmm, Mr. Young back in church. Lord must be working on Gregory Allen. Well Lord since you're working; work on me.

After getting out of bed I ate some toast and called Nate. I left a message; "Hi Nate. I hope your day is going great. I owe you an apology and rather say it face to face. Give me a call back please. Charlotte." Nate called a few minutes after six-thirty p.m. He just left work and heard my message, he will pick me up if I want. I told him to come over and we will work out later what we want to do. I'm not sure how Nate is going to handle this news.

I took a shower and straightened up some then worked on my speech for Nate. I was a nervous wreck. I like Nate but he reminds me of Greg and my feeling guilty about breaking up my marriage makes me feel as though I owe Greg an apology. I need to get closure with Greg before trying to have a relationship with Nate. Maybe Nate is my second chance to get it right. Here he is.

"Hi, come on in." Nate asks, "How are you today after your busy weekend?" "I am rested thank you. You work overtime?" "Only when I need to make some extra cash. Charles is graduating and Amber is in high school. Apparently girls need a lot more clothes than boys. Charlotte you are looking nice today." "Thanks. May I get you something, water, tea?" "Water will work, thanks." I get him some ice water and tell him to have a seat as I place his glass on the coffee table.

"Nate, when you shared with me about your first wife and how you worked to provide for her and your children, I saw my ex. He was what I called a workaholic and I complained constantly about him working. I was young and wanted him with me and the girls all of the time.

Hearing your spin on working to provide for your family Saturday, kinda pricked me at the heart. I have never looked at my ex working as means of provision. I saw his working as an excuse he used to be away from us." I began rubbing my hands; I am so nervous. I stare at Nate's eyes. He is so handsome and there is this tenderness.

I blurt, "I had a hard time swallowing the 'my fault pill.' After self-examining myself, I took a long impartial view at being a provider. I want to thank you for opening the window of my perception and, apologize for not responding to your calls. I was pretty broken up."

Nate says, "Thank you for the explanation. Charlotte I like you and would be very honored if you would give me a chance to know you and vice versa. I admit I was afraid you weren't interested in me. Now I understand." We smile at one another.

Nate asks, "Are you hungry because I am." I nod and reply, "I can eat a little something. What sounds good to you?" Nate tilts his head and says, "I have a taste for Mexican Food, how about you?" As I stand up I say, "Sounds good to me. Let me get my shoes. I'll be right back."

We go to a Mexican Restaurant over on Long Beach Boulevard. I had a Cheese Enchilada and it was heaven! Nate ordered the Carne Asada. He asked about my girls and I asked about his daughter. Being with Nate now, after my revelation of him mirroring Greg, I'm not into sleeping with him as before. I feel as though I might mess up again. So I asked, "Nate do you still work all the time like you did when you were married to Jasmine?"

He told me the financial burden is not as much now as when the children were younger and he had a wife to support. These days his sons ask for money every once in a while but he has money saved and he pays cash for whatever he purchase.

I noticed him using his American Express card the other night and mentioned it. He smiled and said I did not miss too much. Then he explained American Express gives bonus points for you using their card. He pays the card off every month and at the end of the year, he has enough points to get free gift cards. This way he gets free gifts for using his card. 'Hmm, now that's smart money-making right there. I see Nate, as being very wise.'

Nate took me home and when I told him I enjoyed myself and thanked him, he asked if he could come in. I told him I was very tired and would talk to him later. I never heard from Nate again.

For the next few days I was in a funk. I felt depression trying to re-introduce itself.

Irene called that Wednesday evening and told me about the great sex she and Rance had and asked, "Charlotte what did you do to Nate? He told Rance you weren't into him." I was a little relieved. Nate is a good man and I don't want to hurt him. He's right, I'm not ready to get into a serious relationship. I have to get some kinda closure with Greg first. Complete the last chapter of a book before moving to the next or else the storyline gets way too complexed and won't make any sense.

After talking to Irene, when I settled in bed I thought about Blake and Cedrick. Blake had been married for only a year before he divorced. His ex was an I.R.S. Compliance Instructor and traveled quite a bit. Blake said she was cheating on him and when he had evidence, he told her not to come home and she didn't.

He filed for divorce and she left him everything, house, boat and both motorcycles. Blake told me she hurt him very bad and he was angry so he had a lot of one-night stands. He felt it was fate that brought us back together and when I told him my husband and I were not getting along; he was hopeful we would get married.

Blake wanted children and the girls took to him but I was angry and when Gregory left, I really wanted to hurt him. Blake was on me to divorce and move on. It was Blake who advised me to file for divorce and he was with me every step of the way. Blake even appeared in divorce court with me. I was so glad Blake was at my side because I had no clue what to do or expect. Also I wanted Greg to see there are men willing to spend time with the person they love.

After the divorce was final was when Blake started nagging me. "Charlotte, when are you going to let me make an honest woman of you?" Or "Let's stop this game, we are both single now." I was so busy being scared Blake would change on me as Gregory had, I never stopped to see...I didn't love Blake I needed him.

I always put off answering Blake. The divorce was final in December and New Year's Eve Blake gave me an engagement ring. I felt pressured. I thought he was expecting me to marry him, as if I divorced Gregory to be in the position to marry again. What can I say, I was scared!

Greg and I grew up together and I thought I knew him and here he up and changes on me. I thanked Blake for the ring but never said, "Yes, I'll marry you." He caught the insinuation, he just never responded.

Blake and I were a good fit. He let me do pretty much what I wanted like Greg but the longer we were together I realized I didn't love Blake; he was more a friend and companion to me. I needed a friend and having Blake always around, I was never lonely. He didn't mind my rules of him not living with me. We waited until the girls were in bed before we went into my bedroom. Blake was happy to be with me.

The second Christmas we spent together after my divorce Blake asked, "Charlotte when are we going to set a wedding date?" I felt like he sucked all of the oxygen in the room from me. He looked at me waiting for my response. "I don't know Blake, how does next year sound." He looked at me for a minute and I asked to be excused.

I went to the bathroom and gasped. Realizing I didn't love Blake, now I feel if I don't give him a date, he's walking. A few days after New Year's Blake told me his lease was up in February and we needed to set a date for our wedding. I was so scared. I didn't know how to tell him to renew his lease. However, I guess the look on my face spoke for me.

Blake sighed from discuss and asked, "Charlotte do you love me?" My response was, "Blake, I have a great amount of admiration for you…" He cut me off. "I get it. When you uttered Blake, and not yes, I got it. Look Charlotte, I love your dirty bath water and would wait for the date you set and pay for everything you want but, the one thing I refuse to do is allow you to step all over my heart. Woman I love you! What is it about me that makes you not want to commit to me?"

I took a discerning look at him. Blake is so hurt. I felt tears welling up because Blake is a good man, I just don't love him. It was that exact moment I realized, I had used Blake. I felt sorry for him and was thinking now of how to express my feelings without breaking his heart. He was looking me in the eyes and I noticed he began blinking.

Blake cleared his throat, stood up and walked to the front door. We were sitting in the living room and I watched him walk away as I blinked back tears. He opens the door and without turning to face me says, "Goodbye Charlotte Ann Thomas." As the door closes, I give my tears permission to fall.

I blamed Greg for me using Blake, 'All Greg had to do was love me enough to want to spend time with me. Gregory Allen, you have hurt three people now!'

I felt bad I had used Blake and went into a depression. Irene told me I was grieving being divorced and Blake leaving. As long as Blake was around I didn't take time to grieve from the divorce. Irene had experienced a divorce and told me, divorce is as devastating as death. You were married to someone who became one with you and in my case, Greg was my best friend.

Irene said for me to give myself some time to grieve, then get back out there. "Charlotte you are young, beautiful, have a great body and you have a good job. Some man out there is waiting on him some Charlotte. I'm here if you need me. Okay?" I was crying over the phone and all I could utter was, "Okay."

After my conversation with Irene, I sat on my bed and decided to look up the word grief. The definition stated *pain, sorrow, heartache, and torment* as a few descriptions. The word, "torment" made me think of depression. I need to know what it is I'm dealing with. So, I wrote the dictionary definition down for depression; *"feelings of severe despondency [loss of hope] and dejection [low spirits]. Self-doubt creeps in and that swiftly turns into depression."* The thesaurus had this to say; *"unhappiness, sadness, sorrow or heavy heart."*

When I read the word despondency, my mind went back to when Greg first went to work. I was depressed then, I missed him so much. At that time I thought I was depressed because Greg and I were going through an umbilical cord cutting process. Greg and I were always together growing up and I told myself every day, "Charlotte Ann, grow up! Greg is a grown man now and is being responsible. Get over it!"

I remembered Greg telling me he was working for us and each time he told me that I would feel better knowing in the future we would be together. But after a few days not seeing Greg I would feel hopeless again. At that time I was impatient and felt Greg and I would never be together. I thought it wouldn't take much for us to be together as long as we were together that was all that mattered.

Today I remember the definition of depression. That's what I'm trying to sink into, hopelessness. Having to face the truth; *I* destroyed my marriage being impatient and immature. This is awfully hard to deal with. All these years I have blamed Greg…

After Blake and I broke up I took two days off work and cried. I would drag myself from bed, get the girls ready, take them to school then come home and crawl back into bed. I would sit and think of nothing but how I was hurting and break out crying. Crying made me think about not being wanted by Greg and that thought prompted me to cry more intensely.

Getting ready and going to work took great effort on my part. My mind would drift from my conversation with people, to my pain. I would watch the clock wanting to get home to my bed so I could cry; then fight back tears because it seemed the clock wasn't moving. I just wanted to stay in bed and cry.

I would see couples hugging or walking together with hands held and find myself blinking back tears. It seemed every woman was loved but me. Why did Greg not want to be with me? What's wrong with Charlotte Ann huh?

One day while I was home in bed Mother called me about something and asked what was wrong. She could tell by my tone something was going on with me. I told her Blake and I broke up and began sobbing. Mother dropped what she was doing and came over. She sat on my bed and after rocking me and allowing my tears to splatter, Mother took her hand and lovingly brushed back my hair.

While holding me in her arms Mother softly began speaking; "Baby, Proverbs 13: 12 tells us, *"Hope deferred makes the heart sick, but a longing fulfilled is a tree of life."*

Baby you hoped your marriage would be happily ever after. You hoped Blake would do what Gregory was unable too. Baby the word hope in the Bible means "expectation" and when you expect something for a long time, well when it doesn't come to pass like you expect, your hope turns into hopelessness. Depression is hopelessness rewound over and over and over until you make yourself sick.

Baby I love you and it hurts me to see you in pain. Listen good to me now. Put your hope in The Lord. I Hope you find strength to stop rewinding your disappointment. Then you will be able to heal. Can you try that baby? Can you try doing that for your mother? Huh?"

Mother turns my body to face her. I have tears on my face. I heard every word spoken to me, I just can't utter a response, so I shake my head up and down to answer her. Mother has a wrinkled forehead as she gazes into my eyes she says, "Come on let me pray for you."

Mother gently laid my head on her shoulder and held onto my head as she prayed: "Father, my baby hurts. I pray on her behalf that you will heal her heart and reveal to her the plans You have for her. Your plans are good and are not evil. You have my baby's future in the palm of Your hands. Direct her thoughts to be of You and Your will and snatch my baby from the hands of the enemy. In Jesus Name, amen."

Mother rocked me as I silently cried, thinking; 'Lord I want to be happy again, I really do.'

It took me a while before I realized I had to stop myself from thinking about Greg causing me to hurt and hurting Blake. I don't remember when it was but I do remember climbing into bed one night and my mind going to Gregory Allen Young and thinking how he hurt me not wanting me.

As if a light being turned on in a dark room, I heard Mother's voice, 'depression is hopelessness rewound.' I told myself, 'stop it Charlotte! We will not go there tonight.' It wasn't too much longer Pam talked to me in the ladies' room at work about needing my full attention on the upcoming exhibit.

I believe the combination of all those events together helped me snap out of my depression. Alright; I need to put a stop to this hopelessness now before it gets out of hand. Maybe I need to go to a club…Nah I'd better leave that alone!

After Blake and I broke up, maybe just before Easter Irene phoned me late one Thursday. "Okay Charlotte, it's time for you to dust off your stilettos, we are going to paint the town Saturday night, just the two of us single ladies!" I responded, "Single! Girl what happened to Keith?" Irene quickly responded, "Girl you know I can't get too close. He was beginning to grow on me, can't have that. I know just the place we can go. They play music from the Motown Sounds and there's a dance floor. What you say to us leaving here around eight?" I was hesitant. "Come on Charlotte you've had enough time to grieve, it's time to move on.

Be here five minutes to eight so we can walk out of the door at eight sharp. I'm hanging up before you think of some excuse, love you, bye." I'm not up to going anywhere. What if I hear a song that reminds me of Greg or Blake and get weepy… Maybe, this is what the doctor would order for me. I'll see.

Irene and I went to "The Pebble" and we had a ball! I phoned her three times through the week canceling and she would not accept any of my excuses. Half an hour at The Pebble, I was so glad I went.

The Pebble has a huge bar that's about twenty feet long. It's made out of small stones with glass overlay. It really is a conversation piece. I'm not much of a drinker but Irene can get pretty plastered at times. I've known her long enough to figure out when she's troubled, she drinks. When she drinks, she cries when she cries, she drinks. I've had to help her to her bed several times.

Last year Karol, Irene's daughter, decided she is gay and that really had Irene in an upheaval when Karol first told Irene. I would sit and listen to her as she opened up every emotion she felt. Most times I cry with Irene when she cries.

Glen Junior, Irene's son calls Irene on Mother's day, her birthday and Christmas and that bothers her. The day Glen Junior moved his things out of Irene's, she called me that morning to tell me him and her were at it! I dropped everything and went over to her house. Glen Junior was throwing his things into bags and containers. He told her she wasn't a very good mother the way she had so many men in her life and he was going to live with his father and attend college in Oakland, California.

I had to calm Irene down she was yelling at Glen Junior throwing up things she had done for him. Each time she thought of something she had sacrificed to do for him, she would sarcastically add, "Oh yeah! So that's your definition of a mother that's not good!" She finally calmed down and we both stood in the driveway watching Glen Junior drive away.

I went inside and sat with Irene at her place and as we drank she reminisced on all she gave up for Glen Junior to pursue a football scholarship. Glen Junior was great at playing football and received a very lucrative scholarship. Irene was so hurt. And again she drank, and cried, and drank.

I don't judge Irene, my daughters aren't perfect. I thought Tammi might have been gay at one time because she never dated. Talk about relived when she told me she met Justin. Like Irene I would still love my baby but as a mother I want my daughters to have a somewhat normal life.

Life itself brings highs and lows and adding friction to what is already unpredictable seems senseless. Why invite more friction into your life? The way Tammi smiled when she told me she met a nice man, I knew she thought she was in love. I was overjoyed for her.

And when Reece told me crying, Charlie's cheating on her made her feel she couldn't satisfy him sexually. I hugged her while crying along with my baby. I understood her dating every man that asked her, her name during that time. I kept Lexie and Ty day and night for several months because Reece was sleeping her way to recovery. I prayed for my baby daily because I understood how she felt not being wanted by her husband. Also I prayed she wouldn't get pregnant or something that would have her taking penicillin.

In a way work was Greg's other woman so I understood what my baby was going through. So, I don't do anything but listen to Irene and, she listens to me. I guess that's what friends are for. Neither Irene nor I have sisters so we have this sister/friend bond. I do love her like a sister.

Irene and I hit the Pebble every Saturday night I didn't have to work and the last time we went Keith, Irene's old flame, came into the club and Irene was dancing with some guy. Keith was with a lady but he kept his eyes on Irene. She performed something awful. The lady Keith was with started the eye rolling and I told Irene to stop dancing with different men. Keith watched every move Irene made and he was steaming mad.

Irene was dancing real close to some guy and started bending in front of him and moving her hips provocatively. Keith jumped up, ran over to Irene, and grabbed her arm. The guy she was dancing with pushed Keith and Keith's lady friend called his name as she walked towards the door. Keith sneered at Irene and left. I told her we were not going back to The Pebble, Keith knew she was hanging out there. We started bar hopping and I met Cedrick Ballard at The Hub in Redondo Beach.

It was hot that summer and I kept the air conditioner on in my apartment twenty-four seven. I was saving money to buy a house. Pam had given me several bonuses and after spending the first one on clothes, I decided to buy a house. Pam informed me there were first time buyer programs available for me and I needed to buy my own house so there would be stability in my daughters lives. So I looked into it and decided to save for a down payment.

I knew what I could afford monthly and was saving to put additional money down so my payments would be where I could handle them without being strained financially. Greg was paying me four hundred dollars a month for the girls but he was having so many kids, I didn't know if he would stop paying me or not.

When Greg and I went to court to finalize our divorce the judge asked if I wanted court ordered child support payments from Greg, I declined it. Greg was paying me and knowing how he loves his daughters, I knew Greg would never miss a payment.

After that third wife of Greg's dropped babies out like passing gas, I didn't rely on the money Greg gave me. Living with Greg I learned to pay cash for everything except my car. I lease my cars now and write off the payments. I drive luxury cars being I work with people that have large incomes. I am presently in the Lexus SUV and this is my second time leasing one. It's great for when I need to transport paintings.

By the time I met Cedrick I had forgotten about hurting Blake. After considering Blake knew I was married, he was risking me staying with Greg and it just didn't work the way Blake thought. *Well Hello!* Neither did my marriage.

When I met Cedrick I had no intentions of getting serious and was out to have fun. Irene and I were sitting when Cedrick asked me to dance and I agreed. Cedrick is tall and built. He gyms faithfully twice a week, talk about buff! His personality is one of confidence, Cedrick Ballard knows what he wants and does not stop until he has obtained it. After we danced Cedrick sat with Irene and I and asked me to dance again.

I spent the rest of my time with him, he bought all of my drinks besides, I was just having fun, right? Cedrick asked for my phone number, I gave him some bogus number I gave all the guys that asked.

The following Saturday Irene and I decided to check out some other bar. That Monday my air conditioning unit gave out in my apartment. Well guess who the repairman was that came to fix it! Yep, Cedrick Ballard.

I was shocked when I opened the door. He was so professional and acted as if he didn't recognize me. He flashed his badge and asked the appropriate questions about my unit. After he looked at the unit he told me he had to order a part and it might take a few days. I signed the paperwork and he left.

I called Irene and told her what happened. We were both stunned. I didn't know if he would come back now he knew where I lived, or if he would call me since my phone number was on the paperwork. Irene told me to call the office and request another repairman but we realized he already knows everything about me so what's the point. We were both scared so I ended up taking the girls to her place and we stayed with her, it was too hot in that upstairs apartment anyway.

I was at the apartment again when Cedrick returned with the part. I let him in and when he told me the unit was up and running, I asked if he remembered me. "Oh yes I remember you." He says with an attitude. I let him know why I asked. "I was wondering that's all, you never said anything." Minus the attitude Cedrick says, "I called the number you gave me and switched it up so many times. I am not hard up for dates. I happened to like you. I *thought* we hit it off. But I guess it was the J&B talking to me. Anyways, have a nice day." "Thanks, you too. Thank you for fixing my unit."

Cedrick stands outside my apartment, turns around to face me and asks, "If I called you, would you mind?" Feeling bad for lying to him, I softly said, "No, not at all."

Cedrick called that evening and we went to dinner the following evening. He told me he meet a lot of women being in the line of work he's in and he is always professional. Work is work and play is play, he does not mix the two.

Cedrick was divorced also. They married young and his ex, wanted to party a lot and with their two sons, he wanted some stability in his home. She started going out without him and met some guy. End of the marriage. That was two years before we met. Cedrick was a good man, hard worker, clean, great to be with and always the life of a party. The problem with Cedrick was his nasty alter-ego would show up after he drank too much.

We started sleeping together one weekend the girls were at Greg's and Sunday evening I told him my daughters were coming home and he had to stay out of my bedroom. We could only be in here when the girls were in bed for the night. He said, "Hold up. You asking me, a grown man to sneak around when I want to make love to you?" I answered, "No, I'm telling you. I have girls and don't want them sleeping around and shacking up so I'm going to be an example to them."

Cedrick insisted we not sneak around when we slept together and I made him sneak around. The first few months he took me to nice hotels and when the girls were staying with Greg we were at my house. After the hotels played out we went to his studio apartment in West L. A. but the few times we were there it was very noisy. His next-door neighbor kept ongoing parties so Cedrick suggested we go to my place.

When I met Cedrick my three bedroom, two and a half bath Spanish stucco home in Inglewood was already thirty days in escrow. Cedrick helped me move into my house and installed some things for me. He slowly brought some of his things to my house and at least twice a week I had to remind Cedrick I did not want a man living with me. I reminded him that I have girls and find no problem with him waiting until the girls went to bed and were sleep before we went into my bedroom! He would go silent every time I repeated myself.

Thanksgiving Cedrick and I were at my parents and we were all sitting around talking and drinking. Walt and Cedrick were engaged in conversation most of the time we were there and I never noticed how much Cedrick was throwing back.

The girls had gone over to Mother Mays and when they were dropped off at my parents, Greg wanted them to get clothes and spend the rest of the weekend with him so the four of us were headed home. Once we were all seated in Cedrick's car, he told me he didn't think he should drive and for me to take the wheel. I did and he was quiet until we walked in the house. I placed his keys on the kitchen counter and headed for the girls room.

Cedrick says sarcastically, "Do I have permission to go into your bedroom Miss Young!" I turned towards him and noticed he was looking in my liquor cabinet. I walked over to him and asked if he thought he already had enough. He turned towards me so fast he startled me. Cedrick raises his voice while saying, "I am a man. I don't hide and sneak around like some fifteen-year-old. I love you Charlotte. I feel like some kid asking permission to sleep in your bed. I am a grown man!"

I put my hand on the cabinet door while saying, "I think you've had enough to drink." He abruptly stopped the cabinet door from closing. My heart leaped. I was afraid of Cedrick but wasn't about to let him know that!

I snapped, "You can sleep on the couch. And leave first thing in the morning!" I turned around to leave. **"Charlotte!"** He yells. I turned around and see he's stepping towards me.

My heart is beating so fast. I stood looking him directly in the eyes. **"What!"** I yell back. I'm thinking if he hits me Walt will kill him! He stands in front of me slurring, "I love you, I want us to get married. I can't be sleeping in your bed with the clock ticking. Let's get married." He's no longer shouting. Cedrick reaches for my waist but I'm scared and as I push his hands away, I tell him we will talk about this tomorrow.

I go help the girls and as we leave I throw a blanket and pillow on the couch for Cedrick, he can sleep on the couch! The girls and I leave Cedrick sipping his drink at the kitchen counter. Reece tells me they want to stay home with me to make sure I will be alright. I explained how Mr. C had a little too much to drink and everything was alright.

When I returned home from Mother Mays, Cedrick is on the couch passed out sitting up. I go to my room and lock the door. I'm thinking, 'Oh Dude, you are so gone!'

I get up the next morning and Cedrick is gone. He called later and asked what happened. He woke up on my couch and my bedroom door was locked. I couldn't believe he didn't remember. I told him he had too much to drink and raised his voice to me in front of my daughters so I locked my door. He was very apologetic.

When Cedrick saw the girls he apologized to them and said he would make sure to never raise his voice again. Cedrick took me out that Saturday evening to an upscale restaurant in Beverly Hills. I counted his drinks every time he drank after that.

Cedrick never came directly out and said he wanted us to marry when he was sober. He would make statements like, "Hey Miss Young, let's take this relationship to the next level." Or "Miss Young, you think you can stand me around twenty-four seven?" Or "Miss Young, wanna change your last name?"

I would always respond, "This level is just fine thank you." Or "The question is can you stand *me* twenty-four seven." Or "My name has already been changed." I liked Cedrick, he was a lot of fun and easy to talk too, he just had that nasty side when he drank too much. That's when I was afraid of him, but I didn't let him know.

I put it together. Cedrick would drink a lot when he was troubled. Why he wouldn't just ask me straight out what he wanted I could not understand. Greg and I never had a problem talking about what was on our minds. That is when he was home and we talked. I felt, if Cedrick is such a man, he needs to stand up like one and say what he needed to say to me *without a drink.*

One morning Cedrick was getting up to leave before the alarm clock went off and when he said, "Good morning." I could hear he was upset. I started helping him get dressed so he could hurry and go. He says, " Charlotte would the world come to an end if your daughters saw me here with you this morning?"

I was rushing as I said, "We'll talk later, you need to go." He's no longer whispering, "Charlotte are you hearing me!" I'm now agitated. "Cedrick, you need to lower your voice and leave, right now!" He looked me over and his eyes seemed to blow up like someone pumped air in them. He snatched his shoes from my hands and left slinging the door wide open.

He didn't call me and I didn't call him either. To be honest by then I was afraid of Cedrick. I can't be with a man I'm afraid of. Especially when I'm not sure what might set him off. The man just woke up mad!

All that day I thought about how to tell Cedrick we need some space between us.

The next day I pull up into the driveway and Cedrick is parked in front of my house. I pull into the garage and when the girls and I get out of the car, there he stands at the end of my bumper with a large bouquet of assorted flowers and a box of candy. I admire the flowers but at the same time I'm thinking, 'I love these flowers, but Bro, you leaving here!' He walks into the kitchen with us talking to the girls.

As we stand listening to Tammi tell about her day at school, Cedrick interrupts. "That's good Tammi. How would you all like to go to dinner. The girls respond, "Oh yes! Where are we going?" Cedrick is looking into my eyes and says very softly, "Yesterday was our one year knowing each other. That's what the flowers are for. Charlotte forgive me. Please?" I gave in. I hugged him, found a vase for the flowers and we all went to dinner. Cedrick pulled out a ring box and presented an engagement ring to me while we ate and asked me to marry him. I said "Yes." We were engaged.

Cedrick started bringing clothes over and dressing for work at my place but he was always gone when the girls were up for school. On the weekends Cedrick would stay and we had no problems he just kept his feelings in and only told me what was on his mind *after* he had a few drinks. That, I did not like about Cedrick Ballard.

I had a big sixteenth birthday party for Reece at the house. It was top of the line. I bought her the pretty dress she wanted, and there was pink and purple everything. Balloons, streamers, tablecloths, cake, punch, plates, and cups. After she blew out her candles Mother asked what she wished for. Charece Kimberly Young embarrassed me and hurt Greg.

She says with a raised voice and, an attitude, "My wish is that I do not have to spend one more weekend at my fathers house! I think I am old enough now to make that decision. Free me and let me stay here, where I live. That's my wish Grannie Thomas." I immediately looked at Greg. His face drained of blood. He went completely pale. I knew Reece's words hurt him. I was embarrassed for Greg.

Reece had been coming home from Greg's telling me how mean Janice was to her and Tammi but I also know Reece is at the age she gets an attitude with me if she can't have her way. I know Greg, he would never allow anyone to mistreat his kids, ever! I felt today was not the time nor the place for her to air that laundry.

I walked over to Reece and told her, "Look missy! Clean up your attitude. We will talk about this later!" She cut her eyes over at Janice. When Greg and his litter were leaving, I walked over to the door and apologized to Janice. She doesn't seem mean. In fact she seems timid to me. Like had I made a sudden move she would have pissed her draws!

After everyone left, Cedrick asked, "So, does that mean I have to mouse around here on the weekends too now?" I responded, "Let me talk to her and find out where all of this is stemming from." I reached out to hug him but he pushed me away and went for the liquor cabinet.

As I made sure the girls were in their room, I prayed we not argue tonight, I was tired. Cedrick stayed up late drinking and came to bed wanting to talk. I told him tomorrow. He came back with, "Before I sneak out the house like some hardened criminal or after I ring the doorbell pretending to be a welcomed guest?"

I scooted to the end of my side of the bed. Cedrick sarcastically spits out; "Just what I thought, never want to talk when I do." He rolled over and started snoring. I'm thinking, 'dude, talk to me when you will remember we had a conversation!'

Cedrick and I had been together three years when he told me one morning, "Charlotte I'm taking you out tonight. Get a sitter." He leaned over to kiss me bye and whispered, "See you at four-thirty." And he left the house.

I questioned myself what event was Cedrick celebrating! It's not his birthday. I came home early, took the girls to Mother, returned home, showered, dressed in my green short off-one shoulder dress, and waited for Cedrick while I sipped on a glass of wine.

Cedrick entered the house with flowers and a brown paper bag. His J&B. We went to dinner and he was in a mood. Cedrick ordered three drinks on the rocks. I'm tired of this relationship. My stomach gets tied up in knots and my insides shake like I'm being electrocuted.

I'm not living the rest of my life like this, up, down, up, down. Now *I* have an attitude. After the plates were removed Cedrick leans in towards me and starts, "I meet people everyday. Most women I see when they're engaged, that's all the conversation anyone hears. You, Miss Young, have never asked to set a date for our wedding. You wear my ring but I'm treated like a trick that has to leave when my times up. Charlotte, do you want to get married?"

Now I'm pissed! "No I do not!" I hear myself getting loud. I shut up to calm myself. He leans back and says, "Alright. I'll get my things and leave. You ready to go?" I grab my purse and push my chair back to stand up. He quickly sits straight up and sternly says, **"Sit down!"** I jerk my neck back, 'He talkin to me?' "Sit down Charlotte Young!" I look around the room. People have stopped their conversation and are watching us so I sit on the edge of my chair.

He starts, "I love you. I didn't love Monica this much and I have never been treated like this before, ever. I tolerate your treating me like a child because I love you. You don't even realize today is three years we've been together. Three years I hoped every morning, today will be the day you see me as a man. But I will no longer be treated like some young boy by you. I am a man Charlotte. Why can't you see that?" I spoke up as I leaned into the table. "Okay, you want to do this here, let's go for it!

You say you're a man but you can't seem to talk to me like a man without a drink first! Talk to me when you're sober and I'll know for sure you mean what you're telling me. And let's not talk about you remembering the conversation! I love you Cedrick, I just don't like you when you drink. There! Can you handle that mister man?"

He's moving his bottom jaw around. Now he's squinting his eyes at me and jumps up out of his seat. Realizing we were not given the bill, Cedrick snaps his fingers at a waiter and yells, "**Check Please!**"

I head for the ladies room. When I enter the waiting area he's watching me. I'm taking a good long look at him realizing this is it for us. Cedrick is a good-looking man, and when not drinking he's a good man. I'm through with him getting mean when he drinks. I am done!

We ride home in silence. He gets a few grocery bags, takes them into our room and I wait in the living room while he packs up. He stands at the front door looking directly in my eyes. "Your keys are on your dresser. Charlotte I wish you the best. Sorry I couldn't make you happy." He left. As the door closes I'm thinking, 'Thank you very much Gregory Allen. Another three years of my life, gone…'

I missed Cedrick and cried when I felt lonely but being lonely made me realize I should keep to myself. I don't need a man to take care of me. When I need a man sexually, I have one night stands just like Irene. It works for me.

I told myself, 'I have teen girls. Reece is a thirty-six "C" cup bra and Tammi is a thirty-four "C." They are both shaped like me and have big shapely legs like Sam and Mother Mays. I can't have some man that's not their father walking around here eyeing them. I would try my best to kill a man if he tried something with my babies. And whatever is left of that man when I get through would be for Greg and Walt to have!'

From then on I wrapped myself totally into raising my teenaged daughters and doing a great job at the gallery. Like I said, it works for me!

~~~~Gregory~~~~

As I drive home from my counseling session I am so confused. I feel as though someone has stripped me butt naked in front of The Queen Mary and everyone passing by can see me. All Mrs. Judson asked was, "Gregory, why are you holding back tears?" I felt as though she stun gunned me.

I automatically shut my feelings to cry down. I have never felt comfortable crying in front of women. Well, only Char and Mama. Char understood me. So I thought. I cried as I held Char in my arms after we made love the first time. She cried along with me.

When Char and I first lived together we would lie in bed talking. We would share our innermost feelings and one night we were talking about the definition of love. Char told me her definition of her love for me. Man I mean I could feel her heart as she told me how she felt. As tears began to roll down her beautiful face, I teared up. I felt as if every word she uttered was coming straight from her heart out of her mouth. I allowed tears to stream from my eyes as I wiped her tears away. We ended up falling asleep holding one another. Man...

I remember coming home one morning and Char was sitting in the bed breastfeeding Charece. I stood at the foot of our bed, Char looked up at me and smiled while asking how work went. I watched her with our daughter. Char caressed our little infants small head and spoke so softly, "I love you little girl. Mommy loves you." Again I felt a wave of compassion overtake me and tears slowly flowed. Char reached out for me and I sat on the side of the bed next to her and hugged them both.

Char said in a wavering voice, "Greg you are a great husband and now you're a great dad. I love you." We both cried. Char never teased me or brought up my crying. In fact she would hug me and cry along. I mean, I didn't do waterworks, nothing like that. However back then, I felt comfortable enough to express my feelings of compassion.

When Faith was almost seven months pregnant I felt the baby kick for the first time. Faith and I were in bed and she snuggled up behind me and I felt Kozet kick me in my back. I thought, 'My son is making a touch down!' I was so moved and as I turned over, Faith began to straddle me and made a comment, "What's this?" She was making fun of my slowly dripping tear that had made its way to my cheek. She placed her thumb on my cheek and wiped it away.

Faith laughed and said, "I know you're not crying over a little kick in the back. Ha, Gregory as strong as you are, you are not a cry baby are you? Ha, ha, ha. Gregory Young is a cry baby." She looked down at her stomach and said, "Okay little Greg, don't be a wimp like your daddy! Ha, ha, ha!" I looked at her. She was making fun of me. That was the only time I cried in front of her or any other female with the exception of Mama.

After Mrs. Judson asked that question. I thought she was going to make fun of me for wanting to cry. As she sat looking at me I inhaled then responded, "Men don't cry. Everyone knows that." She says to me, " I want you to take your time and think. Then explain to me why you believe that?"

What was I supposed to tell her? No way in hell I am going to cry in front of her and if she thinks I am going to tell her how Faith made fun of me, huh; she is dead wrong. My business is my business!

After staring at her a few minutes, I looked at my watch. I had about nine minutes before our session ends. I put my arm down and stared at the coffee table periodically glancing at my watch. I looked Mrs. Judson in the face and said, "Times up!" And I got out of there.

Now I feel so naked. What is this crap! How many more of these nonproductive sessions must I have? Everyone knows a man ain't supposed to cry…

All through my shift I am rewinding the conversation Faith and I had in bed about me crying. I don't understand why that pisses me off but it does! I'm going to see if I can change from Mrs. Judson to a male counselor, she does not understand men. Mrs. Judson, yeah right, I bet she's divorced! Probably another bitter black female out to belittle every man in her path.

The first four weeks of counseling I went over my relationship with each one of my wives and my childhood with Mrs. Judson then she started with the stupid questions.

By the time I arrived home from work it was settled; I am requesting a male counselor.

This morning while eating breakfast I notice Mama has disappeared. She usually talks to me during my breakfast. Most days she updates me on what's going on in the lives of each one of my kids with the exception of Anna. I call Linda every so often for an update.

Charece married Charles Kennedy when she was eighteen and had Alexus and Tyreke so close together. I think that had barring on their break-up. Charles has a large family and they took his side when Charece and Charlie argued. Money was usually the issue and Charlie's family gave him money when he asked for it but his sisters kept telling Charlie that Charece was extravagant and he needed to put her in check.

Mama told Charece to keep her in-laws at bay but Charlie was the one drafting his family into their affairs. I guess every marriage has its set of problems to solve. I did get two grand kids out of their union. They are both good looking and smart.

Tamera stayed in her books. She reads like I do. I think because I always read around her she picked up a love for reading. She attended Scripps College majoring in Sociology. Tamera is our family Social Worker. I am so proud of her and was surprised yet happy to hear she was serious about the young man she is dating. With all of this homosexual awareness now days and Tamera not dating until she was almost twenty-one, I did wonder about her sexual preference.

Mama tells me this boy is handsome and they will make handsome babies. I thought about making an effort to spend time with my grandchildren. I will not be fathering anymore babies that is for sure. I am working on redeeming my relationship with The Lord. I need His guidance right about now.

I started attending church every Sunday again after moving into my place. I went to Holy Temple however when the kids saw me after church, it was very difficult. I would leave the parking lot thinking all I wanted was a family. Kozet would hug me and I would kiss her forehead and hold onto her while she told me how happy she was to see me. She would lay her head on my chest and wrap her arms around me smiling.

Kozet is very pretty. She looks like Mama and Sam however Kozet has Faith's beautiful, slanted eyes and high cheek bones. I love it when she smiles her full smile. When I say "Okay," she gets serious and as I tell her to have a good week, the girl has the fastest flowing tears I have ever seen!

And David, after he hugs me he stands a few feet away and watches my every move. When he knows I am leaving, he asks, "Dad are you coming back home?" I make sure to look him directly in the eyes and it actually hurts when I tell him every week, "No son, but I love you very much." Man…

After a few months of feeling as though I had not been in the presence of The Lord when leaving church, I decided to attend Morning Star. Now my logic is, I do not miss a day's work therefore I will not miss a Sunday.

This morning during my drive to Morning Star, I feel turbulence within me. I feel as though I am inside a whirlwind and cannot find an exit. Deep inside me there is a void and I cannot for the life of me figure out what it is. Lord, I need a Word from You. What is it I must do?

I enter the sanctuary and was escorted by the usher towards the middle of the sanctuary however, I took a seat on the end pew close to the rear of the church. It was not until the usher stopped to reveal the row she had selected that she realized I had already sat down. She gave me a look like, "Cannot follow directions!" I looked away from her and my eyes went straight to Dad Thomas. He was sitting on the Deacons row and gave me a nod. I nodded back.

Mother Thomas entered the sanctuary and stopped in front of me and told me to get up and give her a hug. As we hugged she whispered in my ear; "Glad to see you in The Lords house. Listen to The Lord Gregory. He has a plan and a purpose for you baby." She let me go and kissed me on my cheek.

As I sat down memories of being married to Char surfaced. I recall Mother Thomas giving her daughter advice. Most of the time Mother Thomas was telling Char, "Love covers faults Charlotte, don't smear his shortcomings all over his face. Concentrate on being a better wife." Char would reply, "Mother, you have always been partial to boys! Why I waste my breath telling you anything..." Sometimes Char would just shake her head at her mother and walk away. Mother Thomas has always had my back.

Lord I just want to settle down with a wife that appreciates me. I am a good hard-working man and want the best for my family that is all. Char was a great wife and I really did not know she was no longer in love with me. I believe that is what hurt me. I did not see her being unhappy. Almost catching her with another man was as if I walked right up on a brick wall and hit my head, I never saw it coming.

Char became whinny when pregnant with Charece. 'This hurt. Stop that's sore.' She complained all of the time. I read all I could about the body changes a female experiences while pregnant and Char was experiencing almost every recorded symptom. I became patient after reading what to expect.

After Charece arrived Char was always busy with "The baby" and I had to wait in line for some attention. I remember the day I decided to work extra overtime since Char was so wrapped up with Charece.

It seemed overnight Char told me she was pregnant again. At least she took birth control pills after Tamera arrived, unlike somebody else I know. I believe the reason it was difficult for me after leaving Char is, aside from being my wife, Char was my best friend. I could talk to her about what I felt and she was a great listener, she understood me.

Char was a sweet person, gentle and very loving. She could be a hellcat when the situation called for one but Char was warm and affectionate. Man…

After I left her I remember missing her so much I would feel like crying every moment I had free. I would picture her in my mind, smiling and giving me her amorous look. Man I loved that girl!

Working overtime allowed me to make a lot of money and I had saved over a thousand dollars to put towards buying our first home when Char realized she was pregnant again. I used the money saved to move us into a two-bedroom apartment in Lomita.

The area we were looking into purchasing our house was more than what I qualified for. Since Char was pregnant again, the bank would not consider her income to qualify for the house. Char worked part-time for The Afrikan Museum of Art downtown Los Angeles. Once Tamera came along, that was the end of her working.

That was when Char began dropping little remarks about me never wanting to spend time with her and the girls. I shrugged it off thinking when I was home, she had a baby in her arms. I just thought Char was whiny, I knew she was spoiled. That I did not mind, I wanted her that way so I could give her what she wanted. I would do anything to see that smile. I just never knew she would cheat on me...

This music is jammin, the choir is great.

I enjoyed the preaching also. Pastor Gray preached from John chapter 2 verses 1 through 11, it reads:

" On the third day there was a wedding in Cana of Galilee, and the mother of Jesus was there. [2] Now both Jesus and His disciples were invited to the wedding. [3] And when they ran out of wine, the mother of Jesus said to Him, "They have no wine."

[4] Jesus said to her, "Woman, what does your concern have to do with Me? My hour has not yet come." [5] His mother said to the servants, "Whatever He says to you, do it." [6] Now there were set there six waterpots of stone, according to the manner of purification of the Jews, containing twenty or thirty gallons apiece. [7] Jesus said to them,

"Fill the waterpots with water." And they filled them up to the brim. [8] And He said to them, "Draw some out now, and take it to the master of the feast." And they took it. [9] When the master of the feast had tasted the water that was made wine, and did not know where it came from (but the servants who had drawn the water knew), the master of the feast called the bridegroom.

[10] And he said to him, "Every man at the beginning sets out the good wine, and when the guests have well drunk, then the inferior. You have kept the good wine until now!" [11] This beginning of signs Jesus did in Cana of Galilee, and manifested His glory; and His disciples believed in Him."

Pastor Gray explained how Jesus was obedient to his mother and performed his first miracle. We must be obedient to God's Word and we too will see miracles in our lives. Pastor stressed Mary's words, **"Whatever He says to you, do it."** Should be what we the church live by, doing His Word!

God will *always* manifest His glory through His Word. We just need to put a demand on His Word. Pastor closed saying, "If you are facing a difficult time in your life today, remember what Jesus has done already and believe in Him for the miracles He has done. That should hold your faith together until this too passes. After all Jesus is the same, yesterday, today, and forever!"

That was a "WOW" statement for me. As I stood for dismissal I closed my eyes and prayed, "Lord knowing You never change, I need you to tell me what my next move should be, amen."

As I turned to leave I heard, "Daddy?" I looked up and into Tamera's beautiful face. She reminds me of Sam when she was growing up. Tall, brown skinned with pretty dark brown eyes that makes you not want to stop looking into them. Tamera's smile is warm like Chars and the young man holding onto her waist is looking directly into my eyes.

Him and I make eye contact and he extends his hand to me. We shake hands and he introduces himself, "Hello Mr. Young. It is good to finally meet you. I am Tamera's fiancée; Justin Moreland." "Hello Justin. Fiancée?" Tamera interrupts, "Daddy I have been meaning to call you lately but we are really busy getting our wedding plans together. The days are zipping by. Justin proposed last year and wanted a Vegas wedding but you know me, this will be my *only* wedding and it will be memorable."

I looked at Tamera and wondered if my invitation was mailed to Stockton Avenue. Mama has not mentioned anything. Now I am wondering if I am invited at all. Tamera pulls me by my arm and takes a few steps away from the isle and asks, "Daddy I want you to give me away. I'm asking you to please be the big person on my wedding day. Mom is too busy trying to talk me out of getting married to think about how to behave with you in the same room. Daddy can I count on you to make peace with her?"

As I look into my beautiful daughter's eyes all I can say is, "Of course." She kisses me on my cheek and Justin gives me a nod while saying, "Nice to meet you." I watch them as they leave waving at and hugging people in the congregation.

This church has been Charece and Tamera's church all their lives. Mother Thomas brought them when Char did not or could not. They had Easter and Christmas recitals here, Heaven and Hell Parties and Youth Days at this church and yes, I missed every last one of them. Look, a man has to provide for his family. Okay I am *not* going to get all guilty for keeping food on the table and clothes on their backs. I cannot believe I am leaving church mad!

On my drive home I remember Char being so excited about the first time Charece said, "Dada." And the night I came home and climbed into bed Char turned over and told me Charece has her first tooth coming in. The day after Charece took her first steps Char brought Charece into the bathroom while I was getting ready for work and had her walk for Daddy. I can see the smile on Char's face now. Man that woman had a smile.

I remember when Tamera was born. Now I am smiling.

Char was up when I arrived home from working twelve hours, and I was tired and sleepy. She began having labor pains around nine-thirty that evening and had Mother Thomas come pick up Charece and was now timing her labor. The pains were almost ten minutes apart.

I sat on the couch and dozed off. Char shook me and said, "let's go the pains are five minutes apart." I was so sleepy I could not move and dozed off again. Char was pacing the room and when another pain hit; she yelled, **"OH MY GOD! COME ON GREG BEFORE I HAVE THIS BABY RIGHT HERE!"**

I jumped up so fast and drove like a maniac.

I slept in the waiting room and when Mama woke me she said Char had another girl. My body felt so heavy like I was full of lead, I could barely move. I went to see Char and Tamera and held my beautiful brown daughter in my arms. She was so small and did I mention beautiful. As I kissed her tiny forehead I almost cried thinking, 'this precious bundle we made depends on me.' As I handed Tamera back to Char I thought, 'I will make sure you have a good life little girl.'

Today Tamera's arrival seems like just a few years ago and now she is getting married. Man did the time fly.

I arrived in LB from church and Sam's car is not in the driveway. I find Mama sitting on the couch in the living room. When she turned to face me I could tell she had been crying. I stood in front of her, waiting to hear her say something. Mr. Mays walks up to the living room doorway and says, "Hi son." Mama looked up at me and said, "Sit down Gregory. Your father Roland Berry called today." I sat but my eyes never left Mama's face.

She continues, "He wants to meet you after all these years. I was so angry I shouted at him over the phone. When he said he wanted to meet you and get to know you I totally lost it. I said, "Well Gregory's wanted to see you and know you too but you ran out on us like a scared bat outta hell. In fact, you can go straight *to* hell!" I slammed the phone down on him." Mama's lower lip is quivering and she looks over at Mr. Mays and continues.

"As I slammed the phone I realized Roland hurt me when he left me pregnant having to face Daddy alone. I was so ashamed being pregnant and Daddy made it his business to let me know how much of a coward Roland was for not taking care of his own child.

Gregory I loved your father and he took advantage of me and ran off. Mays is a good man and I love him dearly but I realize today after I received that phone call, I need to forgive your father and love Mays like he deserves to be loved."

Mama is now crying with her hands covering her face. I sit next to her while fighting back tears. I glance over at Mr. Mays and he is looking at Mama. As I turn my attention back to Mama I am thinking, 'That coward has the nerve to hurt my mother again! Oh yeah I want to meet him.'

Mama calms herself and looks me in the eyes while saying, "I'm sorry I didn't handle that phone call too well. Maybe he'll call again and you can speak to him." I had a visual of myself with a big leather strap giving Mr. Berry a good old-fashioned ass whupping! Mama stood up kitchen bound to warm the foods and I followed her. Mr. Mays walks over to Mama and kisses her forehead. She hugs him so tight she grunts; then tells him she loves him.

Mr. Mays gently lifts Mama's chin up and says to her, "I know you love me and being hurt makes it hard for you to express it sometimes. Phylis, I love you and the life you make for me, for us. If he calls again, I'll take the call. Gregory needs to know who he is and who his father is. We will all get through this. You'll see." He bent down and kissed Mama on the lips, turned around and placed his hand on my shoulder and left the room.

The three of us ate in silence. Mama played with her food and watched Mr. Mays. I noticed he kept his eyes on Mama. I went to the back room and thought about how I never noticed Mr. Mays and Mama interact while I grew up. They were so formal with each other back then. In fact Mr. Mays was invisible until any discipline was needed around here. He would render the whuppings however, Mama would interject very loudly I might add why we were getting what Mama called, "a belting."

Mr. Mays never whupped us when he was angry. One time he told Jamal; "Get out of this room right now! Boy If I hit you your mother will need an undertaker to bury your butt!" Jamal was gone right after the word 'Boy' was uttered. That was the only time I witnessed Mr. Mays being angry.

Jamal had taken Mr. Mays money out of his sock drawer. The dummy was buying ice cream, comic books, and a pair of sunglasses. When Mr. Mays discovered his money was gone, well he put two and two together. Whenever Mama found out one of us had done something to merit a whupping she would meet Mr. Mays at the back door telling him to beat Jamal and whup Samantha's tail.

When it was me that had done something, Mama would always start off saying, "Mays, Gregory needs a belting." Mama would stand in the doorway where Mr. Mays was explaining why what we had just done was wrong. Mama would be yelling with her fist balled up, **"That's enough talk! Beat him, and beat him good!**

When it came to Sam, Mama would go get the belt and hand it to Mr. Mays but he would talk to Sam and not take the belt from Mama until his speech was ended. Sometimes Mama would snap the belt at Sam and roll her eyes. Mama is only five feet, three inches but she can be a fireball.

That night I was thinking, 'I wonder what Roland Berry looks like. I look like Mama but she is brown like milk chocolate and short, so I must get my height and skin tone from Berry. Well now that I am thinking about this, Grand Pop is tall and mama looks like him with Grannie's skin tone. Well I want to meet this coward.'

I remember once when I was little before I started school. It was dark outside and Mama had my hand pulling me headed to the front door of Grannie's house. Grannie followed us and when we entered the living room Grannie yelled, **"He used you and you still holding onto him. You better stay with Mays and be thankful The Lord sent him your way!"**

Mama stopped after she opened the screen door and turned to face Grannie. Grannie continued in a lower tone, "Phylis that baby needs a father. As long as Mays doesn't beat on you and sleep around, make it work!" Mama looked down at me and said, "Come on Gregory!" Grannie grabbed me and picked me up to kiss me bye but I was scared mama was going to leave me. I squirmed to get out of Grannie's arms.

Man, I can't believe I remember that!

I am thinking back to my session Friday with Mrs. Judson. She told me to allow my mind to regress back to my childhood. That is where we develop outlines we use later in life. My childhood was good, so I think.

Grannie spoiled me and Grand Pop sat me down and taught me what things were, how they worked. He was only strict when it came to the Bible and when I asked questions. Yeah, I think I had a pretty good childhood, no mother issues here.

I need to figure out what my image of marriage is. Mrs. Judson said, "Mr. Young every couple enters marriage with two separate views of what marriage is. Working those different views out during marriage is a part of marriage. Examine your definition of marriage. Don't be afraid to embrace your truth. See you next week."

Wow, now I am thinking my grandparents, Mama and Mr. Mays are the only marriages I have as role models. Grand Pop rules over Grannie; telling her what to do all the time. Grannie is very passive and humbly does as told. Mama and Mr. Mays have always been formal. Mama pretty much does as she wants; Mr. Mays goes along with her. The Thomas house has a pretty good marriage. Mother and Dad Thomas are the only couple I have witnessed laughing, hugging, and kissing. He pats her behind a lot.

Hmm, I wonder what Berry has to say.

I am unable to sleep tonight. I lie here thinking about Tamera and Berry. I received shocking news twice in one day. I can handle giving Tamera away, I just do not know if I can handle Char being there with another man. I watched her perform at Charece's wedding. I was mad because I had no idea Char was such a loose woman. She was totally out of character. Then again, I never knew she would allow another man to touch her. Maybe I was mad because as it turned out I did not know Char like I thought.

Even though Janice and I were separated at the time I escorted her and the kids to Charece's wedding and reception. Janice kept her arm wrapped around mine the duration of the wedding and reception. Janice was afraid of Char. The girls had told so many lies about Janice being mean to them. Char would phone us late Sunday nights after the kids were in bed and tell Janice off about mistreating her daughters. Janice told me Char threatened to put sugar in her gas tank if she mistreated her girls one more time.

Janice was in tears that night so I took all of the late-night calls after that. Char and I would have shouting matches. I told her I was their father and would not allow anyone to mistreat my daughters. She always went to, "Oh so now you want to be their father. Sure you have time for that Greg! How you gonna use daddy skills when you're not around, huh!"

I would end up hanging up on her or she would hang up on me. I must admit when I talked to Char, in my mind, all I could see was her with those stupid sheets in her hands. I realize tonight... I was hurt... Maybe I still am.

I worked my butt off making it financially possible for us to live a decent life and all I have ever gotten from every wife I have had is the same recording. I am either cheap or only think about the budget or I never want to spend time with them. Why can't women see it takes money to buy things and someone has to go to work for that money. Man it does not take a rocket scientist to figure that out!

Tamera told me Char is trying to talk her out of marriage. I wonder why. Well, I hope Tamera and Justin makes it. He seems respectable and Tamera has waited this long to marry. I thought Tamera was shy as a little girl until Mama told me I was shy also when I was her age. I knew then Tamera is a thinker. Charece is outgoing like Char, she has never been shy. We had to watch her closely when she was a toddler because Charece went to anyone.

Looking at Tamera today, I realize my daughters are all grown up and I cannot say I was part of their growing up. After Charece and Tamera stopped spending weekends with us I only saw them Christmas and Father's Day. Char would let them come to church with Mama and Mr. Mays every once in a while. Some occasions she would drop them off for a few hours at Mama's.

One Christmas Charece and Tamera came to spend the holiday with us as a family, they had two ponytails and the next Christmas they were wearing bras. They grew up so fast.

Man. I lay here in bed shaking my head because I realize I have married for companionship and, a nice-looking body. Honestly, I really did not want to marry Faith or Linda, what I wanted was to playhouse with them. I knew Faith and I were total opposites.

I believed Faith being different than Char made me think she was possibly the kind of woman I needed. Faith being a hard worker and an hourglass body had a lot to do with me wanting to be with her too.

I also knew Linda's son was going to be a problem the first day I met him. But Linda had such a body on her and the teasing drove me mad. Looking back I see where she lassoed me into her web but I could not take my eyes off her sexy body.

I think I was in lust with my last three wives. I know it was lust with Maria. Janice had a small waist, big hips, and legs. Yep! Lust was leading me then and I was caught way up in it.

Lord I am asking You to deliver me from the lust of my flesh and the lust of my eyes. [1 John 2:15,16] says:

"Do not love the world or the things in the world. If anyone loves the world, the love of the Father is not in him. [16] For all that is in the world—the lust of the flesh, the lust of the eyes, and the pride of life—is not of the Father but is of the world."

Right now Father, I repent of my lustful ways and desire to walk in newness of life. Life guided by You Holy Spirit. Direct my path to righteousness and be with me as I walk in it. I give You permission to take my life and do what You will, because Your ways are exceedingly wise. Teach me to walk upright in Your ways Holy Spirit, is my prayer, In Jesus name, Amen.

I woke this morning and realized it was Monday; therapy session, I regret having to get up.

Just as I thought, Mrs. Judson asks another dumb question. "Gregory what was the constant complaint from each one of your wives. I need you to be honest and remember, I am not here to judge you."

I did not have to think long. " Well, every one of my ex-wives said the same thing. As if they wrote it down on a piece of paper and handed it over to the next Mrs. Young. 'You never want to spend time with me. All you talk about is the budget.' That was the constant complaint."

Mrs. Judson then ask, "Is there any truth to what they all told you?" I looked at her, realizing there was. "Maybe." I was hoping she would let it go.

"How does it make you feel; your ex-wives being right with their complaint?"

"People are entitled to their own feelings."

"True. When more than a few people share the same opinion, do you think there may be some truth in what's being said?"

Now Mrs. Judson is ganging up on me! I look at her. She is looking at me, waiting for my answer. "Look. I am a responsible man. I take care of my wives, children, and myself. I do legitimate work and I mind my own business. They do not understand. In order for them to have a decent roof over their head, nice clothes on their backs, running water and transportation, that stuff costs. And *I* so happen to be the one paying!" My volume is slightly up there.

"Gregory, what are you feeling right now?"

"Pissed!"
"Why?"

"Because she cheated on me and I took real good care of her and the girls!"

"Who?"

Wow! I am still mad. I need to collect myself.

"Who are you referring to Gregory?"

"…Char."

"Your first wife?"

I nod "Yes." I feel as though I want to cry. I clear my throat and sit straight up and say, "Look I do not want to talk about her. Move on to something else."

"Gregory, I am here to walk with you to the truth. Should you choose to ignore the truth, you will remain the same. Should you choose to take a look at the truth, get an understanding of that truth, then and only then are you able to heal. The choice is yours to make. Remember; broken people can only break people. Healed people…"

I have heard enough. "Yeah, yeah, I know!"

"Why are you angry right now. Gregory do you know the reason why you are upset?" I lean forward and say in a calm voice, "All I have ever wanted, was to make my wife happy and give her everything she thought she wanted. I have to work in order to do that. What do I get… cheated on. She had another man *in my bed*!" I feel tears trying to break from me because I am mad enough to hit someone!

I look away from Mrs. Judson, lean back and shut up. "Gregory, God made us to cry when we hurt. It is not a bad emotion. Pain is part of life and some consider crying is a releasing of pain. Cry if you need too. This is one of the places crying is in order. What's said or done here is kept in confidence."

I fought back tears and had nothing more to say. When my time was up, I got up and walked out.

As soon as I unlocked my truck the tears started. I sit down and hit my steering wheel. Not good, my shoulder is still tender. I hurt… I am hurting. Lord I hurt not just my shoulder. Help take this pain in my heart away, please.

I sit in my truck weeping. This hurts so bad. Char broke my heart. I really loved that woman. What hurts me is… I thought she loved me. I thought she understood me and knew I was working to get us a home for her and the girls…

I am done. I will just date and leave the relationship crap alone.

I turn my phone on and start my truck. On my way to work Mama texts me; "He called again. I didn't pick up. Call your father. 954 555-1111" Man. When it rains it pours. I decide to get this over with. I pull up into a parking space at work and look at his number. I am angry. It is best I call tomorrow.

All during my shift I thought of what I would say to my biological father. I have been on light duty since I returned to work. I am in the cage issuing parts and it gets slow so I have plenty time to think. I really want to know what happened to him and my mother. Maybe Berry cannot manage a relationship either.

Mr. Mays is a good man and I never want to make him think I do not appreciate him taking me in and treating me like he does Jamal. I know of a few guys I went to school with whose mothers gave them to their grandparents to raise because their mothers new husbands did not want to be bothered with another man's kid. Not Mr. Mays.

I remember asking Mama about my real father. She always told me he went to the service and never came back. The last time I asked Mama about my father was on a Father's Day. I had to have been twelve or thirteen. She gave me the same line as before and when I asked, "Do you know where he is?" Mama had the look of shock on her face. She said, "Gregory a lot of men go away to fight for our country and just never come back. I have no idea how to get in touch with your father. Mays will just have to do. Hear me?"

After that conversation I never brought up my father again, I just kept the questions to myself. Now my father is reaching out to me so I guess it is time to face him.

I drove home from work thinking why now this father thing, on top of having to deal with these ungrateful wives. I was trying to figure out if my answers to why I feel unappreciated may lie in my being abandoned by my biological father... Who knows.

I woke with Roland Berry on my mind. I am ready to face him and move on. I called him before heading to LB. "Hello, this is Gregory, may I speak to a Mister Roland Berry?" "Speaking. Thank you for returning my phone call." He sounds articulate. In fact his voice sounds like mine. "Gregory I would like to meet with you. There are some things being said face to face gives more clarity. My apology to you for not being active in your life merits a face to face."

"I agree." "Thanks son. When is a good time for you, and do you have a place of preference?" I answer, "This time of day works for me and there is an IHOP on PCH." He asks, "This time tomorrow good for you?" "Yes." "Alright, see you tomorrow. Bye." Did he call me Son? He wants to apologize... huh.

While driving to Mama's I went over the phone conversation with Mr. Berry in my head. The words, "son and apology" kept replaying. While I ate Mama eased herself down in her chair across from me at the kitchen table. I said, "We are meeting tomorrow. He wants to apologize to my face." She looked at me, I mean really looked at my features. I was going to ask if something was wrong but she stood up and told me my lunch was in the fridge and left the room.

That is when it dawned on me tomorrow is session day. Monday, Wednesday, and Friday's are when I meet with Mrs. Judson. Yeah, she is the one benefiting, getting paid and I am still not divorced.

I got up and called Berry. I left a message, "Sorry I will have to meet you Thursday. Tomorrow is not good. Gregory." He has my number now so if he is unable to make it, oh well. I am so tired of doing my best and it is only being misconstrued.

Work was slow and I decided tomorrow I am calling the counseling agency to get another counselor. The more I thought about how I was not getting anywhere with this counseling and still married, the angrier I became. By the time I arrived home I was so agitated I could not sleep. Mrs. Judson was now added to my list of women I cannot wait to be rid of!

After I dressed, before heading to LB I called the number on my court papers and was transferred to two different persons. Finally I talk to the appointment division and after being on hold for over ten minutes, I am told there is no way I can be transferred to another counselor without written approval and my sessions would start over. I was so angry I cussed the lady and hung up on her.

I get to LB and Mama gives me the silent treatment. Oh well.

Now I get to Mrs. Judson's office pissed to the max! Again Mrs. Judson has questions for me. I snapped my answers at her and she sat still for a few minutes and says, "Alright Gregory, you are having a bad day. It's part of life." She tore off a sheet of paper on her tablet and as she handed her tablet to me, she says, "Since you're so angry write your feelings down. Here."

She handed me her ink pen. I took both tablet and pen from her as I say, "I am mad enough to cuss. You sure want to read what I have to say?" She motions for me to write. I hold the pen, look at Mrs. Judson and say, "Roland Berry wants what from me? Why does everyone want a piece of Gregory Allen?"

I slam the tablet down on the small end table next to me. "What is it about Gregory Allen that everyone just has to rip him apart, piece by piece! **I am sick of this! All I want is to make my wife happy and take care of my damn kids!**" I am rapidly blinking back tears.

Mrs. Judson asks, "Why is it alright for Gregory Allen to be pissed but not you?" I sit all the way back in the chair and bow my head. Too ashamed to look at Mrs. Judson. Tears are streaming down my face. I am holding back the dam I feel rumbling around inside me, wanting to break free. I close my eyes. I hear a soft, "Cry Gregory, cry."

The gentleness in Mrs. Judson's voice sounds as if it is a choir directors baton, directing the flow of tears up and out of me. I cried.

I saw in my mind the hurt from each wife. I became aware of the pain from not being understood…

I saw the pain from not being appreciated…

I saw Mr. Roland Berry's silhouette and felt pain from being forgotten. I felt pain from being betrayed and taken for granted. I feel so lonely…

I feel so stupid! I opened my mouth and cried out: **"Lord help me…"**

I cried and snotted so much I was actually tired. I looked up at Mrs. Judson and could care less what she thought of me.

"Gregory share some of the emotions you felt while crying." I told her what I felt.

She says, "It's okay to feel what you feel. What's not okay is bottling our feelings up and refusing to look them in the mirror. Carrying un-productiveness from relationship too relationship is never healthy. Gregory are you a believer?" I told her I was.

"You are open now. You have attached a label to your pain. Now place each label at the foot of the cross, knowing, not doubting, Christ loves you enough to heal you. I will give you a few moments to do that." Mrs. Judson stood up and walked over to her desk and pulled out some files and began writing, never looking up at me.

I had no idea what she wanted me to do so I sat with my head down seeing myself laying my bundle of pain down. I silently prayed:

'Lord you made me. You know my strengths and my weaknesses. I repent now as I lay the pain and hurt down. As I get up from this chair, I will leave every labeled pain here and not take any of it with me. I pray to You believing You are my Healer. And please direct my path. I am so tired of making wrong moves and having to come to You to straighten out the mess I have made. Guide me Lord. I yield to Your way concerning me. In Jesus Name I pray. Amen.'

When I looked over towards Mrs. Judson she comes back to her chair. As she sits she says, "Alright Gregory, you need to think about what would work best for you to improve. I am referring to you improving on what each one of your wives said about you. For instance not spending enough time with your next wife. How would you improve yourself so you won't hear that complaint again?

I thought, 'She never lets up, man!' I sat and looked at her. She looks at me and says, "Want to share with me what you will do?"

"I don't know, spend more time with her. You know it is almost time for me to leave." She glances at her watch and says, "Alright, you did good today. See you Friday."

All during my shift I thought about what Mrs. Judson asked… *"When more than a few people share the same opinion, do you think there may be some truth in what's being said?"*

I know I work a lot. I even asked for overtime when Char first had the girls. She was always into them and I felt like I was waiting my turn for her to get to me. So I decided I could make more money. I never thought Char would ever cheat on me. We were best friends and when she went silent on me, well, I thought she was finally over not being angry.

Faith was extravagant and thought I was cheap. People who come from meager beginnings often tend to be that way.

Janice, she complained after Jonathan started school about us not spending time together. Maybe because Janice refused to take birth control, and gained so much weight I did not want to spend time with her. When she lost that last baby I thought, 'I hardly touch her, how the hell she get pregnant again?' That ended it for me with her. She refused to take birth control and I had enough children to support I could not afford her giving me another mouth to feed. Anyway, looking at her weight helped turn me off.

Linda played the same "lonely" record. She even told me she was not that lonely *before* we were together…

Okay, I will admit I worked a lot. But how does giving a woman what she needs constitutes not wanting to be with her? Not one of my children have ever said their father could not provide for them. Not one Young went hungry or without whatever it was they needed. The lights and water has always been on. Every time pajamas were needed, I made sure no one went without. I really do not get it! How does providing make me a horrible man? Forget this! Three weeks left of this counseling. I will just sit it out the remainder of my sessions. All I want is a divorce!

I went home but could not sleep until the sun came up. Now what does Berry want? I tossed and turned. I envisioned myself jumping the man. Then asking him where has he been all my life. What is this meeting about?   Finally I dosed off but I was tired when my alarm went off.

I called Berry to confirm we were still on. We were. I arrived at the IHOP and had to wait for him to show up. He was easy to pick out of the crowd as my father. I look just like him with the exception of my nose. His is pointed and we are the same complexion. I am a foot taller. I kept staring at him. He looked as though he were my older brother. Maybe that is why he stared at me.

He sat down and started talking…"Well Gregory I cannot deny you, that is for sure." I looked at him. I have nothing to say. He asked for this meeting. He is still talking. "I have never been a talker so, I will get to the point of this meeting. I married Judith three years after I left California. I went to Florida for my Naval training and you have three sisters and a brother. I made a career of the Navy and after retirement, I began attending church with Judith and, well Gregory, I need your forgiveness. I have repented to God, your mother will not let me tell her I am sorry for leaving her pregnant.

Gregory, I was twenty years old and ran women back then. I was scared out of my mind when your Mother told me I had to marry her. I was too young, *we* were too young to be married. The marriage would not have worked and you would have grown up under horrible conditions. I did not settle down until Judith walked into my life.

Gregory, please forgive me for being a coward and running out on you and your mother without an explanation. Is that possible?" I looked him in the eye and said, "Sure." He sat staring at me and I noticed a tear slowly draining from his eye. He quickly wiped it away but continued staring at me.

He says, "As a young man I never cried. You know, Naval training and Barber Shop talk of men don't cry nonsense." I felt myself squirm. "Gregory, real men cry. Compassion is indication of you being sentient of others feelings. Once I began to cry, hours had passed before I was able to collect myself.

I believe I lost ten pounds of retained water." He smiles but I am fighting back tears. I want to punch him in the face and hug the man at the same time. I look away from him and take a deep breath. When I turn my attention back to him, he has a serious look. "Alright. I have taken enough of your time. Should you want to get to know the Berry history, just give me a call."

He rose up while saying, "Son, I deeply regret not getting to know you while you developed but it would be my pleasure to get to know you now. Thanks for allowing this meeting. You may not understand, but I do have love for you, you are my firstborn." He extended his hand to me as I stood up, and I reached out to shake his hand. The man pulled me into his arms, and I hugged the man!

When I felt his strong hand in my back, I whimpered like some woman and shocked myself. He held me tighter as he whispered, "Lord heal my son. Heal my son." Man I broke. My father held me and I felt safe and angry. Emotions were surfacing inside me I never knew I had. I swallowed real hard and let go of him and he sat back down so I followed his lead.

We both pulled napkins from the dispenser and wiped our faces. The waitress came and took our coffee orders and after she left Berry says, "How about some breakfast?" I nodded and we had breakfast together. I felt like a little boy having breakfast with him.

I felt as though he had answers to who I am and yet, I resented his abandoning me and my mother. I guess it was Holy Spirit giving me the ability to sit and listen. My father told me about his childhood.

He has a younger brother, my Uncle Reginald, a year younger. He remembers his parents arguing constantly while growing up and their arguments were mainly about money. By the time he began junior high school, his father left.

His mother did her best but she became religious and made them attend church a lot. He was a ladies man in high school playing basketball gave him a great advantage with the females.

He met Mama in high school, Woodrow Wilson Classical High. He was a senior and she was a sophomore. They secretly saw each other and when my father graduated he began working for Mc Donald's Restaurant in the maintenance department. He was working and giving his mother money.

My grandmother, his mother, Paula Berry, was working a full time and a part-time job. When Mama found out she was pregnant my father joined the Navy so he could leave California. Attending the same church as Mama he knew Grand Pop would make them marry and, he also knew he was not ready to settle down.

At that time he thought about how he grew up having to hear the fights and arguing and figured he would do his kid a favor by leaving. Later he realized he was a coward leaving my mother without saying goodbye, but the damage was done. Now he wants to right some wrongs.

My grandmother Paula lives in Phoenix, Arizona close to my uncle Reggie. It was her who kept in touch with a neighbor who knows my grandparents.

My grandmother Paula kept my father informed of my accomplishments.

My Uncle Reggie married and has three children and because they are spread out over the map, they are not that close. When my father said, "I understand if you choose not to get to know me and family on my side. I just want to extend myself to you."

I wondered if my DNA was limited to his looks. Family has always been important to me. Me not being with my kids made me understand why he was not with me.

We parted agreeing to keep in contact and I went to LB. Mama was at the ironing board. When I walked in the back room she put the iron down and stood waiting for me to say something. After greeting one another she asked what happened. I told her we had breakfast and she sat down on the couch. I explained what my father told me about being scared and too young to settle down.

Mama squinted her eyes and said, "Would'a been nice had he told *me* that!" I said, "He asked for my forgiveness. He also said he would ask you for forgiveness, but you never give him the chance."

Mama folded her arms while sarcastically saying, "OH he did, did he!" I softly said, "Mama, I forgive the man. Life is too short to hold onto hurt.

Besides, forgiveness is for the offended not the offender." She looked at me and tears silently began to fall down her cheeks. I walked over and hugged her while telling her I loved her and appreciate all she has done for me. I walked away letting her know I was on my way to work.

Nine-thirty p.m. I get a text from Tamera... "Daddy we will be having a meeting Sunday evening with the wedding party and you are invited to come. Mom has agreed to be civil. We will meet at our place six p.m. sharp. If you can make it, it would make me happy." Her address was listed and "love always Tammi" was her signature.

Why did I read her signature over and over... Love, always. I was moved every time I read it. My daughter loves me unconditionally. I began to wonder if she knows I love her the same way.

My mind regressed to when Tamera and Charece were growing up. I told my kids that I loved them as much as I could when they were small but I am not sure they know I still love them. They acted as though they did not want to be around me when they became teens. I guess my working so much, caused our time together to diminish.

By the time I clocked out at work, my mind was on whether or not my wives knew I loved them. Not being home left room for doubt. I went to bed and saw Tamera's "Love, always" in my mind. Again I was up questioning how can anyone know they are loved if no time is spent with the person.

Around two a.m., I sat up in my bed and thought about how Char would beg me to spend time with her. I recalled many different occasions she would ask if we could go to the nearby park and just lay on a blanket together. I remembered how before we broke up Char would have tears in her eyes as she asked when I would be able to just hold her like I used to…

A light bulb in my head came on!

I was so busy trying to make her happy buying her things and never wanting her to go without, the thought of hugging her or holding her and expressing how much she meant to me never occurred to me.

I figured our times together earlier in our relationship was a good foundation. Char should have known I loved her. My thoughts were constantly about giving her whatever she wanted.

I really thought Char was experiencing self-esteem issues after the birth of our daughters. She continuously asked if I loved her. I remember thinking, 'How could she possibly think I do not love her?'

I sit here in bed making myself rewind the expressions Char held on her face when she asked, begged, and sometimes cried while asking me to spend time with her…

I now realize Char was wanting, needing my affection, my reassurance…

That realization about Char caused the sound of Janice and Linda's voices to have the same sound; "You never want to spend time together…"

My understanding became enlightened. I could see Char's point. I have to admit, I had fallen short in the "Being There" department concerning my marriage.

Huh, I faced my truth.

Had it been me wanting to spend time with them… Why did I not see this before? I made myself comfortable while sitting up against the headboard and allowed truth to completely take over my thoughts.

Faith was just lust. Her being a hard worker I thought we would work together and have it all. After living with her I realized we had two totally different agendas. Faith wanted better for herself, I wanted better for our family.

Janice, I thought she wanted what I did. A home for us to be a family in. I felt I was drowning in pampers and formula. I could not see us getting ahead, just keeping our heads above water. Janice saw nothing wrong with that. She once told me she wanted to have all the babies I could give her. Had she taken birth control and lost weight, we might still be together.

Linda; lust again. She told me what Char could not. She had to take a lover; I was not home. I am a good provider but when it comes to spending time building our marriage, I lacked in that area.

When I asked Linda if I were a lousy lover, she was quick to tell me on the contrary. My lovemaking was reason she wanted to be with me so much. That was a feather in my hat. I was hurting then… I am being brutally honest. Man!

I finally fell asleep. My alarm went off and I did not want to wake up. I realized it was Friday and Mrs. Judson's face flashed before my mind. I felt broken and if she wants tears; she can have them today!

Mama was in a somber mood and I felt like talking. I looked at my food but drank the coffee and asked, "Mama I realized last night I could have stayed home more while married to Char and she would not have cheated on me. At the time I thought being a provider was most important in a marriage. How can

I make right this wrong I have done?" She got up and left the kitchen.

Mama returned to the table with a notebook and as she sat down she turned several pages in it and says, "Okay, here it is." She looks up at me and says, "Son, the woman was made for the man as a help mate. Most church folk interpret the words help mate as a means of financial help but let me read to you what help mate really means." Mama reads to me what is written in her notebook:

"To surround, support, reinforce." Mama slowly lays the notebook down on the table and looks up at me and continues. "Men always say women are complicated. We are different is all. The woman was made for the man. We need to be wanted, we need to be loved. Gregory us women need to know we are the only woman in this world for you.

We give everything we are and have for who we love. We will surround you with love, kindness, sex, nurturing, and we will support your dreams and visions. We will reinforce whatever you say. Only if, hear me, only if we know we are your one and only love.

The minute a woman doubts her man is not dedicated to only her, like we are to him, huh, you on your own. No more supporting, surrounding and the only thing we will reinforce is nagging! When a woman doubts being her man's one and only you got trouble on your hands.

Now a man was created to create supply and fix. He needs to be appreciated, respected, and given plenty lovin. Females are more emotional than males and get bent outa shape when things are in a mess. We also help you men to look at situations with your emotions and not use logic all the time.

When the woman feels she's not wanted, there will be hell to pay. When a man feels unappreciated or disrespected, there's gonna be hell to pay. Gregory God created us to balance each other that's all. But we end up divorcing and not growing, not learning. If you ask me, we need to be taught what marriage is. Sex ain't all there is."

I asked, "Mama how do you feel about my father?"

Mama folded her arms, tilted her head, and said, "I felt he used me and when he left me; well, you weren't the only thing growing in me, so was malice. I felt like I was just a roll in the hay to him. Women give themselves to a man the first time out of love. After you told me he was sorry… Gregory, I needed to know I wasn't used. That I wasn't just there and he used me.

I was in love with your father and he ran off and without a word. I thought the worse. You know when we don't know the truth, we think the worst. I was seventeen when I was pregnant with you and I was scared to death. Daddy was so angry and when your father left me, my father thought I was just whoring around and got caught."

Mama is blinking back tears as she continues in a trembling voice. "Every ounce of love I had for Roland turned into hate. I'm working on forgiving the man now." She breaks down crying. I sit across from her and allow tears to flow down my face also. I can relate.

After drying my face, I realize tears really are a form of cleansing. I felt sorry for my father and Char. My father because his leaving Mama and me created a pattern of unforgiveness for Mama and I to live by. And I felt sorry for Char because she had no idea I was working to please her so she could be happy having everything she thought she wanted. Sorry for Char because I was young and had no clue building a marriage includes spending time with each other.

Mama is right; male and females balance one another.

On the way to my session I thought about what Mama said regarding male and female roles and how God created us. I recollected my Bible studying days and revelation of us needing one another became clear as a bell.

In 1 Peter 3:7 the scripture tells us husbands to live with our wives with understanding. Respecting them being the weaker one in the relationship. Mama explaining how the woman is more emotional minded, I realized my wives wanted to spend more time being together and us holding each other. Me being a man, thought of the responsibility of providing.

I feel as though my understanding is now clearer than ever. I am shaking my head up and down, yeah, I totally understand why I am on my way to this session.

As I stepped off the elevator to Mrs. Judson, I stood straight up, I am ready for her today.

"Gregory today we are going over all of the definitions for the word "intimacy." They are all written down on this worksheet. I will read the definition and you tell me what the definition means to you and if you have experienced the definition. If so, who with. We are here to heal, not criticize. Your feelings and opinions are yours and we are all entitled to our own opinions. Are you ready for the first definition?"

I shake my head "Yes." "Okay, the first definition is, Close familiarity or friendship." I look at her and ask, "Do you want me to say who my close family members are and close friends?" "Sure, if you would like. I also need to know your opinion of what that definition means.

If I were answering this I would say, I Believe I know what 'Close familiarity' is. My relationship with my friend Stacy since third grade would best describe it. Our friendship has lasted over twenty-five years and we have shared a lot of our life's changes. Something to that effect.

Gregory I need you to examine yourself as to whether or not you have any experiences with these definitions. If you haven't just say so and we will move on to the next definition. Okay?" Again I nodded.

I say to Mrs. Judson, "I have experienced intimacy with my family. Char is my oldest friend; we have known each other since I was eleven and she was nine." Mrs. Judson looked at me and when she realized I was done talking she says, "Alright Gregory, that was very good. Can you tell me who in your family you are most familiar with and why?"

"I am most familiar with my mother. She knows me better than anyone else in my family."

"So, you are not closest to your brother?"

"No, not really. Jamal is five years younger than I am. We did not have much in common growing up, I was mostly his guardian. Our parents worked seven days a week most times."

"May I inquire if you are close now that you are both grown?" "Oh no. I left home when Jamal was almost fourteen." "Okay Gregory, so you are not intimate with your brother Jamal as far as being familiar, what about friends. Did Jamal come to his big brother for girl advice or similar subjects?"

I thought about how Jamal always talked to Mr. Mays and how I would sometimes hear portions of their conversations. "No, he never did."

"Do you know who your brother Jamal went to for such advice?" "Sure, he went to Mr. Mays, his Dad."

"How do you know this?"
"I overheard some of their conversations."
"And what were your reactions when you heard Jamal and his Dad talking?"

"Well if it was a subject I had questions about, I would go to Mama and ask her." "And your Mother would answer you satisfactory?" "Sure. Mama and I have always been close."

"Gregory, have you ever thought about going to Mr. Mays instead of your Mother?"   "No."

"That's great Gregory let's move on to definition number two. Thinking of intimacy, who are you closest too, and why?"

I quickly replied, "My mother and Char!" "Why your Mother?" "Oh that's easy. It was just the two of us for the first five years of my life. I talked to Mama about any and all questions I had." "Why Charlotte. Gregory why are you intimately close to Charlotte.

Remember Gregory this is pertaining to being close, not being sexual, but being comfortable being close with this person."

"I understand. First of all, I *was* intimately close to Char, not anymore. Char and I, well, she was like Mama. I could tell her or ask her anything and like Mama, she never judged me. She understood me." "So Gregory let me ask you this; were you ever intimately close with any of your other wives?"

"Oh no!" I'm shaking my head 'NO' while answering.

Mrs. Judson asks; "Do you think any of your other wives would understand you like Charlotte did? Gregory I ask because of the rapid response you gave." Now Mrs. Judson has me thinking… "Maybe because I knew Char longer than my other wives. She knew me and my other wives did not."

"Gregory, let me get clarity. You didn't know your other wives as long as you knew Charlotte so you didn't feel as close to them as you felt with Charlotte. Am I understanding you?

"Yes." Mrs. Judson continues, "So, did you not allow your other wives to see or get intimately close to you?" I know where she is going with this. She thinks I wore a mask with my other wives.

"Look, I did not wear a mask when I dated my wives. They all knew Gregory Young. They changed into nagging needy women after the wedding. *They were the ones wearing a mask, not me.*"

Mrs. Judson does not skip a beat, "That leads us to our next definition, number three. Have you experienced intimacy in a private cozy atmosphere with someone without the atmosphere being set for sexual activity. Just a private cozy relaxed atmosphere? Gregory do you understand? Intimacy can be very private and shared in a relaxed place without sex ever being the motive. Are you understanding the definition?"

"I understand the question. But men are always working on sex being the goal of anyplace private and cozy. Are you married?"

"Gregory, this is one of many definitions for the word intimacy. A private cozy setting can also be for a time of sharing ones deepest personal feelings and thoughts. And to answer your question, I am very happily married. Can you think of a time when you were with someone and you felt comfortable sharing your personal feelings?   "No."

"Gregory I need you to think about the question. To be in a private cozy place with someone you trust enough to open up too about what you may never share with anyone else. Think for a minute. Is there anyone?"

After I thought about the question I remembered talking to Char like that. But I would never share my deepest feelings with anyone else. So I responded, "Yes, Char."

"Good! Gregory, you are doing great with your answers. Now the next definition is an act of sexual activity. I need you to think please before you answer this definition.

Most people assume if a couple have children intimacy is involved in the relationship. However we can see by these definitions, intimacy is an act of opening oneself up for another to see what is very personal. You might say intimacy is the purest form of truth we humans experience.

Gregory, a lot of people are afraid to reveal their natural selves. Remember, we are only going over the definitions of intimacy to reveal if you have experienced any of them. Alright?"

"Alright. Well honestly, now that your definition is opening ones authentic self-up during the act… well, maybe I have opened myself up like that, maybe a few times. Yeah, a few times."

"And who were you with at the time?" I felt as though I was going to choke. I cleared my throat and looked away from Mrs. Judson. I whispered, "Charlotte."

I felt myself getting angry. Man this is getting nowhere fast. Mrs. Judson handed me a Kleenex and I held it, cleared my throat, and said, "Next definition!"

Alright Gregory, this is the last definition. Intimacy can also be when you are close enough to someone you are comfortable sharing your true observations or knowledge of a subject with. Can you think of anyone you were comfortable enough with to allow that to happen?"

My mind immediately went to a time Char and I were laying in our bed when we were first married. I was holding her and telling her my insight of life. She rubbed my arm and said, "That is so deep. You are a thinker for real. And you know what?" Char turned over to face me and continued, "I love you. Just the way you are."

Yeah, she loved me so much the way I was, she had to sleep with another man and in the very bed I shared my deepest thoughts!

So much for intimacy! I moved my eyes to Mrs. Judson and noticed she was observing me. I looked away from her. I am done with this definition crap. She asks, "Anyone come to mind?" I snapped, "NOPE!"

"Alright Gregory we skimmed over these definitions today. I am giving you this copy of the worksheet we just went over for you to take home. Gregory, your homework will be to examine each definition. Take your time and be truthful. Measure your feelings regarding each definition to see if you can embrace the definition and if not, take time to ask yourself what is hindering you from embracing its meaning.

Remember we are walking to your truth and your feelings can be healed when the reason why you are unable to embrace intimacy is revealed."

Mrs. Judson pulled out a copy from her tablet and handed it to me. I took it to appease her however

I did go over the list and had a good cry while I did. This crying has got to stop.

Today is Saturday, wow this week is over. I went to LB and talked to Mama about Tamera wanting me to join the meeting tomorrow evening. I was having second thoughts about going. Mama told me to go and if I felt uncomfortable, just leave. I didn't want Mama to know I felt uncomfortable about going because I do not know my own daughters anymore.

I fathered them but after they stopped being with us on the weekends, I missed a segment of their development and realize that was the most important segment. They were transitioning into young ladies and I do not know who they are now.

Mama thought Char being at the meeting would make me uncomfortable but Char I can handle. My daughters whom I do not have any idea what they like and dislike, will be interacting with me. I love them so much and hurt when I think of them not wanting to be with me. I do not want to feel as though I am an outsider. Man. Here I am their father, and an outsider…

Before leaving LB headed to work, I texted Tamera I was going to come and did she need me to bring anything. She texted back a smiley face and, "Just the fruit of peace! So happy to have U, love always, Tammi." I found myself smiling as I drove to work. My little girl!

I thought of the intimacy definitions all during my shift. I realized Charlotte Ann Thomas is the only wife I was intimate with. I also realized she hurt me deeply and lust became dominant in every relationship I entered after I left her. I was so caught off guard when I ran into Dude that night I believe the pain rendered me incapable of facing the truth about how I felt.

Maybe I felt inadequate as a lover. Dating on the rebound is what led me into meaningless relationships. Janice was the only other wife I loved and her gaining weight and getting pregnant every time I took my pants off had a lot to do with me not wanting to make love to her. I loved Janice, but never fully allowed intimacy into our relationship.

...I realize now that is because I allowed intimacy with Char and she shattered any chances of me ever opening up again. I was not opening myself up and allowing anyone else access to hurting me, not again.

Truth is, I could have spent more time with Char. Buying things was what I wanted to do for her. She wanted to be with me. I could have taken the time to sit with her and we could have found a happy medium. Alright, I take responsibility for my portion of our marriage failing. But the idea of Char *not* loving me enough to *not* go through with giving herself to another man… hurts.

Lord, heal me. I hurt. Heal Your son… Is that what my biological father prayed?

I went home after my shift and went over a few definitions again. I faced my truth and feel as though I am on the road to healing. I am ready to embrace healing. I am not going to jump into another relationship until I am totally healed. I need to get closer to The Lord and allow His guidance for my future. God knows I have made a mess not considering Him in my plans.

I was able to sleep and felt refreshed Sunday morning. I looked forward to attending church.

While getting dressed for church I had a smile on the inside. I feel as though I understand what makes a marriage and, working to keep the love in a marriage is important. I do not feel like I failed at marriage. I understand going to work and getting a paycheck is reward for the work done.

I also understand now putting time in a marriage with the one you love is work and to have a marriage that will last is the reward. On the drive to church I thanked The Lord for giving me His Holy Spirit. I understand now why Jesus told His disciples

He had to go so the Comforter could come. Revelation brings about understanding and understanding comforts. Lord I thank You!

Today I followed the ushers instruction and sat where he directed me. Praise and Worship was going on and the song, "I Surrender All" was being ministered. I observed the Praise Singers as their eyes were closed and the expressions of being in the presence of The Lord was evident. I listened to The Words. "All to Thee my bless-ed Savior, I surrender all."

I had a brief flashback of myself sitting in that chair in Mrs. Judson's office, laying all of my labels at the foot of the cross. I silently told The Lord I trusted Him. The last song they sang was, "God has not given us the spirit of fear." The Words were up on the screen and second Timothy 1: 7 is what we are singing.

I took time to concentrate on the words and think, 'I am not afraid of anything.' I began thanking The Lord for not giving me the spirit of fear. I noticed Char being seated in the isle across from where I am, a row in front of mine. My heart started beating fast. I do not want to argue with her. As I looked towards the pulpit, I realized, maybe, just maybe I am afraid of Char.

All of this counseling has me facing my truth as Mrs. Judson would say. I am afraid of Char, she is the only woman in my life I loved with my whole heart and she broke it. Lord you did not give me a spirit of fear, so I am good!

Today the church honored some high school students who are planning to go off to college after graduation and awards were given to all those graduating. Pastor Gray preached from the book of Jude, 14-25 and it reads:

"Now Enoch, the seventh from Adam, prophesied about these men also, saying, "Behold, The Lord comes with ten thousands of His saints, [15] to execute judgment on all, to convict all who are ungodly among them of all their ungodly deeds which they have committed in an ungodly way, and of all the harsh things which ungodly sinners have spoken against Him.

[16] These are grumblers, complainers, walking according to their own lusts; and they mouth great swelling words, flattering people to gain advantage. [17] But you, beloved, remember the words which were spoken before by the apostles of our Lord Jesus Christ: [18] how they told you that there would be mockers in the last time who would walk according to their own ungodly lusts.

[19] These are sensual persons, who cause divisions, not having the Spirit. [20] But you, beloved, building yourselves up on your most holy faith, praying in the Holy Spirit, [21] keep yourselves in the

love of God, looking for the mercy of our Lord Jesus Christ unto eternal life. [22] And on some have compassion, making a distinction; [23] but others save with fear, pulling them out of the fire, hating even the garment defiled by the flesh.

[24] Now to Him who is able to keep you from stumbling, And to present you faultless Before the presence of His glory with exceeding joy, [25] To God our Savior, Who alone is wise, Be glory and majesty, Dominion, and power, Both now and forever. Amen."

Pastor Gray took time to warn the graduating students of being persuaded to compromise the godly upbringing they have been raised in concerning The Word of God. Pastor stressed how Jude was warning the church, us, how to hold onto the gospel we have been taught and for us, the church not to cave in when people grumble and complain and even sometimes will make fun of us when we would rather go to church and Bible study and not party and drink excessively or do drugs like a lot of college students.

Pastor Gray encouraged us to build ourselves up in The Word and prayer to equip ourselves against temptations and influences of worldly lifestyles. In doing the right Christian works, we may perhaps become a witness to those who mock our lifestyle and may even get the opportunity to encourage someone watching us to live right for Jesus Christ.

I felt as though Pastor Gray were speaking to me. I remembered being teased as a young man for wanting to attend church and even while being with Faith not fitting in with her lifestyle. I thought about myself being carried away with my own lusts. I mean Holy Spirit was talking to me and not just the graduating class!

I went up to the altar for prayer. When we were dismissed Char was headed over to me. We made eye contact and she nodded as she said, "Hi Gregory." The softness in her voice shocked me at first and I thought 'we are in church that is why she is being nice.' I nodded.

I made it to the back of the church and Tamera was talking to Mother Thomas and Char. Mother Thomas reached out to me and I leaned in and hugged her. "You are beginning to be a regular on Sunday's I see." "Yes Ma'am." Mother Thomas looked at Char and commented, "Maybe you can show up to The Lords House on a regular basis Charlotte, you think?" Char looks me in the eyes and replies, "Mother I think you're right. I need to give The Lord thanks for all He has done for me. Good seeing you Greg."

She smiled and I thought we were back in time. Her smile was warm and captivating. Char's smile always had some mysterious effect on me. I stood still thinking, 'Wow.' Tamera and Justin spoke to me as she hugged me so tight and whispered, "Daddy I love you." "Love you too baby." For some reason I could not take my eyes off Char. I headed to Mamas.

Sam is still living at home and is now saving for her a house in Carson. Leslie, Sam's oldest is fifteen, Lauryn is thirteen and Sam's son, Lil Ricky is eleven. Sam and I get along since I no longer have to live with her. She seems to have softened up. When she first started staying in LB, she was bitter. I think Mama has been sharing bits of godly wisdom with my little sister and it is breaking the fallow ground of her heart.

Rick was the one initiating the divorce and Sam was angry. She felt she had given Rick the best years of her life and he up and decides another woman is best for him. I told Sam I understood her pain and we became closer after that conversation. It also helps I do not have to deal with her kids. Mama tells me Sam is dating again, she has accepted being divorced, buying her own home and her dating again is proof.

After we all ate I went in the living room and called Linda. This is my way of seeing Izzy and Anna. Linda's moving to Kentucky turned out to be a blessing. She has learned all about her mother and that side of her heritage.

Since living in Kentucky Linda has become a regular church attendee and she loves it. Right after Thanksgiving Linda phoned me and shared her experience becoming saved. She said after learning about the love Christ has for her, she repented of her sin and accepted Christ as her savior. She hungers for The Word and is falling in love with Jesus. Linda truly is a changed person; her conversations are more scripture based and she thanks me for encouraging her to find out about her heritage.

I talk to the girls and every once in a while Linda phones me back with FaceTime. Izzy is growing up and looks like Linda and is very smart. She loves history. Anna, my beautiful daughter can stop traffic she is so beautiful. Her eyes are big and a perfect round dark brown. Her eyebrows and eyelashes are dark brown and stands out on her perfect cappuccino skin tone.

All of my daughters are beautiful but Anna, her beauty is inner also. I truly believe Anna has a calling on her life and I see it. Maybe because she is my last kid I feel this way. I do know this one here, she is different. She is smart too; she speaks Spanish and English. Linda says Anna loves church and she listens attentively to Bible stories.

Linda tells me Pedro is in the service and married. I spoke to Pedro once after they had been in Kentucky for almost two months. He apologized to me and said he understood what I was trying to teach him. I told him I accepted his apology and asked him to forgive me, I could have applied a wiser approach.

After talking to Linda and the girls I went to my place and changed clothes then entered Tamera's address into my map app. As I drive to her place I am thinking of my life and how I have come full circle. I had my first place before I married Char at the age of twenty. Here I am forty-one years old, will be forty-two in a few months, still single and living by myself.

Thinking of what Pastor Gray said earlier today makes me remember when life was so simple for me. I thought Char and I would be together the rest of our lives. I never could have dreamed I would be married four times. I like being married and do not mind putting up with females and their drama. We all must tolerate something.

As I walked to Tamera's apartment I remember the first time she smiled at me and said, "Dada." I remember the day I saw her walk by herself for the first time. The first time she opened her mouth for me to see her first tooth. I feel a slight smile as I ring the doorbell.

Justin opens the door addressing me, "Hello Mr. Young. Glad you are able to make it. Come on in we are all in the kitchen as you can hear." A burst of laughter is coming from in front of us as we walk towards the sound. Justin walks into the room headed to Tamera and says, "Baby it's your Dad." It becomes quiet and I feel as if all eyes are on me, the outsider.

I am standing in the door to the kitchen, Char gets up from the counter and comes towards me. I am thinking 'She is going to slap me and they are going to be witnesses. Is this gang up on Greg: Deadbeat Dad Sunday?' I glance at the crowd; Tamera, Justin, Charece, two other men and another young lady and they look as though they are not breathing.

I brace myself for the slap. Char walks up to me and says, "Hi Greg, we are all so glad you were able to make it." She extends her hand out to me. I hesitantly extend my hand to her and we shake hands. Char asks, "Can I get you something to drink?" No thanks, I'm good!

Char turns around and says, "Come on in so we can get started. What's wrong with you all, looking as if you're in shock?" Charece says, "Mom you kept your word and yes, we are in shock!" Tamera walks towards me while saying, "Daddy thanks for coming. You have always kept your word with me, thanks." She reaches up and kisses me on my cheek. Charece comes and hugs me. As my daughters turn to be seated I stick my chest out; I feel as if I am ten feet tall.

The other young lady introduces herself as Tiffany and she is the coordinator and has a paper tablet to prove it and, is waving it around. Justin introduces me to the guys; Anthony, and Shawn. Tiffany starts, "Okay let's get our roles defined."

Justin offers me a seat at the table across from Char. We go over the rehearsal plans, the dates, times, and location. Justin informs us guys of needing to get our tux. He asks for all of our cell numbers so he can text the tuxedo rental address to us.

Tamera looks at me and says, "Traditionally the father of the bride pays for the wedding but because there are so many of us Young's, I have let you off the hook Daddy. It's all paid for." Smiling, she adds; "I want it known to everyone here, my Dad sent money to my Mom every month like clockwork and I was able to attend college, get a good paying job and afford to pay for my wedding." Justin interrupts, "Baby, *our* wedding. I plan on being there." He bends down and kisses Tamera on the forehead. She is sitting in front of him. I can see they really love one another and he is very attentive to my daughter.

I am glad for them and hope they work at keeping their relationship this way. Man, I am sounding like Mrs. Judson. We go over everyones role and Justin prays a closing prayer. We all head for the front door. Char asks, "Greg can you walk me to my car?" Charece says, "Mom, you promised!" Char hugs

Charece and says, "Stay out of grown folks business. Love you!"

I wait for Char to walk up to me and open the door for her. She says to me, "Thanks," and turns to say goodnight to everyone and walks out.

As we walk to the parking lot Char is quiet and I am wondering if she is going to yell at me. We step up to a very nice car and I ask, "This you?" She turns to me and her eyes are glossy while she says, "Please Gregory let me say this while I can talk. I owe you a huge apology." I notice the side of her mouth is slightly jumping as she pauses.

Now she is blinking rapidly but continues, "I am so regretful…of breaking our marriage vows. I was young…and…thought you didn't love me. I only slept with Blake to make you jealous. I was so stupid and became angry with you. I am so sorry." I could hear the remorse in her voice. She lowered her head and cried. I am talking gravely boohooed!

As I stood watching Char, I felt sorry for her. Her body begin to tremble then she let out a deep wrenching sound and buried her face in her hands. I stepped up to her and put my arms around her. She stepped into my arms, and I mean she wept. I blinked back tears because she was in my arms trembling.

When she simmered down, she looked in her purse and pulled out tissue and blew her nose.

Char's voice still trembling she asks, "Greg do you forgive me?" She looks up into my eyes with such softness. I answer, "Yes I do. Forgive me as well Charlotte." She half smiled and said, "Of course I do. Thank you Gregory. You are a good man and I appreciate you having a forgiving heart. Goodnight." She turned and unlocked her door. I held it open for her and watched her pull off. I was numb as I drove to my place. Charlotte Ann Thomas asked *me*, for forgiveness. Man!

When I arrive home I sit in the dark allowing my mind to rewind Char's body trembling from regret. I just sit for a long while. Maybe I dreamed she asked for forgiveness. Me and Charlotte in the same space and there was no yelling? When I stood up I realized tomorrow is Mrs. Judson. I remember our last session now I wonder what she will open up tomorrow.

I awakened visualizing Char weeping in my arms the whole while I was getting ready.

I arrived in LB and Mama looked different, she was actually glowing to me. I asked what was going on? She responded, "Gregory, I have totally forgiven your father Roland Berry! I haven't felt this good since I was in high school. Son your mother is finally free! After Mays left for work this morning I couldn't get back to sleep so I started praying. I prayed in my heavenly language and began to weep. I broke down.

Gregory, I realized I had unforgiveness in me towards Roland Berry. I asked Holy Spirit to take it away and replace forgiveness in its place. I let go of every ounce of hurt I had hidden inside me and let me tell you, it feels good letting it go. Did I cry, weep, sob; you name it, I did it! I bellowed or as the Bible says, I lamented!

It felt like I had a water hose gushing out of my heart. I released all of the hurt, POW! I realized I had emptied myself of unforgiveness and hurt grabbed hold and went out the window along with it. I called your father and told him I needed his forgiveness. Gregory, he told me he forgave me and asked me to forgive him. I tell you; words cannot describe the joy I experienced! After our phone call ended, I came in this kitchen and cooked up a small tornado! Just for my loving, patient husband Mays.

I tell you; it feels so good being free from that weight! You will be forty-two years old and I am finally free from my mistake. Now son don't take this the wrong way. I love you, yes I do. You are not the mistake. But to admit I made a mistake thinking Roland loved me and would marry me because I was carrying you, that was *my* mistake.

Roland lied when he told me he loved me. I tell you! I am so free now." Mama was glowing so bright. I have never seen her this happy, ever! I was smiling because Mama glowed so. I ate and left for my session. Only two more weeks and I am done with counseling. I can truthfully say the sessions helped some.

Mrs. Judson took one look at me and says, "Gregory tell me what's going on with you today." I told her about going over the definitions twice and the revelation I had of Char breaking my heart because I trusted her and shared intimacy with her.

"Did you embrace your truth Gregory?" Yes I did. "And how does that make you feel?" ...As though I can face and embrace any future fears. "Good Gregory. You have gained progress during these sessions. We only have five left after today.

Today there is an exercise for you. It is similar to the definitions. You did very well with the definitions so this will be easy for you." Mrs. Judson walks over to the wall and turns over what looks like a three-foot white presentation board with small colored thermometers.

The top of the board has black capitalized letters titled, "LOVE." Below are the thermometers. Each is labeled underneath:

1. Suffers long and is kind.
2. Does not envy.
3. Does not parade itself.
4. Is not puffed up.
5. Does not behave rudely.
6. Does not seek its own.
7. Is not provoked.
8. Thinks no evil.
9. Does not rejoice in iniquity.
10. Rejoices in the truth.
11. Bears all things.
12. Believes all things.
13. Hopes all things.
14. Endures all things.

At the very bottom of the board, in large red capital bold print letters are the words; "NEVER FAILS."

Each thermometer is colored a different color and only halfway. I knew right away this was from first Corinthians 13. My suspicions are true, Mrs. Judson is a believer. Why the thermometers are half full questioned me. So I listened.

"Gregory it is assumed all who marry are in love. On this board is the *TRUE* definition of love. It's a sad fact, however it is a true fact; few find true love. That's because few know what love is. We have to *work* our marriages. First finding where our relationship is as it pertains to *true* love. Then we work *at* keeping our love balanced in our marriage.

Notice how each thermometer is colored only to the middle?" She points to the chart, then looks at me. I nod "Yes." "That indicates balance in these attributes. Let's go over each attribute to see how balance is necessary. Ready?" Again I nod.

"Love; is both a common and proper noun, circumstances depend on how love is to be applied. Let's do this exercise for each definition. Are you ready?" My reply is, "Yes." "Alright we see here love suffers long and is kind. To suffer long is the act of enduring. We also see, 'and is kind,' immediately following long suffering which tells us kindness is being illustrated *during* the practice of long suffering.

There is no impatient attitude displayed while practicing long suffering. There is no pity party going on. Your mate only feels love and patience while long suffering is being endured by you. Love is producing kindness instead. Can you see where the work comes into play?" My response was another nod.

"Gregory suppose you have made a dinner reservation for you and your wife to dine at a very exclusive restaurant. It has taken over two weeks to get this reservation and she is taking a while getting dressed. You look at your watch and realize if she lingers you will be late. You are getting agitated thinking of how long it will take to get another reservation. And where will you dine as an alternative if this reservation is lost.

You walk to the door where she is and notice she is applying make-up. What would be your *first* reaction? Be honest this is just an exercise."

"I would tell her to hurry, we will miss our reservation." Good. Now take a moment to apply long suffering to your response, what would you say? "I would say the same thing." Okay, think of how much you love your wife. Remember the reason you fell in love with her…

Now, how would you tell her in a loving way. For example; 'Come on you are already beautiful to me. We do not want to be late for our reservation.' See how this works?

Taking a few seconds to apply love can set the atmosphere for a positive response! **Work: when you love, is not laborious**. Gregory are you getting an understanding about love and how working to display love can never fail?"

I *do not* get what Mrs. Judson means. I look at her and she realizes it is not registering. "Let's look at how love does not envy.

The word envy originates from jealousy, ill will and covet. It may seem strange but not putting yourself in her place makes you think about how you could be still getting ready, how you could be watching the game. The thought of you placing importance on being on time may make you resent the fact you are waiting on her and she is not waiting on you.

Love is not envious of your mate making you wait on her. Love causes you to pull out patience and ask for wisdom regarding what to say and the tone best suited, so you won't hurt her feelings; because you love her."

Mrs. Judson turns to the board and says, "Alright Gregory let's look at the word parade and get understanding of what it means because love causes us *not* to parade ourselves. The word parade means to show off, to be boastful and brag.

Looking at the same scenario of the dinner reservation, how would you think bragging or boasting about oneself applies." I think I know what Mrs. Judson wants me to say. "Okay Mrs. Judson maybe I would tell her how I am dressed and she should be also."

"Great. Gregory I believe you have the reasoning to this exercise! Now what do you suppose love would have you to say to your wife using the same reservations example?" I am confident how this exercise works so I answer.

"I guess using love as my compass I would think, okay she is a female and females need more time to get ready. I should have given her more time to get ready. So, I might say, 'I am sorry, I should have given you more time to get ready, but if we miss our reservations it will take weeks before I can get another one. We would end up eating someplace else and I really want to enjoy this special meal with you."

"Gregory that is very good. Working the components of love becomes less stressful the more we apply them. You will have more serious scenarios to handle, but the techniques work the same. What we have to remember is love covers a multitude of faults. We must remember to love and not be critical. When both mates practice loving; you will have a lasting marriage and will model a loving marriage to your children and family."

Mrs. Judson adds, "Gregory these are all components for any form of loving relationships. In marriage it is the responsibility of each mate to make sure all of these components stay balanced. When any one of these components of love becomes imbalanced, and life will give instances for everyone of them to be tried. It is our responsibility to keep that component balanced.

Take anger for example. Life is sure to bring an occurrence when anger will be valid. It is up to us to allow anger to have its experience but, we must keep our anger balanced. Once it fills us completely, our love becomes imbalanced and that is when failure takes over. Anger spills over into vindictiveness and vindictiveness spills over into dishonor and so on.

Do you see the importance of keeping a balance to these components? Love has everything needed in a marriage. Patience, truth, kindness, and trust applied to those components, will bring balance back. *Trust and truth is fueled by intimacy.* Now do you understand why many say love is powerful?"

I nodded.

Mrs. Judson went through each attribute of love. I was speechless and yet felt as though a light bulb had come on in my head. The rest of the day when I went over the chart mentally, I kept saying, 'Yeah' to myself. It was adding up. Spending time, sharing intimate times with the one person you love really feeds and nourishes the love you already have. Nourishing the love you have strengthens the components and causes balance, which creates success. In other words, love will never fail. I get it... I really got it!

During my shift I went down memory lane with each one of my wives and it was apparent, the only wife I started marriage with love and all its components, was Char. Janice came in second but I was looking for another Charlotte Ann Thomas and Janice was the closest I could get.

When I came home after my shift, I grabbed my Bible and slipped into bed and smiled at myself. Gregory Young is in bed with the Bible on his mind and not a woman.

I went to the back of my Bible and looked up the word "Marriage." I went over each scripture and each referencing scripture and wrote them all down. I was so excited; this revelation is invigorating. Man was this a good study.

I slept like a baby and woke Tuesday disappointed I had no session today. All during my shift I thought about how I could have used the love chart in my marriage.

When I slipped into bed I realized I only thought of my marriage with Char. I only applied the love chart to my marriage with my first wife. Oh I know why, If I had gotten it right the first time, there would have been no other wives, yeah that must be why…

I stayed up so late last night when my alarm went off this morning, I hit the off button instead of snooze and went back to sleep. It was twelve-fifteen when I woke and my appointment is from one to one fifty-five. I was rushing so I ended up leaving my apartment with shoes in hand and hopping into my pants as I headed for the front door. I called Mama while at a red light and told her I would see her tomorrow, I overslept. I did not think about what Mrs. Judson would go over until I put my hand on the doorknob to enter her office.

She threw me for a loop. I was ready for more charts. Instead she asked what was my definition of the word forgiveness. I immediately went back to hating being here again. We sit looking at one another then Mrs. Judson says, "The last exercise we took a look at love. We saw how love covers faults. Being able to cover faults with love takes the act of forgiveness. Gregory what do you think forgiveness is and remember this is only an exercise."

I thought for a moment and said, "My definition of forgiveness is simple. Forgive and forget." She looks me in the eyes and asks, "And your process of forgiving is…" "Well, if it is something simple, I just let it go, forget about it." Mrs. Judson asks, "*And,* if it's something major?" I was prompt with my reply, "Now that is different. Depending on what it is, I might take it slow forgiving."

"Okay Gregory tell me why would you quickly forget with one instance and take it slow with another?" "Mrs. Judson some things are not worth the energy and some are."

"Give me an example of what you call not worth the energy. For instance..."

I had to think. "Okay, for instance my wife wanting to talk at three-thirty in the morning when she knows I am tired." Mrs. Judson says, "Okay so, for that instance you would forgive on the spot?" " Yes."

"Alright, now give me an example of something major." "Well, major is when your wife is having an affair. Now that is major." "Gregory have you ever experienced infidelity from any of your wives?"

"Yes I have." "Which wife?" "My first and my last." "Who Charlotte and Linda?" "Yes."

"So because you consider infidelity major you are not willing to forgive Charlotte or Linda?"

"Come on Mrs. Judson would you forgive your husband if you almost caught him? "I'm sorry Gregory we are here to discuss your feelings on this subject. Answer my question as honestly as you can." 'I think Mrs. Judson has been cheated on also.'

"I'm waiting for your answer. I am curious as to your definition of major and not worth the energy." "Mrs. Judson you know a spouse being unfaithful is major, come on." "Gregory why do *you* feel that way?" "Because you make a vow before God and witnesses to be faithful and when you are not, the marriage is over." "Gregory are you saying your wife giving her word and not keeping it is major to you?"

"I am saying, my wife sleeping with another man in my bed while I am at work trying to get us a better life is what I call major!" "Gregory forgiveness is for any and all instances. Here, I have a dictionary. Here read to me what it says." She hands me the small dictionary and there is a marker in the page and the word "forgive and forgiveness" is highlighted in yellow.

I read aloud: **Forgive, verb; stop feeling resentful towards [someone], for an offense, flaw, or mistake. Pardon, excuse, exonerate, absolve; make allowances for, feel no resentment toward, feel no malice toward, harbor no grudge against, bury the hatchet with.**

"Very good Gregory. Do you see some of these same definitions apply to love, can you see it?" I shook my head up and down as I looked at her. "Good, now read the definition for forgiveness."

Forgiveness, noun; the action or process of forgiving or being forgiven. We beg your forgiveness: pardon, absolution, exoneration, remission, dispensation, indulgence, clemency, mercy; reprieve, amnesty.

Mrs. Judson took the dictionary from me while asking, "So Gregory, what is it that you have done in your marriages you consider to be major?" My neck jerked. Where is she going with this?

We sit staring at one another. Mrs. Judson say very softly, "Forgiveness always, always accompanies truth. Gregory you have covered a lot of your truth, now it's time to apply forgiveness.

Counseling is a means of self-examination and, when we understand the process of facing truth, we must forgive ourselves first, then we apply the same principals and techniques when forgiving others. Think about what you have done that is considered major. After you pull that incident up in your mind, share it with me. I will give you a few moments."

I am sitting here going over what my truth is. Okay I may have worked intentionally just to get away from the house when the girls were small. And yes, maybe I could have spent a little more money and not been as restrictive. "Alright Gregory, share what major action of yours you consider unforgivable."

I feel myself squirming as I say, "I maybe could have not worked so much..." Mrs. Judson tilts her head to the side and extends her hand up as she utters, "Hold up. You said you consider major incidences unforgivable. Working too much is major to you?" I quickly respond, Well maybe not to me but it was to my ex-wives.

"Gregory you said unfaithfulness, adultery is what you consider major. Have you ever been unfaithful to any of your wives?" I feel as if Linda caught me in bed with Maria. "Have you?" Mrs. Judson asks sternly. I snap back at her, "Well, yeah!"

"Were you caught?"
"Not in the act but it was revealed, yes."
"Did you want forgiveness at the time?"

'I am thinking about how I regretted being with Maria when the burning started as I urinated.' "Gregory let's go back to when you were unfaithful. Think out loud of your very thoughts the day you knew you had done something major. Are you there?" I nod "yes."

"Okay, walk through it out loud."

"Um, after we committed the act I felt both regretful and pleased. I knew I had made a mistake."

"Gregory be honest, why did you feel regretful?"

"Because I didn't love the woman I had just slept with." Mrs. Judson sits looking at me and says, "Go on."

"I felt pleased because my wife at the time had set me up for marriage and after we said 'I do' she stopped pretending and allowed me to see her true self. I felt I was led into a trap as far as our marriage was concerned."

"Gregory you are doing very good. Now explain why did you become sexually active with a woman you did not love when you knew you did not love her?"

"Because she kept coming on to me and Linda was in her last trimester so the both of us were unable to have sex. Her friend was there and giving me signals she was available."

"Do you, Gregory Young, want to be forgiven for the major act you committed?"

"Yes."

"Have you considered your wives who committed a major act, want you to forgive them?"

I feel myself squirming in my chair.

For a split second my mind went straight to Char in Tamera's parking lot, trembling, and crying in my arms. Mrs. Judson asks, "Have you Gregory?"

"Yes."

"Have you asked Linda for forgiveness?"

"No."

"Why not?"

"She cheated on me so, we are even. "Gregory, keeping score is what's done in a game. Marriage and love is no game. You need to be forgiven just as Linda and Charlotte does. The game playing has to end. Have you forgiven yourself?"

"Mrs. Judson I have never thought about forgiving anyone." "Alright then. Gregory right now, I want you to say out loud while looking me in the eyes, say 'I forgive myself.' " I look her in the eyes and say, "I forgive myself."

"Now Gregory take a moment to see your major act is tied to Linda and also tied to Charlotte, then tell me that you forgive yourself as if you are un-leashing the both of them from your unforgiveness. Take a moment…"

I saw Char in my mind again in the parking lot weeping with her head down. I felt myself blinking back tears. Why was she weeping… was she un-leashing me from her unforgiveness? I looked into Mrs. Judson's eyes and as I opened my mouth, I felt warm tears flowing down my cheeks. I said very softly, "I forgive…" I broke.

I held my head down, closed my eyes and a video began in my head. I saw Char holding those sheets. Faith as she put a cigarette to her mouth while pregnant with Kozet. Janice as she swelled up like a balloon and Linda as she told me she had slept with those other dudes. I raised my head up as I yelled, "**I FORGIVE!**"

I visualized Roland Berry as he held me in the restaurant. I inhaled deeply and as I bow my head, very softly this time I utter "I forgive them and I forgive myself."

Mrs. Judson hands me tissue and I allow the tears to flow. I bent over and put my head in my hands and cried. I asked The Lord to forgive me. I want to be completely un-leashed of any and all unforgiveness. I *need* to be completely un-leashed.

As I lift my head I hear a gentle, "Share your thoughts."

"I have never forgiven Char for breaking my heart. I realize how angry I am because, I never confronted her. In fact; I buried my pain. I allowed unforgiveness to grow in my heart. Sunday Char asked me to forgive her. She wept. I think I know how she felt; I believe she unleashed me. I feel as though the weight from the pain has been removed. Yeah, I have let that mess go."

Mrs. Judson says in a trembling voice, "Gregory I will send the Judge your order of completion. "Gregory you have learned to walk to your truth, face your truth and walk *through* your truth to healing. You now have the tools needed to apply love and forgiveness.

As Mrs. Judson stood she extended her hand. As I stood I extended my hand to her and we shook hands.

"Gregory Young, I have a feeling you will be very successful now in the matters of love and relationship. I wish you the best. She walked toward her desk and I left her office.

I walked to my truck and as I sat down I thought, 'I am finally free. Not only from Linda, but from my past mistakes. Lord help me walk the path You intend for me.'

I pulled out my phone to turn the volume back on and have two text, one from Tamera and one from Char. I read Tamera's; "Good morning Daddy. Just want to say "thanks" for wanting to be part of Justin and my future and let you know I love you, Love always, Tammi." She has a smiley face at the end. I smiled knowing my daughter loves me un-conditionally.

I read Char's text; "Hope you don't mind me getting your number from Reece. I must give you a "Thanks" for allowing me to empty out Sunday night. I need your forgiveness so I can move forward. Now I am working on forgiving myself! Char."

Man, why did she have to add that last part… I picked up a burger and fries and headed to work.

During the drive I realized; I never thought about forgiving Char. I never thought about mending our relationship. I was devastated she betrayed me. I never thought Char would stop loving me. Therefore I never really dealt with her infidelity.

The next morning I headed to LB and talked to Mama while I ate. I told her what happened Sunday night and that my sessions were finished. I told Mama I was working on forgiveness by starting with myself. She was so happy for me. Mama told me she was proud of me getting on the path Jesus has for me.

Mama became serious and said, "Gregory your father showing up now in your life is God's timing. I think The Lord has new beginnings for you son. Include your father in the people you need to forgive. I'm following my own advice. I think we have to understand why our past happened and be okay with it before the future can be given to us. Kinda like learning to add before we can multiply and divide. Know what I mean?"

Mama stood up, kissed me on my cheek and left the kitchen. I thought about the timing of Roland Berry wanting to be part of my life. Now, when I am dealing with forgiveness. I know God's timing is perfect. We humans live in time, God does not.

I thought of how God knew I was going to file for divorce, be ordered to attend counseling and forced to deal with truth, love, and forgiveness when Roland Berry wants to be introduced into my life.

By the time my shift ended, I saw the awesomeness of The Most High God working in my life. I surrendered my will to Him. I am not making another move until I consult God's will for me, that is for certain.

During my drive home from work the words, "Forgiving myself" started to play over and over in my head. Char said she was working on forgiving herself. I need to follow her lead so I can move forward. Lord knows I do not like being alone. I want a loving companion. A woman who understands how I am and loves me for who I am. I will not be so frugal and spend more time being intimate.

I only have six children to pay child support for including Sybil and only seven years left to pay. Then it will only be Anna. Man time flies.

Janice wants to refinance the house and take some money out to do some remodeling. This will allow her to have the mortgage in her name. I will begin paying support by money order. I include Sybil because Janice is raising Kozet. Besides Sybil and Kozet are sisters in every sense of the word and Janice loves Kozet as if she gave birth to her.

The next two weeks I went to physical therapy and while leaving my last session I received a text from Tamera. "Daddy this is my last fourth of July being a Young. The wedding is in three weeks and you need to get your Tux. Here is the address just ask for the Moreland party. I'm getting nervous! Love always, Tammi."

I texted her back, "Thanks baby. How about you clear thirty minutes on your calendar tomorrow at noon and meet your old man close to your job? Love, Dad." "Great! meet me @ "Pappy's Cafe on Hill St. See U then."

I met Tamera and told her I loved her and shared my feelings for her the first time I held her in my arms. She went water works on me. I informed my daughter she will always be a Young in my heart. She was *my love* way before she became Justin's. I held her hand and told her to apply First Corinthians thirteen to her marriage and to allow Justin mistakes and vice-a-versa. God ordained marriage and He must be involved for it to work. I told Tamera I was proud of her and knew in my heart she would be and do great.

She asked if I were relieved she wasn't gay! We laughed. Char told her we were all concerned she was. I hugged her and felt like I was ten feet tall when I left the cafe. I just validated my second daughter; my father skills are still sharp!

Two days later Linda phoned to say she received the divorce papers and was off to a brand-new start. She wished me well and let me talk to Anna. I must admit, I was sad because I knew it would be a long time before l would get to hold my beautiful baby girl again.

I realize the chapters in my past were ending and a whole new book was beginning for me. I am glad. This next book will be about Gregory Allen getting it right.

Our fourth of July was great. Janice dropped off the children and they had a ball with their cousins. Kozet and Sybil are beginning to drive and their conversations were about studying for their drivers permits. I told Janice I will call her so we can discuss me getting them a car to share. Man it is unbelievable they are driving already. We all ended up at the park after five p.m. and played softball until dark. Man, Lil Ricky has an arm on him!

When I dropped the kids off at Cloverleaf, Janice told me she was serious about her friend Ralph Langley. He asked her to marry him. She wanted me to know he was a good man and wants us to meet. He is a Highway Patrolman and wants the two of us to talk. Ralph wants to reassure me he would see to it my kids will be loved and treated appropriately.

Ralph has a son twelve years old and gets along with our kids very well so far. I wished her well and told her to have Ralph call me so we could set up a meeting. I left thinking how I want to evaluate this dude myself. Kozet and Sybil are my concern considering they are becoming young ladies.

During my drive home I am thinking, 'Linda gone and now Janice remarrying. I wonder how Faith is. Huh; I think I will give her a call when I get home.'

The last phone number I had for Faith was old but I dialed it. Faith's sister, Shelia answered. She had me to hold on Faith had walked outside and was on her way. Faith was living with Sheila and their mother, Mae in Victorville. Faith had recently started working for Hughes Aircraft. For several months she fell on some hard times and Sheila is helping her get back on her feet.

Faith went into her room and told me the last man she lived with went to jail and her and the boys were left to fin for themselves. She asked if Kozet was alright and when I told her about my situation she became silent. I asked if she were alright. She cried as she told me she was grateful I loved Kozet enough to take good care of her.

Faith apologized to me saying she did not understand the love a father has for his daughter and thought I was overprotective of Kozet when we were together. I assured Faith that Kozet was loved, safe and happy. Faith told me when she gets her own place she would like to contact Kozet and gradually get to know our daughter. It is just not good right now to have a young girl in the environment she is in.

Jaheim is almost twenty and recently joined the Marines and is now stationed in Twenty-Nine Palms, California. Dameon is eighteen and in continuation school trying to graduate in December. He spent a year with his Dad, ran into some trouble and stayed in Juvenile Hall for five months. Faith told me to kiss Kozet for her and said she would text me her address so if Kozet wanted to, she could write her.

I wished her well. I felt sorry for Faith. Growing up with little to nothing, she wants to have it all and not take time to count the cost. I believe she realizes now that fast money is not worth what you have to pay for it.

Now that leaves Char. I think she does well on her own. I wonder if she will show up with someone at the wedding. Char is almost thirty-nine years old but looks good. Hopefully this wedding we can be civil and have a peaceful alliance. When we see each other at church, she is very cordial. Now that I have made peace with my ex-wives I can settle down with a nice woman whose theory of existence coincides with mine. I am getting lonely.

The wedding is Saturday so I took a week off starting Friday this way I can make the rehearsal. Friday after I left LB I went to the Barber Shop then to pick up my Tux and Justin was there along with three guys, two I know: Shawn and Anthony. Justin introduces me to Devin. They are his three groomsmen.

I pick up my things without trying them on but check the sizes and count the pieces and I am good to go. Justin is standing by the mirror talking to the salesman. I wait until he is done and ask if I may have a word with him.

Justin steps up to me and I walk towards the cash register. When we are alone I tell him; "Justin we do not know one another and I am sure you are a good man or Tamera would not be marrying you. I need to say this too you. I may not be in Tamera's life but take what I am telling you and store it deep in your memory. If you ever physically abuse my daughter, I will give your ass a beating you have *never* had before. Send her home before you hit her. Do I make myself clear?"

Justin's eyes enlarged and he stood straight up and answers, "Yes sir. Let me say Mr. Young, I will never mishandle your daughter in anyway and certainly not physically. I love Tamera and have no intentions of ever hurting her, even emotionally."

"Alright Justin I have to make myself clear." I extended my hand to him and he shook it and pulled me too himself and hugged me.

I had to let Justin know what I will not tolerate when it comes to my daughter. I had the same conversation with Charles on their wedding day. I do not want these young guys thinking because I am not in my daughters lives, I do not care about my daughter. I am a father and father's protect their daughters especially when there is no brother old enough to protect them.

I zip by my place, drop off my Tux and jump in the shower.

I pull up into the parking lot of the church and everyone is here except Tamera and Charece. They are all huddled at the front entry. I walk over to the crowd and Charece pulls up and Tamera is riding with her. Char speaks to me, "Hi Gregory. We're waiting for the key." I nodded. After shaking the guys hands, Charece and Tamera walk up and I embrace them.

Char asks Tamera if she is alright. Justin walks up to Tamera and asks the same question. I am observing Tamera's body language. I think she is scared. As she shakes her head "yes." I grab Tamera and hold her. She cries in my arms and says, "Daddy

I'm scared. What if we change and our marriage won't work!"

I guided Tamera away from the entry and say to her, "Baby you will change, just make sure you do it together." I let her cry in my arms. Char slowly walks up behind Tamera looking me in the eyes. Tamera stops crying and tells me once again she is scared. Char says, "Tammi, baby." Tamera turns around and repeats to her mother that she is scared.

Char extends her arms out and as Tamera walks into the arms of her mother. Char says, "I know. Baby just because me and your Dad didn't make it doesn't mean you and Justin won't make it. Tammi you're older than I was and much smarter. It will work out, you'll see. It will work out." Tamera looks in her mother's eyes and utters, "Mom you think so?" "Yes baby, I know so!"

Justin slowly walks up to Tamera and says, "Tamera Aliyah, I love you and vow to always love you. I am nervous too baby." He hugs her and she buries her face in his chest and says, "Justin I'm so scared." He comforts her saying, "I know baby. I know." Justin rubs her back and turns Tamera towards the entry and slowly leads her into the church. Char and I stand watching them. Char turns to me with tears in her eyes, "That was us at one time. Hard to believe huh."

I stepped up to Char and she lays her head on my shoulder and allows the tears to fall from her eyes. After a few moments she wipes her tears away, looks up at me and says, "Okay let's not have Tammi worrying about our behavior." She grabbed my hand and we walked inside the church and sat on the front row together.

Once Tiffany started giving us directions, we were all busy doing as told. Tiffany is a Wedding Coordinator Authoritarian! She made us go through the mock ceremony three times so we would be confident tomorrow. Before Justin gave a closing prayer, Tiffany told us to be here exactly one hour early and if she thought we were going to be late, someone else resembling us will be taking our position. She does not tolerate CP [Colored People] time!

I waited for Char and walked her out. She held my hand as we walked to the parking lot and when she stood in front of her car door she let go of my hand and said, "Gregory I like being civil. I think it will work for us, what you think?" She was smiling her famous smile. I want to kiss her so I put my hands in my pocket. I do not want to make her mad.

"Char will you be attending the wedding alone?" "Yes, I'm not dating these days." Almost whispering, I ask, "How about I pick you up?" She hesitated answering. I lifted my hand up and said,

"Okay, I understand." She puts her hand on my arm and says, "Oh Greg I don't mind you picking me up. I'm thinking since we're getting along, you might want to come by my place and see something." "Okay, when?" "I mean now. Are you busy?" I shake my head 'No.' She smiles and says, "Okay, follow me home. You will get a kick out of this!" She turns to open her car door. As I hold the door for her, I respond, "Alright."

We get inside of Char's living room and she offers me a drink. I tell her I am good. The whole drive here I am wondering what is it she wants to show me. I do not think she is trying to trick me; Char seems sincere. As she takes her shoes off she says, "That's right you don't drink." She places her hands on her hips and asks, "Greg how do you not drink with all of those kids running around?" Char is smiling. Man I wish she would not do that! Char always could get anything out of me when she smiled. I hunch my shoulders.

"Well I'm getting myself a glass of wine. Hold on, I'll be right back." She disappears.

I am standing so I look around the room. She enters, "Greg you've never drank all these years, not even when you went through your divorces?" She walks up to me. "Nope." "Here, take a swig of this. It's Moscato wine. It is sweet. Really it's a dessert wine but we all drink it before dessert." Char hands me the glass and I taste it. I respond, "Fruity. And you are right, it is sweet." I hand her the glass. "There were nights I wouldn't have made it without Mr. Moscato!" She drinks some of her wine. "Um, wait until you see this. Come on, there're in my room."

She grabs my hand and pulls me behind her. After she takes a couple steps she stops, turns to me and with a serious look says, "Greg I'm sorry. I felt like you were my friend again. I'm sorry. I have been looking at old pictures and laid aside a pile of Tammi from when she was an infant until now. I thought you would appreciate seeing them."

Char walks back to the cocktail table and puts her glass down. I walk over to her and she says, "I realize it looks like I'm trying to seduce you. You know, pulling you into my bedroom. I didn't mean to imply. I mean, if you're uncomfortable being in my bedroom, I'll bring the pictures out here. I don't mean anything by, I mean. It seems like we have never been apart. Kinda like old times.

Gregory, I'm drowning here. I really didn't mean anything. Honest." I nodded and said, "Okay, I understand. I really don't mind seeing the pictures in your bedroom Char I do not want you uncomfortable. Besides, you have decorated this room so well, I am curious how the rest of the house looks." She half smiles and grabs my hand as she goes into her full-blown smile. "Come on!"

Char pulls me into her bedroom and bounces down on her bed next to the pictures. "I knew you would appreciate these. I have been staying up late lately going through these and the memories!" She picks up a pile close to her pillow and hands them to me. "Look, look at how beautiful she was. Greg it's hard to believe our baby is getting married! Here, look at this one."

I stood looking at a picture of Tamera when she was a few days old. I remember the day we took this. Man she was so beautiful. I sat on the bed and Char and I went through each pile on her bed and we laughed as we reminisced and shared the events that led up to the taking of each picture. I felt as though Char and I had stepped into a time zone. We walked down memory lane while we held each picture in our hand.

Char picked up the last pile and while holding the last picture in her hand, she looks up at me and says, "Wow. We had some good times huh?" I felt sad our trip was over. I have always felt comfortable being with Char. She was my best friend. Now looking at her, seeing sadness covering her face, I want to hold her and reassure her Tamera will be fine. But I know if I hold her, I will kiss her.

I stood up and said, "It has been fun but I gotta run." I jogged out of her bedroom. When I put my hand on the front doorknob I stopped and turned towards Char and said, "Goodnight Char. I will pick you up at noon. Cannot have Tiffany finding replacements for us." Char was standing in the doorway to her hall with her shoulder and head leaning on the door opening. "Yeah, can't have that. Goodnight Greg."

I got out of Char's house and had to take several deep breaths. It has been a while for me and, "WELL!" Go home Greg. A cold shower is what you need, go home!

I crawled into bed and thought about the pictures and how easy it is to be with Char. I tossed and turned. I thought; 'going down memory lane with Char has me wound up!' But around two-thirty in the morning, I realized… I still love Char. Man!

I woke and realized I was taking Char to our daughters wedding today and I smiled. Man I felt as though we were going to my high school prom. I shaved real close and practiced walking, pretending Tamera was on my arm while looking at myself in the mirror. Yep! I am ready to give my daughter away. I left my place with time to spare so I stopped and picked up some mints.

Char was not ready. Man this woman has not changed. I thought about what Mrs. Judson went over with me on her chart, about the dinner reservation and went through each step we talked about.

Patience, Gregory, patience. Char yelled, "**Okay, here I come!**" I stood up and watched the door for her to appear. Char stood in the doorway with her, "How do I look?" Expression. She is beautiful.

I eyed her from head to toe and back to her eyes. I felt a slow smile become visible on my face. Char smiles. "You like what you see don't you!" She bats her eyes while saying, "Have me home at a decent hour. Ha, ha!" Now her smile drops. "Greg I'm joking, you do know that right?"

I walk towards her and reply, "Of course. I think the mother of the bride is nervous." I stand in front of her and she says, "You always know my expressions. Thanks Gregory for being here." "Hey, Char, what is with this Greg one minute then Gregory the next?" She shyly replies; "Well, I have to remind myself we are exes now. Greg since we're civil I feel as though we were on vacation from each other."

I take hold of her arm and say, "Really. Let's get going before Tiffany interviews a couple that resembles us." Char gets her purse and off we go. I say, "By the way, you look stunning." "Why thank you very much. You're looking handsome in that Tux." Char is smiling and I resist the urge to lean in and kiss her. Man!

Char and I agreed I would drive her Lexus since we were so eloquently dressed. We arrived at the church to see the parking lot almost full and it is forty-five minutes before the wedding begin. I overheard one of the guest turn to tell another guest, "Hurry up! Tiffany is the planner and she starts on time. She will make you wait outside while the bride marches in." I now understand why the parking lot is so full.

I walk Char to the Brides dressing room and go over to the Grooms side and Justin is sweating bullets. He has a towel in his hand wiping his face and neck. It is late July but Justin has more than the weather going on.

I walk up to him and ask if his father were here. "No sir. Would you like to pretend you're him. Please. Somebody tell me something. What if I get laid off or can't support her? What if.." I put both my hands on his shoulders and turn him so he is facing me. "Justin, you are very intelligent. You will always find a means of supporting her. Think about you are marrying the one woman you want to spend the rest of your life with. Imagine her coming down that isle presenting herself to you; the man who won her heart. Do you know how blessed you are marrying my daughter?"

Justin stands completely still, with his eyes locked to mine says, "You are absolutely right. Tammi waited just for me. Yeah, just for me." Justin hits his own chest and says in a deep Hulk voice, "Yeah!" He looks at his watch and tells us, "Let's get this show on the road!" I'm getting married!" We all follow the leader. I stand at the rear door watching the guy's head for the front of the sanctuary. Now I am sweating.

I look at my watch, three minutes to one. I hear Tiffany, "Chop, chop ladies!" I turn to see Char and Tamera. Char looks so good in that soft coral dress. She turns to kiss Tamera and as she turns towards me, she is blinking back tears. My eyes follow Char and the door closes.

Tamera walks up to me and when I look at my daughter, she is glowing! My daughters are all beautiful but Tamera resembles my side of the family, but she is Chars' skin tone. I ask, "You alright?" "Yes." She smiles and I see her mother's smile on her. Man. She places her arm in mine. When we hear the organist hit the first note of, "Here comes The Bride," the door opens. Here we go.

I announce, "Her mother and I do." And back up as Tiffany has instructed. I sit next to Char and she whispers, "You did great." I glance at her and place my arm around her shoulders. Char leaned into me. Tamera is absolutely elegant and gorgeous. I have never been so proud of her. I felt myself blinking.

The reception is in the church Fellowship Hall. It has a large veranda where there is a DJ and dancing. After the picture taking I went to visit Janice, Ralph, and the kids table. I sat with them and after Ralph, or I should say Langley; [he prefers it to Ralph] after we introduced ourselves I spent time talking with the kids. I noticed how attentive Ralph was to Janice and when she got up headed to the ladies room I noticed she has lost a lot of weight. Janice looks like she did when we first met minus the small waist.

My sons are growing. David looks like me as a young man, he has signs of hair stubble on his face now. James looks like both Janice and myself and Jon looks like me but he is brown skinned. They were impressed with the ice sculpture of the two hearts.

Kozet and Sybil each sat on both sides of me and we talked about when they get married. Sybil wants a wedding like Tamera's. Kozet wants a huge wedding. I asked how they feel about Mr. Langley. They said he was nice and kisses Mom in front of them. And they were excited to be in Janice wedding. They told me about their dresses. The boys could care less.

Char came over to the table and went straight to Janice. I watched her in case I had to come between them. Janice had the look of fright on her face however as Char extended her hand out to Janice, Janice smiled and extended her hand. Char bent over and hugged Janice and after saying how happy she was to see her, Char thanked Janice for her part in helping to get Tamera here today.

Char said, "Janice you know it takes a village. I want to apologize for not trusting you with my girls. I need you to forgive me. I appreciate you teaching them to be responsible. Forgiven?" Janice answers, "Of course." And reaches for Char to hug again. My thought was, 'Thank You Jesus!'

I spent time at Mama's table and talked to Grannie and Grand Pop. Grannie has a bad back and both her and Grand Pop rarely get out these days. I swing by their house at least twice a month briefly to check on them. Sundays Grannie stops by Mama's and makes dinner plates for her and Grand Pop but they very seldom come inside and eat with us. Grannie says Grand Pop tires after service and needs his rest.

I found my table and sat in front of my place card. When Char came to the table and saw the grandkids were placed between us she laughed. As she switched the names she says, "They put distance between us." She sat next to me and says, "I'm so glad we are pass that. It feels so good to forgive." She tilts her head and asks, "You alright?" I nod 'yes' and lean into her as I say, "This is great compared to Charece's wedding." I half smiled having a flashback.

Char places her hand over mine and tells me, "I was so jealous, you had a wife and kids and I thought you were happy without me." Greg that man I was with is gay. He does hair in the salon I frequent and me talking about how good I wanted to look, he offered to escort me.

His name is "Zip" that's why you were never introduced. He cuts hair as good as he dances. She smiles, "We never know what The Lord has for us. I'm so glad we've come full circle. Greg…" She's blinking back tears. I say, "I know." As I place my hand over hers.

We all toasted to the newlyweds and ate then the music began. I was totally surprised when the DJ announced, "And now a tradition requested by the newlyweds. The bride's parents will dance as a demonstration of unity." I looked at Char and she was just as surprised as I am. I stand and take her hand as she stands and we walk to the center of the dance floor. The music begins.

The DJ has selected "We Go A Long Way Back, by Bloodstone." I held Char in my arms and closed my eyes. She moves perfectly with me. Man…

The music stops and we are applauded. Char takes my hand and introduces her boss to me. Pam and her date, Thurman. I help Jamal take Grannie and Grand Pop to their car then go sit with Mama and Mr. Mays. Jamal and Tina stay on the dance floor. Sam introduces me to her date; Eugene Alexander and we all talk for a while.

Kozet comes and asks me for a dance. I have no rhythm at all. How do you tell your daughter you cannot dance? I decide to appease her and move from side to side as she dances all over the place. Sybil joins her and Kozet has moves, she gets it from Faith. That woman was a dancing machine. The boys come join us and I ease away to my seat. I enjoyed every minute.

When time to pack up I helped with the gifts and had to put some in back of Char's car. We followed Tamera and Justin and after the gifts were stacked in their living room Justin asked if I would like a drink. I told him I was not a drinker. He told me they had cider he nor Tamera drink alcohol. Char and I stayed for half hour and left the wedding party and Charece going over the wedding events.

When I pulled up in Char's driveway she grabbed my hand, looked me in the eyes and said, "I need to talk to you." She was silent the ride here so I had no idea what she had to say but I wanted to find out.

We go to the living room and she takes her shoes off and sits down. After I take a seat I motion to her for her feet. I used to massage her feet it relaxes her. I start massaging and she tells me to wait and goes into her bedroom. Char returns and has removed her stockings and has on a long animal print caftan. "Okay now work your magic."

After a few moments of me massaging Char says, "Remember that time you massaged my feet and I woke myself snoring? I had no idea I was pregnant." She smiles and I remember that night and smile.

"Greg I like being with you and love having you as a friend again but, I need to know if I'm spending time with you again to prove to myself I can have a friendship with you and not screw it up. I have to be sure I can move pass the mistake I made. I don't want to rekindle this friendship and when you do something dumb, say, 'ah ha, I knew you were the reason I screwed up, not me.' I need to know I have truly forgiven myself. Understand?"

Char is looking at me but her eyes contain that distant stare, as if she is pondering. I know that look so I let her finish her thought. Sure enough, she continues; "I mean I need to know if I want to be friends with you again for the right reason. Know what I mean?" I answer, "I think so." We look at each other until it feels uncomfortable. Char went to get a glass of wine. I watch her every move.

She sat down and asked if I wanted something to drink, she had juice in the fridge. I kept looking at her, I want to make love to Char. She takes a sip from her glass and as she sits her glass down on the table she slides over to me and tries to snatch my bow tie off while saying, "This has gotta go! OOPS. I'm so sorry!"

Char was choking me. The elastic on the bow tie was tightening up. I grab her hand and pull her to me and kiss her. We both become worked up and made love on her couch. It was so similar to our first time in the back seat of Mr. Mays car.

Char cried in my arms. I was busy trying to catch my breath. She laid on my chest and said, "I missed you. You're the only man that makes me feel complete." She started crying again. I wrapped my arms around her and started blinking back tears. I feel the same way about her.

I automatically take in deep breathes to stop the tears, then I thought, 'Char is the only woman I can cry with. Oh what the hell.'

I allowed the tears to stream down my face. I feel one with her. "I love you Charlotte." She raises up and kiss my lips. "I love you too Greg." We laid on the couch together and no words were uttered. I begin to thank The Lord for giving Char back to me.

Char and I became inseparable after Tamera and Justin were married. We talk every day and spend our weekends together. I know you are not surprised to hear we will be married in October. Nothing fancy,

Justice Of The Peace and a three-hour reception on the Queen Mary.

We attend church together every Sunday and we are both growing spiritually. I shared the tools Mrs. Judson taught me with Char and we both know firsthand, Love truly never fails.

When Char and I sit and talk, most times we end up thankful we have one another in our lives. I have found intimacy in my worship also and let me tell you, it is an awesome fulfilling experience.

No longer do I entertain fear of intimacy…